"ANIMUS"

BY

PHIL KEITH

SOUTHAMPTON, NEW YORK

2008

ISBN: 1-4196-9962-8
ISBN-13: 9781419699627

DEDICATION

TO LOLLY and PIERCE

with thanks for all your
unconditional love and inspiration

FOREWORD

The first major event in this novel is inspired by an actual murder, as yet unresolved, that took place many years ago in Elliston Park in Southampton, New York. The real murder also involved a young serviceman and some bizarre sexual circumstances. The rest of the story is pure fiction. The resemblance of any of the characters in this book to actual persons either living or dead is purely coincidental.

Phil Keith

Southampton, NY

Summer, 2008

TABLE OF CONTENTS

Prologue

Mike Carmody was well on his way to being a stumbling, incoherent drunk. The boozy high that brings gentle waves of euphoria was long gone. He had tilted way over to the dark side of being completely smashed. The blood pounded in his brain with every exaggerated heartbeat. A persistent pain throbbed between his ears. He was having trouble focusing. Words and phrases spoken by others were still quite clear to him but his own body was not in sync with his mind. Everything he tried to do with his appendages was an effort, and he was not coordinating well at all. He had dry mouth and craved another drink. His tongue was thick, his nose stuffy and his vision, for some very strange reason, reflected nearly everything in vivid shades of sky blue.

The only part of him that seemed to be having a good time at this very moment was his dick. Oh yeah, his dick was doing just fine. He was as hard as a rock and, as he looked down at his naked crotch once more, the woman he had met at the bar just a couple of hours ago was still all over him with her mouth, lips, tongue and hands. There was limited room in the back of the big Mercedes for sexual gymnastics, but what they were able to do pushed most of the drunken discomforts aside. Man, she was good, and clearly enjoying herself. Only two things intruded on Carmody's sexual reverie. Where were they going? He couldn't quite remember. The big kid who was with the woman when she came into the bar was now driving, but where was he heading? He dully remembered he had to be at work by nine tomorrow morning. The other question disturbing Carmody was, why wasn't he coming? This woman was clearly an expert and he was clearly in ecstasy, but she'd been at this for longer than he could usually make it before bursting at the sperm-spraying seams. This was not a great concern; mind you, just a small curiosity. Who would want this to stop, after all? Was he that drunk?

The car suddenly turned sharply to the left. The hum of rubber on asphalt seemed to change to the rattle of stones or small gravel. The vehicle slowed and came to a stop. The woman climbed off, opened the door on her side of the car and disappeared. Carmody could smell the crispness of a cold gentle rain mixing with the odor of warm and sweaty leather. The door on his side of the car opened. The large arms of the man-child pulled him roughly from the sedan. He tried to stand. He was successful but definitely unsteady.

The chilly droplets began to gather on his naked body. All he had on was a pair of heavy wool socks. But the cold did not bother him. It felt invigorating, in fact. The cooling rain began to revive him. The boy led him to the front of the car, where the fog lights cast an eerie yellowish glow. A large blanket was spread on the ground in front of the car. The woman stood squarely in the middle of the blanket, now totally naked. She had quite a figure, Carmody had to admit. Large pendulous breasts, trim waist, short but finely shaped legs. Her crotch was nearly shaved clean, just a thin vertical stripe what was it called? A Brazilian? She smiled and motioned him to join her on the blanket. Carmody looked down at himself. Still erect, still sticking eight full inches straight ahead. He giggled and stumbled onto the blanket. The woman ripped open a small packet and had him sheathed in an instant. She whipped around and fell on her knees and elbows. She thrust her ass up toward him and slowly wiggled it from side to side. She took her right hand and thrust it between her legs, using her index and middle fingers to spread her vulva and reveal her vagina. A small puff of steam escaped her vaginal lips as she exposed her hot inner pubic area to the cold night air. It was clear what she wanted Carmody to do. He dropped to his knees, grabbed her and with both hands, shoved his entire cock into her with one hard stroke. She yelled with delight and started to slam her ass onto him harder and harder. He didn't have to do any work. This was sheer sexual heaven.

She pushed back on him and she pushed him up. She wanted Carmody on his feet and bending over her. It was easy and pleasurable to comply. Carmody was like a dog in heat. Then suddenly she stopped. She was half crouched, half on the ground. Carmody was deep inside her, draped over her butt, panting with pleasure.

Two strong arms encircled Carmody's waist and he felt what seemed like a hard rubber handle slam into his anus. Whatever it was it was suddenly deep inside him. And it hurt like hell. He gasped in pain and looked over his left shoulder. It was the boy-the kid-and now he was naked and it was suddenly clear to Carmody that the fuck-er was becoming the fuck-ee. And he was too drunk to move. Carmody was now a coital sandwich being pile driven from behind and bush-whacked from ahead. One moment of penis-slick joy was immediately followed by a twinge of ass-wracking pain, over and over. He finally passed out.

He did not know how long he was unconscious, but when he came to he was still naked, it was still night, and it was still cold and rainy. But he awoke to new physical sensations: his asshole was on fire, his whole butt hurt like hell, his back was a mass of prickly scratches and he couldn't move his arms. The rain on his face helped dissipate a little of his fog. He shook his head vigorously from side to side. That seemed to clear enough of the cobwebs to help him understand his back was hard against a tree trunk and his hands were somehow tied behind the tree. This could not be good, he managed to tell himself. Then there was another sensation. It was nowhere near as bad as the others. In fact, it was pretty damn good. Carmody glanced downward. Unbelievably, his pecker was still as hard, and it was being worked over by a hungry, happy mouth. It took a few seconds for Carmody to realize it was not the woman he had recently been fucking. She stood just off to his side, draped in a fur coat, calmly smoking a cigarette. So-who? Jesus! It was the kid! No...No...No. And worst of all he was finally going to come. He could feel it and there was no way he was going to be able to stop it. His whole body tensed for the explosion. He could only moan. He started to convulse. Seeing this, the woman was quickly at his side. What...what is she doing? Carmody panicked. Just as he started his orgasm she slipped a plastic bag over his head and closed it around his neck with her bare hands. Carmody freaked and took deep choking breaths against the smothering plastic. When no air came into his lungs Carmody's body tensed even more causing blood to flow thicker and faster to all parts of his body, including his engorged penis. This gave his orgasm the force of a fire hydrant. Then his heart seized. All the blood that had been pumped to wherever it was going simply stopped and stayed where it was. Carmody died in a furious spasm of terror and ecstasy.

1

Disruption

After thirty-two years in the business, you'd think I'd have seen it all. Much to my ultimate regret, today would prove that I hadn't.

I was cruising east down Sunrise Highway just west of Hampton Bays, coming up on Exit 64. Tomorrow was Gracie's birthday and I wanted to stop at Macy's and pick up something she might actually like. With my taste, getting the right gift for Gracie, or any woman for that matter, was an iffy bet. But I kept trying.

My cell phone chirped. I glanced at the caller ID. It was my deputy, Beth Cantwell. I picked up the phone and opened the flip. "Yeah, Beth, what's up?" I greeted her wearily. In my mind what I was really saying was, *Jesus, Beth, hasn't it been a long enough day already? I mean, we started at seven-thirty this morning and here it is a little after eight at night!*

"Sorry to bother you, Chief, but there's been a murder."

"Ok, hold on a sec." As if that didn't happen a hundred times a year in this county. That's why we had fifty homicide detectives on the payroll. I put my phone down on the empty passenger seat and fumbled for the headset. I rarely used it but knew it was somewhere in the center console. Shit. Where was it? It was highly unlikely that I was going to get pulled over for talking on my cell phone. I mean, Christ, I have official plates that scream *I'm the Chief of Fucking Detectives for Suffolk County, New York.* Most every cop in the County knows my car anyway. Only some rookie who would get his ass handed to him would even attempt it… still, it was the law and I should try to use the damn thing. After sifting through all kinds of crap in the dark and sticking my index finger with an uncapped pen, I gave up. I grabbed the phone and hit the talk button.

"OK…I'm with you…and?" I asked while sucking on my wounded finger.

"Well, sorry to tell you this Chief, but it's someone you know," Beth said, almost too clinically.

Chills ran down my spine and I felt that prickly, tingly feeling guys get in their balls when they know bad news is coming.

I could only think of Gracie and my son, Kyle. *Please, God, no!*

"Whaddya mean 'someone I know'?" I snapped back.

"The detectives on scene called in about twenty minutes after you left. They specifically asked for you. When they couldn't get you, they asked for me. They know I have your private cell number."

It was true. I only gave a very tight circle of trusted friends, family and associates my private cell phone number. Live by the phone, die by the phone...I hated cell phones and

unlike most Chiefs I didn't carry a police scanner in my car, either. I like some private time in my day and, unfortunately, the only time I get some private time is usually when I'm driving from meeting to meeting or crime scene to crime scene.

"Don't worry Chief. It's not about Gracie or Kyle," Beth instantly reassured me. *Thank God.* Somewhat more controlled, my sphincter returned to its normal shape and I asked with trepidation, "So who's the unlucky vic?"

"One of your Navy pals. Name's Carmody. Michael Carmody."

My heart sank. Mike Carmody was a clean kid from a good family. He was, indeed, 'one of my boys,' as in a member of the Navy Reserve unit that I currently commanded. He and I had been called up with the rest of our unit for Iraq. We had just served a shitty thirteen-month tour overseas, having returned only two months ago. Who the hell would want to whack Mike Carmody? He was a happy-go-lucky kid with a cute girl-friend, no enemies, a new truck and bright future. Murdered? Didn't make sense to me. Had to be an accident.

"Who's on scene?" I asked.

"Garwood and Wysocki."

Good. Both men were solid detectives. Lifers. They knew their shit.

"OK, Beth, where?"

"Not far from you. Crime Scene's on site, too. Location is Emma Rose Elliston Park, off Millstone and North Sea Roads in Southampton. You know where it is?"

"Yeah, I know where it is. I can be there in fifteen."

"You want me to come out?" Beth seemed quite concerned.

"Let me get there first then I'll call you back if I need you."

"OK. Sorry. Good luck. Hope everything is OK."

Jesus. "Yeah, sure, thanks." If Mike Carmody was dead it would not be OK. "Back at you later," I signed off.

I pushed the accelerator down and cranked the windshield

wipers up. It had been raining lightly all day but now it was coming down harder and the temperature was dropping into the low 30's. We'd surely have some snow tonight. But it was the first of December, after all, and snow couldn't be far off anyway.

My Mercedes 300 C, ten years old but lovingly maintained, dropped its rear end a little closer to the highway. As the tires dug in I surged ahead. Out of the corner of my right eye I noticed—ruefully—that I was zipping past the Macy's exit.

Sorry Gracie, I'll try again tomorrow.

2.

"You Haven't Seen it All..."

Emma Rose Elliston Memorial Park was a postage-stamp sized county park consisting of a dirt apron, a few scattered picnic tables and a couple of short nature trails. Even though it was illegal, many people ran their dogs here and the park rangers, who hardly ever were there anyway, looked the other way. It was, in fact, an elderly couple with a big old golden lab who made the troubling discovery that would change my life considerably.

The wide tires of my Mercedes rolled through the fenced gate a little after 8:20 p.m. Elliston has a fan-shaped, gravel-covered parking lot that rarely contained more than one or two cars at a time. Except tonight. I counted at least six police vehicles: three black-and-whites, a blue job, and two unmarked but unmistakably dreary sedans that all but shouted "Cops!" The unmarked sedans, I knew, belonged to my detectives. Among the black-and-whites, two were from Southampton Town, and one from the Suffolk County Sheriff. The blue sedan was New York State Police. *God, I hope we're not going to have a jurisdictional squabble. That's all I'd need.* I pulled into a spot away from all the other cars. I hate getting my doors "dinged."

The crime had certainly happened within the jurisdiction of Southampton Town, but the Town usually referred capital crimes, like murders, to the Sheriff. If they were particularly gruesome the Sheriff usually tossed them to us. The State only got involved if the crime happened on State property, but technically everything in New York is State property, so they could poke their noses in wherever they wanted. This was a County park, I reasoned, so we'd\ probably not have to fight about it, but even if we did I was pretty sure everyone would back off seeing that I was likely to get personally involved.

As I got out of my car I also took note that there was a Southampton Village Volunteer ambulance, its blinkers slowly flashing, and one of our Suffolk County CSI vans. Good. With medical and forensics support already on site we could analyze and wrap things faster. There were two other vehicles present. One was a NEWS 12 van; its telescopic microwave relay pole already extended high into the night sky. That could only mean some reporter was trying to beam in a story for the eleven o'clock news. That could be irksome.

But the presence of the other car really gave me pause. It was an all-black sedan with government plates and "USN" and some ID numbers stenciled on the doors. What the hell was the Navy doing here? All of a sudden I had a very bad feeling about all this.

I stepped away from my car and my shoes, which were clearly meant for show and not field work, sank into the chilly, sandy muck. Instantly I felt my socks go "squishy." Fuck. I hated having wet feet. Went back to my jungle days in Vietnam.

Behind the phalanx of vehicles yellow police tape ringed almost the entire perimeter of the tiny park. Some attempt, at least, was being made to preserve what was surely a crime scene of growing importance. Behind the taped barrier flashlight beams danced back and forth, like a bunch of Jedi and Imperial Storm troopers were having a light saber battle deep in the woods. But just a moment later a set of Klieg lights snapped on and the entire forest was turned from night into day. Silhouetted about twenty yards into the trees was a small blue hut of some kind, and behind the hut was a large group of officers encircling what was probably the victim.

I turned up the collar to my Burberry, popped open an umbrella, and strode toward the tape. Two uniformed officers and one plain-clothes type barricaded a portion of the tape against what looked like a very insistent female and a very aggressive man shouldering a large video camera. Words were being exchanged and even though I wasn't close yet, I knew they were not all pleasantries.

Drawing closer to the banded perimeter I could see Tim Garwood arguing loudly with the feisty lady who tried to jam a microphone down his throat. The other two cops, one from Southampton Town and one from the Sheriff's Department, pushed back on the cameraman, and none too gently. I frowned. Finally, when I was about six feet away, I caught Tim's eye. He breathed a big sigh of relief. "The brass" was finally on scene. Soon he'd be out of this witch's clutches and could get back to a more hospitable zone.

"Hey, Chief." Tim smiled sheepishly.

"Hi, Tim, howzit goin'?"

Catching the interchange, both the cameraman and reporter whirled around. The camera guy I didn't recognize. The reporter, unfortunately, I did. Jenna. Jenna Walden. A thoroughly venomous little bitch with whom I had clashed many times. I knew a bad night had just gotten worse. Even in the depths of this darkness Jenna's slashing blue eyes shone in recognition and her sinuous red lips curled into a fake smile.

"Why if it isn't Chief of Detectives, Jim Griffin!"

"James."

"Yes, sorry, 'James.'"

I hate to be called "Jim." My Mom and my 'Da' named me James for a reason, I figured. Plus, every James in the world is called 'Jim' and I liked being different. Jenna knew this. So did every reporter covering a Suffolk County beat. She was just being at ass, knew it, and loved it. Jenna was bright; I had to give her that. Attractive, too. Very attractive. She also knew that. And she'd used it to her advantage. Tried it with me once. Fortunately, my common sense and the desire to keep my balls prevailed.

The real problem with Jenna, though, was her aggressiveness. She was "going network" someday, no doubt about it, but was stuck in this metro-market independent station. She made no bones about it—as soon as a network anchor desk or big station reporting job opened up for her she was gone from this confining "little" island. All it would take would be one major story she could break first and call her own. Was this murder mystery going to be it? With all due respect to Mike Carmody, who couldn't really care about it one way or another, I secretly hoped so. Maybe I could be rid of her.

The strobe on the camera blasted into my eyeballs painfully and the microphone was now two inches from my face instead of Tim's.

"So, what brings the Suffolk County Chief of Detectives out on a night like this, 'James' Griffin?" she drawled.

"Jenna, turn off that camera and take that microphone out of my face now or I will have you escorted out of this park immediately." I growled.

"Oh, Chief..." Jenna pouted.

"NOW!"

"OK, turn it off, Dan."

Mercifully, the strobe went dark. We all stood there stone silent for a few seconds. I could hear fat, heavy droplets of water from the pine boughs plopping into the sand.

"Well..." Jenna said smirking and folding her arms across her sizeable chest, "your turn, Chief. What's going on here? All we heard on the scanner was something about a naked man tied to a tree, dead, probably murdered. Comments?"

Jenna truly knew more than I did at this point. And that really pissed me off. "Jenna, I just arrived on scene, as you can see, and I need to familiarize myself with the situation before I can give you any comments. Would you be OK with that for a few minutes until I can get my bearings?"

"Hah! I know more this than you do, don't I?" she trumpet-ed.

"You don't know what I know, Jenna," I shot back defiantly. "Now stay here. And I mean stay here, and I'll get back to you shortly."

She glared at me silently, one boot tapping the mud.

"Good. We understand each other then." I turned toward the crime scene, grabbed Tim by a shoulder and practically dragged him after me. Another ten yards into the woods and I stopped. I leaned into Tim's ear and whispered, "You keep that miserable harpy out of this crime scene even if you have to handcuff her to a post, get me?"

An evil smile warmed Tim's face. "You got it Chief."

"Now what's going on here, Tim? But tell me quietly. She's still straining to listen."

"OK, Chief. Well, it's a Tasmanian cluster fuck for sure." Tim frowned and dutifully flipped open his note pad. He read and reviewed the facts he had gathered so far even though he knew it all by heart already. "So, about seven-thirty this elderly couple, Mr. And Mrs. Vignoli, drove into the park to crap their dog a big golden retriever. Well as soon as they let the dog out of the car, he starts acting strange, like all yippy and barky and weird. They say he's not normally like that. Pretty gentle, peaceful dog. Well before Mr. Vignoli could get a leash on ol' Skippy – that's the dog's name, Chief, Skippy."

"Yes, Tim I'm with you. Go on."

"Well, ol' Skippy, who's, like, as old in dog years as the Vignolis, mid-70's, takes off like a bat outta hell, running straight back into the park. The Vignoli's are freakin' now. Neither one of 'em has the gas to run after this mutt, ya know what I mean? But just behind this pump shed, that's the little blue building you can see just ahead, Chief. You got it, Chief? The mutt comes to a halt."

"Yes, Tim. I see it."

"Well, the dog's dead in his tracks and barkin' like an idiot. The Vignolis finally catch up with Skippy and he's yelping away at this tree. Mr. Vignoli has a flashlight, so he shines it on the tree to see why Skippy's makin' such a fuss. Well, the geezer sure got an eyeful. He jumped on his cell and called 9-1-1. Southampton PD was here in minutes." Tim stopped and looked straight down at the ground, nervously shifting his feet.

"Tim?" I leaned down slightly trying to look into his eyes.

Tim took a deep breath, let it out heavily, cleared his throat and said, "Chief…It's…well, you better just come. I have to show you, OK?"

I was irritated, but Tim was an excellent detective. I decided to go along. "OK, let's go." I turned to walk toward the lights. Tim grabbed my elbow, stopping me.

"Chief," he struggled quietly. "It's real bad, Chief. Sick-bad ya know? And him being a friend of yours and all."

I looked at Tim. He'd been on the force nearly two decades. Like me, he thought he'd seen it all. Like me, he hadn't. "OK, Tim," I calmed him, "Let's get this over with."

But I stopped again. "Tim…How did you know it was Mike Carmody, I mean so quickly?"

"Found his clothes in a pile in the parking lot. Wallet, too. Still had some cash and credit cards."

"Oh," I sighed, and we started to trudge ahead.

The small and deathly quiet circle of police surrounding a particular tree behind the pump house widened to let me into their reverent midst. CSI Frank Tartaglia was studiously investigating the body. As soon as I saw it with my own eyes my left hand went to quickly cover my mouth. I felt sick. I pressed my eyes shut tightly. I lowered my umbrella until it hit the ground. The rain no longer mattered.

"Get him down, Frank," I hissed, waves of nausea rising higher.

"Oh, Chief," Frank now recognized my presence, "You're here…"

"Get him down, Frank."

"But, Chief," Frank protested, "if we take him down now we might compromise some trace evi-"

"Now, Frank, now!" I shouted. Every officer present jumped back. "Do it *now*!"

"Yeah, OK, sure, Chief," Frank mumbled. "We'll do it now. No problem."

I opened my eyes again, hoping the horrid, sickening sight before me would somehow be gone. It wasn't, of course. How could this be? Who could be so twisted, so sick? It was almost too much to absorb, but there it was.

A young man, a decent, hard-working kid I knew very well, was handcuffed to a tree that measured about a foot in diameter. He was standing up, back to the tree, his arms shackled behind the trunk. He was naked, except for his socks. And he was very dead. The last time I had seen him alive he was laughing loudly, white teeth flashing in the sun, trim and tan. The klieg lights made his skin look a whitish, cobalt blue. Rain ran off his rigid body in rivulets. A length of rope, maybe nylon line, was tied around his neck and wrapped tightly around the tree. The line and cuffs were enough to keep him standing, even in death. A plastic bag, probably a dry cleaning bag, now shredded, dangled about his neck. Some of the plastic was still stuck under the rope.

A small trickle of dried blood hung from the left corner of his open mouth. His dead eyes stared straight ahead, open wide in terror. There was no other obvious blood, but the rain may have had something to do with that. Frank would tell me. What looked to be a steel spike of some kind protruded from the chest. It stuck out from his flesh about four inches. It was impossible to tell how far it had been imbedded.

The truly weirdest part of this sick, horrible tableau, however, was that Mike's penis was, even in death, stiff. The apparently still hard-as-a-rock erection pointed straight ahead into the floodlit night.

"Somebody get the cuffs, I'll get the rope," Frank pleaded with the throng. Instantly, several officers started fingering keys attached to their belts. Handcuffs were pretty standard. Surely one of these officers would have a key that fit. Mercifully, the cuffs clicked open on the second try. Frank slit the rope around Mike's neck and four officers gently lowered the body to the ground. I sent for the ambulance crew who came forward quickly with a body bag and a wheeled gurney. One of them threw up. I felt like I should, too.

"Frank…" I motioned to Tartaglia, asking him to come closer.

He came to my side. "Yes, Chief."

"What's your take?" I asked quietly. "And let's keep it down, OK?"

"Yeah, sure, of course…Well, I can only give you preliminaries, as you know. Nothing totally definitive until we get him back to the morgue."

I put an arm across his shoulders. "I know, Frank. Just give me what you've got right now."

"Well, probable cause of death was suffocation. Plastic bag was over his face when I arrived. Had to open it up to make out the face and all. Some bruising around the neck but probably not enough to warrant strangulation as the COD. Bruising on the wrists. Probably fought the cuffs. Some signs of a struggle. Peticheal hemorrhaging in the eyes, indicative of suffocation. I'd say that the metal spike or whatever the hell is in his chest was placed post mortem. No blood or arterial splatter, very little blood from or around the wound. Almost no blood on the ground, despite the rain. Hasn't been dead long. A couple of hours, maybe. Liver temp is still 92.5."

"That's it?" I didn't know how much more I wanted or could take, but felt duty-bound to ask.

"Well, for now, unless you are as curious about his dick as everyone else is."

"Well, it is a little strange, Frank, don't you think? How does that happen? After you're dead, I mean?"

"Well, Chief, it's actually not that unusual. We see it a lot these days, now that we have Viagra, the four hour hard on and all that shit. It's all about blood flow, Chief. Blood flow is what makes your dick hard. After you shoot your wad, the penis relaxes and lets the blood back out, but if you die at the time of ejaculation, the penis stops working, the blood stays put and you stay hard. We see a lot of old guys at the morgue these days wheeled in with their flags still flyin,' so to speak. Most of them have a load of ED drugs in 'em and they've been fucking their brains out one last time when the ol' ticker just stops. At least most of them have smiles on their faces."

"Jesus, Frank."

"OK, bad joke. But that's what happens. My bet is once we get this guy's tox screens back he'll have a boatload of Levitra or Viagra in him."

"So, Frank, you're saying this is a sex crime? Carmody was having sex when he died?"

"Yeah. I'm pretty sure about that. Looks to me like there are some signs of sexual activity, although I don't think this kid was *having* sex so much as he was being *given* sex. I mean, maybe it started out as a sport fuck, but it definitely looks like it got out of control somehow. Just a guess."

"But, Frank, this is a young guy. He's only twenty-six! What the hell does he need Viagra for to get laid?"

"If you were twenty-six and *didn't* want to get laid, you'd need something – a lot of something – to get the weenie workin'! This guy probably didn't want to get fucked, seeing his fate and all. If he *was* fucked, I'll have evidence on that."

"Dear God," I moaned.

"Let me get him back. I'll have it all for you by nine a.m."

"Yeah, OK. Thanks, Frank. And look, I'm sorry for shouting at you."

"No problem, Chief. You know the guy, huh?"

"Yes, I do – did."

"All right, boss. We're outta here. I'll see you in the morning?"

"Yes. I'll be there. Nine a.m. sharp."

"Oh, Chief, one more thing. The plastic bag…"

I knew I probably didn't want to hear this, but I said to Frank. "Yeah?"

"The bag is probably what killed him. It wasn't that steel pin or whatever the hell it is in his chest. And it wasn't the rope around his neck; at least I don't think so. I'll bet it was the plastic bag. The reason I bring this up now is that it might help point your investigation in a specific direction, if I could be so bold as to suggest…"

"And what direction would that be, Frank?"

"People who are into really kinky sex will sometimes tie plastic bags around their heads. Learned this at my last forensics seminar on sex crimes. They say the sensation of suffocation can enhance an orgasm and it can definitely increase blood flow to certain parts of the body during sex. Dangerous game if you're a willing participant. Deadly game if you're not. You might be lookin' for a pervert, maybe a couple, who're into weird sex."

The wheels of the gurney snapped into position and Frank and the EMTs wheeled Mike's body toward the waiting ambulance. The klieg lights went out and the crime scene was plunged into dank, chilly darkness. My heart and soul felt just about the same.

3.

Naval Intelligence?

"Sir, excuse me, are you Commander Griffin?" The soft voice came from behind my left shoulder. I turned slowly. A young Navy officer stood stiffly at attention. He looked miserable with the rain dripping off the visor of his bill cap. He was clad in a black, standard Navy greatcoat, double rows of brass buttons gleaming. The two solid gold stripes on each shoulder told me he was a Lieutenant. "Yes, Lieutenant," I said absently, "I'm Commander, uh, I mean, Chief Griffin. How can I help you? And you can relax…at ease."

"Yessir. Thank you, sir." With that his stance collapsed just a fraction. "Well, sir, I believe you are acquainted with the, ah – deceased?"

"Yes I am, Lieutenant." I glared at him. "Now who the hell are you and how can I help you?"

Even in the darkness I could see the young officer blanch.

"Sir, I'm Lieutenant Scott Overton, ONI."

"ONI?" My eyes widened. "What interest does the Office of Naval Intelligence have in this case?"

"Well, sir, the deceased, Petty Officer Carmody, was a member of your Reserve Unit, yes?"

"Yes," I replied cautiously.

"You served with him in Iraq, sir?"

"Yes again, Lieutenant, but you already know all this, don't you?"

"Sir, yes, I do."

"So, I ask you again, what's ONI got to do with this?"

"Well, I believe you and your unit returned from Iraq just last month?"

"Correct."

"Sir, I'm sorry, but it's just pretty routine, actually. The Navy would have an interest in any post-deployment deaths of recently returned veterans, but, as you well know, a petty officer of Carmody's rating, well, that could cause a few extra questions to be asked..."

"Look Lieutenant, I'm sorry. I'm being rude. I'm just a little upset, as you can well imagine. Let's get out of this damn rain."

"Thank you, sir." Overton smiled. "That would be most appreciated."

"OK. Let's get some coffee."

We walked silently to the parking area. *Shit! Walden! How am I going to get by her?* I peered into the darkness. Good. She and her cameraman were busy by the ambulance.

"Lieutenant, we'll take my car. It's over here. Leave your sedan here. We'll pick it up later."

"Roger that, sir. I'm with you."

Overton and I snaked around the perimeter of the lot, jumped in my sedan and rode away before Jenna Walden knew we were gone. Fifteen minutes later we sat in a quiet spot at the Southampton Publick House, sipping coffee, and waiting for hot soup and sandwiches.

"So, sir, was it bad over there?" Overton inquired.

I was still distracted with the disturbing images of Mike Carmody lashed to the tree. "Over where? Iraq?"

"Yes, sir."

"Look, Scott—can I call you Scott?"

"Certainly, sir."

"Scott, it's 'James' or 'Chief' if you're uncomfortable with James, but, please, not 'Sir' or 'Commander.' At least not here, in my civilian world. OK?"

"No problem…Chief."

The hot soup arrived, accompanied by sandwiches. We ate silently for a few moments. The steam rose from the coffee. It smelled great and tasted better. It helped wash away the visual stench of the past hour.

"Yes, it was bad over there, Scott," I finally offered. "Very bad."

"So I've heard." The boyish-looking officer—they all looked so damn young these days—gazed pensively into his simmering bowl. "I'm scheduled to go to Iraq in about a week. Any advice?"

"What do your orders read?" I asked, now interested. God, he looked too young…

"I'm going into Tikrit as Assistant O-I-C (Officer-In-Charge) of the Joint Intelligence Task Force stationed there."

My eyes widened. "Colonel Chalabi's command?"

"Yes, sir… I mean Chief. What do you know about him?"

I pondered this silently for a few seconds. *What shall I tell this kid? That he's going to be working for a certifiable psycho who's off the charts? Nah. He'll find that out soon enough. Why get him all worked up before he deploys?* I dodged the question. "What's your background, Scott?"

"Naval Academy, Class of 99, Chief. Second in my class. Missed the top spot by two one hundredths of GPA. Went to sea for a year on the *Ticonderoga* as Assistant Weapons Officer. *Tico's* a guided missile cruiser, Chief, if you didn't know."

I didn't. To me, all boats are 'gray' and can't be distinguished much, one from another, except for the big ones with the flat decks. I can usually tell those apart from the rest. I'd spent my whole Navy career, active duty and Reserve, in land-based aircraft or on shore duty. I avoided sea duty like the plague. I get seasick very easily. My two mercifully short cruises aboard big gray boats had been pure misery.

"...then I requested grad school, so the Navy sent me for my Masters at Georgetown. International Relations. Middle East specialty. I speak passable Arabic. Now I'm working on my PhD, but only part-time. When I finished my Masters I was shipped out to Staff, Sixth Fleet, working for the fleet Intelligence Officer. After eighteen months there I requested to go back aboard a cruiser or a missile shooter, you know, get my first department head tour..."

Very ambitious kid, this Lt. Overton. I glanced down at his double-breasted blues and noticed for the first time that he sported two neat rows of ribbons. Six in all. Below his SWO

(Surface Warfare Officer) pin his highest ranking decorations were the Navy Commendation Medal and the Navy Achievement Medal. The green and white striped Commendation Medal had a gold star affixed, meaning a "second award." Impressive. And only six years out of school. Overton was on a fast track.

"... but I didn't get the Department Head assignment. Not yet anyway," Overton sighed.

"What happened?" I asked, knowing full well that the Navy was probably jerking around one of its future stars for some totally stupid reason. They had a habit of doing that, especially when tribal jealousies between different specialties within the same service came into play. Pilots looked down their noses at submariners, who looked down their noses at ship drivers. "Ring knockers" (Academy grads) sneered at ROTC commissions who sneered, in turn, at officers like me who started as Enlisted, and so it went.

"Well, my old boss at Sixth Fleet, Captain Cooper, got his flag..." [Which I knew meant promoted to Rear Admiral or 'Flag rank']. "...and Admiral Cooper has a lot of pull with the Pentagon..." [Which I knew, too, having crossed swords with Tim Cooper once or twice in my past.] "...and he specifically requested that I be assigned to him at ONI. And, well, here I am, and I can't say too much more or I'd have to shoot you." He grinned, for the first time since we met.

I smiled back. "Sometimes we keep too many secrets, I think."

Overton nodded in agreement. We fell quiet again, sipping at the coffee, biting half-heartedly into the sandwiches.

"Petty Officer Carmody was one of my best, you know," I offered, breaking the brief silence. "And he was Chalabi's chief cryptanalyst while we were deployed. Good sailor. Very smart. But you already know this too, don't you Scott? This is why you're in, of all places, Southampton, New York, on a black-ass, miserably cold and wet December night. So let's you and I cut the crap and be honest with each other, OK? I'll tell you what I know about this if you tell me why you're really interested in a pretty twisted but nonetheless rural murder way out here in the sticks of eastern Long Island. And don't give me the bullshit again about caring about every serviceman who comes home from the war and all of a sudden gets whacked."

Overton's eyes narrowed a fraction, grew decidedly colder and bored into mine. "OK," he exhaled slowly. "I'll tell you what I can tell you at this point."

"Let's hear it," I replied coolly.

"Since you have worked with Colonel Chalabi you know his background? That his parents were Iraqi but that he was born in the US Embassy Hospital in Baghdad thus making him an American citizen? That his father was an Arab doctor and his mother Jewish? That Saddam had all of Chalabi's family slaughtered? That Chalabi only escaped because he was in school in the embassy at the time? That he joined the army and went into intelligence work with a passionate sense of revenge against Saddam?"

"Yes, I intoned "I know that story well. I also know that Colonel Chalabi has had a remarkably distinguished career, that he has risen in rank quickly and, by all reports, he has done nothing but bestow honor on himself while in service to his country." I was probing, because I knew far more about Achmed Chalabi. I knew, for starters, that he was a borderline sociopath with homicidal tendencies.

Overton leaned across the table and, like in a bad spy movie, glanced around the nearly empty room before continuing. "ONI thinks he's gone a little nutty, you know, like '*Apocalypse Now*.' I'm going over there, as his deputy, to find out for sure, one way or another."

Feeling a little uncomfortable, I leaned against the back of the booth. I folded my arms across my chest. "What's that got to do with this murder investigation and me?" Mike Carmody had been dead for less than four hours and ONI already knew about it in record time. How was that possible?

Overton smiled and relaxed a little. "Well, Chief, to be honest with you, I knew nothing about Petty Officer Carmody's unfortunate murder before I hopped in my car at six-thirty this morning. I was on my way to Long Island to see you."

"Me?" I answered warily.

"Yes. Because of your recent Iraq experience and your contacts with my soon-to-be new boss. I looked up records of all officers who have served under Chalabi since he's been in Iraq. Your name, because of your background and experience, and because you're back home now, immediately jumped out at me, so I decided to take a couple of days leave and try and track you down. I'm afraid, sir, I'm flying under a false flag. I'm just here to talk with you. I'm not here, despite uniform and staff car, in any official capacity whatsoever. It's all a ruse. If that's offensive, I apologize."

My ass. Should I believe this kid? He is, after all, like me, a trained spy. And dumb ass me, have I yet asked to see some ID? This could be a complete con job. I had let my grief and revulsion get the better of me. Damn!

"I stopped by your office right after lunch. You were in a meeting. I decided to go find a motel room and try to catch you later. I got a room at the Marriott down the street from your office. Frankly, I was tired so I bagged it for a few hours. I got back in my car about six o'clock. I was going to try and catch you at home. I flipped on the scanner. All our sedans carry pretty sophisticated scanners, Chief."

"I'll bet they do."

"I heard some interesting chatter, something about a 'Navy guy' being involved in a murder, and decided to drive directly to the crime scene. GPS got me there, no problem. I figured you'd turn up eventually. And you did, so, here we are." Overton smiled, a little too triumphantly.

"Yes, and here we are," I mocked him.

"Chief, I have to think Carmody's murder has to have something to do with Chalabi, don't you?"

"Why do you leap to that conclusion, Lieutenant?" By reverting to rank instead of name I was putting Overton on notice that our relationship was, once again, formal. I could see his antennae go up.

"Look, Chief, sir...Carmody was so close to Chalabi while he was there that he had to have seen something...heard something. Maybe something so incriminating that Chalabi was afraid he'd say something to someone once he got back to civilian life. Maybe Chalabi felt that he had to have Carmody iced...maybe..."

"Whoa, stop there!" My voice had risen and I was too loud—a couple of heads turned. I lowered my voice again and leaned into Overton's face. "Look, Lieutenant, Mike Carmody is-was- a good kid. I know his family, farmers out here on Long Island. I got him into the Navy after he graduated high school. He was looking around for something to do. I convinced him he could save some dough for college and basically get a free ride when he was done with his active duty. He signed up. Because he was also a very smart kid, he got into cryptanalysis and spent his whole tour in the Intel unit aboard the carrier Kennedy. When he got off of active duty and came back home I snapped him up in a heartbeat for my reserve unit. He started college at Hofstra. He worked construction when he wasn't busy studying and God damn my influence in his life decided he wanted to become a cop. He just found out yesterday he was accepted for the Sheriff's Academy and now he's dead. That's all I know."

For a few uncomfortable seconds we simply stared at each other across the table. Was I revealing too much? My heart was pounding. I knew my blood pressure was up and I had forgotten to take my pills. Just then my cell phone chirped. I damn near jumped out of my skin, my anxiety level was so high. I glanced at the call window. Jesus. It was Gracie. Shit! I had forgotten. I told her I'd be home by eight. She'd rented one of our favorite movies and we were going to spend a quiet evening at home.

I raised an index finger in front of Overton's face silently signaling 'just a minute' and flipped open the phone. "Hi, Hon. I'm so sorry....yeah...yeah...I know. Yeah, something really, truly important came up. Yes. Yes. OK. I'll be home soon. Soon, yes.

No more than an hour. Yes, I love you. Thanks. Bye." I felt like a shit. "Look, Scott, I've got to run," I said, softening my stance a bit. "Let's take this up again in the morning. Why don't you come by my office, around ten o'clock?"

"OK, that's fine, Chief. It has been a long day." He stifled a yawn. "I could use a little rest. And again, I'm sorry if..."

"Enough for now. Let's start again tomorrow with fresh eyes. And do me a favor, can you change into civvies?"

Overton smiled, "Sure. No problem."

We left the Publick House and I drove him back to his car. Elliston Park was now dark, deserted and draped with yellow tape. The last exchange I had with Scott Overton went something like this: "Scott, you know, this could just be what it appears, a rotten, random murder of an innocent kid. I mean, if this was an assassination, why all the extra crap? The...uh...performance enhancing drugs? The sexual melodrama? If this involved Chalabi, wouldn't someone just pump a couple of slugs into Carmody and disappear in the night?"

Lt. Overton was getting out of my car. He stopped, turned to me and said, "Or create a clever ruse to make you think that."

We exchanged looks and shook hands.

"Tomorrow, then," I said.

"Yes, sir. Tomorrow morning. See you then."

Overton walked to his car, started it, and pulled away. I followed for a few minutes but at Montauk Highway he turned right and I turned left, headed for home.

Lt. Overton never showed up the next day. Or any day. Two days later I called a buddy at the Pentagon. A Lt. Scott Overton was indeed assigned there. He was, indeed, USNA Class of 99 and all the other things Scott Overton had said he was. I left a message for him. He never called back. He went off to Iraq and two weeks later, he came home again, this time in a metal casket covered with an American flag, a slug in the back of his brain. Case unresolved.

4.

Home at Last

By the time my faithful Mercedes pulled into the driveway it was 10:35. What a long, shitty day. I opened the front door slowly, thinking Gracie might have gone to bed. She hadn't. She was curled up on the couch, feet tucked up under her cute little butt, chenille throw covering her lap, peacefully reading a book. The stereo was on. Classical music flowed softly from the speaker. That was a good sign. Classical is not Gracie's favorite genre. I love it even though I can rarely tell one composer or piece from another. If she had some classical on, I wasn't in too much trouble and that was one way she could silently express that she wasn't angry with me. I also noticed an unopened bottle of sparkling cider chilling in an ice bucket. Crystal goblets sat waiting. Another good sign. I'd have preferred a double Dewar's, truth be told, but that wasn't going to happen. Gracie had been totally dry for twenty years now. I hadn't had a drink in over a year. I hadn't planned on giving it up but thirteen months in an Arab country had given me a good excuse to get a grip on a thirty-year habit. Being clear-eyed when people were constantly shooting at you also added some motivation. Still, I missed it terribly. Especially after days like today.

"Hi, darling," Gracie smiled coyly lifting her eyes from her book.

"Hey, lover." I sighed, sloughing off coat, scarf, gloves and wet shoes. "I'm sorry about tonight."

"No problem, I was in the mood to get cozy and finish this book. Look, almost done!" She beamed.

I swear, Gracie must read a library a month. She was always next to a book. I had no idea what she was reading but knew she had started this eight-hundred-page monster just the other day, and as she proudly showed me now, had about a half-inch of text to go. She patted the cushion next to her. "Come, sit, tell me about your day."

I did, grateful for her sense of warmth and companionship. I walked over, and gladly sank my aching tush into the padding next to her. She leaned over for a kiss and as she did the front of her robe fell open and both of her wonderfully large breasts popped into full view. I had to shift my crotch instantly to give it some room to expand.

"Oops! The pups are loose!" she giggled.

"Yea, who let the dogs out? Woof-woof, woof-woof!" I mimicked the popular Baja Men refrain.

We laughed. She took both my hands in hers and placed my palms strategically on top of each hard pink nipple. My God, she was a magnificent woman. At forty-five she had a body truly twenty years younger. At ten years her senior I wasn't as ravenous for sex as I had been when I was thirty but I'd had more and better with Gracie in the three years we'd been together than in a long, long time.

We had fucked like rabbits when we first became serious about one another. Gracie liked it all the ways that I did which meant pretty traditional and nothing weird, but vigorous and often. She liked to laugh and tell me she had to use it up before menopause got her. I'm convinced that won't stop her. It's me I'm worried about. I had to admit to myself there were times I couldn't quite keep up. She was always loving and understanding. I had asked my doctor about the little blue pills. He had given me a prescription before I went off to Iraq but I'd never had the nerve to use them or talk to Gracie about it. Fortunately, since I'd only been back a month, I was still felling as horny as a three-peckered billy goat after a full year of abstention. We kissed again, and I gently massaged her breasts.

"Just checking," I whispered in her left ear. "Breast exams are my specialty."

She shoved a hand in my pants, just behind the belt buckle. "Oooh." She chuckled sexily, "I wanted to hear about your day but I see something has come up!"

"Yeah…" I croaked, "I'll tell you about it later."

"C'mon old man," Gracie challenged, jumping from the couch and dropping all her clothes on the floor. "Fuck the birthday girl."

One look at those big tits, long luscious legs, and her magnificently tufted crotch and I was a babbling idiot with a hard-on. The little blue pills could stay safely hidden in my sock drawer for one more night.

5.

Autopsies Suck

I strode into the County Morgue in Hauppauge just after nine o'clock the next morning.

"Where's Tartaglia?" I boomed to no one in particular.

Several technicians snapped to attention. Someone responded, "Exam Room 3, Chief, right over there on your left."

I didn't break stride, just changed course, and saw a door off to the left clearly labeled "Exam Room 3, Authorized Medical Staff Only! No Exceptions!" Except me, that is. I pushed through the double doors. Frank Tartaglia was standing over an exam table, feet spread, hands on hips, shaking his head. I couldn't tell if it was in disgust or pity.

He didn't even look up. "Morning, Chief." He knew it would be me.

"Morning, Frank. Whaddya got?" I walked slowly to where Frank stood, next to Mike Carmody's lifeless form. Mike's lower torso was covered with a large white towel. His pale blue eyes stared openly at the overhead, seeing nothing. And then it started to assault me. The smell or rather, all the smells. It took a special breed to work the morgue. I couldn't stand being in the place for more than a few moments at a time and only when I absolutely had to be there. The odors of death were too personal, too creepy for me. Despite the cleanest environments, there was the ever-present scent of fecal matter, the coppery tang of blood. The smells crept into your nostrils and hung there, assaulting your olfactory senses. The inevitable stink of chemicals, usually a strong blast of bleach and faint whiffs of formaldehyde made quite a bilious stew. It was awful and it made my stomach churn but for Mike Carmody's sake, and in his honor, I stood rooted next to Frank. My brain kept telling me, *"you need to leave now or you're going to puke."* But as others know, I don't always listen to what my brain is telling me.

Frank looked like he'd been up all night. "Well," he said puffing out his cheeks, "cause of death was suffocation, as I suspected. It was, indeed, the plastic bag we found over his head that became the instrument for Carmody's demise."

I wasn't surprised. I looked hard at Frank. "You get any sleep last night?"

He took off his glasses and rubbed his eyes. "Yeah, coupla hours. I sacked out in the back."

Frank was known to keep all kinds of odd hours, sometimes running through three straight shifts. During the TWA 800 tragedy ten years back he didn't go home for over a week. He was a good investigator; no, strike that, he was the best.

"I also ran the tox screens, twice to be sure. Carmody had a blood alcohol of 2.1. He also had some Quaaludes in there. He was totally whacked. Surprised he could even stand up. No wonder he offered so little resistance. Whoever whacked him slipped him one helluva 'Mickey.' He had also ingested a minimum of 400 mgs of Viagra—enough to keep his cock hard for a week."

My eyes strayed to the towel across Mikes thighs. The erection was gone.

"I drained it," Frank said casually.

"You *what*?" I choked.

"I drained it with a syringe. Sucked out the blood in the penis from behind his scrotum. Otherwise that towel would still have a tent pole."

"Jesus, Frank. That's ...that's..."

"Sick, yeah, I know, but you want his mother looking for a coffin with extra room in the lid?"

"Oh, man, Frank..."

"OK, then, let's move on shall we?" Frank smiled weakly.

"First there's the bad bruising about the wrists: at some point he struggled against the handcuffs. Probably when he began to realize he was being smothered by the plastic bag. Interestingly, there was minimal neck bruising from the rope. My guess is that the rope was wrapped around his neck after he expired."

"Why would anyone do that?" I blanched.

"Only a theory, mind you, but probably to keep his head up. Maybe these sick fucks wanted to take pictures after they were done. The rope was pulled back and up from underneath the chin and tied higher on the tree, behind his head."

"Man, if that's true, these are sick . . . wait a minute," I stopped, suddenly realizing what Frank was telling me. "You said 'fucks'. As in plural. More than one. Do you know that for sure now?"

"Don't know for sure, but it seems likely that there were at least two people involved."

"Ugh." My eyes narrowed as I smelled much more than my clinical surroundings.

"First, as you can no doubt see, this is a big guy. Powerfully built."

Indeed, Mike had been a wrestler and football player in high school, and when he wasn't on duty in Iraq, he was always working the weights in our makeshift gym.

Frank continued, "And I bet despite being drunk, hopped up and stoned, he couldn't have been manhandled like this by one person."

I nodded in agreement.

"Secondly, he was raped, to use one of your navy phrases, fore and aft."

"What the hell?!" My stomach flipped again.

"There was a small amount of blood, his own blood, in his rectum and small tears around his asshole. Something was shoved up his butt and from the lack of any splinters, fibers, metal residue or whatever; it wasn't something artificial, like a plunger, metal rod or broomstick. It was probably a dick, wrapped in a condom. I didn't find any used condoms at the scene, but I did find minute traces of condom lubricant lining his lower rectal aperture. I could also tell from the lack of scarring or hemorrhoids that butt fucking wasn't Carmody's preferred form of coitus."

"Is this going to get any worse?" I groaned.

"'Fraid so. Carmody was also fucked from the front. Scared as he undoubtedly was, he probably couldn't help getting a hard on. With all that Viagra in him, he would be locked and loaded, especially if someone was…ah…manipulating his penis. The skin on his penis was slightly chafed, indicating someone was stroking him hard, either by hand or mouth.

The plastic bag over his head also contributed to increasing blood flow to his extremities, like his penis, as I said to you last night."

I closed my eyes tightly, not wanting to see what my mind's eye was trying to formulate. I also knew my dick was a little chafed this morning and now I felt very guilty about it.

"I also found a little dust in the cracked skin of his penis."

"Dust? Whaddya mean 'dust'?"

"The kind of powder you find inside condoms. To help you slide them on. Someone put a raincoat on him and then probably mounted him from the front. Don't know if it was an ass or a pussy that got stuck on the end of Carmody's dick, but one or the other, for sure. Unfortunately, the rain washed away any trace DNA and these animals, whoever they are, were careful about collecting all the wrappers. Couldn't find any distinctive footprints or tire tracks that would help us, either. Even if it hadn't rained the stampeding herd of cops and press saw to that."

"So, bottom line, what you're telling me is that Mike Carmody either got drunk or was made to get drunk, then someone or a couple of someones slipped him drugs and Viagra, dragged him out to Elliston Park, disrobed him, raped him, chained him to a tree and suffocated him?"

"Yep, that's about the size of it, Chief."

"What about the metal spike in the chest?"

"Oh, sorry, almost forgot about that. It had nothing to do with Carmody's death. It was hammered in, probably with a rock—there was stone dust on the exposed end of the spike—and it was done post mortem. Sort of a last 'fuck you' to the victim, probably. It penetrated the heart, but the heart had already stopped beating by the time the pointed end plunged into the pericardium."

"What kind of spike was it?" I was almost afraid to ask.

"Well, here it is. Take a look." With that Tartaglia picked up a metallic object that was resting on the examining table next to Carmody's body. He tossed it to me. Thank goodness it wasn't particularly sharp—and Frank had mercifully cleaned it off. It was about twelve inches long. The handle end was about a half inch in diameter, tapering down to a point that was oddly shaped. Rather than a blade or a sharp tip the business end of whatever it was took the form of a human hand, coiled into a fist, with the index finger pointing straight ahead. It was light but sturdy and seemed to be made of sterling silver.

"What the hell is it, Frank?" I was genuinely puzzled.

"You'll have to get a better expert than me on this, but the shape looked vaguely familiar. I went on the internet to check and I think it's one of those Torah tools, or whatever they're called in Hebrew."

"Huh?" Now I was totally lost.

Frank smiled crookedly, knowing he had me. "You ever been inside a synagogue?"

"No." I had to admit, that was one place where my Irish Catholic feet had never strayed.

"Well, next time you're not busy on a Saturday, stop by for services. What you're holding is what the rabbi uses to read from the Torah. It's kind of like a pointer. The Rabbis use them to follow the text without putting their fingers on the holy script. That's what was pounded into Mike Carmody's chest. What that means, I'm not even going to guess. That's your department."

My mind raced. *Was this a random act of homo-erotic sadism? A ritual murder? A revenge killing? Military retaliation? All of the above? And what significance to lend to the religious overtones? Arabs? Jews? Terrorists? Just plain sickos?* My thoughts grew leaden. I couldn't get my head around it. Not yet anyway. But I would. And when I did, someone would be mighty fucking sorry. I looked down one last time on poor Mike Carmody's violated body. I put my hand on Mike's right shoulder and swore,

"Don't worry Petty Officer. Someone's going to pay for this. I promise you, Mikey, someone's going to pay."

6.

"Stopping By Woods on a Snowy Evening…"

The steady downpour turned to freezing rain and snow. His footfalls began to crunch on an icy crust forming on the fallen oak leaves. The bunker was somewhere just ahead but he couldn't see it yet. It had been dark for nearly an hour now, and he was disoriented, late. He cursed the cold. It felt so strange to someone who had never before in his life seen snow. There was no light. He couldn't risk using the small penlight in his jacket pocket. He would just have to feel his way forward. He begged Allah to be merciful and guide him. Unexpectedly, his right foot snagged a tree root. He pushed with his left to maintain some balance but the ice defeated him. He went down hard, face first. His outstretched arms cushioned the fall a bit, but his chest hit the ground with a muffled thud and the air fled from his lungs in a painful rush. He heard a snap, but it took a moment for the pain to materialize. Once it did, agony shot through his right calf, rocketed up his torso and exploded in his brain. He tried not to scream but before he could jam a fist into his mouth a tortured shriek welled up in his throat and gained partial expression in the ink-black air. A night bird of some kind took frightened wing from a nearby pine. He couldn't feel anything in his right foot but agony. His ankle was broken, that he knew. He also knew that if he didn't get help, and quickly, he would die of exposure in this cursed place. His mind raced. What to do? Rational thought wrestled with the pain and panic.

He tried to roll over on his back. It was impossible. The pain and the tree root kept him pinned to the ground. He could not reach his shattered ankle with either hand to free it. Cautiously, he dragged his left foot to the snag. Using the toe of his left foot for leverage he slowly, agonizingly, pushed the twisted root up and over the heel of his right foot. He had been beaten several times in his young life, but he could not recall a pain quite as intense or as exquisitely brutal as this. His breaths came in sharp, rapid gasps as he struggled. The misery sent his brain into self-preservation mode and he passed out for several seconds at a time. He also pissed his pants. He couldn't know how long it took but his right foot was finally free. Gathering all his remaining strength he rolled on his back, crawled to the base of a nearby tree, and pulled himself erect. Gingerly, he tested the right foot to see if it could take any weight. The pain and sickening cracks of splintered bone told him it would not. He was in the dark in the middle of nowhere and he was going to die. Unless he could get help. He didn't mind dying—he fully expected to die soon for what he believed in. But not like this. Not this way. This would be wasteful and not in accordance with the plan. He craved martyrdom but not alone in a dark, freezing woods. He wanted his death to be a glorious one. A death remembered in song. A death with Paradise and the seventy promised virgins. This death would be stupid and meaningless.

It was this final rationalization that drove him to extract the cell phone from his left breast pocket and flip it open. He punched a speed dial number. After just one ring a whispered voice answered, "Where are you?"

"I do not know. I am somewhere near the bunker but I don't know how far. I am hurt. Please…I cannot be far away. Help me."

"Shit! Fuck! How could you be so stupid?" The voice suddenly erupted.

"Please," the injured man wailed softly.

"Shut up! Get off the phone!"

The connection was gone. He was once again alone in the dark with his pain. He whimpered and rapidly spiraled into panic. Then seconds later, as a gift from God, he heard a heavy metal door creak somewhere just ahead. A narrow shaft of light spilled into the forest like a ray from heaven, but was quickly gone again. Two angry voices began to move toward him, softly calling and cursing his name simultaneously. They couldn't be more than two hundred yards away. "I am saved. Allah be praised!" he murmured.

One hundred miles overhead, an NSA satellite parked in a stationery orbit over the east coast and trained to intercept foreign language phone calls, primarily those in Arabic, snatched a conversation out of the air of just eighteen seconds. It was, indeed, in Arabic. It seemed to be some sort of plea for help. The on-board computers instantly flashed the intercept to the duty officer for this satellite, sitting at a console in Langley, Virginia. The watch officer punched a code into his keyboard. A few seconds later another computer pinpointed the exact location of the cell tower that handled the call. The GPS coordinates indicated "Montauk, NY." Someplace within Camp Hero, a County Park. From the late 1920's to the late 1970's, Camp Hero had been an active military installation, mostly old coastal artillery but in the 60's and 70's, it was a highly classified US Air Force communications station. "Hmm," the watch officer mused. "That's the most interesting intercept I've had so far tonight." He logged it, taped it, downloaded it to the server, and went back to his crossword puzzle. One of the analysts would parse it out tomorrow morning and figure out what to do next.

7.

"In My Own Words..."

I walked the four flights of stairs from the Morgue to my office. I needed clean air in my lungs and the strain of the climb would pump the oxygen faster. I brusquely told my secretary to hold my calls and not to interrupt me until I told her it was OK. I slumped in my leather chair behind my desk and spun to gaze out the lone window. The view was panoramic but not particularly scenic. Bare branches swayed in a cold December breeze. Cops, lawyers, and civil servants scurried with members of the general public anxious to cross the stone-cold surfaces of the quadrangle below and find somewhere warm. Heavy traffic along the Southern State Parkway, just visible through the naked brush a quarter mille away, thrummed steadily.

Jesus, Jesus, I said to myself. What a cluster fuck. Poor Mike. I was dreading going to see his parents, which I knew I would have to do later in the day. I flashed back to my own family. There were some very happy memories but the good times always seemed to get book-ended by periods of excruciating pain. *So much has changed,* I sighed to myself.

My folks came straight from Ireland in 1950. My "Da" had a cousin who had a friend who was in construction. The friend promised there'd be jobs for my parents. Carpenter work for Dad and a maid's position for Mom in one of the resorts that were beginning to pop up along the pristine beaches of Montauk. Anything seemed better than the abject poverty that strangled my parents in Dublin. What being poor didn't kill, the whiskey would, so off they went to this strange new land. This was one of those rare instances when promises were kept. My father got a good job right away as an apprentice carpenter and my mom became a maid at Gurney's Inn. Within six years they had five kids. I was the second born, the first son, and I came along in 1952. Mom stopped working after my youngest brother was born. My father did well enough to buy a small farm in Amagansett. He said the soil there was so rich you could poke a Popsicle stick in the ground and it would sprout. The whole family pitched in to grow anything that would make money, mostly potatoes and tomatoes. What we couldn't sell to the farmer's markets in Manhattan we'd try and hawk at the family's modest roadside stand.

"Da" died two years ago after a long and mostly happy life. Mom is in assisted living now. My brother, Terry and I see each other occasionally. He got the farm although ownership stays with the five of us, split evenly, after Mom is gone. My older sister, Rebecca, who has moved and lives in San Diego, says the twenty-two acres should be worth a couple of million now. Maybe so. I don't pay much attention to those things. But it's a comfort to think there might be something more to retirement than my two pensions, which won't support the lifestyle to which I had become accustomed. Of my two younger sisters, one died in a car accident when she was 18. A drunk driver plowed into a car in which Colleen was riding. She and three friends were killed. It was the biggest tragedy in East Hampton in 1972. The drunk died, too. If he hadn't I would have killed him myself. The family, being Irish and stoic, never fully recovered. I think it's the major reason I am no longer close with my siblings. No one wants to experience that pain again. My baby sister is a crack addicted whore somewhere in Nevada. No one has heard from her directly in over a year. With my police connections, I can reach out and find out where she is at any time, if she's alive. I try to determine that every few weeks, for Mother's sake if nothing else. It's always the first question when I visit her, "Jimmy" (yes, I do let my mother call me that), "have ya heard of our Betsey, now?"

Looking back, I don't think I've ever been more blissful than when I was an ignorant teenager humping fifty pound bags of spuds and trying to hump the girls from East Hampton High. That was the late 60's. The craziness that became "The Hamptons" hadn't really started yet and it was a great time to be alive. And then "the draft" descended on all of us boys unlucky enough to have been born in that window from 46 to 56. I was smack dab in the middle. We had all heard "that word," meaning "Vietnam," but we never paid much attention to it. Turning eighteen suddenly put a pucker in your sphincter and as soon as I did I was promptly classified as "one-A" by my local Draft Board.

I knew nothing about the military and Vietnam except what John Wayne had taught us in '*The Green Berets.*' It didn't really look all that glamorous and we had already had one East Hampton High alum shipped home from Southeast Asia in a box. CPL Jimmy Collins, USMC, was a local hero. They talked about naming the Legion Hall in his honor but I couldn't help thinking he was nonetheless dead at the tender age of 19. His example was sobering to say the least.

A cousin (my family is a giant web of cousins) had already overcome the challenge of the draft by enlisting in the Navy Reserve. No fox holes, no mud, and a college deferment. Sounded good to me. I visited the Navy recruiting office on Main Street in beautiful (it wasn't) downtown Riverhead. It should have told me something that the recruiting office was sandwiched between the State Unemployment Office and the local IRS headquarters. Nonetheless, I believed the petty officer's mesmerizing recruiting spiel, so I signed up and went back home to apply for colleges. I was content in my naïve belief that I was safe.

I did pretty well in high school, despite losing my virginity on several occasions and being introduced to the wonderful world of beer. I set my sights high and with all my clubs and sports, I managed to get into Brown, Boston University and my safety school, U-Mass Amherst (yes, I wanted to get off the East End at that time in my life. I had this vague notion rattling around somewhere in the back of my brain that I could "make something" of myself, at least more than a potato farmer who liked to drink beer and chase women.) I opted for the Ivy League and the bright lights of Providence. I couldn't afford it, and my "Da" was spat tacks about the cost of tuition, but—God bless the Ivy League – admission was "need blind," which meant, in those days, if they were dumb enough to let me in, I couldn't get kicked out for financial reasons alone. The University would help its students find a way to pay the tab. For me, this meant a couple of pitifully small scholarships, a ton of financial aid and a million part-time jobs.

I settled in, and took turns doing handyman tasks, babysitting professors' kids and driving a cab in Providence. I struggled to stay awake in class. Somehow, probably out of fear of failure and my Da's promise to cut my balls off if I flunked out, I just missed making the Dean's List at the end of my freshman year. Exhausted, whipped and broke I went home for the summer hoping to make enough money bartending at the Shagwong to get a good start on my sophomore year.

A week after I returned to Amagansett, I got my call to active duty from the Navy. The Petty Officer recruiter who had lulled me into a false sense of security about a college deferment was now somewhere on a big fat aircraft carrier in the Mediterranean. He was far away from the war and decidedly removed from my desire to rip his dick off and stomp on it. Dumb kid that I was, I did, of course, fail to read the fine print. Right below the paragraph talking about my "college deferment" was the little hidden phrase that said "subject to the needs of the service." That seemingly innocuous catch-all, I later learned, conned thousands of stupefied guys like me. Bottom line, whatever the service "needed" they could snag by dipping into the pool of talent they had already gotten to sign on the dotted line. The meat grinder now simply known as 'Nam was churning through all the available gristle at an ever accelerating pace. Only the guys with the dads who had the strongest connections could keep their sons from being called up. Those with the best pull got their kids stashed in stateside National Guard Units, that way, they could claim, somewhat speciously, they had still "done their duty." My dad was not among those elite. He did call our Congressman, with whom he'd had a couple of small dealings but the fifty dollars Dad had kicked into this guys campaign once was not enough to keep me from packing my sea bag. Running off to Canada or returning to

Ireland was never an option, not if I didn't want to be disinherited.

The days immediately before and after my 19th birthday were crazy, a truly drunken affair, held mostly on our back deck. Two weeks before I should have been heading back for sophomore year at Brown, I was, instead, hung over and on a slow train headed to the Naval Training Center, Great Lakes.

My reverie was broken by the intercom. *Damn it! I said 'no calls!'*

My mind-reading, ever loyal, incredibly efficient pain-in-the-ass secretary Tilly Stumpp's voice blared through the speaker, "Yes, Chief, I know you said 'no calls,' but you'll take this one. It's Gracie."

"OK, where is she?"

"Line two."

"Thanks." I stabbed one of the blinking buttons. "Hi, Sweetie, what's up?"

"Thought you'd like to know that your 'other girlfriend' was just on the local news with her story of last night's murder."

Oh, shit, Jenna Walden. Gracie took perverse pleasure in needling me about Jenna. "So, what was her take? And, please, she's not my girlfriend." I thought I heard a little giggle, but Gracie quickly got serious.

"She's trying to make it sound pretty sensational, loverman. She's tossing out lots of hints about sex, drugs and mayhem. She's a dog on a bone and it sounds like she'd like to make a big deal out of this. Just a heads-up."

"Thanks, I think. Unfortunately we know what happened but not why and we're a long ways from who."

"Well, good luck. I know it's a tough one for you. If you want, I'll go with you to visit Mike's family."

What a sweetheart this lady was. "Thanks, hon, that's a nice offer, but I think I'd better do this myself. It's going to be ugly, and painful."

"OK, but if you change your mind just let me know. And don't forget Kyle's coming over for dinner tonight."

"Yeah, I remember. I should be home by six. If I get held up I'll call you."

"Promise?" Obviously, she was thinking about my faux pas of last night.

"Promise. I love you. Talk to you later."

"Love you, too. Bye." With a click she was gone. I punched line two off.

My mind's eye callously and cruelly transposed by beautiful son Kyle to the slab now occupied by Mike Carmody. Involuntarily I doubled over in a spasm of panic.

8.

"I Love You, Too, Mom..."

One hundred rivulets of silken warmth cascaded downward from the ornate Italian showerhead. Soft jets of steam rose upward from a dozen vents evenly spaced around a marble shower pan some ten feet on each side. Naked boys, frozen in the tile, gamboled in the swirling mists. Except for the sound of the thrice-conditioned pure artesian well water sliding down the gold plated drain, the world was blissfully warm and silent.

The young man stood under the flowing stream quivering involuntarily. Yes, the water felt good, and the hand-milled oatmeal soap would cleanse his skin roughly, the rougher the better. He felt a need to be really clean, but not to wash away the images—no, not those delicious images—it was the evidence he wanted to scrub away. The images thrilled him still and it was all he could do not to grasp his penis right then and masturbate. He desperately wanted to relive, in fantasy, the most delicious physical and sexual experience of his sixteen years. Just thinking about it made his dick start to stiffen. It was exquisite, ramming his cock up the guy's ass while the man's dying, terrified eyes bulged outward as he gasped for air. Climaxing while the guy choked on his last breath was the best part of all. What a rush. He was especially proud of his last touch. His father had recently given him his very own reader for the Torah. What a stupid gift. He hated Synagogue. He hated being Jewish. Mostly, he hated his father. He had tossed the vulgar pointer in the trunk of his mother's car intending to ditch it at the first opportunity. Tonight, he had found a much better use for it. Pounding it into that guy's chest with a rock he had found nearby seemed perfect retribution.

He reached for his penis until his right hand began to cradle it lovingly. The skin was red and a little raw with all the night's activity but maybe one more…

The shower door clicked open unexpectedly. His reverie was broken and he turned in a start.

"Aw, sweetie, did you have a good time?" an older woman's voice gently purred. She was naked and stepped into the expansive shower with him. She giggled. "I see you want to take matters into your own hand."

9.

Garwood and Wysocki, Yin and Yang

The spasm passed but it seemed to take an eternity. I straightened up again and took a deep breath. Somehow, I managed to push the frightening image from my mind. The intercom blared—again. *Jesus!*

Tilly growled, "Garwood and Wysocki are here."

"OK, give me a minute."

"Buzz me back when you're ready."

Detectives Tim Garwood and Gerry Wysocki sat in Chief Griffin's outer office waiting, mulling over similar thoughts. He had said promptly at ten a.m. and they had both gotten there on the dot. The Chief was a good man, a fair man, but you never wanted to piss him off. He had been known to bust really senior detectives back to traffic control for obstinate behavior and God forbid you ever did anything outside the law. Three former Suffolk detectives were now serving time upstate because they went afoul of Chief Griffin and the law. And both Garwood and Wysocki knew that the Chief was going to be even more riled up this morning about the case the two of them had caught last night, being that the vic was a friend and all. Yes, they were both more than a little nervous.

Tim Garwood, eighteen years on the force, nine in uniform and nine as a detective, was as solid as they came: a good husband, father and Little League coach. He was not overly burdened with intellectual prowess or ambition, but he was dogged, determined and loyal. Gerry Wysocki (everyone called him "the Pollock"), sixteen years on the job, ten as a uniformed Deputy Sheriff, six now as a Detective, was a ladies man, a poker player and a lover of single malt scotch. He had gotten both a Bachelor's and Master's at night, the former from Long Island University, the latter from Hofstra, and was reportedly working on a PhD. He was imaginative, reckless and sometimes cavalier with the truth in order to nail a perp. You couldn't find a greater mismatch between two partners on the entire force, yet their "cases-closed" rating was the highest in the whole department. Go figure.

Garwood tapped his fingers on the arm of his chair. Wysocki, who had given up smoking just last month, was fiercely chewing two sticks of Trident. At that moment Deputy Chief sailed through the outer door. She nodded to the two detectives and to Tilly. As if on cue, the Chief's inner door popped open and Griffin stuck his head out. He looked grim-faced and he did not speak. He locked eyes on the trio and with a jerk of his head motioned both into his inner sanctum.

Chief Griffin's office was spare but not Spartan. Above all it was always neat. Not a piece of paper out of place. Not a coffee cup without a coaster. The only luxuries the Chief allowed himself were a large, flat desk whose highly polished oaken top had once been a slab of the deck of the USS Constitution, "Old Ironsides," a gift of some mysterious origin and something to do with the Chief's clandestine work with the Navy. The Chief also indulged his collector's side with plaques representing all the places where he had been stationed or ships on which he had served while on active duty. There had to be nearly three dozen of them. Lastly, there was the small stereo with its ever-present low-key classical music.

The Chief lowered himself into his chair and motioned to the other three to take chairs facing him. He quietly folded his hands and placed them on the desktop.

"Sorry for the delay," he started.

"No problem, Chief," Wysocki opined for all.

"I just finished with Tartaglia. Make Carmody's prelim. It was nasty."

All three of the Chief's compatriots suddenly needed to check their shoe tips.

"As you might have guessed," the Chief went on sternly, "I'm going to be taking a personal interest in this case."

"Yes, sir," they replied in unison.

"Garwood. Wysocki. I want you both on this 24/7. Any other active cases you have, give the files to Beth. She'll assign additional detectives to help you clear them."

Garwood and Wysocki looked at each other and exchanged a silent signal that said, simply, "Shit. This is one fucking serious case." Turning back to the Chief they both opened their mouths to speak simultaneously.

Griffin cut them off before they could talk. "No questions. No objections. No protests. No shit."

Defeated before they could even get going, both detectives fell back in their chairs and dutifully answered, "Yes, sir." Having worked with this Chief for several years now they knew when to push and when to hold back. This was definitely one of the times to hold back.

"Keep Beth just as up-to-speed on this case as you do me.

She is my backup. I want her 100% involved. I will also give you whatever you need from the department's resources. Just ask. Any questions?"

The two detectives glanced at one another again. There was obviously something that needed saying, but they remained silent. It was Beth Cantwell that broke the ice.

"Chief," Beth drawled in her Houston, Texas-born lilt, "we all know that the vic was a friend and co-worker of yours, and that certainly makes this case special to you, but..."

The Chief locked eyes with each of them in succession, screwing them firmly to their chairs. A long moment passed.

"Beth," the Chief finally said, "that is exactly the type of question you, as my Deputy, should ask. I take no offense from it. Yes, this man was a friend and colleague of mine. I know his family well and it will be my sad duty to pay a call on them today. There is, however, absolutely no reason for me to treat this vicious, horrendous homicide any differently than any other case we have. Except for one thing."

The three leaned forward.

"I smell a rat."

And that was all it took to justify the orders the Chief had given. It was well-known in the department that the Chief never used the phrase "I smell a rat" unless there was, indeed, a rat to be smelled. He had only used that phrase three times before today in the ten years he'd been in Suffolk County. Every one of those three cases had ballooned into major probes and events of real importance in this small corner of the world. One case had brought down a County Executive in bribery disgrace. Another had stopped the mafia from gaining a toehold in Suffolk County. The third had been a messy celebrity murder involving infidelity, drugs and a bloody baseball bat. Yes, when the Chief smelled a rat, it was wise to sniff the air for oneself.

Now that the tension had been broken and the stage had been set, coffee could be served-the Chief buzzed Tilly, and in it came.

"OK, Tim, Gerry, what've you got?" the Chief intoned.

The Pollock took the lead. "Well, Chief, not much more than you already know, but we're trying to piece together Mike Carmody's last hours."

Tim Garwood chimed in, "We know this: Carmody was last seen alive at Buckley's. Do you know it, Chief? In Southampton? Right at the end of Job's Lane?"

"Unfortunately." The Chief smiled, remembering a few nights of ribaldry from his hard-drinking days.

Wysocki came back on cue, "Apparently, Carmody found out

yesterday morning that he passed the entrance exam and had gotten a date for the Police Academy. He called a couple of his buddies from Village PD and invited them to lunch. They went to the Driver's Seat and had lunch at the bar. Mostly liquid lunch was the story we got from the bartender. Then Carmody's buddies called a few of their buddies who called some of their pals and their girlfriends and by three o'clock, they had a pretty big party goin'. The Driver's Seat bar gets a little crowded so the group rolls down the block to Buckley's. By 4:30 their crowd numbers about fifteen and everyone's pretty much loaded. We've got all the names and we're going to start taking statements as soon as we're done here."

"But there's a twist, Chief," Garwood added. "About four o'clock this couple comes in. A woman, towing a kid with her. I mean, not a kid, kid. From what we know so far he's like a teenager, but a big kid, too, well over six feet, around two hundred pounds. And this lady is dressed to kill, I hear. I mean really turned out, and partially undressed, if you know what I mean? Low cut and all. She's blonde, maybe mid thirties and built like a brick shit house." Garwood reddened and glanced at Deputy Chief Cantwell. "Uh, sorry, m'aam. No offense." Cantwell is thirty-five, also blonde, stacked, and built like a brick shit house.

"None taken, Detective." Cantwell smiled wryly, wondering if Garwood knows she's a dedicated lesbian. He does, as does everyone else in the Department.

"Yes, m'aam. Anyway, barkeep says he's never seen her before and he classified her as not a 'Buckley's type'. More of a Hamptons type, you know? She starts ordering Stoli shooters. The kid gets Diet Cokes. About 4:30 the lady and the kid strike up a conversation with Carmody and some of his pals."

"Pretty soon this lady, the kid, Carmody and his buddies are all one big happy party, laughin' and scratchin', and tossing back the drinks," Wysocki continued. "Everyone's ripped, except, apparently, the kid."

Garwood looked at some notes. "Now, here it gets a little sketchy. That's why we need to get back out there and get to these guys as they sober up. Apparently the party starts to break up about six o'clock and recollections start to get a little fuzzy, but at least two people, including the bartender, seem to think that Carmody, who was clearly loaded, drifted out with this broad and the kid. After that, we got nothin' –yet."

"Well, actually, Tim," Wysocki reminded, "there's a couple more things."

"Oh yeah, sorry." Garwood flipped over a page, "A couple of guys and the bartender seem to remember hearing the woman being called 'Vick' or 'Vicky,' and the kid 'Vincent' or 'Vincenzo,' or something like that. And the woman drove a big, dark blue Mercedes."

"Hmm," the Chief intoned. "Well, that gives us a place to start. You gentlemen know what to do. Beth, get these guys what they need and let's get moving."

The three police professionals knew they had been given their marching orders. They got up hurriedly and quietly, leaving the Chief alone with his thoughts. Griffin pulled open the top right hand drawer of his desk. He pulled out a small album of 5x7 photos, all from the recent tour of duty in Iraq. He flipped to a picture of Mike Carmody, dressed in his desert fatigues, all smiles and full of life. Griffin tried to hold this image in his mind instead of the one he had seen on Tartaglia's cold, stainless steel table.

10.

Drifting Back...

I am not one for nostalgic rumination, but I had to admit, on this cold and dreary morning, I was pretty depressed and I found myself drifting back, remembering how the hell I had gotten where I am today--and that Mike Carmody's days were already done and over. The Navy had been our common denominator...

My six months in boot camp were less than memorable, but not awful, actually. After a couple of weeks of self-pity I finally decided to "get with the program," as my drill instructor yelled at us non-stop. Once I did things actually became tolerable, if not enjoyable. Toward the end of 'Basic' those guys who were "adapting militarily" and getting the best grades on the PT tests and the written exams got some choice as to where they might end up in the Navy's vast hierarchy of jobs. Luckily, I was in the top 5% of my battalion, academically and physically. It was time to choose a rating. Having always liked to tinker, especially with Da's farm machinery and my junker cars, I thought I'd become a Machinist Mate. These were the guys with really big wrenches who tackled monstrous engines on the fleet's aircraft carriers, cruisers and destroyers. According to barracks scuttlebutt it was also a safe rating. "MMs," as they were called, were given the cushy postings, far away from harm, deep within the bowels of big, grey boats. I'd do my two years at sea, get out and be back at college with the GI Bill to back me up and a lot of money saved. Once again I signed on the dotted line and once again, I got fucked.

I failed to perceive that the Navy had a lot of small engines, too. Some of the smallest yet most powerful were on the patrol boats the Navy was using to sweep up and down the Mekong River and its hundreds of miles of long, muddy tributaries. These particular craft were the genealogical successors to the WWII PT boats that had been so romanticized by Hollywood, not to mention the legacy of our deeply lamented hero president, JFK. Their newer version of the PT was called the SWIFT boat. It was indeed fast, and better armored than its flimsy plywood predecessor, but SWIFT boats were always going in harm's way in search of the Viet Cong. This also meant that the crews on Swift boats were always getting shot at. Being on a Swift boat was the navy's liquid equivalent to a foxhole. It was not fun.

Six months later I was "in country" on a thirteen month tour stationed aboard a Swift boat that was part of a squadron of boats operating in The Mekong Delta. I was surrounded by a crew of psychotic crazies who loved machine gun oil as much as they loved booze, which they drank constantly, even on duty. They never stopped calling me "college boy" and I never stopped ragging them for their stupid, hell-bent desire to get into action anywhere it could be had. The skipper of our boat was a particular loony – a Lieutenant, Junior Grade, from the Naval Academy Class of '70 who was on a mission to get himself medaled up. He took stupid risks, constantly tried to exceed his orders, and went in search of the enemy everywhere, even where they didn't exist. He continually badgered people to write him up for citations. He managed to get himself shot twice. But only a little bit shot: just enough to qualify him for Purple Hearts but not badly enough to cripple him or deter his quest for naval immortality. The crew hated him. We came close to fragging him a couple of times but couldn't quite figure out how not to get caught. Somehow, he survived the war. Many years later he became an Admiral. Such is the stuff of which our senior brass is sometimes made.

As for me, I just tried to keep my head down and figure out how to keep The Psycho from killing us all. Then, three months into my tour, we got a call to chase some VC from an up river hamlet about five clicks away. Off we roared on another glorious mission. Long story short, it was a setup.

The VC were good at feeding us bad intel- the kind of stuff we'd just love to believe so idiots like our skipper could run off in search of a Silver Star. We got hammered in a deadly crossfire at a bend in the river just two clicks upstream from Base. Two of our crew were killed outright and two more wounded. Including me. I took two AK-47 rounds, one through my right thigh that thankfully missed all my bones, and a second round that clipped a big chunk out of my right ass cheek. Our valiant captain was knocked unconscious by a ricochet slamming into his helmet and it was only because our XO, a senior Navy chief who quickly took command, that the rest of us got the hell out of there alive.

I was medivaced to the USS Sanctuary where I was patched up and given a Purple Heart of my very own. Later I found out our glory-bound CO had nominated everyone on the mission, including himself, for the Bronze Star, with Combat "V." Incredibly, we all got the decoration. I had done nothing to deserve it except survive the lunacy that was Vietnam, but I didn't turn it down either. I think all of us thought we probably deserved it for just being there and making it out alive.

The Sanctuary needed my bunk, so they sent me to a regional hospital just outside of Saigon. My butt healed up OK but my thigh wound kept festering in the jungle miasmic atmosphere that was Southeast Asia. The doctors wouldn't let me back on my boat (what a shame!) until it fully healed and they wouldn't send me home either. Worse, I was not incapacitated enough to allow the Navy to let me sit around with nothing to do, so, I was sent LD/TAD (Limited duty/ temporary additional duty) to a NIS (Naval Investigative Service) unit in Saigon that was short a "body." They needed someone to process paper and felt that I, being a "college boy," could perform what amounted to a secretary's job until I was fit enough to go back to my boat or my tour expired, whichever happened first. I knew fervently, desperately, which option I wanted.

The NIS (these days the NCIS, just like the successful TV show) was the Navy's own in-house police force and investigative branch. They had facilities worldwide, generally wherever there was a substantial Navy presence. NIS agents went anywhere they were needed to look into crimes "within the family." They cooperated and shared cases with the other "alphabet soup" government agencies responsible for combating nefarious behavior, and worked with the CIA, FBI, DEA, and so forth.

Life is what happens to you when you make plans, as they say. The NIS branch in Saigon was populated by a lot of guys who were smart, savvy, educated and dedicated. It didn't hurt that nearly all of them had experience and training from some of the best urban police departments in the country before they came to NIS. NIS was also one of those hybrid units that had civilian officers as well as guys who were on active duty and uniformed. Consequently, it had some military aspects but it was also partly civilian, i.e., "normal." I couldn't help it. It began to appeal to me.

By carefully working the guys in the unit, and taking on more and more responsibility, I wormed my way into their professional affection. My wound finally healed completely. The doctors were going to send me back to the Swift boats, but several of the NIS agents who had become my friends pulled some strings and got my TAD changed to permanent duty. It was how I first got into police work.

At the end of my tour I went home in one piece, newly promoted to Petty Officer Second Class (E-5) and sporting two full rows of ribbons on my dress blues. I wasn't yet 21. My family was proud. But the rest of society, I quickly discovered, wasn't interested in my Vietnam sacrifice. I got spat on by a group of hippie freaks as I got off the plane.

So, after a two year hiatus, I was finally back in Providence. Since I had (eagerly) taken an early out from active duty, I still owed the Navy two years of Reserve duty. That meant one weekend a month of drill and two weeks of active duty in the summer. Fortunately, there was a NIS Reserve Unit in nearby Newport so fulfilling my remaining obligation was not stressful.

I graduated from Brown with the Class of 75, BA in history. We were just bailing out of Vietnam then and the economy sucked. Yes, I had an Ivy League degree, but unless I wanted to go to Wall Street or off to graduate school, there wasn't too much out there. Finance didn't appeal to me and I was heartily sick of academia, so I drifted for a summer. My active duty stint took me to the Naval Base in Rota, Spain, which was very pleasant and by chance, one of my old NIS buddies from Saigon was now O-I-C (Officer in Charge) of the NIS detachment in Rota. One of his buddies was now the Deputy Commissioner of police in NYC in charge of the Police Academy.

Flash forward: valedictorian of the Police Academy graduating class, three years of foot patrol in the Bronx, six years as a homicide detective and I was a "comer" rising fast through the ranks. Hard days, long nights, lots of booze, one divorce. Along the way I signed up for another tour of Reserve duty. What the heck, I needed the money to make alimony payments and the summer tours were pretty neat. I was promoted to Petty Officer First and in 1979 I was offered the opportunity to become an officer in the navy's direct commissioning program. I traded my bell bottoms for gold braid and started to climb through the officer ranks of the Naval Reserve.

Still driven, I charged ahead. Youngest Captain in the NYPD at the time, two years as head of the mayor's protection detail, and on my 20th anniversary of joining the Department, Deputy Chief, Homicide Division. In the Navy Reserve I had been successfully promoted from Ensign to Lieutenant (jg), full Lieutenant and then to Lieutenant Commander; and, yes, one more divorce.

But I was getting worn out. I began to think maybe it was time to smell the roses and get a grip. I wanted to go back home. The Deputy Chief of Detectives job for Suffolk County was open. I applied for it and was hired. That was 1995. When the Chief of Detectives retired in 2000, I was promoted to the top spot. I also made full Commander in the Naval Reserve and mostly sobered up. Happily, no more divorces.

Haven't been married for a while but did get serious with a girl fifteen years younger who wanted to have a baby. I agreed, thus my only son, Kyle, now eight. We see each other all the time, his mother and I are on decent terms and Gracie, thank God, is in love with Kyle. She never had any kids of her own, and she tells me she's not about to start, which is fine with me. I'm only fifty-six and can barely keep up with Kyle.

And that, as they say is "the book" on me—pretty much. Not many regrets, except the lousy marriages. I'm professionally at the top of the heap in my small pond, I make good money, I love a wonderful woman and I live in one of the most beautiful places in America. All in all, I'm pretty lucky, which, sad to say, was not the case for poor Mike.

I sighed heavily. I had no idea where this case was headed. All I knew was that I had to get my head into it and damn fast.

11.

The Turk

The light was very dim, purposefully so, yet the eyestrain annoyed him. He also did not like being so close to this fat Jew he didn't really trust.

"So, my friend, did all of our boys pass the test?" The large man purred quietly as he poured tea.

"All but one," the Turk replied flatly.

"Which one?" the pourer of tea inquired.

No, I do not like this man at all, the Turk said to himself. *But I am told to obey him, that it will be a service to Allah and our cause, so I obey him I must.*

The two men of such very different backgrounds and religions were sitting at the furthest table from the front of the chic new Italian eatery on Newtown Lane. It was owned by the Turk's host and his host's gay lover. The place was all the rage and quite the "in" scene in the Hamptons last summer, but on this chilly December evening, it was all but deserted.

"Ibrahim," was all the Turk allowed. "The younger Ibrahim. We have two in our group, as you may recall."

"Ah." His host sighed, "Yes, I remember him. He had such promise--and a nice little ass," the big man chuckled.

God, how I hate this pig, the Turk cursed silently.

"So, how will you handle it?" the restaurant owner asked.

I will handle it how I handle it, you Hebrew fuck! the Turk's brain shouted to his tongue, but somehow the tongue stayed quiet. *Am I not the Turk, you idiot? Am I not Ottmar Germella, the enforcer of God, whom all men fear, except you, you stinking pile of camel dung? You may think your money and your connections will save you, you fat, fucking Hebrew dog! Don't you know you're being used you sheep-fucking moron? Don't you know someday I will enjoy slicing the fat off your bones pound by pound as you watch and shit yourself in terror?*

A few silent seconds passed. The Turk's blood pressure began to throb at his temples. "It has already been taken care of. Ibrahim will no longer be a problem," he said quietly.

Even in the darkness the Turk could see the large man's eyes narrow. He also stopped stirring his tea.

"What exactly does that mean, Ottmar?"

It means what it means you putrid, ass-fucking, man-whore! Germella's brain began to ache. He had to stop. He had to get out of here and soon.

"It means, sir that I have taken care of the problem."

"Don't fuck with me, Germella," the host hissed. "I want to know how. I need to know how."

Germella involuntarily fingered the razor sharp stiletto he kept hidden behind the lapel in his sport coat. He ached to whip it out and slice through the right carotid artery of the man sitting across from him. It would be over in a fraction of a second. The sheer mass of the man would spray blood ten feet in every direction and they would both be covered in gore, but it would be worth it to watch this man seize in horror as he choked to death on his own vital fluids.

The Turk took a deep breath. He had lost count of the number of men, women and, yes, children he had killed during his thirty-seven years of toiling for the cause. They had stopped having meaning. But this man's death would have meaning for Ottmar; it would make him feel good about killing again. This would feel good, truly good. But this man's death, which, in Germella's mind was only a matter of timing, must wait. Now was not the right moment. The detestable Jew-pig had money and resources that he, Ottmar the Turk, and his bosses in Al Qaeda needed. That the Jew was willing to commit those resources to turn on his own people, his own family, did not matter to Germella. If he was willing to be used, so much the better. He would soon be joining Ibrahim anyway, although he doubted this man would want the same seventy virgins in paradise Ibrahim so desperately craved--at least not seventy female virgins.

"Ibrahim has been sent to Paradise. He will not trouble me, you or the plan any further. His mistake in the woods was fatal to him," Germella finally offered. "He failed the tracking and stealth exercise. He got lost. Worse than that, he injured himself so badly he would not have been any use to us. He also broke the strictest protocol and used his cell phone to try and call for help."

"He used his cell phone? Jesus! How stupid was this fucking raghead? Who did he call?" The man quivered with anger.

The Turk found it somewhat ludicrous for this Jewish butt fucker to be calling on Jesus, even if only in curses. He was also offended by the term "raghead." Strictly speaking, having been born in Istanbul, Germella was Turkish, but he had been raised in Baghdad and he considered himself an Arab.

"Do not concern yourself. He called me. Fortunately, Achmed and I were only moments away. He had broken his ankle in the forest and we hauled him inside quickly. No one saw us. The cell phone was a throw-away. It cannot be traced."

"Thank God for small favors." The big man exhaled. "What did you do with him?"

"We disposed of him in such a manner that the police will be chasing ghosts for weeks."

"Why didn't you just toss him off the cliffs at Camp Hero? If he were to be found, the cops would think he took a tumble in the dark. Or why not just cut him up and dump him at sea? Or just fucking bury him ten feet deep? He's a god dammed undocumented fucking Palestinian for Christ sake--who's going to care?"

Germella could not help it. He leaned across the table close enough to smell the sweet tea on the fat man's lips. "You, perhaps, would like to tell the Turk how best to run his business? No, my friend, I do not tell you how to run your businesses. Do not tell me how to run mine." The Turk nearly spat on him. "It is harder than you think to hide a body. Pieces of cut up bodies wash ashore. Bodies thrown off cliffs, especially at former military installations, will be treated as suspicious. Bodies buried even ten feet deep have a nasty habit of being found by dumb luck or someone seeing something they shouldn't. No, sir, I decided to hide the body in plain sight. That will confuse the authorities even more."

Somewhat subdued by the Turk's menacing demeanor, the big man leaned back in his chair, crossed his flab-draped arms over his massive chest and asked quietly, "So what did you do?"

The Turk smiled sinisterly. "Two days ago the local police found a man cruelly murdered. It was a sex crime, they say. It's been all over the news. I'm sure you heard about it. It is said to be a gay murder, or perhaps a gay hate crime."

The big man squirmed in obvious discomfort. *Oh, yes.* Ottmar beamed to himself. *You are a very gay man with some very gay issues and now I can tell you have, indeed, heard about this crime.*

"So we made Ibrahim drink alcohol. A lot of alcohol. We told him if he didn't we would kill him. We told him it was to punish him for being so stupid and careless. When he was thoroughly drunk we strangled him. We also rammed a broomstick up his ass a few times. Wasn't that a nice touch? To make it seem he had been violated in a well… you know… homosexual sort of way?"

The big man swallowed hard.

"Then we took him to Cedar Point County Park, way out toward the lighthouse. We covered his head with a plastic bag, handcuffed him to a tree, wrapped rope around his neck and left him to be found. We copied the other murder.

Hidden in plain sight. The police will think they have a gay serial killer or a gay hating serial killer on their hands. They will go crazy looking for everyone but us. Clever, don't you think?" The Turk grinned.

"Yes, clever…now leave me alone. Get out of here until I call you again."

"Certainly sir, but there's one more matter we must take care of right away."

"What's that?"

"I will need $25,000 to send to Ibrahim's family. The death guarantee, as I am sure you remember. We promised each family of the martyrs the $25,000 death payment."

"Yes…yes. OK…sure," the big man mumbled, realizing that real deaths were starting to be tallied against his plan. "Go see Birdsall. He'll have the money wired. Now leave me."

"Certainly, sir. Have a good evening." Germella stood and walked to the front entry, and out into the cold night air. The chill felt cleansing compared to the fetid space he had just shared with this fucker. He started his Jeep and pulled out into Newtown Lane. He turned left onto the highway headed to Montauk. He reveled in a vision of having that fat Jew on the end of his knife some day. His reverie did not permit him to see a black sedan pull out of a parking space three spots behind him and begin to follow.

12.

Ivan the Terrible

Ivan Centpied nervously swirled his Cosmopolitan. It was his third in thirty minutes. The crowd at the bar at World Pie in Bridgehampton was growing larger and louder and his appointment was now a half hour late.

"Damn, where is this bastard?" he cursed to his glass. At that very moment, the front door opened and with a blast of wintry air his appointment walked in. They spotted one another instantly. The new man strode quickly to the far end of the bar where Ivan had been guarding an empty stool. Centpied's contact was impeccably dressed and looked as if he just stepped off the set of 'The Sopranos.' He was, indeed, of Italian descent with gray, slicked-back hair and shining eyes. He was not, however a 'made man', like Tony, but rather the head of a private security firm and a former mercenary soldier. He slipped onto the stool next to Centpied.

"You're late," Centpied growled.

"Traffic." The man shrugged.

"Well, you called me. What's so damn urgent? Wanna drink?"

"Club soda with lemon, thanks."

Centpied practically recoiled at the man's inability to take a real drink, like him, but he got the bartender's eye and ordered the club soda and a fourth Cosmo.

The man looked around, assessing the crowd. "You sure you want to talk here?" the man asked incredulously.

"Good a place as any. I'm a regular. Everyone knows me here. Can't hear yourself think above this noise anyway. No one will be the wiser, so what's up? I've got a dinner party in an hour."

"OK, then. Here's a little news flash for you."

The man drew uncomfortably close to Centpied's right ear. "Vicky and the little bastard went out yesterday afternoon. Cruising. Looking for a party."

"Schlit!" Centpied slurred noisily.

"They ended up at Buckley's in Southampton and started hangin' with a party of local cowboys."

"So? Did they behave?"

"Don't know really. I wasn't on their tail myself last night, Derrick was."

"Derrick? Who the hell is Derrick?" Centpied bellowed, startling a couple next to them at the bar.

"Hey! Hey! Pipe down will you? Derrick is one of my boys. He's a good one, too, but since he's done one stretch of hard time, he's a little skittish around cops and the VR's were hanging around with a party of cops, would you believe!"

"So, what happened?"

"Well the party's over about 6:30 and the VR's head out but Derrick, he thinks one of the cops at the party has made him, so he beats feet."

"Damn you, I pay you to watch those two anytime they go out and you know why!"

"Yeah, yeah, but yesterday was my day off, man, and I had this cute little thing cuddling up to me…"

"I don't give a fuck about your love life you asshole I pay you…"

"Back off Centpied." The man stiffened, "I'm not your lapdog and I don't need this crap from you. I'm trying to help you out here, but if this is the way it's gonna be, fuck you and see you later!"

The man stood up from the bar stool. Centpied grabbed his elbow.

"OK, OK! Look, I'm sorry. It was a rough day. I apologize. Please. Sit. Tell me what you have to tell me."

Smoothing the lapels of his sport coat the man resumed his perch. "Well, that's better."

"Please go on."

"So anyway, Derrick splits for a while. He goes back to the bar about a half hour later but everyone's gone. He's a little panicked now, so he heads back to the ranch. The dynamic duo, thank goodness, shows up about nine o'clock and all in one piece and seemingly none the worse for wear.

"Thank God." Centpied sighed.

"But here's the not-so-good part."

"Jesus, what?" Centpied's heart sinks.

"Well, I'm back on duty this morning about seven o'clock and I've got the police scanner going in the car, right? Well all the cops are buzzing about some sort of sex murder that took place last night."

"So?"

"Well, here's the really interesting part. The dead guy is one of the cops from the party at the bar –or I think he's a cop; I couldn't really get that part. Anyway, one of the guys Vicky and Vincenzo were partying with turns up dead, tied to a tree."

"But...but...what can that possibly have to do with them?" Centpied sputtered.

"Uh, well, the only thing I heard was that the cops are looking for a good looking-broad with a kid and a big blue Mercedes."

Centpied's vodka flushed face went deathly pale.

13.

Mindset

He sat alone in his second-floor study, his back to the room, and stared through the expansive windows behind his desk. From this vantage point Milos Rubino could gaze down the entire length of his vast front lawn, all the way to the ornate gates and guard shack. He leaned back in his massive leather chair, folded his hands across his impressive belly and smiled to himself. *A few more days. In just a few more days they will know what Milos can do. Once and for all they will know.*

Rubino was not one to reflect on life very much but at this moment, he couldn't help wandering back. It would only be natural. What he had been through was clearly driving the events that were about to unfold. *They will be sorry—all of them.*

He had conceived a plot that he thought quite brilliant. He

had not confided all the details to any one person thereby insuring that he alone would hold the reins and drive the process without interference. If he was the only one who knew all the facets of his master plan there would be no possibility of betrayal, or so he believed.

It was too bad his father was not alive to see this. The old bastard had been dead several years now, and good riddance as far as Milos was concerned, but it was still regrettable that he couldn't twist this dagger of a scheme deep into his father's heart. His mother was still around although she had been nothing more than a cipher to his old man. Still, he somehow felt he could channel his revenge through her. She and his father had been so symbiotic in life that he was convinced that wherever his father was now, hopefully some form of hell, his message would get through to him and make his afterlife more hideous and miserable.

And then there was his brother, Omri. *Omri the Magnificent! Omri the Favored One.* Rubino shuddered involuntarily just thinking about his vaunted older brother, the favorite son, the one who could never do anything wrong in their parents eyes. But Milo's experiences with his older brother were quite different than his parents would ever acknowledge. The adolescent teasing, the natural dominance of an older brother, was not unusual, but when Milos finally revealed that his sexual preferences were not directed toward the female species, Omri's attentions turned decidedly vicious and brutal. And because Omri could do no wrong, he was never chastised or punished. *Until now!* Rubino smiled again to himself. *Yes, won't Omri be surprised!*

Then there was also the matter of inheriting the family fortune. Omri, as the oldest, had a natural line of succession, but what had happened when their father died was still not fair. Their mother received the bulk of the estate for use in her lifetime but everything else went to Omri—there was no provision for Milos. Yes, it was true, his father, while still alive, had set up a trust for Milos, which essentially gave him two billion dollars, but it was under the condition that he go away and never darken the family doorstep again. All of that had been arranged by Omri and acquiesced to by their ill and dying father. Milos had never gotten over the insult.

Milos Rubino was particularly proud of that part of his master plan that included Al Qaeda. What a deliciously satisfying touch that the explosive end of his machinations would be carried out by some of the most vicious anti-Semitic terrorists in the world, all financed and arranged by a Jew! The very thought of it gave him goose bumps. And it had been deceptively simple. A friend had a friend. The once-removed friend, formerly with the State Department but fired for an unfortunate sexual peccadillo with his boss, the male Ambassador to Qatar, put him in touch with someone who knew someone. The second someone could get to the Al Qaeda head man in Iraq. After almost a million dollars in bribes had been paid a meeting was arranged. Naturally, the Al Qaeda representative was quite skeptical but after a promise of twenty-five million was laid on the table with an immediate down payment of half that amount, the skepticism somehow dissolved. The leaders of Al Qaeda suddenly began to appreciate the irony: a prominent Jew paying to attack a target that would be a profound statement for their cause. So, the deal was made.

Forty years of taunting and disgrace is coming home to roost, Omri, for you, our mother and the Jewish Mafia in America, too! Milos was proud to be a Jew, but he had never felt much included. Jews, in general, frown on homosexuality, and even more so among their own. It was only until he got his hands on his large trust fund and started tossing it around for Jewish causes that Jewish leadership began to pay attention. Rubino's interesting family life simply ceased being much of a concern. But in Rubino's mind it was time to change the leadership dynamic and one way to do that was to wipe out a goodly portion of it in one fell swoop. Terrorism would be held responsible. Then he, Milos Rubino, and some of his selected friends, could step into the leadership gap.

There were other things to prove to the world: that he could be a successful businessman, for example. He had tried many ventures and none of them had amounted to anything. Once he had left an entire company and its two hundred employees in bankruptcy and without paychecks overnight. *But all of that had been because of the interference of others,* he rationalized. *This is my plan, mine alone, no partners to screw it up, except for that creep Centpied, but I'll deal with him after the plan has been carried out.*

Secretly, he knew, he could also use the money. He had been bleeding money in recent years and he knew it wouldn't last forever. That's why the real estate and casino aspects of his plan were so important—and appealing. He'd turn the Hamptons real estate scene inside out, smash it down, buy it up cheap and make millions, no, billions. And on top of that he'd be the majority owner in a casino that would make Donald Trump pale.

One day, he hoped, he could turn the casino over to his boy. Maybe that would be something Vincenzo could handle because, sadly, Rubino knew Vincenzo wouldn't be good for much in the traditional sense of the business world. He had tried to shelter his only child, and he did have a real soft spot for the kid, but he understood Vincenzo had "issues." No amount of expensive counseling and psychological testing had worked, at least not so far. Vincenzo just didn't fit in. He couldn't be sent off to school, couldn't mix in with any group. *Maybe it was my fault* Rubino sighed. *I gave him everything—too much.* Rubino had even bought control of an entire private school hoping he could get Vincenzo to somehow function in some form of traditional education. It had been a miserable failure. Now the school was worth nothing more to Rubino than the twenty acres of prime real estate that it occupied. On a whim, he decided to try and turn it into an "alternative school" for his gay friends who had either adopted or somehow conceived their own children. He would make it a model for gay education. *But not right now. There'll be time for that later. Right now the school will serve an even better and more immediate purpose.*

Vincenzo's challenges had been evident since he was a small boy. It was the main reason Rubino kept his mother, Vicky, around. She was no walk in the park either but she had proven to be loyal to Milos and caring of Vincenzo. Milos was sure Vicky loved her son but he had no illusions that she also stuck around for the unlimited piles of money and the sex—not from Milos, of course, but from all the boy-toys her money could buy. *Well, I can't worry about them right now. There's too much to do. Besides, they know absolutely nothing about my plan. There's nothing they can do to screw it up.*

14.

Implausible Denial

Morton Rivkin was a nervous little man by nature, but this situation had kept him saturated in sweat and awake the last three nights. *This wasn't the way it was supposed to be,* he wailed to himself. A knock on his office door nearly sent him bouncing off the ceiling. But it was only his bookkeeper, Edith. She peeked in.

"Hey. Some of us are going out to lunch at the Golden Pear. You wanna come? Or can I get you anything?" Edith asked with genuine concern.

"No, no, that's OK. Thanks. I want to look at these numbers one more time." Morton smiled, distracted.

"OK, suit yourself. I'll be out for about an hour. That OK with you?"

"Huh? Oh…Sure, fine. See you later."

The outer office door opened and closed with a click. His office window on the second floor overlooked the staff parking lot and he saw Edith join up with a couple of her teacher friends. Laughing, they all got in one car and drove off to lunch.

A simple laugh. How long had it been since he'd had a simple laugh? It was damned unfair. After twenty-five years in public accounting and God knew how many awful hours commuting by train to Manhattan, what had seemed like the dream job had finally come along. Now it was becoming a nightmare.

Everything had changed after 9-11, including the little Rivkin family. No longer did it feel "safe" to live in the Jewish enclave in Plainview and go from home to work to synagogue and back. Terrorists, real anti-Jewish terrorists, had struck America and Morton had felt personally assaulted. All he'd ever wanted was a life with numbers, a good Jewish wife and maybe a kid or two. Accounting was his professional passion. He was good enough to be pushing steadily toward a six figure salary with a big brokerage firm headquartered in Manhattan. He'd gotten the good Jewish wife, too. (Maybe a little shrewish at times, but who was perfect?) One child, a daughter, not the desired son, but all in all, not bad.

Except for the terrorists. Morton knew he had to do something.

A friend at Temple came to Mort one day and said, "Here's something you should look at! A beautiful little private school in the country, it's been around for decades. It's just been taken over by a big Jewish businessman and he's making lots of changes. He's pouring money into the school. He's offering big salaries and best of all he needs a good Jewish accountant to be his CFO. Of course, he can't say 'Jewish Accountant Wanted' in the job advertisements but everyone knows what everyone knows!"

Mort applied. He was interviewed by several people on the new Board of Directors including the "Big Man's" personal CFO, Manny Birdsall, and by the "Big Man's" partner, Israel Sokolin. And in this case, he knew, the "Big Man's" partner meant they were a gay couple, but they were good Jews and who cared? Amazingly, he got the job--and he knew why. It wasn't because he was the best candidate. Many good accountants and finance officers had applied. It was because he was the safest candidate – a competent guy with the numbers who wouldn't say shit if he had a mouthful. He could be relied on to take orders –and he was of the correct religious persuasion.

So Morton chucked his insulated life, gave up his small corner office and staff of three and took on the job of CFO of the Irving Center School in Bridgehampton. His wife begged and pleaded not to go. She couldn't bear not being one block away from her mother. His daughter, Esther, cried her eyes out for weeks over leaving her life-long friends for a room full of strangers in the 7th grade class at this little hick school in the country. Despite the wailing and gnashing of teeth and all bets to the contrary among co-workers and friends, Morton stood his ground and packed up his totally disenfranchised wife and daughter and moved to that Sodom and Gomorrah known as "The Hamptons." They bought a modest house in Springs and tried to settle in.

Now, six months later, he knew he had made a grave, possibly fatal, mistake. But not for the reasons his wife and child had feared. It was worse than any of them could have ever imagined and it could no longer be denied. Something was wrong, very wrong, and he knew it. Nothing made sense. The spreadsheets didn't connect the dots and the 990 forms the IRS would soon require him to file on behalf of the school didn't add up to the right numbers. They were going to blame it all on him.

He had been hosed. Used. He was smack dab in the middle of a giant ruse. Money was coming in and going out, but it wasn't all tuition payments and school expenses. There was too much money, and he couldn't account for the origins of all of it. There were too many expenses, many totally unrelated to the operation of the school. He feared—no--hell he knew money was being laundered, in and out. The Head of School was clueless, the Board members were useless, and the "Big Man's" personal chief financial officer, Birdsall, was ruthless making Rivkin a cipher in their fraudulent game.

Now he was being directed to send a $25,000 payment to a blind account in a Palestinian bank in Gaza. A Palestinian bank! He was told to take the funds out of the school's "special operating account" and record it as a "miscellaneous curriculum expense—consulting." He had balked. Birdsall had threatened to fire him if he didn't do it. Rivkin was not afraid of the firing. He was afraid of the implications—and lying to the authorities and the IRS when and if it ever came time to account for where this money had actually been spent. It was, after all, his signature, not anyone else's, on the check. And even though the school processed hundreds of checks a year and the likelihood of getting caught was very minimal, it was still not the way things were done. And he didn't like the idea of sending money to Palestinians one little bit, even for a legitimate expense--which he knew, in his heart, this wasn't. But he did it. And he knew why he did it. It would give him time. Time to dig deeper, which he had done, and now, after several sleepless nights, he was getting a much clearer picture of what was really happening. And it scared the shit out of him. Actually, he couldn't quite believe it was all true, but the one thing Morton Rivkin knew, because he loved numbers so well, was that numbers, unlike people, can't lie. After hours, when everyone else had gone home, he began making copies. When he finally got home each night the copies went beneath the floorboards of the closet in his den.

Why me? he asked himself again, for the hundred thousandth time. But he knew why. He had been chosen to perform one and only one task. If the shit hit the fan, he was the one who was going to be covered in it.

15.

Copycat

The cell phone on Griffin's nightstand chirped annoyingly. He slowly opened one eye. The blue LED said "6:14." Every-one on the staff knew not to call his cell after hours unless it was urgent. "This better be serious," he griped sleepily. The phone beeped a second time. The caller ID read "Garwood." Gracie stirred next to him. He patted her butt and told her to go back to sleep.

He grabbed the phone and opened the flip. "Hold on a sec-ond, Tim," he whispered.

"Sure, boss," he whispered back.

"Why is he whispering?" Griffin wondered.

He fumbled for his robe, found it half under the bed, retrieved it and pulled it on. He headed for the kitchen. This call would no doubt require coffee. *God bless Gracie* she had set up the coffee pot the night before. All he had to do was push the "on" button, which he did. "Yeah, Tim…what's up?"

"Real sorry to bother you so early, boss. I got rousted out myself about a half hour ago. Night watch called. Some clam man who was getting an early start out at Three Mile Harbor was flashing his lantern around, you know, looking for a good spot to start raking. He's right at the edge of Cedar Point, near the old lighthouse? Lantern beam catches what he thinks is a naked guy takin' a piss behind a tree. So the Bonaker calls out to the guy. No response. He rows in a little closer. Then he sees the guy is tied to the tree and he ain't movin'! He hops on his cell and calls 911. East Hampton PD rolls out. Looks like we got another dead guy tied to a tree, boss."

"Shit," was all Griffin could manage as he fumbled in a cabinet for a coffee cup. "All right, Tim. I can be there in about a half hour, forty five tops. Get forensics out there before the local yokels get on this."

"Already on it, Chief. Tartaglia's comin' out with his crew and a meat wagon."

"Good. Good. You'll be there, Tim?"

"On my way now, Chief. Gerry, too. He's rollin' from Yaphank. Hey, boss…"

"Yeah, Tim?"

"You think we got, you know, some kind of homo serial nut job runnin' around the East End?"

"Sure looks that way, Tim. Two of these within a week aren't encouraging. If you get there before me you nail that crime scene down, you understand? I don't want any evidence lost in the mud or whatever this time."

"You got it, Chief. I should be there in fifteen."

"Thanks, Tim. See you there."

A little over an hour later Griffin rolled to a stop at the end of a small lane far back into Cedar Point County Park. He pulled up next to Tartaglia's crime scene truck. It was full daylight but gray and overcast. A light snow was predicted for the afternoon. Leaves and twigs crunched softly underfoot in the overnight frost. Exiting the car he could see a small group working near a large locust tree at the edge of the harbor fifty feet ahead. There were only a half dozen and thank God no press – at least not yet. Another car rolled to a stop behind him. It was Wysocki. Griffin stopped to wait.

"Morning, Chief." Wysocki blew warm air into cupped, gloveless hands.

"Hi, Gerry."

"We got another one?"

"Looks like it. Let's go see." They trudged off together.

The group around the body consisted of two uniformed East Hampton cops, one female, who seemed clearly distressed, and an East Hampton detective Griffin knew slightly. Also present were Tim Garwood, Frank Tartaglia and one of Tartaglia's assistants, Jimmy Oakes.

"Here we go again, Frank, eh?" Griffin greeted Tartaglia after shaking hands all around.

"Maybe. Maybe not," Tartaglia mused.

"Go on," the Chief said warily.

"W-e-l-l..." Tartaglia hesitated before continuing. "At first glance, it looks an awful lot like what happened to poor Carmody, and that may well be the case, but there are some subtle differences. I'm gonna have to give you the standard spiel, Chief. The one that goes 'we'll know more as soon as I get him back to the lab.'"

Griffin stamped his feet in the cold and wrapped his arms more tightly around his torso. *Should have worn thicker socks* he chided himself.

"OK, Frank, I'll buy that, but tell me what you have now, OK? Best you can?"

"Right, well, COD appears to be strangulation, not suffocation, even though we have a plastic bag, knotted rope, handcuffs, same stuff as before. See here?" Tartaglia pointed a gloved hand to the purplish red area around the dead man's larynx. "Bruising about the neck is much more pronounced in this case than with Carmody. Vic is an Arab or Middle-Eastern man, probably mid to late twenties, about 5'10", 150 to 160. No ID, of course. It appears he's been anally assaulted."

This was the point of no return for the young female officer. She turned, bent over and vomited. Griffin motioned to the East Hampton detective and leaned close. "Detective Corwith, you can dismiss the uniforms. We'll manage from here. Suffolk County is taking jurisdiction of this case as of now and I don't need any more puke on my crime scene, OK?"

"Uh, sure, Chief. But I'll have to stay with this until you leave the scene. And we'll have to be kept up to speed. It did occur on our turf..."

Griffin cut him off with a wave of his hand. "You and your department will be given copies of everything we get and you or whomever your Chief assigns can be part of our task force on this case. Will that be all right?"

"More than fair, Chief. Thanks." Corwith looked relieved to be both rid of responsibility for the case as well as off the hook with his boss.

Griffin turned back to Tartaglia. "Continue, Frank."

"OK, then…here's what's got me curious. I don't think this guy was brutalized or killed here. Carmody, we know, was killed where he was left. Even though Carmody's crime scene was a mess of mud and destroyed evidence, his bodily fluids were at the scene, disturbed bark on the tree where he had struggled against the rope and cuffs, and a few blood drops at the base of the tree. If you'll look, Chief," Tartaglia said pointing to where the dead guy's hands were still shackled to the trunk, "there's no evidence of any struggle with the tree either here or up here, where his neck is tied to the tree with the rope.

"Also, look at this." Tartaglia referred to the rope itself, "Different kind of rope. This one is plain braided sisal. The one around Carmody's neck was nylon. Now, that's not a big thing--to most people rope is rope and they'll use whatever is handy, and that could be the case here--but serial killers are creatures of habit. They'll use the same signature items over and over. Same weapons, same restraints, same tape, same rope and the same knots. The knot on this rope is a simple shoelace-type knot. Carmody's knot was a clove hitch – something that would get tighter the more you strained against it. Very sadistic.

"Then there's this," Tartaglia signaled Griffin to look to the ground. "Whoever did this tried very hard to erase any evidence they were here. They even brushed away tire tracks all the way out to the paved road so we can't get any tire prints. But the ground cover, being frosted as it is, will hold its shape somewhat until the sun or higher daytime temperatures warms it, even if you try to brush it back. I can definitely tell that this body was dragged to the tree, probably by at least two people, one on each side of the body. I also thought the drag marks were a little weird. It looked to me like one foot was rigid and one was flopping around, so I looked at this guy's feet. Look ..." Tartaglia, Garwood, Wysocki and Griffin bent over the body and looked closely at the victim's feet.

"...at the right ankle. It's badly broken. And freshly broken, probably in the last day or so. And it's never been set or tended to as far as I can tell. Notice the severe swelling, purpling and broken skin, where pieces of bone are starting to wear through to the surface? This guy sure didn't walk here on his own, and he must have been in excruciating pain—before he was killed, that is. We also have no blood droplets or bodily fluids from the vic here, meaning, to me, he was killed elsewhere and manhandled to this site."

Griffin was beginning to see where Tartaglia was going. His mind started racing for similarities and differences.

"Socks!" he blurted. "Carmody was wearing socks. This guy isn't."

Tartaglia grinned at Griffin, "Now you're cookin', Chief. Two more things and we'll be on the same page."

Griffin looked at the spike sticking out of this guy's chest, just as Carmody had been spiked, but Griffin knew instantly this was different.

"Frank…This spike was pounded in, after death, correct? Just like Carmody?"

"Yes, that's true…"

"But it's not the same, it's not a …what was it?"

"A Torah tool. No, this is not a Torah tool. It appears to be a plain, metal tent peg. A big one, for a big tent, like a party tent or something similar."

"OK, Frank. That's one, but you said 'two more things'. What did I miss?"

"Well, his dick."

How could they have forgotten? The bizarre twist that had fascinated morbidly with Carmody was missing here. This man's uncircumcised penis was absolutely shriveled.

"Damn, Frank. You're right."

"Now, Chief, connect the dots and I'll make you an honorary CSI."

Griffin mulled it over for a few seconds. He was close to pulling all the threads together but they wouldn't yet weave a strand. It was Wysocki who finally got it first.

"Jesus. The newspapers!" he blurted out.

"Bingo, Gerry, excellent!" Tartaglia congratulated.

"Sorry guys, I'm still not there..." Griffin confessed.

"You wanna tell him Gerry, or me?" Tartaglia was obviously enjoying this.

"Go ahead, Frank." Gerry offered. "You collected all the pieces first."

Tartaglia summed it up and Griffin finally got it. "OK, Chief, there are certain things we gave the media about Carmody's killing and there are certain things we held back. Handcuffs, plastic bag, sexually assaulted, tied to a tree, naked; we gave up all those details. So here we have, with this vic, a tree, handcuffs, a plastic bag, and sexual assault. With Carmody we said 'naked' so this guy is naked. We forgot to say 'socks'. With Carmody we said, 'spike' protruding from the chest postmortem. We didn't say 'Torah tool'. We held that one back out of concern for Jewish sensibilities, so not knowing that, this killer or these killers simply shoved in a 'spike,' whatever they had at hand, and this is one mother of a spike. We said of Carmody, 'sexually assaulted'. Out of sensitivity for his family's feelings we left out the info about his stiff cock and *how* he was sexually assaulted. This victim has been anally assaulted even though I don't know by what or whom as of yet; but in the male-dominated Arab world--and this guy is definitely an Arab--male sexual assault is both common and assumed to be anal, so that's what he got."

It finally dawned on me. "Frank, what you're saying is..."

"Yes, Chief. This may be a copy cat killing. We may well have more than one sick, twisted puppy on our hands."

A collective groan went up from all of them. Now they'd be chasing more than one psychotic killer which meant more time, more work and spreading the resources thinner. This was turning into a real nightmare. As bad as it looked, little did they know then just how black the clouds were about to become.

16.

"You May Interrogate With Extreme Prejudice..."

[FLASHBACK FIFTEEN MONTHS]

Armored personnel carriers do not have great shock absorbers. But considering that we tore through openly hostile streets I was more grateful for the armor plating than cruising in comfort. I was annoyed by the dust, however. The dust inside an APC traveling at 40 mph can be truly awful. I was already caked with it and the fine, particulate sand common to Northern Iraq was choking me to the point of remembering what it felt like when I smoked two packs a day.

My team and I were headed for our appointed rendezvous with our new boss. Our impossibly baby-faced driver, a young marine Lance Corporal who looked like he should be in middle school, was clearly enjoying our discomfort.

"Shit stinks, don't it Come-an-duh?" he yelled over the roar of the 500 horsepower engine and the rattle of machinery and chattering teeth.

"Yes Corp-or-al," I answered between jolts. "It stinks. How much farther?"

"'Bout fifteen minutes, suh! Unless, of course, we get blow-ed up by a freaking IED!" he whooped in what I believe was a West Virginia accent. He pounded the steering wheel, laughing at his own black humor. A dribble of tobacco juice ran from the corner of his mouth which he whisked away with his gloved right hand. The steel pot on his head wob-bled from side to side like some ridiculously oversized Darth Vader helmet. He slammed the shifter into overdrive and the powerful motor growled up another octave.

"Make it ten minutes, suh! Road ahead just cleared up a bit!"

"Um-hum," I choked over the grit.

I stared down at my boots, wondering why I hadn't taken the goggles offered me back at the LZ. My eyes were water-ing like crazy. Why the hell would anyone need goggles rid-ing inside an armored vehicle? I now knew why.

Boots. Boots...dull, black and tan desert boondockers. I suppressed a laugh. Just a few days ago I was sporting wingtips, polished to a high gloss. My de-rigueur $200 wingtips…It seemed like eons. What day was it, exactly?

It had started off innocently enough. My secretary brought me a priority Fed Ex and plopped it on my desk about 9:30 a.m. Since I got those all the time, I pushed it aside to finish tackling my email. But something kept drawing my brain back to the purple and red envelope. My sixth sense was radiating a small warning signal but I didn't know why. I had, however, learned to trust that sense implicitly. With a sigh I pushed my keyboard back under the lip of my desk and picked up the package.

As I read the "sender" info the hackles on the back of my neck came straight up: "Dept. of the Navy, Chief of Naval Operations, ONI Section, Washington, DC 20012, URGENT."

This could not be good. I zipped open the packet and pulled out a sheaf of documents about a quarter-inch thick. Before I got to the first page, a smaller packet, the familiar airline ticket envelope, plopped on my desk. Now I really knew this was not good.

Pushing my reading glasses a little higher up my short and twice broken nose, I read with fear and trepidation, "under the authority of Public Law 13T-Sec.7, para.12, the Chief of Naval Operations hereby directs CDR. James Allen Griffin, USNR-R, 147-062-9981, Commanding Office of Naval Reserve ONI Det. 71-A to report for active duty per the instructions enclosed." My heart sank.

I mean, I'd known this was a possibility, but here I was, fucked again. I could only stare at the horrible papers and mutter over and over, "Not now, shit, not now!"

The war in Iraq was a year old. Stunning initial success was settling into a staggeringly stubborn routine of chaos and destruction. Saddam had just been pried out of his hidey-hole and was now in our custody but the euphoria was short-lived. Organized resistance increased instead of slacking off like the Pentagon brain trust had confidently predicted. Our young men and distressingly, to this old troglodyte, young women were dying every day and this mess looked for all the world like another Vietnam.

As Commanding Officer of a highly classified, highly sensitive Office of Naval Intelligence detachment whose specialty was Interrogation Tactics, I had known for months that there was a big, fat bull's-eye painted on my back. If the shit got any deeper over in Iraq and we stayed much longer the odds were very high that I and my unit would be yanked out of our peacetime jobs, recalled to active duty and asked to start humping sand.

The timing sucked. But when does the timing of war ever *not* suck? Things were going great with Gracie; I was really enjoying watching Kyle grow out of his baby fat into a fine little boy. My police department was in great shape and humming along. I had just bought a 28′ motor home for me and Gracie to use to cruise around the countryside.

Now, called up, I'd be away for probably a year, maybe more. I'd have to turn over the Department to Beth who was good but not quite ready, in my view, to be Acting Chief. I'd lose a chunk of Kyle's development, have to put the RV in storage and be in a country where you couldn't drink. Worst of all I'd be without Gracie's alluring charms for far too long.

I could have gotten out of it, if I had wanted to take early retirement or resign my commission. But that wouldn't be right, and I couldn't bring myself to do it. It also hadn't helped that I had written my Master's Thesis at the Naval War College on "Effective Interrogation Tactics for POWs." Male ego firmly intact, there I was, two weeks later bouncing around in a Marine Corps APC, covered with dirt, roasting like barbeque pig waiting for bullets to start ricocheting off the sides of the truck.

My team bounced along with me in silence. My XO, LDCR Tim Stevenson, is an investment banker from Patchogue; my OPS officer, Lt. Ron Civilletti, a Captain in the NYS Police, POI Franklin Goins, an African-American race relations specialist with the NYPD and PO2 Mike Carmody, construction worker from Southampton and police officer wannabe.

The rest of my unit had been split into two other detachments, one assigned to the 3rd Marines in Baghdad and the other to work with the Brits in Basra. All of us were either cops, had been cops or wanted to be cops. We were also one of only two reserve units in the whole US Navy who worked exclusively in interrogation tactics and methods. Our job was to "out process" Iraqi POWs, which the coalition forces were scooping up in droves, and get as much useful intel out of them as possible. Once we were done wringing out their brains (if they had any) and separating chicken shit from chicken salad, we also had to decide which POWs got to go back to their families, which should be detained for further interrogation and which ones were the truly the hard cases that needed to be shipped off to the main detention centers like Abu Graib and Gitmo.

The hard work would be done by my officers and men. I was pretty much along for the ride and to coordinate activities between all three detachments. In the field I worked directly for an Army Colonel whose boss was a Marine Brigadier General attached to headquarters in Baghdad. A shitty job, but somebody had to do it. And if we did it well and kept our heads down we could all go home in about thirteen months, covered in "glory."

The APC suddenly slid to a stop and all of us held on to keep from tumbling into a heap.

"Made it, Come-an-duh! We're here. We done cheated

death once again and lived to tell the tale," our little Lance Corporal proudly announced.

"Great. Thanks, Lance Corporal. Keep your head down now, ya hear?" I offered hopefully.

"Yes-sir! I'm a short-timer. Two weeks and a wake-up and I'm outta here!"

"Well, good luck. Thanks for the ride," I said as we all stumbled from the truck, patting ourselves down, dust clouds billowing from our obviously new and far too clean desert cammies.

"Yes-suh. Thanks and here comes Sar-jint Francis, right ovah yonda, suh," the corporal pointed to the right.

A Marine Corp. Gunnery Sergeant strode up to my disheveled group, came to attention in front of me and snapped off a salute right out of Parris Island. I returned the salute in my nonchalant, devil-may-care fashion, and I could practically hear him sneer, "Reservists!" Was he looking down his nose at me? Fuck him...

"Commander Griffin?" he inquired, disdain in his voice.

"That's what my name tag says, Gunnery Sergeant, so it must be!" I said, probably a little too sarcastically.

He reddened in I-hate-officers fury. "Uh...yes, sir. I'll take your group with me sir, to check in. Colonel Chalabi wants to see you right away, Commander. He's in that building right over there."

The Gunnery Sergeants' left arm shot straight out to my right pointing at a low, windowless metal structure about 25 x 150, with a single metal door and a flat roof. It was guarded by what looked like two marines who were fully and grimly armed.

"Very well, Sergeant. Guys? Go with the Gunnery Sergeant here and I'll catch up with you as soon as I pay my respects to the Colonel."

My team gathered up their gear, mouthed their "yes-sirs" to me and ambled off with GYSGT Francis. I adjusted my web belt with its holstered .45 and slung one strap of my 50 pound pack over my left shoulder. The .45 is not my favorite sidearm. It's big, heavy and generally inaccurate. But it throws out a slug that will level a target with brute force if you hit it anywhere. That's why the Navy prefers to issue it to officers who don't generally carry firearms. It'll keep you out of trouble, but I much prefer my police .38. I had not been allowed to ship out with it, but Gracie said she'd try to sneak it into my first care package. I hoped she was kidding. I was sure I could find one here, on the black market if not in the supply system.

I walked over to the building that Chalabi was supposed to

be in. It was the middle of July. It had to be 110 degrees and it was only 9:00 a.m. I felt weak. It was definitely going to take some getting used to the heat. A section of three F/A -18s roared directly overhead. The whop-whop of rotor blades was a constant. Machinery rumbled everywhere around me. And what was around me was a temporary compound for the 2nd Brigade, 5th Marines, just on the outskirts of Tikrit, Saddam's family stomping grounds.

Tikrit, in northeastern Iraq, was very much a hot spot. It was still not under any sort of Coalition control although almost all uniformed and organized military resistance had been killed, captured or fled. The people who lived here were hostile, infested with insurgents and mad as hornets that we had captured their beloved dictator. We were slogging through the city block by block and also looking for the illusive WMDs we knew had to be here. And somewhere nearby were half a dozen terrorist training camps we were still trying to neutralize.

The 2/5 was doing a lot of heavy lifting and taking a lot of casualties but they were making progress. They were turning up suspected hard core Saddam lovers and possible terrorists by the truckload. All of these suspects were now being processed and filtered through here, and the job of pushing human flotsam and jetsam through the pipeline in this part of the world had fallen to one of the most interesting military characters to emerge from the conflict so far: a regular Army full bird colonel by the name of Achmed Chalabi.

I had been briefed on my new boss at the Pentagon before hopping the flight to Germany then on via MAC transport to Iraq. Pretty interesting guy, so it seemed. As might be readily guessed from his name, he was not Irish. He had been born in Iraq in fact, but on the grounds of the American Embassy in Baghdad, in the compound hospital, where his father worked as a contract doctor to the Embassy. Technically, he had been born on "American soil" which made him a bona fide citizen of both Iraq and the United States. This had not happened by accident. Chalabi's father snuck his pregnant wife into the Embassy hospital right after her water broke with the express purpose of making sure Achmed could take advantage of dual citizenship. This had been thirty-eight years ago when Iraq was in political turmoil. The leadership of the country was becoming more corrupt and indolent and a young Baath Party military officer by the name of Hussein would soon seize power.

Chalabi was practically raised inside the Embassy compound until he was eight at which time his father was offered the job of Chief of Staff at Baghdad's leading hospital. Another interesting fact I learned about Chalabi was that he was a Jew. His mother had been born Jewish in a very small and isolated Iraqi Jewish enclave in Southeast Baghdad. She had met Chalabi's father quite by accident when, as a young doctor, Chalabi's father had been part of a rescue team sent into the Jewish quarter to treat burn victims. A group of young radicals had set fire to the synagogue school. Dozens of children and teachers had been burned. Twenty who couldn't get out of the school during the fire had died. The arsonists had chained some of the doors shut – from the outside. Chalabi's mother was one of the teachers who had been badly burned. She was treated by young Mehmet Chalabi and an improbable romance blossomed.

Mehmet converted to Judaism and married Rachel. It was a brave and not so easy thing to do in Iraq in those days--even more so in these days. Mehmet's work with the Americans offered him a measure of protection from the hate mongers who seemed to be taking over in Iraq, but he knew the odds were stacked against him. Being a native doctor in a society where doctors were still a rare commodity also worked in Mehmet's favor but his life, absent any major political change, for which he fervently hoped, was a ticking time bomb.

The bomb went off when Achmed was fifteen. Saddam had come to power the year before and Hussein decided it was time to clean house. Jews, Sunni Muslims and Kurds were all in trouble. One day, while Achmed labored at his studies at the American Embassy School, his parents simply disappeared. He never saw them again. He, himself, narrowly escaped being rounded up and only because he was at school at the time. A sympathetic American Ambassador, who knew Chalabi's father, granted Achmed asylum and shipped him off to an uncle who had managed to immigrate to America.

Young Chalabi was devastated. His grief morphed to hatred of everything Hussein, and began a life-long quest to avenge his parents, country and religion. He buckled down to his studies again, in America, and a sympathetic Jewish Congressman in his uncle's hometown of Marlton, New Jersey, gave Chalabi his desired appointment to West Point, Class of '88. Chalabi, his outrage burning brightly, excelled at the Point. He graduated 3rd in his class. He selected Armor since this branch of the Army seemed to be advancing more quickly into desert warfare tactics than any other. He was a young First Lieutenant in charge of a section of Abrams tanks in the 3rd Armored when Saddam marched into Kuwait in 1990. Chalabi was ecstatic. He would get a chance to go back to his native land and liberate it from the beast he abhorred.

Chalabi did not disappoint his superiors or himself. Leading six main battle tanks across the desert, day after day, he charged first, drove the hardest, destroyed the most opposing tanks and slaughtered more Republican Guards than any unit of similar size. He was a man possessed. If the opposition had been more capable some might have branded him reckless, but because the enemy was essentially a paper tiger, his sometimes foolish aggressiveness was overlooked. After all, it didn't result in any excess casualties to his own troops. He wound up with a battlefield promotion to Captain, a Bronze Star with Combat "V" and a Silver Star. He was, however, horrified when President Bush called a halt to hostilities after just 100 days of combat. There would be no tank charge into Baghdad. No capture of Saddam. Not this time. Chalabi seethed but he did so in private. He would just have to be more patient than he had planned. The Army was still going to be his best avenue for revenge. He knew this just as surely as he knew his own name because he knew his enemy better than anyone. Unlike his then Commander in Chief Achmed Chalabi knew that Saddam would never give up power—ever—and that no one in Iraq would ever dare take it from him. He would bide his time.

The Army became Chalabi's life so much so that he rarely went off post, wherever he was stationed. He did not socialize much and only when it was necessary for military functions. He dated infrequently and had yet to marry or even come close. Had he not been a devoted reader of the Torah and a regular at synagogue his Army peers would have thought of him as a monk. He was not charming or particularly likeable, but everyone agreed he was as smart as any officer in the Army and probably destined for General's stars.

After Gulf One, Chalabi was rotated back to the Point to instruct Arabic and desert warfare tactics. He excelled at both and was promoted to Major at the tender age of thirty. Worried that bouncing around in tanks might not be the quickest way to get to slit Saddam's throat next time, Chalabi requested, and was granted, a transfer to Army Intel. The Army might lose a hell of a tanker, but they were more interested in Chalabi's insight into the language, culture and religions of Iraq than his fighting skills. Someone in the Army brain trust felt, and rightfully so that there'd be a Gulf Two. Chalabi could become key to the battle plan.

The next eight years of active duty for Chalabi saw tours as a Briefing Officer, Joint Chiefs of Staff, Army Command and General Staff College, G-2 for the 101st Airborne Division and Deputy Assistant to the honorable Donald Rumsfeld. Just promoted to full Colonel, one of the youngest in the Army, Chalabi was now in Iraq, under orders direct from Sec Def, to figure which direction the wind was going to blow next. Chalabi had what amounted to a blank set of orders. He could roam free in just about any direction he chose and the Army brass would back him.

To me, it sounded a little scary and it was an awful lot of responsibility to put on a pair of relatively young shoulders, even if he was wearing eagles. I guess I was also thinking I was seventeen years older and he outranked me. Sure, I had spent almost ten years enlisted before becoming an officer but even if you counted that time, he still outranked me and would be younger. Maybe I was a little jealous…

The Marines guarding the door to this whatever-it-was building came smartly to attention as I approached, but they made no move to open the door to let me in. Neither did they challenge me. After a few moments of uncomfortable silence, during which none of us moved a muscle I announced, "I'm Commander Griffin." Again, no reaction, no movement.

"I'm here to see Colonel Chalabi. He sent for me." At least this brought an exchange of nervous glances between the sentinels.

"Gunnery Sergeant Francis told me to come over to this building and check in with Colonel Chalabi." Ah! Finally. That was the magic phrase. I had learned over the years that Chief Petty Officers really run the Navy, not its officers, and that a CPO's word is God as far as a sailor is concerned. I had heard it was the same in the Corps in relation to Gunnery and Master Sergeants. I was getting living proof.

At the mention of Gunnery Sergeant Francis' name both guards came to life. The senior of the two, a corporal, finally said, "ID, sir!"

I handed over both my ID and a copy of my orders, which the corporal eyeballed closely. He handed them back to me, saluted crisply, and nodded to the other gatekeeper to unlock and open the door. I returned their salutes and stepped through the portal. The metal door slammed quickly behind me.

The temperature immediately dropped twenty degrees, which still made it ninety inside but it certainly felt cooler. At least I was out of the sun. I dropped my rucksack to the floor. There was no one in sight. I was staring down a single central corridor maybe fifty feet long. There were rooms of indistinguishable size on either side of the hallway – ten doors in total, all of them closed. Two standard fluorescent light fixtures illuminated the center of the building. Somewhere a fan was humming. At least the building had some ventilation, if not air conditioning.

The structure looked to be standard Army corrugated tin with ready made doors and a poorly poured concrete floor. It had obviously been put up in a hurry. But to what purpose? Was this Chalabi's office? Command Post? And why no windows?

Then it hit me. The stench. Feces and urine mixed with the coppery tang of blood. Just then, somewhere down the hall, behind one of the closed doors a chair scraped across a floor. That sound was followed quickly by a piercing shriek. Someone was shouting. I couldn't make out the words, but I knew it wasn't English. Another voice, also not in English, seemed to keen in response, almost begging. A loud crack, like a stick hitting leather. Another shriek and then more screaming. I heard muffled noises behind some of the other doors. Whispered prayers? Labored breathing? Where the hell was I? Some sort of jail? A detention center? Worse, some kind of torture chamber?

A moment later, a door opened far down the hallway, the last door on the left. A figure in desert fatigues emerged, using a dirty towel to wipe his hands. He turned and closed the door from which he had just emerged and set some sort of lock. The man finally looked up, directly at me. He tossed the towel aside and strode toward me. As the man neared I could see he was about six-feet tall, maybe 170 pounds, slightly hunched over as if he were carrying a great weight on his back. He was dark complected but still somehow sallow looking, like he hadn't been out in the sun much. How was that possible in this baking, God forsaken shithole? His features were definitely Arabic with high cheek bones and a prominent, hawk-like nose. He bore black eagles on each collar tab. Chalabi. I finally recognized him from his briefing photo. His eyes were dark, piercing and on fire. They were also red-rimmed as if from lack of sleep. He stopped two feet in front of me and looked me over from head to toe. I did not salute. The Navy doesn't salute indoors or uncovered. Instead I stuck out my hand and said, "I'm Command..."

"I know who you are. Come." He cut me off. He left my extended hand unshaken, wheeled around and started walking back down the corridor. Without turning, he impatiently motioned me to follow. We returned to the room Chalabi had just exited a few moments before. He removed a pass key from his left blouse pocket, swiped it in the electronic lock and the door popped open an inch. He pushed through, again motioning me to follow.

Inside the airless, windowless room a single naked light bulb hung from the ceiling. It cast an eerie, lifeless glow. A quick glance of my detective's eye also told me there were no one-way mirrors or hidden cameras. Sitting on a metal chair in the middle of the room, the only piece of furniture in the room, was a naked man who appeared to be Arabic. His ankles were tied to the chair legs with what seemed to be strands of barbed wire. His hands were tied together behind the back of the chair with more metal wire and with such tension that it looked as if his shoulders would pop out of their sockets at any moment. He was blindfolded. Blood ran from his nose down to his hairy chest all the way to his groin. He was bleeding from both ears. His body was a mass of purple welts, jagged cuts and small circular burn marks. His fingernails had been removed. Several of them littered the floor beneath the chair. Blood puddled under the chair, mixing with the man's urine. He sat in his own shit, some of which dribbled down the back chair legs. His testicles were being squeezed bloody by two large alligator clips, one on each ball, and connected by wires snaking back to a rather large sized truck battery. The man sat there quivering, whimpering, and tenaciously clinging to both life and sanity. On the floor near the chair was a pair of heavy duty leather gloves, now bloody, a braided whip, a three foot long hickory stick covered with gore and a pair of large snub-nosed pliers.

Chalabi circled around to the back of the man's chair. I stood rooted to the spot where I had stopped, hardly able to take in this horrendous scene.

Chalabi finally spoke. His voice was even but full of venom. "This worthless piece of camel dung is Machmoud Tikriti. He is, as you will no doubt quickly surmise, a native of this area. He was also, until most recently, a major in Saddam's beloved Republican Guard. He was in charge of intelligence operations in this sector."

Chalabi now leaned close to the man's right ear and bellowed, "He is also a worthless son of a whore! A rapist! A murderer! A buggerer of young boys! A piece of pig filth!" The rant ended. The man was crying, his breaths coming unevenly.

"He has just spent the last two days giving up all he knows, including the names and whereabouts of all his senior and junior officers, the ones we have not yet captured. He has also promised me his virgin sister to fuck anyway I please and told me I could ram hot pokers up his mother's cunt if I would just let him go. As such, he has ceased to be of use to me."

At that moment Chalabi unholstered his pistol, a Glock, placed the muzzle at the base of the man's neck and pulled the trigger. The man and the chair flew forward five feet, spun around and fell. The man came to rest on his right side. The blindfold had flown off and the man's dead but wide eyes stared into space. There was a giant hole where the man's Adam's apple had been. One of the man's testicles remained attached to an alligator clip. Fresh blood and other bits of flesh oozed down the opposite wall. The echoes of the shot still reverberated around the enclosed space.

My eyes narrowed. I had seen a lot in my time, but nothing quite like this. All I could say was, "What the fuck…"

Chalabi holstered his weapon. "Yes, Griffin, 'What the fuck!' But, Commander, what the fuck did just happen here? You tell me." Chalabi crossed his arms and stood staring at me.

"Well, in my book, an execution, or depending on the circumstances, maybe even a cold blooded murder."

"Wrong on both counts, Griffin. What you just witnessed was a highly dangerous prisoner shot while attempting escape from lawful authority."

"You can't be serious!" I choked.

"I am serious. Quite serious. That's how the report will read. And you will sign it as witness."

"The hell I will!" I shouted.

Chalabi sighed and shook his head. "You're going to be here a while. You'll figure it out. Let's get some coffee."

"Coffee! You just blew a man's brains out and you want to go for coffee? Are you nuts?!"

"Some people think so, but no, I'm not. I'm an Arab, and a Jew and that's a pretty interesting combination that gives me some unique insights into this part of the world. For example, there are nine other rooms in this building, all like this one, and each room contains, as we speak, animals like Tikriti here. They will soon know, if they don't already, what happened in this room. They will give up the information I need much more quickly than Tikriti did and if they do they'll live to see another day and we will save God knows how many Sunnis and Kurds and, I would guess, a bunch of our guys, too. It's a means to an end. And by the way I didn't blow his brains out. I blew his neck out. He choked to death on his own blood would be my guess. Or died of shock or fear, but who gives a shit. He really was a murderer, rapist and pedophile. Welcome to Iraq. How do you take your coffee?"

That was my introduction to Colonel Achmed Chalabi.

17.

Gracie

Gracie is absolutely the best person I know. Probably the best person I've ever known. And I'm in love. It started out quite innocently enough. Gracie is a Professor of Criminology at John Jay College, part of the CUNY system, in Manhattan. She teaches three courses but her most popular, by far, is "Great Detectives-Case Studies in Successful Methods for Catching Crooks." The course is part history, part practical application, and throughout each semester, when the course is taught, she asks real detectives, like me, to be guest lecturers and share all our hard-won knowledge of the mean streets. She contacted me three years ago and asked if I'd come to one of her night classes. I wasn't really interested and didn't think I'd make much of a case study or be a great instructor, but there was something in her voice and the way she subtlety stroked my ego, so I said, "What the hell. Sure."

I showed up one night to a packed lecture hall with over 100 students, and was stunned. Not by the turnout. By her. It was love at first sight. I was totally smitten and I hadn't felt so boyishly giddy since feeling my first naked breast at age fifteen. After the class we went out for coffee. I thought this was a hint from her that she was also smitten with me. My fragile ego was bruised when I learned that she took out all of her guest lecturers for post-class coffee as a "thank you for coming."

I sat there entranced for over an hour. I didn't remember much about what she said. I just kept staring into those dancing brown eyes. When I put her in a cab at Lincoln Center at about 11:00 p.m. I sheepishly asked if I could see her again, maybe have dinner next week when I was back in the city. She looked at me, giggled, then flashed her dazzling smile.

"Well, I don't know, James. I'll check with my husband and get back to you!"

The cab door clicked shut and she sped up Broadway to 87th. Husband! Man, I really had not been paying attention. I was crushed. I moped for days. My staff thought someone close to me had died. Little did they know someone had-me!

Imagine my surprise when Tilly buzzed me at 4:00 p.m. on Tuesday of the following week and said, "There's a Professor

Gracie Connors from John Jay on line two for you. Shall I take a message?"

"Huh?" I was in shock. Seconds passed.

"Chief? You there? Shall I take a message?"

"Uh, no! I'll take the call." I let the light for line two flash for what seemed an eternity while I composed myself. I finally picked up the receiver and stabbed at button two.

"Chief Griffin," I said coldly, while trying to untangle my thoughts and my tongue.

"Hi!" The luscious voice came through the earpiece like warm butter. "I checked with my husband. He said it was OK if we had dinner. You still want to?"

What the hell was this? "Well…yes," I stammered, "I'd love to but, what was that about your husband-again?" I was totally confused.

She giggled. "Sorry, James. I just had to think about you for a while before I reacted. I felt pretty good about you last week, but a girl can't be too careful these days…"

"Gracie! I'm a cop, not an axe murderer," I laughed back.

"That's the problem. I'd probably feel more at ease with an axe murderer. I study them for a living."

"So, the husband is the axe murderer then?" It was a weak attempt at humor.

"No, he's a cop. Now do you get it?"

"Yes, I guess I do."

There was a moment of silence. She resumed the conversation with, "James, I am married. But I haven't lived with Bill for more than two years. We truly have gone our separate ways but we've just never gotten around to getting divorced. And sometimes, for a single girl in Manhattan, it's better to give the impression that you're not single. Do you understand?"

"Yes" I said warming, "I do."

"So...How about that dinner? When will you be back in the city?" she purred.

I glanced at my watch. "For you? In about two hours. Where can I meet you?"

Six months later we started living together. Mostly at my place in Southampton, but Gracie kept her apartment in the city, too, which was a place for her to stay on the days she taught classes. It was also a pied-a-terre for us, and that turned out to be a wonderful thing from time to time.

Gracie cut back on her schedule some. She had been teaching for over twenty years and although she still loved it, she was starting to think about maybe someday retiring and writing a book or two. She had classes on Tuesdays and Thursdays so she'd usually stay in the city on those days, have office hours for her students on Wednesdays and be home in the Hamptons Thursday night through Tuesday morning. It was a pretty decent arrangement and one the college was happy to accept. The alternative would be losing Professor Connors for good and that they were not yet prepared to do. Gracie was one of their best and the administration knew it. Gracie was a rarity in Criminology. She was a pure academic. She had never been a practitioner. Most criminal justice educators have some experience in the system, either as a cop, district attorney, criminal lawyer, military police work, FBI, DEA, whatever. Gracie had never carried a badge or a gun, yet she knew her stuff as well as anyone in the system and was widely recognized for what she knew.

Born and raised in Valhalla, up in Westchester County, she had been a pretty good student but hadn't found much to focus on. She could have gone anywhere to college but she drifted into SUNY New Paltz, which, in the late '70's was a pretty big hippie hangout and a huge party school. Perfect for what Gracie had in mind which, at that point, was to get as high and as drunk as possible and have the best times that could be had. Her upbringing had been pretty strict.

She was loose now and determined to enjoy life. Then, as with a lot of us, there was that defining event that would change everything.

Her college roommate, Caroline, was the closest friend that Gracie had ever had. Friends of some of their friends got wind of a party that was going down across town one April Saturday night in Gracie's junior year. There was going to be a lot of great drugs, so they said. Gracie was still hung-over from the night before and she had just gotten her period. She decided not to go. Caroline did.

Caroline's bruised and battered body was found in an abandoned drug den two days later. She had been raped repeatedly and strangled. The police were never able to make any arrests. Although they had a lot of suspects, there was very little hard evidence. The local DA couldn't make a single solid case against anyone. Gracie was outraged. Furious. And she'd found a purpose in life. She became a criminologist to teach people how to be good cops and prosecutors so cases like Caroline's might not happen, at least not with frequency.

After Caroline's murder, Gracie sobered up. Overnight. She hasn't had a drink or a recreational drug since the day Caroline was buried over 20 years ago.

Gracie finished at SUNY the following year, with honors, and went on to grad school at Columbia and got a Master's in

Behavioral Science. She followed that up with a PhD in Psychology at Stanford. She's been teaching and writing ever since, including a dozen of the very top textbooks in the field of criminal behavior. A few years back she fell in love with a cop. They got married but it sputtered out quickly. Bill transferred from NYPD to Baltimore. They are still friends. I've met him and he's a decent guy.

In addition to being my partner and lover, she is sometimes my sounding board. We try very hard not to mix our personal lives with work, but sometimes it can't be helped. This was one of those times. I needed Gracie's eyes and instincts on this case. That's why we were sitting at a quiet table at Le Chef on Jobs Lane in Southampton, sharing dinner and coffees. I had just finished filling her in on all the details of where we were or weren't.

"My bet's on the second murder being a copycat killing. I think Frank Tartaglia's right about that," Gracie said with great seriousness.

I quietly stirred my coffee. I knew she wasn't done yet.

"But I think you've got two other problems, lover man."

"And they are, my darling professor?"

"The second killing, I'll bet you my next paycheck, it's a cover up."

"Meaning?" I toyed.

"You can be such a smart ass," she said with a smile. "You know damn well what I mean. We know the second guy was not killed where he was found. I'll bet he was killed for some specific reason and then some bright bulb said, 'Hmm. The cops have this juicy woodland sex murder on their hands already, why not make this one look like that one and keep the pricks running in circles all day?' At the very least it's going to split your forces and slow you down."

"Darling, I believe you may be right, I'm sorry to say," I sighed. "But we can't drop one murder and prosecute the other."

"Why not?" she shrugged with nonchalance.

I was taken aback. "Well…Because. That's not how things are done."

She reached across the table and patted my hand. "James, James. I really have to get you to think outside the box once in a while."

"The only box I care about is…"

Now she slapped my hand. "Oh! You and your dirty little mind! You are so bad! Now, pay attention!"

"OK, I'll be good," I laughed.

"Seriously, now. You've got two dead guys. One you know. The other you don't. One has friends and a family that need closure. The other is a complete mystery. Concentrate on the one. The other will follow. It has to. They are related in some fashion. We don't know how just yet, but my guess is one will help solve the other."

I began to see where she was going, and it was pretty brilliant.

"But you have an even bigger challenge, call it problem number two."

"Yeah. You mentioned two problems. What's the other one?"

"Well, dearest, here it is, and you're not going to like it. My gut tells me the first killing, despite your possible conspiracy theories, your mystery Navy Lieutenant and that awful Chalabi guy you worked for in Iraq, is not political or in any way connected to all that military intel mumbo jumbo you love so much."

"You think it's coincidental?"

"Yes, I do."

"Then, what…?"

"Honey, it was a thrill killing. It has all the classic markings.

It was a random act of violence. Poor Mike Carmody was in the wrong place at the wrong time."

"You really believe that?"

"I do. But there's more: once these killings start, they don't stop. Not until you catch whoever did this. No one knows why a thrill killer starts killing, but there's always a trigger. Sometimes it takes a long time for the trigger to be pulled, but once it is, the gun just keeps on firing. That's the other reason you need to put more emphasis on Carmody's murder right now as opposed to your copy-cat "John Doe Hammad." The guy or guys who butchered Mike Carmody will strike again and keep on striking until they're killed or captured."

"Jesus, Gracie. Sometimes I wish you weren't so damn smart."

18.

Prep Time…

"You 'bout ready?" Tim Garwood asked, trying to prod his partner into action.

"Yeah…Just gimme another minute," Gerry Wysocki responded distractedly. He was flipping pages of his notebook back and forth, as if looking for something he had missed or wanted to make sure he hadn't.

The waitress came by the booth for the umpteenth time. "Refills, gentlemen?" It was said without annoyance. Even though the two detectives had been monopolizing one of Martha's best booths at the Princess Diner in Southampton for over an hour on a busy Tuesday morning, she didn't mind. These guys were regulars and tipped well for the use of the space as sort of a surrogate office.

"No, thanks, Martha." Garwood waved her pot away.

"Half a cup, dear," Wysocki asked. Garwood glanced at his watch, for no particular reason other than he wanted to get going.

Wysocki's half cup was poured and sat steaming, untouched. "OK, Tim. Let's go over this one more time. I wanna get this right in my head."

Garwood sighed. This was unlike his partner, who tended to be flashier and a lot more impulsive than Garwood himself.

"Gerry, for Chrissakes, what's eatin' you? Let's just head out there. We can learn a lot more if we find these people and ask 'em some questions!"

"Dunno, Tim. Normally I'd agree with you, but there's something missing and I'm not quite seeing it. Humor me. Let me run it by you one more time, OK? Please?"

"Sure...fine," Garwood said as he held his empty cup aloft so that Martha could see it from across the room, "We should get paid by the hour."

Wysocki flipped back a few pages. "OK, so, we've got shaky statements from five inebriated cops who were at the bar at Buckley's the night Carmody was murdered. The statements wouldn't be worth a cup of piss if they weren't from cops, even if they were shit-faced cops."

"Correct."

"They all agree that Carmody exited the bar with the woman and the young kid. One cop, who left two minutes later, thinks that Carmody was getting into this big blue Mercedes with the kid and this woman."

"Yup."

"Now the cop, this, uh, Sergeant Ferris, SHPD, thinks this is strange for two reasons. Carmody drives a Ford F-150 which is still parked in the lot, a few spaces away, but, hey, Carmody's pretty drunk, maybe he's just getting a ride home, which, in his condition, is the smart thing to do. But why not go with one of his other buddies? Why with these two strangers? People he had met only a couple of hours before? But then again, guys do pick up strange girls in bars, so what's different here? Except the girl is picking up the guy and she's got a kid with her."

"Right."

"But here's where we catch a break. The sergeant recalls the first three letters of the car's plate: A-L-F. He only remembers this because, one, it's his wife's initials, ALF, and two, "ALF" was one of his favorite TV shows from 20 years ago. Nutty logic, but hey, it works. The sarge and a couple of our other boozing brothers also remember this gal calling herself 'Vic' or 'Vicky'." Wysocki flips the page. "So, a check of the

DMV for late model blue Mercedes with at least A-L-F on the plate registered to anyone named Vic or Vicky gets us a 2006 Mercedes 500 SE, license tag ALF-7651 registered to one Victoria Rubino of Number 37 Georgica Pond, East Hampton."

"So, far, so good."

"'Vic' or 'Vicky' is described variously, but nearly unanimously, as late thirties, early forties, 5'6 to 5'7, about 130 pounds, short blond hair, nice ass, great legs, big tits and a body covered in designer clothes and massive pieces of gold jewelry with several large- sized stones. The kid, called 'Vincent' or maybe 'Vincenzo,' is late teens, over six foot, over 200 pounds, olive skinned or very tan, dark, curly hair, big smile, lots of pearly whites and wandering hands, like maybe he's gay or at least really juiced on raging teenage hormones. Couple of the cops say they felt 'creeped out' like the kid was eyeing them sexually and he was all over Carmody, but Carmody's too drunk to notice."

"Um, hmm."

"The System [the FBI National Database System on convictions and arrests] has nothing on the kid, no shock there, but there's stuff on Miss Vicky. Three arrests over the past eight years, one in '98 for DWI and possession, less than an ounce of marijuana. One in 01 for shoplifting at Saks--a bottle of Chanel, she was drunk at the time of arrest--and one in 05 for possession of 'drug paraphernalia' at a beach party in Amagansett that got raided by DEA. Real party girl, our Miss Vicky."

"Sounds like it," Garwood echoed.

"These busts aren't crimes of the century, that's for sure, but all three charges get kicked without any prosecution or further adjudication of any kind. They just disappear off the blotter without any explanation. Now knowing who her husband is, it makes sense."

"That's the Rubino guy, right?"

"Right. Milos Rubino. He's got some serious money, like billions, they say, and I guess he's got some serious pull with someone in the DA's office, too."

"But now maybe little Miss Vicky has started to step it up a notch, eh?"

"Possible, but it's a long stretch from getting busted for drugs or drunken driving to sadistic sex and murder, don't you think?"

"That what's bothering you?"

"Yep. That and a couple of other things. Victoria does have a son, named Vincenzo Rubino, aged sixteen, son of Milos. Seems to fit the description of the kid who was seen in Buckley's. But why is she taking her son, if that was him, out while she cruises the bars?"

"Don't have the answer there, partner, but we do know why she's hitting the bars lookin' for love, right?"

"Well, yeah, maybe. Old Milos is as queer as a three peckered billy goat, they say. Notorious fag. So, Miss Vicky ain't getting any at home, least not these days."

"Kid's supposed to be gay, too. Like father, like son. You don't suppose she's training him, do you?"

"What do you mean?"

"Well, she ain't got a dick, least as far as we know. Maybe she's, you know, introducing him."

"Pretty sick, if true. But where does Dad fit in here? Is he the real dad? Does he know about this? His son?"

"Well, we ain't getting' any answers sittin' here on our asses. Let's roll."

"You're right. Let's go. On to Georgica Lane."

With that the two detectives each pitch in a ten on two five-dollar tabs and head to East Hampton.

19.

The First Confrontation

The intercom on Milos Rubino's massive desk chimed faintly. Rubino stabbed a chubby index finger on a button that opened both an audio circuit and a video link to the estate's front gate.

"What is it?" Rubino snarled curtly.

"Sir, it's Danny, at the front gate. Sorry to bother you but there are two guys here to see Vicky."

"Perlman, you know damn well we don't let people just knock on the door and come in. Who the hell are they and what do they want with Victoria?"

The guard responded nervously, "Well, they're detectives. From Suffolk County. They said they had a few questions to ask Vicky, but they won't tell me any more. What do I do?"

"Damn, I knew it!" This from Ivan Centpied who was sitting in Rubino's study on the other side of the desk.

Rubino's eyes narrowed. "Hold on a second, Danny." Rubino pressed the mute button and turned to Centpied.

"You know something about what's going on here, Ivan?"

"Well…maybe. I don't know…It was something I was going to bring up later in this meeting." Centpied squirmed in his chair.

"Maybe you better bring it up now," Rubino hissed.

"Uh, well, Vicky and Vincenzo went out the other afternoon and the ...um... tail we had on them lost them for a few hours."

"LOST THEM?" Rubino thundered, slamming a ham-like hand on the polished walnut surface. "What do you mean 'lost them'?"

"The idiot on the detail that day followed them to a bar on Job's Lane in Southampton. Turns out the place was full of cops having a party. Our guy got nervous when the cops started leaving. Seems there's a criminal history of some kind on this guy and he decided to drive around the block. By the time he got back, Vicky had left and he... ah…didn't pick them up again for several hours. Until they showed up back here."

"I want that man castrated; do you hear me, Centpied? Castrated! I want his balls on my desk by noon!" Rubino bellowed like a gored bull.

"Well, that might be a little hard, Milos. He's since disappeared and no one knows where."

"Then fire that idiot who runs our protection service."

"I thought about it, Milos, but he's really the best at what he does, despite this lapse, and he knows too much. I'd rather keep him on a short leash until our plans have been executed, then we can, of course, do whatever you want," Centpied replied soothingly.

Rubino thought about this for a moment. "Perhaps you're right. But if there's one more fuck up, even a tiny one, that bastard will be a eunuch, and you tell him that."

"I already have, in much the same words. He assures me he'll double his efforts and this won't happen again."

"Better not," Rubino threatened. "Now let's get rid of the cops."

Rubino moved to push the talk button but Centpied pleaded, "Wait, maybe we should talk to them."

"Are you crazy? I don't want any cops sniffing around here, not now, for God's sake!"

"I know, I know, but they're cops. And cops always get

pissed off if you don't give them what they think they want. Worse than that, they get even more suspicious. Besides, if we send them away, they'll just get more insistent and go get a warrant or something."

Rubino allowed his massive body to rock back in his chair. "Hmm. Maybe you're right. By the way, is Vicky here? And Vincenzo?"

"I'm not sure. I think so. I thought I heard Maria getting them breakfast when I came in."

Rubino stabbed another button. "Israel!" he shouted, "You down there?"

A high-pitched voice with a definite lisp came back obsequiously, "Yes love, I'm here."

"Are Vicky and Vincenzo down there?"

"Yes, love. We're having tea."

"Get them into the panic room now and don't come out until I tell you."

"Lover!" the voice squealed in fear, "what's wrong?"

"Nothing, Israel. I'm just being cautious. Now be a good boy and do what I tell you."

"Oh, Oh! Okay…"

"Now, go quickly," Rubino soothed the other man. "I'll buzz you when I want you to come up."

Rubino hit the button to the guard shack. "Danny, Let the gentlemen come up. I'll meet them in the foyer."

An obviously relieved sentinel responded, "Yes, sir. Right away, sir." He stepped from the booth and back out to the car where Wysocki and Garwood idled, cooling their heels.

"OK, gentlemen. I'll open the gates. Please drive straight ahead and park under the portico at the end of this lane. Someone will meet you there," the guard pointed.

"'Bout damn time," Garwood muttered from the passenger seat.

"Don't mind my partner," Wysocki smiled at the nervous sentry. "He didn't get any last night." With that the massive and ornate iron gates swung open and Wysocki tapped the accelerator.

The driveway was crushed white chips and had to be a quarter-mile long. Small chunks of marble rattled off the bottom of the four-door Ford sedan that screamed "Cop Car!" in its bleak silver tones and non-adorned exterior. All along the approach to what appeared to be the main house at 37 Georgica the plants and trees lining the driveway were dressed in burlap, prepped for what was predicted to be a long, cold winter. The lawns surrounding the center of the property seemed to slope away in all directions in a sea of dull grey-green. Even for the expected opulence of a Georgica address in the Hamptons, this was a place more spectacular than most.

Then the main house came into view as Wysocki rounded the turn at the end of the driveway. The three-story expanse had to be 20,000 square feet, minimum, and looked as if it had been uprooted from beside a canal in Venice. It was definitely Italian, definitely ornate and definitely cost a fortune.

Garwood let out a low whistle. "Whoa! I guess this guy has the money they say he has."

"Appears so," Wysocki echoed with a little jealous sarcasm in his voice.

Two large, dark-suited men awaited the car under the portico. Wysocki slid slowly to a stop at the bottom of a rise of marble steps that lead to a huge front door.

Garwood whispered to Wysocki, "Hey Ger. Both these guys are packin', see?" The obvious bulges under the men's jackets were meant to impress.

"Yeah. I see. Shall we ask them for their permits?"

Both detectives stepped from their respective car doors. Neither guard moved but the one on the right said, "Leave the car right here. Toss me the keys. We'll take care of it. You can go up."

Wysocki pitched the key ring to the man. He snatched it out of the air and pocketed the keys without flinching.

"Don't scratch the paint, please. Our boss is very sensitive about the condition of his fleet," Wysocki wisecracked. Neither guard moved a facial muscle.

Wysocki and Garwood mounted the steps and before they could knock, the heavy doors swung open, guided by some unseen hands or, more likely, a set of silent motors. The two men walked into a large foyer which towered some thirty feet and was decorated with art from floor to ceiling. There were paintings and sculptures everywhere. All of it, both detectives noted with a professional eye, was masculine. Men everywhere, alone and in small groups, mostly nude, posing in stone or renaissance oils. There wasn't a naked woman to be seen anywhere.

Garwood said it first. "I guess we're setting a tone, here, don't you think?"

"Appears so. Guess the stories are true," Wysocki responded wryly.

At that moment another set of doors opened at the far end

of the foyer. Two men walked through, and both detectives independently came to the same conclusion, in their own way, and that was: it would be hard to find a stranger looking pair of male forms anywhere. The two detectives exchanged a look that betrayed both amusement and astonishment.

The man in the lead, now moving toward them, looked for the entire world like a tanned version of the Michelin Man in designer jeans. A huge Polo shirt draped his upper torso and hung over the waistband of the jeans. Both shirt and jeans looked as if they had been made by Omar the Tentmaker. He was huge, and his near 400-pound frame rocked from side to side as he walked. *Actually, he's waddling,* Wysocki thought. His upper arms were too fat to hang by his enormous sides so they sort of stuck out like the appendages on an over-inflated balloon from the Macy's Thanksgiving Day Parade. His moon-shaped face radiated a perfect grin under close-cropped black hair, but his eyes betrayed the smile. They were stone-cold black, and full of fire. As he drew closer, a large diamond-encrusted Star of David dangled from a thick gold chain that, despite its broad links, was smothered under the rolls of fat in his neck. The star flopped noisily on the man's chest as he moved. This ostentatious bit of "bling" was also meant to be a statement.

The other man trailed slightly behind. He was a good six inches shorter than the massive mountain of flesh in front of him, and he, too, was decidedly overweight, but not nearly as much as the other man. It was his shape that defined him. His body looked like a giant Bosc pear come to life. Most of his mass was below his waist on top of short legs, and he walked with arms tightly folded across his chest. He looked like one of those Russian nested dolls come to life. What made him ever more striking was a pair of massively bushy eyebrows that encased a pair of beady brown eyes. The brows were thick and curly enough to make Andy Rooney jealous. And the man drew attention to them even more by trying to hide them behind a pair of oversized black-framed eyeglasses. The effect was to make him look like a raccoon. He also appeared nervous, and sweaty, even in the December chill, and his mouth seemed permanently frozen in a tight little smile.

The mountain spoke first, thrusting forward a huge hand. "Good day, gentlemen. My name is Milos Rubino. This is an associate of mine, Ivan Centpied. What can I do for you?"

Garwood and Wysocki shook hands with Rubino. Centpied kept his arms clasped to his torso and said nothing. Garwood later recalled that shaking Rubino's hand was like trying to dribble a basketball made of dough.

No other pleasantries were exchanged. All four men stood rooted to the slick and highly polished marble floor. No offer of coffee, tea or water. No invitation to sit or retire to any other room was generated. It was clear to both detectives that this was as far as they were going to go into the sanctum, at least on this trip, and if they were going to get anything at all for their troubles, it was going to be here and now, with words echoing around a cold and sterile gallery.

Garwood spoke for both, "Mr. Rubino, we appreciate you seeing us, but it's actually Victoria Rubino we would like to talk with. Is she here?"

Rubino's ferret-like eyes flashed from one cop to the other incessantly, trying to pick up some unspoken intelligence. "Actually, no, she's out. She took my son shopping."

Centpied cringed slightly. A mistake had been made and he knew it. Wysocki caught it.

"Oh, really? I would have thought your son would be in school at this time on a Tuesday morning."

Rubino knew instantly he'd been caught in his lie, but he parried swiftly, "My son is home schooled."

Garwood now got in on the hunt, sniffing a scent. "But aren't you the Chairman of the Board of the Irving Center? That's a local private school, right?"

Rubino was becoming more uncomfortable and started to sway slightly, like a giant cargo ship wallowing at sea. Wysocki, who got deathly seasick on ferry boats, started to feel slightly nauseous just watching him.

Rubino ignored the uncomfortable line of questioning, "You said you were here to talk to Victoria, I believe, not me, so could I ask why you're interested in speaking with her? I am her husband, after all."

Garwood pressed, "Well, we can't really say too much at this point, but we'd just like to ask her a few questions. She may have been a witness to an event, or possible events that took place the other evening."

"Such as?" Rubino tried to pry further.

"Well, sir, as my partner said," Wysocki responded, "We can't really discuss that, except with Mrs. Rubino, and possibly your son."

"My son?" Rubino's eyes widened.

"Yes." Wysocki was now enjoying this, "He might have been a witness, too. Do you know when they'll be back? We could wait…"

"No, no," Rubino blew them off by waving a slab of his beefy arm in their faces," I'm afraid they won't be back for many hours. I believe they went up island, to Roosevelt Mall, maybe even to Manhattan. With Vicky's shopping habits, one never knows."

"OK, then," Garwood added, "we'll give you our cards. Please have Mrs. Rubino call us as soon as she returns. We'll make arrangements to speak to her directly."

Garwood and Wysocki each produced an official business card which Rubino accepted as if he were picking up dog turds. He immediately passed the cards to Centpied, who stuffed them into his shirt pocket with clear disdain.

"So, then, thank you for stopping by, Detectives. We're busy people but we're always happy to cooperate with the authorities," Rubino said mockingly.

"No problem, sir." Wysocki smiled back with equal facetiousness. "But do have Mrs. Rubino call sometime in the next 24 hours, or we'll have to come back and interrupt another busy day. Sorry, but that's just the nature of the game."

"I will do that. Good day, gentleman," And with that, Rubino wheeled his bulk around and with Centpied in trail, lumbered back down the hallway from whence he had come some minutes before.

Again, by magic, the front doors swung open behind the two detectives.

"Guess that's our cue to leave, eh Ger?" Garwood smirked.

"Guess so, Tim. Let's get the hell out of here."

As they walked down the entry steps, the two suits instantly re-appeared. A key ring flew at Wysocki's head. Garwood deftly caught it. "I'll drive," he said.

The two cops switched sides and got into the sedan. The bigger of the two guards croaked, "Have a nice day."

"Yeah, you too," Garwood shot back as he put the big Ford in gear. He gunned the engine and the car leapt ahead, leaving both thugs to duck flying chunks of marble.

"Nice touch, there Timmy." Wysocki smiled.

"Yeah, they deserved it. So whaddya think?"

Wysocki sat silently for a few moments. After the car slid through the front gate and headed back to Montauk Highway all he could say was, "After spending fifteen minutes with those two, I feel like I need a shower."

Back in the comfort zone of his study, Rubino was seething. "How could that bitch be so stupid?" he wailed at Centpied. "Get her up here now! Vincenzo, too. And get that good for nothing, fucking attorney, Bruce Stuyvesant on the phone. I want him all over this!"

20.

Rabbinical Deception

What was I thinking? The disheveled man berated himself over and over as he paced his spacious bedroom in an elegant robe and Stubbs & Wooten embroidered slippers. He hadn't shaved in two days, had barely eaten and told his worried wife and staff that he had a migraine and simply wished to be left alone.

"I knew better than to believe that awful man," he moaned for the hundredth time. "I knew he was evil the moment I met him yet I let him seduce me. Seduce me! With promises of huge contributions to the synagogue. And supporting my plans for expansion. And the trips and dinners and speeches! What was I thinking?" There was no one there to answer the question. A question to which there was only one answer. You weren't thinking.

The Rabbi Baruch Feldman was in a box, a golden box. And the lid had been slammed shut on him by his benefactor and it now seemed the box was mysteriously, magically shrinking and crushing him to death.

Just a year ago he had been so happy – so professionally fulfilled, and now he was miserable, beyond despair, and probably about to lose the one job he loved more than any other.

The Rabbi had been called to lead the ultra-chic, semi-Orthodox Hamptons Synagogue five years ago. As one of the wealthiest synagogues in the country, with an A-list of Jews from the Hamptons, Manhattan, Hollywood, even some from overseas to call upon, the Rabbi felt as if he were in rabbinical paradise. The synagogue itself, situated on five prime acres of real estate in the heart of trendy East Hampton was well-maintained, but a tad old. Part of the plan was to revitalize the entire footprint with a new Temple, teaching center, Hebrew School and event site. It was hard work, but challenging and uplifting. "Until that bastard Rubino came into my life," the Rabbi cursed to the walls. He spat three times on the solid oak floor.

At first Milos Rubino had seemed an answer to his prayers. Yes, a very big man, in more ways than one, he had often laughed with the Rabbi that he wanted to be "the biggest

Jew in the Hamptons," both literally and figuratively. He had certainly achieved his first goal with his obese pulchritude, and with his family's money, he was trying to achieve the second as well.

With promises of immense monetary support and "an open checkbook" for the Rabbi, Rubino had bought his way onto the synagogue's Board of Directors. In the process Rubino had offended a number of the temple's long-time supporters, including many names on that all important A-list. The Rabbi now knew—too late—that he had been blinded by Rubino's golden light and had neglected too many of his faithful flock.

Rubino, having packed the Board with his friends, now controlled it, and he wanted, apparently, his "own" Rabbi to place under his considerable thumb. It had been a masterfully devious scheme. Rubino secretly bankrolled dozens of foreign trips for the Rabbi and his family to "consult" other successful congregations on major expansion plans. There had been glittering trips to Hollywood, Las Vegas and Miami. There had been somber and newsworthy pilgrimages to Jerusalem, Warsaw, Moscow, Buenos Aires and of all places-Honolulu. There had been sober and well-received lectures and speeches delivered by the Rabbi at first-rate universities and synagogues all around the country.

The Rabbi had bought into it, taken all of it, believing

somewhere in his secret heart that he was doing it all to enhance the prestige of his Temple, to make his glorious plans come to fruition. But deep down he knew different and he pushed aside that little strident voice inside that shouted, "Don't do it!" And now the voice wasn't so little anymore. It was, in fact, quite loud, insistent and throbbing painfully just behind his eyeballs.

Rubino kept upping the Rabbi's bonuses, kept encouraging him to hold more services, to keep Temple on the beach, open up the closed and secret liturgies. He insisted that the Rabbi add more and more of Rubino's friends to the membership rolls. It did seem curious to the Rabbi that these friends were almost always male, almost none with wives but a great many of them with adopted children. "Well, what's the difference?" he rationalized. "We're all God's children, aren't we?"

Too late now he realized he was driving solid, traditional Jewish families from the Temple. Too late now he understood that many of those glorious speeches and sermons Rubino had supplied were plagiarized from great sermons of other Rabbis and Jewish secular leaders. Too late now he understood that Rubino had cleverly disguised the funds used for the Rabbi's many trips as coming--somehow-- from the operating funds of the Temple school. Too late he now realized, thanks to his accountant, that he had been paid more than $450,000 last year--more than the President of the United States! And he had no way to justify how that had happened. Too late he knew that he'd been "had." And now Rubino would be able to take over the entire temple and Feldman had handed it to him on a golden platter.

The congregation was in an uproar. All of this had gotten into the local papers and even *The New York Times,* and a general meeting of the congregation had been called to elect new Board members and decide if the Rabbi was to stay or go. The meeting would be next week and from all he had heard nearly every member of the congregation would be there. And why not? It would be Chanukah and most of the Temple's members would be in town for family celebrations anyway. Spielberg was coming. So was Perelman and every other member of the A-list as far as Feldman could determine. It was going to be a disaster and Feldman knew he was going to be ruined. Just as Rubino had planned.

21.

Blended Families

One of Gracie's favorite things to do, no matter what time of year, was to drive by Cooper's Beach and just look at the ocean. On this cool, clear December night blessed with a full moon, the view was particularly mesmerizing. They sat huddled in the warm leather of the idling Mercedes and just stared at the surf, moonlit waves crashing on the empty beach. Gracie's head fell against Griffin's right shoulder and he could hear her breathing change to that of someone drifting off to a gentle sleep. He leaned down and gently kissed the top of her head.

Griffin's thoughts drifted. The warm air blowing across the dashboard and the bliss of the wonderful dinner they had just shared made his eyelids heavy, too. He thought of his son, Kyle, and wished, for the thousandth time, that he belonged to him and Gracie. Life would truly be different. It wasn't that Myrna, Kyle's biological mother, was such a bad person. She wasn't. Just different—in almost every respect—from any woman that Griffin had ever been with. Maybe that had been the attraction, her difference. After two blown marriages and a long period without constant female companionship Griffin had fallen for Myrna—hard. Their furious courtship and frantic desires overcome their better judgments and once the fires banked the relationship flamed out after just a year. But during that year, Myrna had become pregnant, and Kyle was the result. Myrna was a great mother, from a nurturing and physical standpoint, but Griffin rarely agreed with anything she did with Kyle from a developmental or emotional point of view. Kyle loved his mother, that was certain, but the two of them fought like cats and dogs—every day. There was little Griffin could do about it except try and referee when he was with them, but then he hated being with them because they needed a constant referee. Gracie was just the opposite of Myrna from an emotional and volatility point of view and she had been fantastic about accepting and nurturing Kyle. Gracie was, in Griffin's mind, the ideal female role model for his son, but they could only spend a limited amount of time together due to everyone's schedules and the custody agreement, which was reasonably generous, but far from even. Complicating this amalgamated arrangement was the fact that Gracie and Myrna absolutely detested each other.

The two of them had met just after Griffin and Gracie had hooked up. It was a big cocktail party at Long Beach on a Fourth of July. Griffin, Gracie and Kyle were parked peacefully on the sand, luxuriating on a beach blanket staring up at the fireworks display when Myrna unexpectedly walked into their circle of light. It was all quite innocent. None of them had known the others were there. Myrna was hand-in-hand with a local dentist that Griffin casually knew—her date for the night. After pleasant introductions Myrna, for whatever reason, decided to get in Gracie's face.

"You just remember whose son you're trying to alienate. You'll never take him away from me!"

The shock was palpable. Neither Griffin nor Gracie had ever entertained any thoughts of trying to do anything like change the mother-son-father-girlfriend dynamic, but apparently Myrna had seen it otherwise. Perhaps she felt threatened by the comfort and ease with which Kyle related to his dad's girlfriend. Perhaps it was just old-fashioned jealousy. Maybe it was just too many holiday libations.

Gracie will never run from a fight, but this time she just turned and walked away. It was probably the right thing to do. Fortunately, Myrna's date was able to steer her away and skulk off into the night, but the damage had been done. Griffin stood there mouth agape, Kyle was teary-eyed and Gracie was walking away down the beach alone.

The two women have only spoken perfunctory words to one another since, mostly when answering respective home phones. Gracie refuses to discuss it, Myrna will never stop discussing it and Griffin and Kyle just try to do the best they can to function in the middle.

Isn't life interesting Griffin sighed to himself, *especially when the dynamic involves strong personalities. I know they'll never have tea together but I just wish--*

There was a loud rap-rap-rap of wood on glass. Griffin was startled from his semi-conscious state so hard that he cracked both knees on the steering wheel trying to reach for his gun. Gracie bolted upright and whacked her head on the padded interior ceiling. A bright light blazed all over the two of them and a muffled voice from outside said, "Roll down your window, please!"

Griffin twisted in his seat just enough to see, reflected in the glass, the glint of a badge and the baton that had been used to knock on the window. "It's OK, Gracie, I think it's a cop." Griffin hit the button to open the driver's side window, but kept his right hand on the butt of his pistol just in case.

Frosty air coursed through the car as the window descended. A very bright flashlight searched the car's interior and nearly blinded both Griffin and Gracie. After a moment, the light went off. A voiced tinged with amusement said, "Aren't you two a little—ah—old to be out here necking on a cold night like this?"

Griffin relaxed, slightly. "If I ever get that old you can shoot me, Officer--?"

"Reynolds, sir. Southampton Village PD. I was just doing my rounds when I saw your taillights. Just wanted to be sure everything was OK. Could I see some ID sir?"

Griffin and Gracie's eyes met. Gracie stifled a laugh. "Why, sure," Griffin responded, as he reached in his suit coat jacket for his badge and ID. He handed the leather case to Patrolman Reynolds.

Reynolds flipped it open and he, too, tried hard to stifle a laugh, but didn't quite succeed. "Sorry, sir," he chortled, "just doing my job," and Reynolds handed the wallet back. "You two have a nice night, now, hear?"

"We'll try. But just one thing, Reynolds."

"Sir?" Reynolds was barely able to contain his mirth.

"When this story starts to go around the locker room, please be sure to tell them I still had my pants on."

After a moment of silence all three of them broke into gales of laughter.

22.

Boys Will be Boys...

It was late, approaching six o'clock. The campus was nearly deserted and decidedly dark. The weather was turning nasty. Snow was expected later that night. But the cold air helped clear the head so Morton Rivkin decided to take a stroll around the grounds before continuing with his thievery. Even with all his fear and insecurities, he still liked the campus. It was only seven developed acres among two dozen that the school owned but after twenty-five years living on a quarter-acre lot and working in cramped cubicles these seven acres seemed to Rivkin as vast as Central Park.

He ambled toward the large field house. He distractedly wondered why some lights were still on. Basketball practice was over, the kids should be gone. Probably the cleaning crew or maybe one of the adult ed classes. Across the campus and once around the field house and back would be about a half-mile walk. Good exercise and Lord knew he needed it. *It has to be below freezing.* Shivering, he pulled his jacket tighter around his ample frame.

He figured he could get the next batch of documents done in about another hour, and then he could go home. His wife would have dinner waiting and he'd help Esther with her homework. Everyone on the staff thought he was putting in extra hours working on the school's complicated finances. Some commended his dedication; others thought he was just being his usual, paranoid, wonkish self. *If only they knew!* He laughed to himself expelling a billowy breath into the frigid night air. What he was actually doing was frantically copying as many of the schools internal financial documents as possible before they were taken away from him. He was hacking and downloading emails by the score. He was opening personnel files and confidential papers on students and parents. He was reading and taking data from highly sensitive financial aid applications. Worst of all, as facilities manager, with a complete set of duplicate keys to every locked cabinet, desk drawer and safe in the place, he was plundering any and all of the school's murky secrets that he could find. At least one, and sometimes two cartons of internal documents, or copies thereof, were stuffed into Rivkin's trunk each night as he left work. It helped immensely that he was nearly always the last to leave and that at this time of year it was dark by five.

As he turned the corner on the back side of the field house, an enormous structure of wood and glass, he giggled to himself maniacally. *Oh, yes,* he smiled to himself. *If they're going to try and pin this shit mess on ol' Morty, they are going to be surprised! I'll have copies of everything including all the emails that no one was supposed to see. Huh?!* He stopped in his tracks. He heard voices.

He glanced around nervously. Was that a child? Crying? He couldn't see a thing ahead. Coming out of his Machiavellian reverie he suddenly realized where he was: standing under the raised and elongated windows of the boys' locker room which was situated on the far side of the gym, in the back of the field house. He looked up. One of the windows was open a crack and wispy tendrils of steam snaked upward into the moonless sky.

A young voice whispered softly, "Please…please…. enough…please." Then the voice started sobbing quietly.

Another voice, surely a man's, was making guttural sounds and also trying to be reassuring at the same time.

"Uh...Uh…Okay…Uh...Uh….OK...Now, now…."

The young voice again, "OK …coach. Please…stop…now!"

The man again, "Yeah, Yeah…Oooh…yeah….!" This exclamation came with a loud exhale of breath. Now there was just soft crying.

"Aw for God's sake!" the man whispered violently. "You're such a baby!" The man laughed and then said, in a normal tone, "Now get dressed and get the hell outta here."

There were the shifting sounds of feet running. The shower stopped. A chill ran down Rivkin's spine. He recognized the voice. And "Coach." It was the school's PE teacher, Barry Logamin. *What the hell is going on?!* Rivkin said to himself in genuine fear and concern. He knew, but didn't want to know, so shoved the image from his mind. But it came flooding back. He couldn't help it. *My God, what else can go on at this abominable place?* Rivkin cursed to himself. He stepped out of the shadow of the back of the building just in time to see a boy, probably one of the older boys at the school, judging from his size, race from the gym door and head to the parking lot. He couldn't tell who it was. It was too dark. Then a pair of headlights on a big SUV came on and a horn beeped twice, as a welcoming signal. The boy ran to the car, opened the passenger door, and jumped in. A few seconds later the SUV pulled out of its parking spot and sped down the driveway to the highway. It was then that Rivkin recognized the car and thus the student. Rivkin had a nearly photographic memory, which was a big help in his profession. And one of the things he liked to do to exercise his mind was read license plates. He played a game of reading and memorizing all the license plates of all the cars he passed on the way to work each day. "License Tag" he called it. He mentally catalogued each car, every plate number, in sequence, and by state. It was, he felt, a great way to limber up his mind every morning.

He had, of course, just for fun, also memorized the license plate numbers of every staff member, teacher and parent at the school. And Morton had a theory. They say that some people, after a while, begin to resemble their pets. Rivkin felt that cars and vanity license plates really said a lot about the car owners and their egos. This SUV was no exception. It was bigger and more complicated than the driver could ever safely handle. It was over-equipped, oversized and over the top, just like its driver. There was a large white oval in the back with the letters 'VT' in green to remind everyone of the driver's palatial weekend retreat in Vermont. The license plate read "BD CHAIR" to let everyone know that this car belonged to the Chairman of the Board of the School, Janice Brighton. Among the staff and definitely behind her back, Mrs. Brighton had two not-so-flattering nicknames. One was "Clueless" because she was, indeed, without a clue as to what was happening around her, especially with the inner workings of the school; and, the other was "Little Lotta," after the stumpy character from the comic strips. Unfortunately for Mrs. Brighton, despite the fabulous sums of money earned by her corporate lawyer husband and the talents of any fashion designer and personal trainer she cared to hire, she remained firmly, decidedly plump and shaped from top to bottom, like an overstuffed tree stump. As a result, her usual outfit was a pair of jeans and a pullover. Once an attorney herself, she hadn't practiced law in many years, instead devoting her time to raising a family and running the Irving Center's parent association. Last year, she had been rewarded for all her efforts on behalf of the school when the "big man" himself made her co-chair of the Board. Manny had another nickname for her: "Machine Gun Mouth." She had a habit of speaking in rapid bursts, trying to mow down anything else anyone was saying, and usually not making any sense.

So. Morton exhaled nervously. *It was your oldest son I heard.* She must have been waiting for him in the parking lot after basketball practice. *If you don't know what's going on with your own children, you are truly 'clueless.'* The thought trailed away in his mind, too painful, as a parent himself, to contemplate.

At that instant, Rivkin felt himself being slammed, face first, into the side of the building. His right arm twisted painfully upward behind his back, his wrist locked in a viselike grip, and another powerful arm encircled his neck, slowly pushing the breath from his lungs. His left cheek pressed forcefully into the shingles on the side of the field house. Panic began to flood his brain.

A voice—that voice!—echoed into his right ear. "What are you doing here, Rivkin?"

It was the coach, Logamin. "I....I....can't...breathe...!" Rivkin gasped.

"Damn right." Logamin pushed harder. "And you're not going to be breathing at all unless you tell me what you're doing here!"

Rivkin felt consciousness beginning to slip away. Already his peripheral vision was narrowing. "Please...stop...can't..." He was truly desperate but powerless against the much bigger and better conditioned man.

With blinding speed, he was spun around and his back slammed into the wall. His head bounced off the side of the building, but at least he could take in a breath. Logamin's long and powerful arms caged him in--each hand pressed firmly against the wall on either side of his ears, palms flat. Logamin's enraged and puffy face was just inches from Rivkin's nose. Rivkin could feel the other man's exhalations being forced into his own nostrils. Logamin's eyes flared in the dark. It was the middle of winter and freezing cold, but all Logamin wore was a pair of shower sandals and a terry-cloth towel around his waist.

"I'm waiting, Rivkin," Logamin hissed, very much like the evil snake some said he was.

"Back off, asshole," Rivkin squeaked, slapping Logamin's hairy chest with one hand as hard as he could. It was like a pebble bouncing off a granite slab.

The futile gesture from someone as weak and helpless as

Rivkin seemed to amuse Logamin. He barked a short "Hah!" and backed up one step, hands now on his hips. His entire body steamed in the night air and he had the appearance of a shimmering wraith.

"I want to know what you're doing here, Rivkin. And don't bullshit me or I'll break your scrawny pencil neck!"

Rivkin rubbed his shoulder. That and his arm were very sore. His left cheek felt like a washboard from the imprint of the shingles. "I was just out walking you jerk! And what right do you have assaulting me like this?" Rivkin's righteous indignation was finally stiffening his backbone.

Logamin's face alternated between ghoulish grin and stone-faced rage. "Looked to me like some pervert was hanging around outside the boy's locker room. That what you are, Rivkin? Some kind of pervert? Likes to peek in the windows outside the boys' locker room?"

Rivkin stared long and hard at Logamin. The fear and loathing that had been building inside him for weeks was finally beginning to crystallize into hate and disgust. Rivkin stepped a few inches away from the side of the structure, toward Logamin, and pushed an index finger firmly into the fur covering Logamin's breast bone. "Seems to me that *you* should not be calling *me* the pervert…you…you…pervert! I heard what was going on in there." Rivkin jerked a thumb up and behind him, "You left the window open, *pervert*!"

"Shut the fuck up!" Logamin growled, but his eyes wandered upward to the open window. "Shit…" he admitted ruefully.

"Yes, shit," Rivkin countered, "as in you're in a lot of shit, Logamin, if I tell people what's going on here!"

Logamin actually chuckled at this. "So little man, what do you think is going on here?"

"I heard you, you disgusting man! I heard you in there, with Brighton's son doing…doing…whatever disgusting things you do to little boys! Just wait until I tell--"

At this Logamin leapt forward, raising his right fist. Rivkin involuntarily backed into the wall once more and waited for the blow to fall, but Logamin's cocked arm just hung in the air. The coach stared intently, threateningly. The reflected light from the window above bathed Logamin's skin in a sickly, yellowish glow. Absently, Rivkin could see goose bumps forming on Logamin's bare flesh. The heat of the shower was finally wearing off. If he could hold on a few more moments maybe this nemesis would finally need to seek shelter, and he'd be free.

Logamin's lips curled upward in a faint smile. "You really don't know what's going on here?"

"What…what are you talking about? I don't …" Rivkin's voice trailed off.

"Well, I'll be damned. You don't know, do you?" Logamin lowered his hand and backed away, genuinely surprised. "I thought since you were the big man's hand-picked number cruncher you were in on the plan. But I guess you're not. Hmm..."

"Plan? What plan?" Rivkin was now very perplexed.

"You do know that Rubino and Sokolin are lovers, don't you?"

"Well, of course I do. Everyone does. What difference does that make?"

"Have you been that busy sharpening your pencils that you haven't noticed what's going on at this school?"

"I…I don't know what you mean..."

"Jesus, I guess not. Take a look at the enrollment over last year, idiot. Wouldn't you say that there's a rather large, disproportionate number of gay parents enrolling their children here? Friends of the big man and his lover?"

"I...I really hadn't noticed."

"Well, duh! Wake up, Rivkin! It's all part of Rubino's master plan! He's going to turn this bastion of country wealth into his own little private school for all his gay buddies and their kids. And he's looking for gay kids of straight parents, like

Janice Fucking Brighton, whose little boy begs me to do him practically every damn day before he runs home to finish his homework!"

"I'm going to be sick…" Rivkin paled.

"You do that, geek. It's cold out here. I'm going to get some clothes on. Welcome to the real world of the Irving Center."

Rivkin slid down the wall. He wanted to curl up into the fetal position and have all this go away. He knew that Rubino was using the school as a conduit for some kind of money laundering scheme, although he had not yet uncovered its actual purpose, but now this, too? He was actually creating an educational enclave for his homosexual friends and gay kids? And if Logamin was taking advantage of that to satisfy his perversity, was anyone else? Were there others preying on innocent children? What he already knew was wrong with this place had just gotten immeasurably worse.

Logamin was at the gym door. He opened it to step inside, but hesitated to look back again at Rivkin squatting in the dirt. It was starting to snow.

"Hey, Rivkin," Logamin aimed, "now you'll understand why your daughter really hates it here. Just ask her when you get home tonight."

With that, the gym door slammed shut. Rivkin was alone in

the cold. He could hear Logamin's baritone laughter echo through the open window.

"Esther…Esther…" he moaned as he pitched over and puked.

23.

"Brawny"

"Brawny" Harris and I had been friends since college, and we had both played football for the Brown University Bears. We came from wildly different backgrounds though: my family was poor, his was filthy rich. But Brawny was a regular guy, the money didn't really mean much to him. It only counted in relation to how close it could get him to cute girls and race cars. It didn't make much sense that we would be friends, but we kind of hit it off somehow. It started on the football field.

Ivy League football hadn't been a serious threat since the 1930's but it was still a big draw for the rich alums. If we could beat Yale, Harvard or both in any given season it was considered a huge success for the program. We beat both squads my junior year, which was Brawny's senior year, and he had been the hero of the Yale game and I in the Harvard contest.

After the Harvard game he pulled me aside in the locker room and asked if I had any plans for the weekend. I had nothing in particular going on, besides maybe going to downtown Providence to get drunk and celebrate the win. I was then informed that I was going with him. He had a date and a whole Saturday night and Sunday planned in Newport. He'd set me up with a friend of his girlfriend, there'd be a great party, boating on Sunday on Narragansett Bay, and so forth. He then dug into the pockets of his blue blazer and pulled out two fistfuls of crumpled bills. He told me to hold onto the money for us and if we needed more, he'd go get some. A little more than three thousand dollars was our initial stake for the next two days of festivities. Needless to say, we had a great time. When we sobered up the following Monday morning, I gave back a little over six hundred. He looked at me as if I were from Mars. "Nobody's ever given me any money back before," was all he would say. From that day on, he was one of my closest friends. I guess he just trusted me.

Brawny was a big guy, as the nickname might suggest. He stood a little over 6' 2" and hadn't weighed much less than 250 pounds since high school. "John Reynolds" was his given name, but those were seldom spoken and hardly ever used except at the Board meetings he was forced to attend. At the tender age of twenty-four, just after his college graduation, he found himself an orphan. His father, one of three heirs to the family's publishing and transportation empires, had dropped dead of a heart attack in his mistresses' bed when Brawny was in high school. His mother started drinking day and night and didn't stop until she, too, was dead of a stroke eight years later. As an only child Brawny now had to hold up his end of one third of the family's estimated fifteen billion dollar fortune. That meant a seat on the Board of the Corporation that controlled the family's wealth. It was the only real job he'd ever held – except for the two years he spent in the Army.

He probably could have avoided it, with his family's money and connections and all, but he volunteered anyway. Probably just to piss off his mother, whom he never got along with very well. So, Private Harris went off to boot camp, fully expecting to end up, like me, in Vietnam. But much to Brawny's disgust the Harris name still had some magic, and the Army sent him, like Elvis, to Germany, out of harm's way. They made him a photographer for the base newspaper. He was actually good at it. Good enough to get a couple of front page covers in *Stars and Stripes* and of course, in several of the family's magazines. Having drunk half the beer in Germany and deflowered a goodly portion of the local maidens, Sergeant Harris left active duty after completion of his required two years of service and went off to college. That was something else I always thought bonded the two of us. We had both gone off and done our duty to God and country, albeit in vastly different circumstances. We never talked about it much, though.

After college we stayed close, but didn't run around in the same circles. I remember one time, when I was still a beat cop in the Bronx, Brawny dragged me off to lunch at the New York Yacht Club. He bribed my Sergeant to let me off the rest of the day, and there I was, a New York City cop, in uniform, dining at the home of the America's Cup (It was still there in those days). From the looks we got from the members in pearls and cravats, it was as if someone had let a giant fart in the middle of their famous dining room. We had a great time and Brawny just loved rubbing their blue-blooded noses in it.

We'd see each other two, maybe three times a year and we'd commiserate with each other over lost loves and ex-wives (I had two, he had four). Brawny also kept a couple of boats out in Sag Harbor and owned a huge summer home in Bridgehampton. He adored Gracie; he was always trying to cop a feel, and told her every time he saw her to dump me so he could treat her like a royal princess. We all laughed about it, but sometimes I thought he might be more than half-serious.

We both knew he'd never get into Gracie's pants. That was a given –not only out of respect for me and Gracie's loyalty, which he would honor, but also because he couldn't. Sadly, my old friend had spun a Lotus into a ditch at Watkins Glen five years ago. The car rolled over on him and crushed his spine just above the waist. Not even a billion dollars worth of medical care would ever get Brawny back the use of his legs or the feeling in his dick and God knows he'd tried. He was now confined to a wheelchair and had 'round-the-clock nursing. It certainly didn't slow him down much otherwise--he still went deep sea fishing in a specially fitted fighting chair and harness, and drove like a madman, when his head nurse would let him, in a specially configured hand-control operated Rolls. He was still mad for the ladies and had strippers over on weekends. His parties continued to be legendary, especially now that he was temporarily between wives. In short, paralysis hadn't slowed him down much but I could see, I knew, the great sadness behind his sparkling blue eyes and dashing smiles.

If I ever needed information on anyone, especially those in the *Blue Book* or anyone who was someone or trying to be someone, Brawny was my 'go–to' guy. He was a walking –oops, bad analogy, encyclopedia of who was who, who was doing who, who was hosing who and who was, after all, OK, or not. I don't know where or how he got some of his information; maybe, ultimately as a cop, I didn't want to know. But because I now needed to know something about a specific someone I was sitting in the back room of John Duck's, Brawny's favorite restaurant in the Hamptons, waiting for him to be wheeled in. He was late. He was always late.

A great commotion at the main entrance with lots of laughter and shouting told me he had finally arrived. He was a favorite, wherever he went. I think he liked the place better than any other because it was a throwback to the days of our youth. Plus, if he was discreet about it, and because he laid down $100 tips everywhere, they let him smoke.

Trailed by his favorite waitress, his favorite bartender, and one of the owners and pushed along by his favorite nurse, Helen Stull, he made his grand entrance. Half the busy Friday lunch crowd knew him or wanted to know him, and shouts and waves were exchanged all across the room.

I stood to shake his hand. Instead, I got a snappy salute. "Griffin, how the hell are ya?"

Grinning, I saluted back. "Fine my old friend. How are you?"

"Can't complain much. Even if I did, who'd listen anyway?" he chortled.

"Sweetie," he said, smiling at the pretty young bartender, "get us a Stoli Bloody Mary, will ya? Thanks. And James, old pal, what are you having?"

"Just a tonic with lime for now, thanks. I'm sorta on duty."

"Shit. You're not gonna be any fun today," Brawny grumbled good-naturedly.

I turned to Helen. "Hey, Helen. Nice to see you. How are you?"

"Just great, thanks, Superintendent. And you?" A very pleasant but efficient guardian was Helen.

"Great, great, thanks. Uh, Helen…"

"OK, I thought so." She smiled. "This is going to be official and private. Fine. No problem. I've jacked up his meds enough so he should be safe for an hour. Just don't let him over-eat and only one Bloody Mary, OK?"

I smiled back, grateful for her efficiency and sensitivity. "You're the best, Helen. Thanks. I'll take good care of him, I promise."

"OK, you've got the watch and I'm off. I'll be shopping. I have the pager if you need me. Bye!"

And with that she turned on her heels and headed back to the limo. I knew I had about an hour of privacy.

The drinks came quickly, thanks to Margaret, Brawny's all-time favorite server. She leaned over in front of Brawny, bending at the waist. The restaurant didn't allow scanty attire on the part of their female employees, but I noted with amusement that the rather buxom Margaret had somehow managed to unbutton the top two buttons of her blouse sometime after Brawny's arrival. The view was rather spectacular. Brawny smiled broadly. Margaret, a single mom, mid-forties, and one of Brawny's drunken one-night stands years back, still carried a torch for the big man, even in his present condition. I couldn't tell if it was the man or the money, though. She laid the drinks slowly and carefully in front of us, turning to wink knowingly at me. There was just the tiniest of jerking movements, as if Margaret had been surprised by a fly landing on her leg, and then she blushed. I saw Brawny's right hand come out from underneath the table and grasp his cocktail. I knew the drill. He had deftly slipped his hand between Margaret's legs, up under her skirt, past the thigh and like lightning had tucked a $100 bill in the front of her underwear, right on top of her pubic hair.

Margaret knew the drill, too. She straightened, smoothed the front of her skirt, and announced she'd be back in a few minutes to take our lunch orders.

"You know, big guy, you're going to get in trouble for that one of these days," I dead panned, to let him know that I knew.

He took a noisy slurp of his cocktail. "Ahhh, that's tasty. Already have, James, my boy. Been sued twice. Settled before trial. Corporation paid them off. So, what can I do for you, lad? I take it we're not here to brag about our love lives. Hah! You'd win. How's that delicious little tart Gracie anyway?"

You couldn't help but love him. "She's fine, thanks. Said to say hello." I sipped my tonic. "Well, old friend, I need your help or maybe some info, if you know anything about a particular someone who's in your financial league. Actually, a family of 'someones'. At least I think they're a family. I don't really know. They're very secretive and they've got an army of lawyers to try and stonewall our every move."

"You hungry? Let's get Margaret back. Her pants ought to be good and wet by now." He turned in his wheelchair to signal for Margaret. He didn't need to. As soon as he began to turn Margaret was on her way. "So, who's got your knickers in a knot?"

I squeezed the crescent of lime into my soda. "Ever hear of Milos Rubino?"

I don't often catch Brawny Harris by surprise, but I did today. He froze for a moment and looked hard at me. His mask of joviality fell and he got very quiet for a few seconds. He shook his head and let out a low whistle.

"Jesus, Jamesy, if you're looking into Rubino, you've got one bad mother fucker on your hands. He's a nasty piece of shit."

"What'll it be, gentlemen?" Margaret was once again at Brawny's elbow, all a-quiver.

"Huh? Oh, yeah, OK sweetie, I'll have the shrimp cocktail, cuppa chowder and the steak sandwich, cooked just like I like it, OK, honey?"

"You got it, Mr. Harris," Margaret purred. "And you, Mr. Griffin?"

"Cobb salad, please. Russian dressing on the side."

"Is that it, then?"

I think Margaret was hoping she was going to be dealt another quick hand, but Brawny just sat there in silent contemplation. I had to break the ice. "I think that'll do for now, Margaret, thanks."

"Uh, OK…"

Was that a pout as she turned toward the kitchen?

"So, Rubino, eh?" Brawny sighed.

"Well, actually his wife, Victoria, and his son, Vincenzo. They're potential witnesses or maybe even parties of interest in a case. It's a case in which I've taken a personal interest."

"I figured you would. The Carmody case, right? You knew the kid?"

"Yes, knew him well. Good kid. Good sailor. Part of my

Navy Reserve Unit. Was going to the police academy, wanted to be a cop."

"You think Rubino's whore and his whacked-out kid are involved?"

"Don't know. Witnesses place the two of them at a bar where Carmody was last seen alive. One witness says he's pretty sure Carmody left the bar with them. Whore? Whacked-out kid?"

"Yeah. I'll get to that, but you can't interrogate them?"

"Tried. I have two of my best detectives on this. They've had them in for questioning but they came with a phalanx of lawyers who wouldn't let either one give us anything more than name and address."

"No hard evidence?"

"Nothing to directly connect them with Carmody's murder—yet—but some interesting circumstantial stuff."

"Scuttlebutt is that Carmody was strapped to a tree and died with a hard on!"

"Aw, geez, Brawny, c'mon. Is that all you ever think about? Your dick?"

"Hey, pal, all I got to work with these days are my hands and if I'm really lucky my tongue. Fortunately, they stay pretty busy. I can get a hard on, you know. Damndest thing. Viagra will make me hard as a rock for about an hour, but I can't feel a thing. But I can watch and that's still fun. Sometimes I think God's fucking with me, ya know what I mean?"

Sadly, I did.

"I also heard a rumor,'" he continued, "that you have another dead body that was tied to a tree. Some A-rab, they say."

I leaned across the table. "How the hell did you hear that? I put a lid on that case tighter than your Uncle Ted's sphincter." (Uncle Ted was a notorious tightwad and self-appointed guardian of the Harris family's good name. Brawny was never any help in that regard.)

Brawny smiled with great satisfaction. "Well, we all have our own resources, don't we?"

"Well, do me a favor. Just keep it quiet. I'm trying not to deal with a major panic right now. I have enough on my plate. I don't want the good citizens of the East End thinking there's some kind of perverted serial killer on the loose. At least not yet. I'm not sure what we've got, to tell you the truth. Gracie thinks the second murder's a copycat killing."

"Well, my money's on Gracie. I'll back any play she wants to make. She's smarter than you and a hell of a lot better lookin'!"

"Well, you're right there, my friend, but now tell me about Rubino. Or 'the Rubinos.'"

"OK, but it's a long story. And a pretty weird one."

"I've got all day."

"Rubino--Milos, that is--is a member of the Lucky Sperm Club, just like me."

"The what club?!"

"The Lucky Sperm Club. Born into money. Didn't have to do a thing to become filthy rich except pick the right womb. But I would like to point out that as far as he and I are concerned, that's where the similarities end."

"OK, tell me more."

"Rubino's father made all the family money. In the shipping business. Dangerous cargos at first, then later the regular stuff--bulk freight, car carriers, grain, some oil."

"You said, 'dangerous cargos. You mean drugs? Contraband?"

"No, no. The cargos were legal, just dangerous. Here's what I mean. Giuseppe Rubino that's the old man, he sounds Italian, with 'Giuseppe' and 'Rubino' and all, but he and the family are Jews and the Fascists knew it. They all got rounded up by Mussolini and shipped off to the death camps. Giuseppe was a heartbeat away from the gas chambers in Auschwitz in 45 when the Americans finally liberated the place. Rest of the family wasn't so lucky. Seven years later, 52 I think it was, he's a little Jewish nobody down on the docks in Trieste with two old tramp steamers hauling pigs and shit between Sicily and Malta and Crete. Along come a couple of Zionists who need to sneak guns and bullets into the newly minted state of Israel. They hire one of Giuseppe's rust buckets to haul ammo to the Holy Land. They pay him a hundred times what he can make on a single run with one of his tubs. Not being stupid, Giuseppe starts looking around for trips like this. Next thing he does, and it's a legend in the shipping business, he takes an entire tanker-load of nitroglycerine from Africa to Galveston. The US Navy desperately needed the nitro to make bombs for the Korean War. Nobody in the shipping business would take on that cargo, let alone get a crew crazy enough to sign on. Can you imagine what would happen if an entire ship full of nitro blew? You wouldn't find a piece bigger than your toenail. He rounded up his family and friends and got them to man the tanker. Somehow, they got good weather and made it. Giuseppe made a million dollars, net, on that one trip. From there on, he was King. By 1960 he was a billionaire and had more ships than all but six of the world's navies.

"Giuseppe had two sons, Omri and Milos. He settled them and his wife into a palazzo in Venice. Both boys went into the business. Omri had a knack for it. Milos didn't. Omri was the dutiful son and Milos was the family clown. Omri took a wife-female-and Milos took a partner –male. Giuseppe watched in horror as his gay son botched one deal after another and went from boyfriend to boyfriend, usually after a messy public fag-spat. It broke his heart and it was more than he could stand. Before Giuseppe died ten years ago, he fired his own son from the family business, handed the entire company to Omri and basically washed his hands of Milos. But as a parting gift, and in consideration for relinquishing any and all claims in perpetuity on the family's property or holdings, he gave Milos two and a half billion--that's with a 'b', billion--and told him never to darken the family door again. Two and a half billion. Can you imagine? It's even more than I got."

"Certainly more than I've got. Do go on, this is good."

"Well the two and a half billion, which by the way, was ten percent of what the family was worth at the time, has, thanks to Milos' adept handling, turned into slightly less than one billion in ten years, but hey, what's a few hundred million among friends?"

My turn to whistle. "You mean to tell me that this character has, in one decade, managed to lose a billion and a half dollars? Shit, even if you bought T-Bills with it, you would have doubled your money! Who's managing this idiot's fortune?"

"Well, that's just it. The family won't have anything to do with him, although Mommy still has a soft spot for poor Milos--when he runs a few million short, she'll cover for him. All he has to do is run home and beg and promise not to suck any more dicks for a while. She always caves. But here's the even queerer thing, if you'll pardon the pun: most of what he's lost has been pissed away in the past five years alone, after he hooked up with his latest partner, Israel Sokolin. This little weasel is supposed to be some piece of work. First of all, he is little. He's not even half Rubino's size and he's a whiny little Jewish princess in tight Calvin's. I can't even imagine what that looks like when those two try and get it on; I mean here's one guy at 400 plus pounds and this other little wiener at 150 soaking wet. How does that work? Does anybody know? Who's on top, or who's in the back, or…Oh, fuck, it's just too stupid to try and visualize."

"Yeah, and how do a wife and kid fit in the picture?" I was truly curious now.

"Well, before Milos got kicked out of the family he made many attempts to make his old man love him. He even took a real wife twenty years ago to make his father happy. That's Victoria. But old Milos is apparently so fucking gay he couldn't consummate the marriage, so he whacked off into a tube, got her artificially inseminated and she had Vincenzo. That was sixteen years ago. Milos trotted out his wife and son whenever he needed them, mostly for family functions but when his old man disinherited him, Milos gave up the pretense. But he kept Victoria. He never divorced her and she's been raising Vincenzo. Sweet deal. Milos gets to blow or butt fuck anybody he wants and she can get laid by anyone to whom she takes a liking. Israel, now he's the unknown factor here. Like I said, half a billion gone since he's been in Rubino's life. Where's it all going? And why doesn't Rubino get rid of him? Is he that good in bed? Nobody's half a billion good in bed-male or female. Hah!"

On that note, lunch arrived. Margaret hovered for a few moments but then went away. With a mouthful of shrimp firmly in place, Brawny went on. "So anyway, there's all kinds of rumors. The money's going into drugs, gambling, secret Jewish causes, the usual shit. But no one really knows. Sokolin probably knows. Maybe Centpied knows."

"Centpied?" I stopped mid-forkful of salad. "That's his business manager?"

"Major Domo, more likely. Or maybe 'major dumb-o.' He's a weird duck."

"Should I know about him, too?"

"Probably. He could be a key piece. Ivan the Terrible we call him here in our socially connected little community. Ivan Centpied's mother was, and I emphasize *was,* an heiress to a major fortune in the retail business--the old Peabody Chain, remember?"

"Sure do. Didn't they have stores nationwide?"

"Yup. Hundreds. Madge Peabody was in line to inherit a ton. She fell in love with this good-for-nothing French-Russian ballet star with the really ironic name of "Centpied--literally translated from the French words to mean "one hundred feet." Great name for a guy who makes his living prancing around in tights, eh? Anyway, she ran off with him and Ivan was the result. Meanwhile, back at the ranch, it turns out Madge's old man has been falsifying the company books for years. The whole chain goes into bankruptcy and the family is ruined. Since Madge is now broke and no longer any fun, Ivan's philandering dancing dad waltzes out of his life. Mother promptly goes off the deep end and winds up in the loony bin. No more private English boarding schools for poor little Ivan. Word is he learned to swing both ways while he was in merry ol' England. But Ivan is nothing if not resourceful. Even if he's been cut out of a huge inheritance, which he's constantly letting everyone know about, he still has all his blue blood connections. Fancying himself some sort of financial wizard he manages to talk a number of his now ex-dearest friends into putting up millions for a high-tech hedge fund just as the bottom is ready to fall out of the first internet bubble. He and they lost everything and Ivan even gets slapped with a big fine and a permanent disbarment from the securities business. By this time in his life Ivan is truly desperate. He's got a Stepford wife, three whiny kids in private school, a huge over mortgaged manse in Bridgehampton, six cars he can't afford, the IRS breathing down his neck and a pill popping boyfriend on the side. Way deep on the side.

"Out of nowhere appears Milos Rubino. The 'big man' wants to make a big splash in the Hamptons pond but doesn't know anybody here. He's an outsider. A rich outsider, to be sure, but even a rich outsider needs to be properly introduced. Centpied, with his connections, those he has left anyway, are key to introducing the Rubinos to polite society here in the Hamptons.

"I don't like Centpied one bit." Now Brawny is masticating his steak sandwich with gusto and gulping his third Bloody Mary.

Helen would kill him and probably will if she finds out. But Margaret will never tell. I sure won't. The alcohol is loosening his tongue and as much as I like my old friend, I need to know what he knows.

"No, not one bit. Don't trust him. Never have. Something really evil and dishonest about him. Angry, too. All the time angry. And those fucking ridiculous eyebrows. Have you seen them?"

"Can't say as I have. Haven't met Mr. Centpied yet."

"Like two giant fucking wooly caterpillars crawling across his forehead."

"Sounds like a great guy."

"Still, hard to think they're somehow tied up in the Carmody mess. Fucked up as they are, that's still a stretch for me. But there's one more thing." Brawny said, now more soberly.

"What's that?"

"The kid. He's really messed up."

"Whaddya mean?"

"Now James, you know I'm not a prejudicial kinda guy, right?"

"Yeah, right! Except when it comes to Republicans!"

"Don't get me started!" He waved a fork at me. "But seriously, all bullshit aside, I'm OK with most everything. I mean, I'm no saint, but everybody's got a right, you know?"

I could see he was fumbling. "What are you driving at, Brawny?"

"Hell, I don't care one way or another about fags. It doesn't work for me, but, hey, whatever, ya know? I'm no gay basher."

That was true, I knew. In fact, there was a very generous side to Brawny and he had quietly given many millions to a number of charitable causes, including, I knew, a local gay rights organization.

"Vincenzo. He's really a mess. He's as queer as queer can be, but, hell, hanging around gay men for so long and having a very strange family life, maybe this apple doesn't fall far from the tree, ya know? But it's more than that. He's never been able to adjust to a normal school life. He's out of control around other kids. In his own mind he's always better, richer, smarter. He usually gets the crap beaten out of him by the other boys. And sadly, he's not as smart as he thinks he is. He's being treated for all kinds of learning disorders. He's on anti-depressants, they say. Sad. He's only sixteen. And worst of all, Sokolin's all over him, and I think maybe sexually. They've been seen kissing in public, and not the kind of kissing a 'step-dad' gives his 'step-son', if that makes any sense. The kid's really a mess. Maybe he's too much of a mess. Some people say he's crazy already."

By now I had the picture. It was certainly not a pretty one. "You've met him? Been around him?"

"Yeah. Creepy kid. Seen him at a coupla charity parties. They don't let him out much. Understand he's got shrinks up the ying yang and lots of meds." At this, Brawny shuddered involuntarily.

"Wow, he must really get to you," I observed.

Brawny stopped his compulsive attack on lunch and actually put down his sandwich. "I remember, back in the Army, we had a lecture one day on hand grenades. We all thought it was great fun until the Instructor, this crusty old bastard First Sergeant, pulled the pin on one and made me take it from his hand. Then he handed me the pin. He said we'd all be dead if I couldn't re-insert that pin. We all stopped laughing. I was a wreck until I managed to get that pin back in. This kid, this Vincenzo? I'm tellin' ya, somebody's pulled his pin and thrown it away."

24.

Reality's End

She threw herself onto the bed, naked, and stretched out everywhere. Rolling over on her back she looked up at the ornately painted ceiling. Twisted coils of lovers depicting two dozen of the most pornographic scenes from the *Kama Sutra* writhed and gamboled in positions that she thought might not be humanely possible. From instinct, from habit, she stuck her right hand between her legs and closed her thighs tightly around her wandering fingers. She felt herself sink deeper into the five-thousand dollar comforter and further into the blissed-out state caused by the Ecstasy she had just ingested.

Yes, Victoria, you do have the life, don't you? She giggled to herself while working her clitoris ever harder. *And we aren't in Kansas any more!*

She loved that tag line because in Vicky Rubino's case it happened to be true. The middle-class cheerleader from Topeka had worked very hard to escape the mid-West. Excellent grades and lots of extra curricular activities in high school had gotten her a scholarship to the University of Chicago. She majored in economics (the school's toughest discipline), graduated summa cum laude, and went off to business school at Columbia. It was in New York as a summer intern between her graduate MBA years that she had met Milos Rubino. Her marketing professor, who was decidedly gay and reputedly a very close friend of Rubino's, had suggested she take a summer job with Rubino's high-flying technology company. *Why not?* She reasoned. *They're paying stupidly high sums for very little work.* Later, she learned that not only was her professor one of Milo's lovers but also a heavy investor in Milo's firm.

Rubino's company, FEMRAD, had reportedly made a breakthrough in magnetic resonance imaging. The resultant product was a much smaller, more powerful, hand-held device that could be used to scan women's breasts and—so it was touted—detect breast cancer as much as three to five months earlier than was possible with present-day equipment. If true, it would be a revolution for women's health. Vicky was intrigued, even to the point of volunteering her own proud breasts for scanning.

Her first meeting with Rubino, at a company cocktail party,

had left her less than impressed. Actually, she had felt repulsed by this oversized beast of a man with an ego to match. He was loud, obnoxious and definitely not the raging heterosexual she was proud to be. Still, she found him mildly amusing and the fact that he was rolling around in a money pit of some two billion definitely got her attention. For his part, he was not attracted to Victoria's stunning good looks, but rather to her intellect, which was also beautifully shaped.

They waltzed around each other all summer, coyly teasing one another. Vicky enjoyed the money she made, $50,000 for a scant eight weeks of marketing studies, and prepared to go back to school. From her close work with the company she knew that something wasn't quite right. The clinical studies that her marketing materials relied on to attract additional investors kept getting delayed. One medical director after another came and went with shocking frequency. One lasted only two days.

On her next to last day of work, as she prepared to go off with three of her girlfriends to one last summer fling in the Hamptons, the Manhattan District Attorney, the SEC, the FTC, the FDA and a phalanx of menacing lawyers showed up in FEMRAD's conference room. They shut the company down instantly. Fortunately for Vicky, she'd already been paid.

Milos was ultimately cleared of any criminal wrong-doing. Apparently, he had been duped by his partners who had only needed him for his money. The "breakthrough" technology had turned out to be nothing more than a super-bright flashlight with a vibrating device that emitted a low hum when switched on. Milo's business reputation, which hadn't been very good to begin with, suffered yet another ego-crushing and humiliating blow.

Vicky was surprised when Milos called her three weeks later. He said he just wanted to apologize for wasting her time on FEMRAD and he wanted to "make things right." She had really not wanted anything to do with Rubino any more, but that little dollar sign went off in her head again and she acquiesced. Rubino invited her aboard his yacht for the weekend—a yacht that, at the time, happened to parked in Gustavia Harbor, the new ultra-chic spot for the rich and famous on the island of St. Barth's. He had her picked up at Teterboro Airport in his Lear. It would be a weekend that would change her life.

When she came back from St. Barth's she shocked her friends and family by dropping out of Columbia immediately. She married Rubino the next week. Ten months later she had a boy, Vincenzo, and a Swiss bank account in her name alone with $50 million.

That had been seventeen years and over two hundred lovers ago. During those years Vicky had lacked nothing her imagination could concoct. No, she was not in Kansas any more, but the drugs, alcohol and excesses too numerous to catalog had also assured her that she wasn't quite here any more either.

25.

Disinformation

Jenna Walden knew this story was going to be her ticket to the "big time." When she broke this piece on the six o'clock news tonight she could already see herself being interviewed on *Good Morning America* tomorrow morning. And that wasn't just wishful thinking. She'd already clued in her agent, although the agent didn't know any of the story's real details, and the agent had made some calls. If this piece was as big as Jenna said it was, GMA was going to put her on.

She'd spent two solid weeks on this. She'd worked on it day and night since Mike Carmody had been found tied to that tree in Southampton. She'd called in favors, even given out a couple, to piece it all together. Now she had enough to go with. When this hit the airwaves it would be sensational. No more reporting on the local high school science fair. No more 'in depth' stories on the unexpected resurgence of the previously devastated Peconic Bay Scallop. No more "live from this weekend's walk-for Poor Timmy's Fund to Beat his Brain Cancer Bills." No. This would finally show those bastards at network that there was some real talent out here wasting away in hick-land and they damn well better begin to pay some fucking attention. And an extra bonus to this piece was going to be sticking it to that smug prick, Chief Superintendent "James" Allen Griffin. This was going to rock his world and probably bring him down. And about damn time. He had kept her out of the thick of many juicy stories over the past couple of years and now he was going to regret it. Oh, yes, it's payback time!

Now she had the last piece of the puzzle and raced back through East Hampton to get to the studios in Hauppauge by four o'clock. That would give her just enough time to edit the video and get her notes into the teleprompter. Her editor had cleared space for her story to lead the six o'clock news. Her camera man, Dan, was at the wheel of the news van as Jenna sat in the passenger seat and hammered away at her Blackberry, loading the last data onto her PC at the studio.

Officer Janie Reyer at East Hampton PD had provided the final confirmation to her hypothesis. Jenna came out to interview Detective Ned Corwith based on a tip she had received from a Southampton PD Officer. Corwith had been reluctant and tight-lipped, but she knew from her questions and his nervous, guarded responses that she was onto something. And as luck would have it, a chance encounter in the police department ladies room with a female cop who had actually been at the crime scene, clinched it. The young, obviously nervous and very distraught officer had overheard a couple of Jenna's questions to Lt. Corwith in the squad room. As Jenna adjusted her bra and freshened her lipstick, the female officer approached her at the washroom mirror.

"Uh, M'aam, are you doing a story on, uh, the murder we discovered at Cedar Point?"

Jenna's eyes lit up and she stared at the girl's reflection in the mirror. "Why, yes. Yes, I am. Do you know anything that might be helpful?"

The officer glanced around nervously. "I was there."

Jenna ran cool water over her hands, shut off the tap and slowly reached for a paper towel. She could tell the girl was uncomfortable and could be scared off easily, yet Jenna's mind was racing. "Really! So, what did you see?" Jenna smiled as motherly as she could.

"I…I don't know if I should be talking to you…" the officer was now getting apprehensive.

Jenna knew she had about two seconds to get this girl to give up what she knew or she'd be gone. "It's OK, Officer…?"

"Reyer," the young cop responded, "Janie Reyer."

"I'm working with the Suffolk County Supervisor on this investigation," Jenna said smoothly. "His office is very interested in this story." Well, that wasn't too much of a lie. The supervisor's office would certainly be interested in this story after she went public with it.

"Really?" Officer Reyer's eyes widened. "Well, I guess it's OK then."

"Look, Officer Reyer, Janie...May I call you Janie?"

"Sure, OK."

"Janie, the camera is off. No microphone and I'm not wired up!" Jenna laughed, trying to make Reyer feel more at ease. "I won't use anything you don't want me to use and I don't even have to quote you. I'll just say 'informed sources,' OK?"

"Well, I guess so. I could lose my job if--"

"Oh, heavens, please! Don't worry about that. If it ever came to that I can make it right for you. I even know the Chief of Detectives. We're old friends."

"Superintendent Griffin? He was there, too, you know."

"You mean at Cedar Point?" Jenna was near to wetting her pants. This was even better than she'd hoped. This was the perfect tie-in and it proved there was a cover up at the highest levels.

"Uh, yeah. He was there. With the M.E. and a couple of other Suffolk detectives."

"Well, of course, I knew that," Walden lied again with a little laugh. "I just don't know much about the victim you found there, that's all." This was a definite gamble. Up until this moment Jenna had no hard evidence that there even was a victim. Corwith would not confirm it and none of her other sources had actually been at the scene-until now.

"It was...it was...awful!" Reyer suddenly put her face in both her hands and started sobbing. Jenna put an arm around the girl's shoulders and with the other hand, locked the bathroom door.

In the next three minutes Officer Reyer gave Jenna her somewhat limited take on what she had seen that morning a week ago. She described the initial call from the fisherman, her partner and herself arriving on scene, the disturbing tableau of this naked man tied to a tree, quite dead; then, the arrival of the CSI team, the Suffolk County detectives and Chief Griffin. She did leave out the part about throwing up.

"....and that's all I saw. And, please, M'aam, don't use my name. Please!"

"Don't worry. Your story is safe with me. You've been really, really helpful. Thank you so much."

"I'd better go."

"Yes, sure! Thanks again." Jenna reached for the lock, undid it, and the bathroom door clicked open then shut. Jenna turned to the mirror. Her cheeks, she could see, were slightly flushed with excitement.

"There is a God." She sighed with obvious delight.

Now she and Dan sped down Daniel's Hole Road toward East Hampton Airport. The station manager had called her. He wanted her back to the studio ASAP, so had sent the station's news chopper to East Hampton to pick her up. It would save at least an hour.

She sat back in the seat and smiled to herself. In just a couple of hours she'd be staring into that red light, earnestly breaking a story of murder, corruption and cover up. It was time for dress rehearsal. It would go something like this:

"Channel 15 News has been able to confirm today a shocking story of possible sadistic killing, corruption and a cover up within the ranks of the Suffolk County Police that has lead to yet another possible murder, this one of an eyewitness to the first murder, a brutal crime that occurred two weeks ago in Southampton.

"You may recall that early December night when we brought you the gruesome story of Michael Carmody, a young police recruit who was found dead, tied to a tree in Elliston Park in

Southampton. He had been brutalized before being murdered, probably gang raped by one or more policemen with whom he had been drinking at a local bar a few hours before. Reliable sources have told Channel 15 that a group of known Suffolk County gay police officers had gathered for an informal meeting of the "gay pride" group within their ranks. Apparently, something went very wrong or something got very out of control and Michael Carmody, a decorated Army veteran just home from Iraq, ended up sodomized, tortured and strangled in Elliston Park.

"Channel 15 was on scene that night, as viewers may recall, but our investigation was thwarted then and is still being blocked now by Suffolk County Chief of Detectives James Griffin, who has steadfastly refused access to any facts in this case.

"Now Channel 15 has learned that a second victim has surfaced. This victim, also male, and reportedly an eyewitness to the first murder, was discovered four days ago in Cedar Point County Park in East Hampton. The second victim, who has yet to be identified, was found similarly tied to a tree, strangled and mutilated. These details were confirmed today to this reporter by Officer Janie Reyer of the East Hampton Police Department.

"Is there a group of homo-erotic serial killer cops among our own county police forces? If not, are there one or more rogue killer cops preying on innocent victims for perverse pleasure?

Was this a tragic accident among gay police officers that went horribly wrong and is now being hushed, along with additional murders? Is there an ongoing cover-up at the very highest level of the police hierarchy in Suffolk County? And what is Superintendent Griffin's role in all this? Why was he personally on-scene, reportedly at both homicides? What is he trying to hide?

"You can be assured we will stay on top of this story as it develops and bring you all the latest details as we obtain them. This is Jenna Walden, reporting for Channel 15 News."

Yes, this is going to be good, so very good, Jenna said to herself with eminent satisfaction.

It was freezing up again and the skies were dark, but the chopper would have enough visibility to get in and out quickly. The road was clear but black ice was always a danger and Dan was going a little too fast for Jenna. They were just about to the railroad bridge, a dangerous point where the road narrows precipitously.

"Hey, Dan, slow down a lit--"

A black sedan suddenly shot past the van from behind and pulled in front, slamming on its brakes.

"Whoa!" Dan shouted as he stomped on the van's brakes, firmly locking them in place. The van skidded, then spun in a slow spiral until it slammed the driver's side directly into the unbending metal frame of the railroad bridge. Dan's entire left side was crushed into the van's frame and his skull splintered sickeningly as it ground itself into the doorframe. It was later determined that he died instantly.

Jenna was tossed violently leftward but her shoulder belt saved her from any serious injury. She would, however, have a number of black and blue abrasions where the belt securely cinched her body. Something flying around the interior of the van bounced off her left temple, leaving her in a temporary daze. As the sounds of grinding metal, breaking glass and muffled booms subsided there was a moment of complete silence. Every ounce of air had been forcibly compressed from Jenna's lungs by the impact. She was still too stunned to feel the pains that would soon engulf her. Dust motes danced before her eyes. Her head pounded and her ears rung.

Surprisingly, the passenger door clicked open quickly. Someone undid her seatbelt. Two hands under her armpits lifted her roughly out of the van. The pain was beginning to come. *How did help get here so quickly*, she wondered abstractly? She felt the tiniest prick of a needle just above her right elbow. *Where did that black sedan come from?* The last thing she remembered before passing out was, *Why are they putting me in the back of a car? Where's the ambulance?*

26.

Animus Horribilus

The meeting had been exceedingly difficult to arrange, but it was clear that it had to take place. It was only a question of where and under what conditions. Rubino couldn't stall it forever. But he did have enough influential and paid-for "friends" among judges, lawyers and probably cops in Suffolk County that he could dictate some of the terms.

Rubino had wanted the get-together at his restaurant in East Hampton. Griffin felt that gave Rubino too much control and possible leverage. Rubino refused to come to police headquarters for probably the same reasons, in reverse. It was certainly too cold for a stroll in the park, so, they had agreed on a semi-neutral spot. Rubino and Griffin would sit down together in the middle of the basketball court in the cavernous field house of the Irving Center School. Yes,

Rubino was on the Board of the school and he reportedly had closed an iron fist around it, like he tried to do with everything else he touched, but it was, after all, a school. *How threatening could that be?* Griffin reasoned. He tried to push discomforting thoughts about the possibilities aside. The truth was, he was pretty desperate to get somewhere with this case and this looked to be about the only way to get some leverage.

It would be just the two of them. No other aides for Rubino or cops for Griffin. Not even any lawyers. And recording devices were definitely taboo. It was the best Griffin could do under the circumstances. He needed information and he needed it quickly, and if he didn't agree to these terms lawyers and judges would be thrown in front of him in increasing doses and the investigation, which was effectively stalled now, would continue to go nowhere. Griffin was also worried that someone else would end up tied to a tree if he didn't act. Yes, this was the best he could do, for now.

Griffin had learned that the Irving Center, once the proud, old, established blue-blooded East End Day School, had been effectively "purchased" by Rubino in exchange for a $10 million core "donation." The school had recently fallen on hard times and needed money to stay afloat. Rubino provided the cash and, in exchange, was made co-chair of the Board, giving him effective control. He had only insisted on one thing in exchange for his donation: that the school be renamed. Irving, it turned out, was Rubino's pet cat.

Some people found this amusing. Many others found it in poor taste, disrespectful and a clear sign of just how desperate the school had become and how cynical and manipulative Rubino could be.

Big, fat flakes of snow were falling gently as Griffin turned onto the long driveway at the southern end of the campus. He could make out the silhouette of the massive field house about two hundred yards ahead. He eased into a parking spot near the main entrance. It was late on a Friday afternoon and there was only one other car near the gym. It was a Bentley. The personalized plates said simply "BJITH." It had to be Rubino's car. Even in the Hamptons a $300,000 sedan stood out. But what about the license tags? Was it a Hebrew phrase of some sort, which would certainly escape him? A "BJ" with an "ITH" it made no sense. Then it came to him. Something Brawny Harris had said to him at lunch the other day. "Rubino likes to tell everyone he's going to be the biggest Jew in the Hamptons, and not just because he weighs a ton!" B-J-I-T-H. Biggest Jew in the Hamptons. The man was fearless. Griffin had to give him that much.

Griffin shut off the engine. This was not going to be fun, that he knew, but, truly, secretly, deep down Griffin was looking forward to this. He loved confrontation. It was one of his dirty little secrets. Getting in someone's face was a sort of combat and, he couldn't help it, it gave him a rush.

As he exited the comforting warmth of the car a frigid gust kicked up and dashed across the potato fields bordering the school. The snow went from gentle vertical puffs to frosty particles driven sideways. They stung a bit and he turned up the collar of his overcoat to better protect his rugged face. He had dressed the part—how many times do you meet a billionaire?—including the pin stripe suit and regimental tie. He regretted the choice of standard wing tips though. Boots would have been much more practical, and a lot warmer.

His feet made soft crunching sounds as he navigated his way to the doors. The interior seemed well-lit. As he went to grasp the handles the main door swung open. Holding the door for him was a large man, dark haired, dark skinned. Middle-Eastern. Maybe Turkish. Thin mustache. Dark eyes, fake crooked smile.

Griffin stepped in and shook the snow from his coat. "There were to be no others," Griffin said evenly but with obvious displeasure.

The man's smile broadened a bit to show tobacco stained teeth. "I'll be leaving in just a moment, but first I must search you."

Griffin seethed, but he knew this was all a mind game. If he put up a fuss he'd be at an instant disadvantage, mentally, and he wasn't prepared to cede the initiative. "Certainly.

Be my guest." Griffin smiled back coldly. He extended his arms straight out to each side. But instead of the rough pat down he was sure would follow, the Turk, if he was a Turk, produced an electronic wand from his coat and slowly ran it up and down Griffin's frame. Griffin was familiar with the equipment. It was highly sensitive and had he been carrying a gun, knife or any sort of weapon or any electronic device the very expensive probe would have chirped insistently. It stayed silent. He had even left his cell phone in the car.

The Turk emitted a grunt. This probably meant he was satisfied that Griffin was "clean" as well as surprised he hadn't tried to smuggle something in. He looked disappointed that he couldn't nail Griffin with something. He reluctantly waved the chief ahead, then opened the door and disappeared into the gathering snowstorm. He left Griffin with the whirrs and clicks of the fieldhouse heating system.

A deep voice that was also very nasal and perceptibly whiny urged him forward. "Mr. Griffin! This way, if you please. To your right."

Griffin took off his overcoat and hung it over his left arm. Turning to his right he could see all the way across the vast field house interior. Seated squarely in the center of the parquet floor was this massively obese individual that he presumed to be Milos Rubino. He sat uncomfortably it seemed to Griffin, across not one but two, maybe three, standard metal folding chairs. Even with his breadth spread across multiple seats Griffin found it difficult to understand why the metal wasn't groaning in protest.

He sat behind a simple, everyday cafeteria table, arms on top, hands clasped in front of him where Griffin could see them. There appeared to be no one else in the gym and the space was clear of any other furniture or exercise apparatus. A single metal folding chair opposite Rubino had been allotted to the Chief.

Griffin walked slowly and purposefully toward the man. The man did not move, nor did he stand to greet Griffin or extend one of his meat hook hands to shake in polite recognition. He simply glared at Griffin with obvious loathing and distrust. With a cursory wave he offered Griffin a spot at the table.

"Please, superintendent. Have a seat." It was said without warmth, without respect and without any crack in his stony expression.

"Thank you." Taking his time, Griffin folded his overcoat neatly, laid it across the table, and continued to size him up. Griffin collected many impressions in just a few seconds. The first thing he noticed were the eyes: they are, as the poet says, the windows to the soul, and if true, it seemed to Griffin that this man's soul must be very black and full of hate.

The roundness of Rubino's features and his outlandish girth served to betray an inner steeliness and there was a slight smell of sweat; not the sweat of fear, but the odor of a man who was mentally armed and ready for a contest. Griffin had to admit to himself, despite his mental preparation for this meeting, that for an instant, he was scared. There was definitely something evil, unbalanced and fearsome lurking here.

Griffin pulled the folding chair slowly back from the table. The rubber feet chung-chung-chunged across the highly waxed boards. Griffin placed the chair far enough back so that he could sit comfortably and not be directly in the man's face. The Chief slowly and casually crossed his right leg over his left. Rubino continued to glare at him. His labored breathing was obvious and there was a whiff of some sort of too-sweet cologne. Rubino was dressed very casually in the biggest pair of blue jeans Griffin had ever seen. He wore a bright pink polo shirt that had to have been custom-made, even if it did have the Polo logo. A huge gold chain hung around his neck but most of it remained hidden by multiple chins. Griffin sat quietly for a moment, staring at the snow melting from the tips of his shoes. Old negotiation rule: "He who speaks first, loses."

Apparently Rubino was unfamiliar with the axiom. He began the dance with: "What makes you think you can fuck with me and my family without consequence?"

"Ah," Griffin countered, "so much for the niceties."

"I don't have time for them – or you. Now, back the fuck off or I will crush you."

"Mr. Rubino-Milos-may I call you Milos?" It was an obvious ploy to piss him off even more. Angry suspects often shoot their mouths off more than they should.

"You may not!" he snarled. "Only my friends call me by my first name."

"Then I gather your first name is seldom spoken."

Blood filled Rubino's cheeks, turning them beet red. "Griffin, I want to be crystal clear with you. I only agreed to this meeting for one reason: to get you and your people out of my life."

He started to wag a finger in Griffin's face. Griffin amusedly thought it looked as if Rubino was trying to beat him with a sausage. Then Griffin shot forward, startling Rubino. The Chief's right fist came down on the table right under Rubino's chins, making them wobble. The loud, thundering slam of Griffin's hand reverberated for several seconds around the gym. Griffin's face was now six inches away from Rubino's. Griffin could smell coffee and sickly sweet peppermint on the fat man's breath.

Griffin whispered with clenched teeth, "Rubino, you don't intimidate me. I don't care how many fucking lawyers, judges, politicians or body guards you have. You and your family are not above the law and if you or anyone close to you, including anyone in your family, has done any thing wrong in my county, you can bet your big fat ass I will pursue you to the ends of the fucking earth if I have to, to bring you or them to justice. Do you understand me?"

Rubino fairly staggered to his feet. He started back pedaling to gain some space between himself and Griffin. One of the metal chairs he had been abusing fell over and clattered noisily. For a moment Rubino stood there, now about six feet behind the table, and rocked back and forth. Griffin didn't know if Rubino was having a heart attack, about to fall on his face or getting ready to charge. Griffin began to feel slightly uncomfortable and began to seriously contemplate escape routes. But in a moment or two Rubino seemed to recover some of his composure. He stopped rocking. He took a step forward, but stopped again. He wasn't used to being talked to this way.

The two men stared at each other for what seemed like an eternity. In reality it was just a few seconds. Rubino finally took in an enormous breath. Griffin braced for the gale.

"You miserable fuck," he hissed. "don't you know who I am? What I can do to you? Your family? Your girlfriend Gracie? Your son, Kyle? Your career? Your people? You can't fuckin' touch me or any member of my family."

How the hell did he know Gracie's name? Or anything about Kyle? Griffin was startled. It was his turn to step back an inch or two.

Rubino continued his tirade, "I know I can't bribe you. If I could I would have tried already, but apparently, you're one of those fools who still think that principle counts for something. How pathetic. How amusing."

"Money isn't everything, Rubino," Griffin interjected a little too haughtily. It seemed to ring a bit hollow.

"Correct. Power, prestige, revenge and crushing your competition are also important," Rubino shot back.

Griffin tried to mollify his opponent a bit. "Look, all I want to do is ask a few simple questions…"

"Fuck you!" Rubino roared. He was regaining his bravado. He started pacing from side to side. "I'm not answering any of your damn questions!"

"Then why the hell did you agree to this meeting?" Griffin shouted back. "You knew the purpose was to ask you some questions relevant to an ongoing investigation that may involve members of your family!"

Rubino took another step forward. Griffin took another step back and instantly regretted it. Griffin couldn't show Rubino he was backing down in any way. But it was too late. Rubino seized the initiative.

His porcine eyes narrowed by half. He stared spitting as he spewed his venom. "I told you, Griffin. There is only one purpose for this meeting and it's mine, not yours. You back off, asshole. You fucking back off or I will have you destroyed. You drop this investigation of my family or I will bring down such a shit storm on you that you will wish you'd never left your family's fucking potato patch, you hear me?" He reached into his jeans pocket. Griffin flinched. If Rubino had a gun-Griffin didn't- Griffin was a dead man. But it was only a cell phone. He flipped it open, punched one button and growled into the phone, "Car! Now!" He snapped the cover shut and stuffed the phone back in his pocket. "This meeting is over Griffin. You have my message. You'd be wise to heed it." He circled around the table and headed for the doors. An arc of headlights flashed through the windows.

Griffin turned. He watched Rubino's barn-sided back head toward the exit.

"Rubino!" he called after him. "This doesn't finish it!"

Rubino didn't stop or turn. He just kept on going but Griffin could clearly hear him say, "Oh, yes, it does, Griffin. Oh yes it does…"

The double doors flew open. Two bodyguards threw a huge overcoat over Rubino and whisked him away. Griffin was left there standing in silence. This hadn't gone anywhere near as well as he had hoped and despite his best efforts at self control, Griffin was unsettled.

What the hell does he know about Gracie? And Kyle? Why tell me? Griffin's mind raced. *What the fuck is he up to?*

The field house air exchangers came to life again and Griffin knew the heat was on—in more ways than one.

27.

Brother Fox

The Slackwater catered to an eclectic mix of thrill-seeking college kids, blue collar locals and tax free cigarette shoppers. It was definitely not the tony, high brow, Hamptons sort of place that Ivan Centpied would frequent. This spot was not to his liking and the polar opposite of the much more upscale confines he preferred. Instead of smelling like rosemary and brick oven wood fires, the Slackwater stank of stale beer and piss. No, he normally wouldn't be caught dead in a place like this, not even on a bad day.

The Slackwater Pub on Old Montauk Highway was as "local" as a local bar can get. Just down the road from the community college campus it sat on a small hells-half-acre plot studded with weeds and loose gravel, and adjacent to the Shinnecock Indian Reservation. Chicken wings, juke box music and watered down drinks were its specialties. It was dark and dank with a sordid history. A decade back, in the second floor apartment over the bar, a young couple had been savagely murdered. It apparently started as an argument over the possession of a new color TV. The girl and young man had been brutally stabbed and gruesomely dismembered. Patrons swear they can still smell blood in the bathrooms and once in a while a red stained rivulet slides down a wall. (It's only sap seeping from the cheap pine boards but the effect is definitely creepy.) The principal killer was caught shortly thereafter, drunk, with the TV in his car, and a bloody butcher knife in the trunk. He was currently "upstate" in a maximum security prison serving two consecutive life sentences without the possibility of parole. Unfortunately for the reputation of the local tribe, the murderer was from the reservation bordering the Slackwater. There were rumors of an accomplice, who was now a respected member of the tribal council, but nothing could be proven. The chief perpetrator had kept his mouth firmly shut, but his formerly destitute wife and twelve children now lived in middle class style with no visible means of support.

The Slackwater hadn't changed a great deal in the past few years, since the notorious murders, besides becoming a little seedier, darker, noisier and more blue collar. The drinks were still watered down and everybody who wanted to ignore the smoking ban. The reservation "tax free" smoke shops are next door.

But this had been an exceptionally piss poor day so far, so Ivan did, indeed, find himself hunkered down on an uncomfortable wooden stool at the far end of the Slackwater bar. The busty and totally clueless young bartender didn't know what a "Cosmopolitan" was; consequently, Centpied found himself nursing a vodka and cranberry juice that suspiciously tasted much more of cranberry than vodka. He found himself, once again, waiting in yet another bar for yet another clandestine contact.

Where is this idiot? Centpied mumbled unhappily to himself. The news he'd received today had decidedly unnerved him. The plan was still on track but the authorities were getting uncomfortably close. He was totally positive that they didn't have a real clue as to what was afoot, but they were sniffing around diligently, and even a blind pig will find a truffle once in a while. Centpied was hoping desperately that the probing would remain random and sporadic. Just one well-placed inquiry could ruin plans that had taken months to pull together. All they needed was one more week. Then the plan, which ironically kicked into motion with this very meeting, tonight, would be damn near impossible to stop. Just seven more days…

He glanced at his watch again, and ordered another drink with a surly admonition to "Put some vodka in it this time"

Rubino, had, of course, related to Centpied all the details of his nasty confrontation with Superintendent Griffin earlier that day. It sounded damn ugly and disturbing, but no matter. Griffin would be taken out of the picture soon. Centpied felt very confident about that.

Centpied had finally gotten Rubino to put Victoria and Vincenzo under lock and key, at least for now. The two of them were, in fact, under virtual house arrest with double shifts of bodyguards watching them night and day. He almost felt sorry for Rubino. His only son was mentally deranged and his faithless wife was certainly somewhere over the edge. Sometime tomorrow Rubino's private jet would whisk them away to a sanatorium in Geneva where they could begin to get some serious help. Better for The Plan, they'd be beyond the tightening grasp of the law. Centpied shuddered to think what the two of them had done to that poor kid, Carmody. Sick. Truly sick. But more critically, as far as Centpied was concerned, they had almost brought The Plan to ruin. They had known nothing about it, but had almost blown it before it could get rolling.

Then Germella's handling of that idiot rag-head Ibrahim had been both stupid and brilliant. Stupid in that he had killed the bastard at all, but brilliant in that he had made it look like a copy of Carmody's murder. Thank God Germella knew nothing about Vicky and Vincenzo's involvement. It was just blind luck that Germella had concocted his scheme to draw attention to the other murder. Germella's morbid perversity had successfully sent the cops in too many directions for them to continually focus on the Rubinos.

He also smiled to himself concerning his cleverness with that bitch Jenna Walden. He had bribed two local cops with Rubino's money, of course, to send Walden off on a wild goose chase that would muddy the waters even more. He had thought her story was to have been on the local news that very night, but nothing had been mentioned. Strange. But maybe she needed more time. Probably tomorrow. He couldn't wait to see the impact of that! It would cloud things over even further and create even more confusion. And at this critical juncture they needed the cops and everyone else outside their crowd as confused and as unfocused as possible.

He didn't particularly like all the aspects of Rubino's plan. A lot of people were going to get hurt, many of them killed. Some would be friends of his. But then again, some were likely to be enemies too. Centpied mused to himself that somewhere in his worthless meanderings through boarding school one of his history professors had mentioned some Pope or other from the Middle Ages, who, worried about heretics, had instructed his rampaging Inquisitors to, "Kill them all. Let God sort them out."

Rubino had his objectives, Centpied had his. Rubino's goals, sick and senseless as they sometimes seemed, would still help Centpied re-establish himself as a money maker and re-burnish the family's tarnished reputation. That was all that mattered to him.

At that moment, his contact entered the Slackwater through the back door, the "locals only" entrance. Henry Brother Fox was a big man, well over six feet and nearly 300 pounds, but all muscle and tattoos. He wore his graying hair in a ponytail and favored leather pants and vests adorned with Indian beadwork. A deep facial scar from right eye to jaw line made him the perfect caricature for the wild and crazy Indian warrior you didn't want to meet in a dark alley.

The truth was, Henry's act was mostly just that—an act. The scar was from a wound won honorably in Vietnam many years ago when Henry was a young Infantryman. The leathers would give way to tailored suits when he made arguments in front of judges on behalf of his numerous clients. The tattoos, he often joked, gave him added respect among the bikers he rode Harleys with on weekends. Brother Fox was a lawyer, about as wily as his namesake and the head of the Shinnecock Tribal Council.

Henry's biggest client was, in fact, the tribe and his most important case was the one he had been working on with limited success for over twenty years: formal Bureau of Indian Affairs recognition for the Shinnecocks. Recognition as a bona-fide Indian Nation under the BIA would open up fabulous economic possibilities for Henry's people, much greater than the profits from selling tax free cigarettes.

Henry was no great saint. But he was no great sinner either. He was first and foremost an Indian who wanted to see, once and for all, his people become financially secure and independent. To achieve that goal he would do almost anything which was why, much to his own chagrin, he was having anything whatsoever to do with this noxious little man, Centpied, and his even more repulsive boss, Rubino.

"You're late, Henry," Centpied grumbled.

"You're always early, I'm always late. It is what it is, Ivan." Brother Fox parked his outsized frame on a bar stool next to Centpied. The stool post groaned in protest. "Beer!" Brother Fox boomed across the nearly empty bar. The bartendress jumped and the racked glasses above the bar rattled. The girl seemed to know which brand Henry wanted—Rolling Rock—and it was delivered with a frosty mug and a plate full of hot and spicy chicken wings. Henry chugged the beer from the bottle leaving the mug untouched. He then dove into the chicken wings, two and three at a time, before pushing the plate toward Centpied.

Centpied eyed the diminishing pile of steaming spices and grease with unveiled contempt. "No…thanks. Just ate." This was a lie.

"Didja bring the papers?" Brother Fox managed to choke out between mouthfuls of meat and crunched bone.

Was he actually eating the bones too? Centpied shuddered. "I did. Did you?"

"Yep." Brother Fox stopped long enough to wipe the grease from his face and fingers with an old bar towel. He pulled a fat manila envelope from somewhere underneath his leather vest.

Even in the dim light of the bar Centpied could see several stains on the wrinkled envelope. He hoped desperately it wasn't Brother Fox's body sweat. In turn, Centpied reached down under his bar stool and retrieved a fancy Italian leather briefcase which he hesitated to place on the stained bar. He popped the gold plated latches open one at a time. The sweet smell of freshly cured leather wafted upward from the open case. Centpied picked up his own fat manila envelope and he laid it gingerly on the bar next to Brother Fox's.

Henry picked up Centpied's envelope and stuffed it under his vest next to his bare skin and went after his second beer.

"Uh...don't you want to look at the papers? To make sure they're all in order?"

"Nope, it's after business hours. I'll look tomorrow morning. 'Sides if something's wrong or missing, I know where to find you. And I spent all afternoon sharpening my scalping knife. Hah!" Brother Fox guffawed into his beer. "That's a joke, Ivan."

But Centpied had no doubt that if Brother Fox felt cheated, he'd use the scalping knife-- and probably not on Centpied's hairpiece, but on his balls.

Centpied picked up Brother Fox's envelope. He wondered what to do. He was desperate to rip it open and look inside. But should he? Could he? Was this some sort of perverse test of trust?

"Go ahead, white man. You can open it if you want to. It's all in order."

"Uh, well…No. That's OK. I have to be going anyway." Truly, the place was beginning to make his skin crawl and he was sure he would catch some miserable disease or dysentery if he stayed much longer.

"Suit yourself. I'm gonna stay here and drink for a while. Toast your boss."

"Fine. I'll be going then. See you next week."

Centpied jumped off the bar stool.

"Hey!" Brother Fox stopped him. "Who's paying the tab?"

Centpied had had enough of this boorish, smelly, greasy-fingered fraud. His eyes narrowed and he said as firmly as his minimal courage would allow, "I think you'll find the check inside your envelope more than adequate to pay your tab."

"All right, all right! Don't get your tighty-whities in a knot. Can't blame a guy for trying."

"Until the meeting next Wednesday, then. Don't be late," Centpied admonished.

"Don't be an asshole. Oops! Too late! You already are!" Brother Fox banged on the bar and laughed at his own joke.

Centpied stomped out and scuttled crab-like across the gravel to his Audi TT. He fumbled for the keys, opened the door and slid into the cold, cluttered interior. Crumpled cigarette packs and discarded Starbucks cups filled the passenger seat. He retrieved Brother Fox's envelope from the attaché, tore it open and scanned the contents, page after page. He'd read it again in greater detail later, but at first glance it all seemed to be there, including the notarized signatures of all the members of the Shinnecock Tribal Council. He exhaled a long sigh of relief. Behind all the whys, wherefores and whereases; it seemed that they had a deal. He could hardly believe it. Even though the contract ran to nearly one hundred pages the gist of it was quite straightforward. In exchange for $50 million in immediate cash (a certified check in that amount was in Brother Fox's envelope) Milos Rubino and his partners, including one Ivan Centpied, were granted a 49% interest in any gambling enterprise, including casinos that might at any time hereafter, in perpetuity, be built and operated on

Shinnecock Indian lands. It was a pure gamble whether or not any such enterprise would ever be built and operated. First, it required official Bureau of Indian Affairs recognition of the Shinnecocks as a bona-fide tribe under BIA and Federal rules. Second, even if tribal recognition were granted it was clear that the Town of Southampton, who owned all the land surrounding the reservation and therefore access to it, was dead set against another Foxwoods type casino operation near their precious beachfront digs. After intense and secret negotiations with Rubino, Centpied acting as his go between, the Indians had decided to take the $50 million dollar bird in the hand. The tribe was lobbying hard to gain recognition but it was no sure thing. And even if they got approval there would be more bitter battles with the Town, County and State to face. The Shinnecock Casino could take another decade, maybe two or three, to become reality. In the meantime, $50 million, $5 million of which went into the pockets of the Tribal Council, including Henry Brother Fox's $2.5 million, would go a long way toward schools, housing and other improvements the reservation desperately needed. The tribal council was secretly laughing at the stupidity of this too rich white Jew who had more money than sense. Besides, even if they were wrong and Rubino was right or lucky they'd still have controlling interest in a franchise that could easily rake in billions over time.

But they didn't know what Centpied knew. And that was this: Another $5 million dollars had secretly been transferred to the Bahamian bank account of the BIA official directly responsible for deciding on tribal recognition for the Shinnecocks. He would be retiring next month on his $35,000 a year pension after 36 years of service to the BIA- but not before rendering a decision, in two weeks , that would open the floodgates for Casino development in The Hamptons. And neither the BIA turncoat nor the Tribal council had any clue that the entire economic structure of the Hamptons, the one built on peaceful security and sky-rocketing land values was about to be destroyed overnight. Once this unexpected change occurred, any opposition to new forms of economic development would dry up and blow away in a New York minute. Rebuilding and revitalizing a devastated local economy, even with something as odious as a casino, would no longer be so onerous and Centpied would own 10% of Rubino's 49%. He would be rich beyond his family's wildest aspirations for ill gotten gain. He quivered with joy just sitting there in the car thinking about it. He couldn't decide between getting drunk, fucking his clueless trophy wife or screwing his boyfriend. "Maybe," he mused, "I'll do all three..."

28.

Recall

James Griffin was very troubled and made no bones about it to Gracie. He couldn't get the day out of his mind. He was desperately hoping Gracie could talk him through it.

"Damn, I'd love a double scotch," he admitted.

"Don't do it," Gracie breathed softly in his ear. "You're doing so well. Do you really want to go back there?"

"Maybe," Griffin grumped testily. "No. I don't know. There are times, like now."

"They never stop. Trust me, I know."

"So what's my compensation? What offsets the wonderful buzzes? The great highs? The occasional oblivion?" he mocked, only half in jest.

"Well for one thing, you'll probably live another ten or twenty years longer," Gracie offered.

"Ten years semi-drunk, twenty years sober, I'll take the ten," he argued back.

"OK, your erections are harder and last longer when you haven't been drinking. How's that grab you?" Gracie gave him a smug little grin.

"Well, now you're making more sense." He smiled for the first time since he had come home, all tense and irritable, a half hour before.

Gracie tried to draw him out a little more. "Pretty bad day, I take it."

"Yeah. Pretty bad." He proceeded to give her a blow-by-blow of the confrontation with Rubino. Just as he finished the phone rang.

"Don't pick it up. It's trouble." Gracie scowled.

How does she know these things? Still, they were at a critical stage and even if the news was bad, he had to know what it was. He picked up the phone on the third ring, just ahead of the answering machine.

"Griffin."

"Chalabi."

Griffin's heart went cold. "What can I do for you, Colonel?"

"It's General. I'm now Brigadier General, Commander."

"Congratulations." He didn't mean it. All he could wonder was, *What are those idiots in the Puzzle Palace thinking, promoting this psychopath to General?*

"With apologies for disturbing you at home, let me get right to the point."

"Please do."

"I need you here in D.C. Immediately. Tonight if I could arrange it, but I can't, so first thing in the morning."

"You what?" Griffin was incredulous. He sat bolt upright. Gracie fell back on the sofa in defeat.

"I'm sending a Pentagon Gulfstream for you. It'll be at East Hampton Airport at seven a.m. Be on it."

"Now just a second Chalabi...General...who do you think you are that you can--"

"I think I am your superior officer, I think I have just given you an order, and I think you had better obey it."

"Look, I'm not one of your regulars, you can't just yank me around when you feel like it. I've done my part! I'm a civilian again!" He was beginning to shout.

Gracie left the room, near tears.

"Not as of two hours ago. I've had TAD orders cut for you. They'll be waiting for you when the plane lands. Don't bother to pack. You'll be coming right back. But do come in uniform. It makes people around here less nervous. We're suspicious of civilians."

"You damn well should be! Civilians are in control of this government, including you!" Now he was shouting too loudly.

"Calm down, Commander. If it's compensation to your shocked state of mind, I can assure you this is for your own good. I will inconvenience you as little as possible and your orders, although somewhat vague, are not for an extended period, a few days, maybe two weeks at most."

"Look, General, you don't understand…"

Once again, Chalabi cut him off. "I do understand. Carmody, your dead Arab, the Rubinos. I understand."

Griffin was shocked, "You're telling me this is about my case…cases?"

"Partly. But I'm not sure about your phones so I can't discuss it further. Be at the airport at seven." The line went dead.

Griffin held the receiver to his ear dumbly for another few

seconds before putting it down. Gracie returned with two mugs of steaming Earl Grey. Moisture welled in the corners of her soft brown eyes.

29.

Posturing

The East Hampton Airport was not used to handling military air traffic or the presence of uniformed personnel in its miniscule terminal. The controllers were much more adept at guiding in corporate Lears and dealing with loopy drunks trying to kill themselves in single-engine Cessnas.

The sleek Air Force Gulfstream with its distinctive military markings swooped in low and quietly. It kissed the runway with exact precision, pulled swiftly onto the taxiway and rolled up to the terminal. The cabin door popped open with a slight whoosh of pressurized air. An automated stairway scissored to the tarmac and locked in place. An Air Force TSGT in working blues scurried down the ladder, quickly spied Griffin decked out in his Navy great coat with three gold stripes on each shoulder board, and came to a stiff and proper salute at the bottom of the ladder. Griffin returned the salute and wordlessly stepped aboard. In the space of three minutes the Gulfstream had rolled to a stop, picked up its single passenger, closed the hatch and begun to roll again.

The sergeant made Griffin comfortable, saw that he was strapped in properly, informed him that he'd bring coffee as soon as they were airborne, then ducked into the cockpit. In the brief seconds the cockpit door was open Griffin could see the two pilots in place, one man, and one woman. The sergeant doubled as steward and flight engineer, and as he closed the cockpit door, he took his position on the jump seat behind the pilots. The jet began to accelerate and in moments it was airborne again.

The coffee came, along with a *Washington Post*, a *New York Times* and boxed breakfast. Today's in-flight menu consisted of a small carton of milk, one carton of strawberry yogurt, a banana, an individual portion of boxed Cheerios and a cellophane-wrapped raspberry Danish. He was amused. In the nearly thirty years he'd been in the military, in-flight box lunches hadn't changed much. And no matter which meal a box lunch was intended to cover, it was still called a lunch. Never a "box breakfast" or a "box dinner." He passed on all but the coffee.

Soon the Lear was above the cloud layer blanketing eastern Long Island. The small executive jet, probably meant for much higher ranking passengers, was instantly bathed in bright sunshine. It was a warm and welcome respite from the grayness of both the weather below and his current mood.

Seven other leather seats seemed to mock his loneliness. The ozone charged air hummed relentlessly and his coffee steamed in the chilled cabin atmosphere. He was also alone with his thoughts.

What the hell is Chalabi up to? he wondered to himself for the hundredth time. *Why is the Pentagon taking such an interest in a civilian police matter? It had to have something to do with Carmody's quasi-military status, and the as yet unidentified Arab we found at Cedar Point.* That's all he could come up with. *But why all this high drama? And why hadn't Chalabi just sent someone up to talk to him, like that young Lieutenant what was his name? that appeared out of nowhere on the night of Carmody's murder? Why hadn't Chalabi come up himself for that matter?*

Griffin was also irritated about being taken out of the field for a day-at least he thought it was for one day, but he didn't really know. He had called Beth Cantwell an hour ago to tell her he'd be out of town for the day and to take over. She seemed strangely, uncharacteristically unnerved by his call. He had wondered why but only in a distracted sense. There had been much on his mind when she had asked where he was going and he had been somewhat surprised by his own answer. Something in his primeval brain had alerted him to say, "Out of town. Can't say where right now. I'll call you later." He had now begun to seriously wonder why he had done that. Later, he'd be very glad he had.

The TSGT came back again to check on him. He was informed that ATC had cleared them direct-priority traffic. They'd be landing in less than an hour. He could also tell that the sergeant wanted to know more about him. Apparently Chalabi had some "pull." Mere Commanders don't get treated like this, at least not normally. He would have loved to tell the Air Force non-com that he was being called in by the President for a strategic meeting or how to finally close out the war in Iraq, or some other oblique nonsense but, of course, he couldn't. He didn't even know why he was there himself. So, he smiled in thanks and turned to stare out the window. The sergeant got the hint and disappeared back into the cockpit.

The steady whine of the engines became his airborne accompaniment. He had an hour to kill. He thumbed through the newspapers. Not even the Metro section of *The New York Times* had picked up anything about the current goings-on in his cases. There had been about four column inches on Carmody's murder and its lurid details but nothing since, which, he reflected, was probably just as well. He was tired. Bone tired. He put down the paper.

I'm getting too old for this, he said to himself. *Maybe it's time I retired for good, from the force and the Navy.* He had more than enough time in service to do both. And Gracie had assured him at least a part-time teaching gig at John Jay. "Professor Griffin" was sounding a lot better to him today.

But not now, he told himself. *I can't stop until I close this one. I just have to. I have to see this one through.* The problem was, and he knew it, the "next one" would be staring at him just as soon as he was done with this one. Then what?

His reverie was broken by a marked deceleration in the engines and the slight downward pitch of the aircraft's nose.

"Are we there already?" he wondered aloud. He glanced at his watch. Nearly an hour had passed. He must have dozed off.

The intercom came to life. "We'll be landing at Reagan in ten minutes, Commander. Please be sure you're still buckled up."

Reagan? Why Reagan? He would have expected to land at Andrews. But Reagan was much closer to the Pentagon than Andrews. Jesus. Chalabi did have some pull, or he was operating outside the box, which Griffin knew full well he was capable of doing.

The Washington Monument and the Potomac approach to Ronald Reagan International slid by. Again, the landing was smooth as glass and the jet taxied to the far end of the airport—the military end. A black sedan was waiting. With a nod and a thanks to the flight crew Griffin was down the ladder and into the car before his cheeks chilled from the frosty December air.

The driver was a Navy Petty Officer Second Class. Christmas music blared from the radio. The petty officer immediately turned it down as soon as Griffin was in and buckled up.

"Morning, sir." The petty officer smiled into the rearview mirror. "Your trip was OK?"

"Yes, Petty Officer, it was. Pleasantly brief. I presume you know where to take me because I sure as hell don't know where to tell you to go."

"No problem, sir. My orders are pretty specific. Straight to the Pentagon, East Side garage, 5th level VIP entrance. Someone will meet you there."

"OK by me. Let's roll."

"Yessir!" The sedan accelerated across the tarmac, out the back gate and onto an airport exit ramp.

He had only been to the Pentagon a couple of times before, and once was on a guided tour. But he did know the East Garage was definitely not for tourists. And the 5th level was reserved for people like the Sec Def, and the Joint Chiefs and their staffs. He was getting truly preferential treatment--or a path straight to hell. Either way, he was wary and very uncomfortable.

The drive took less than fifteen minutes, most of it against the morning rush. Griffin had given no signal to his driver that he wished to engage in idle chit chat, so the ride was conducted in silence. When the sedan rolled to a stop at the 5th level VIP entrance, a Marine Corps lieutenant colonel stood waiting. He popped the door, looked in, glanced at a card he was holding, gave Griffin the once over and motioned for Griffin to exit the vehicle.

The Marine was all business. "Good Morning, Commander. Please follow me." With that, he did a near perfect about face maneuver and headed toward the double doors ten feet away. Before the Colonel could slide the card he was holding completely into his pocket, Griffin could see that it was actually a frontal face shot of himself. Interesting. It was also unusual for an officer of equal rank to act as escort, a duty usually reserved for officers junior to the expected visitor. But nothing in the last twelve hours had been "as usual," so why would they be now?

Inside the double doors to the VIP entrance stood two Marine guards, fully armed, locked and loaded. Beyond the first two guards were two more Marines standing behind the metal detectors he'd be required to pass through.

He slowly and carefully shed his bridge coat. The colonel obligingly held it for him as he produced his military ID from inside his dress blue jacket. He handed the card to the first Marine guard, who scanned it carefully. While this dance went on in silence, another began, a pas-de-deux he knew he'd win, but that would end up being very uncomfortable—for the colonel.

While Griffin remained bundled in his hefty, double-breasted, gold buttoned, knee length bridge coat, all the colonel could see of Griffin's military regalia were the three broad gold stripes on each shoulder signaling his rank of "Commander" and his cover (hat) with the "scrambled eggs" on his visor signaling that he was a senior officer, although in the Navy Griffin held the lowest rank for which this visor decoration was appropriate.

But once the outer coat was removed, the inner blue dress coat would carry any badges, military decorations or insignia to which the wearer was also entitled. Medals bestowed were represented by ribbons and commonly referred to as "fruit salad." These colorful strips were worn in rows of three over the left breast. Griffin could see the colonel's eyes widen just a tad when his eyes caught Griffin's impressive display.

Griffin was extremely proud of his decorations—all of them--but he knew they could be intimidating, especially to others who thought of themselves as "warriors." Who was wearing what decorations would, in an instant, reveal to another trained eye where, generally, the wearer had served, what scrapes he had been in and whether he had received any kudos for valor or extraordinary service. The ribbons also went from lowest precedence to highest, with the most important decorations sitting at the left of the topmost row. Griffin had seven full rows plus one, or twenty-two awards in all. His highest decoration, the Silver Star, earned recently in Iraq, stood out, all alone at the apex of his colorful pyramid.

Griffin also wore ribbons for his Bronze Star, the Purple Heart, Navy Commendation Medal, Navy Achievement Medal, Joint Service Commendation Medal, Combat Action Ribbon, and a whole slew of other campaign ribbons indicating service in Korea, Kuwait, Gulf One, Iraq, and of course Vietnam. But tucked in among all these multi-colored awards was another, rather plain looking, single-colored ribbon of dull magenta. It told the world that the wearer had earned the Navy's "Good Conduct Medal." It stood for four years of "good conduct" or sort of a, "no-black-marks-on-your-record" award. For each additional four years of good conduct the wearer was entitled to another medal but awardees would put a tiny star on the first ribbon for each subsequent award. But here was the thing: the Good Conduct Medal was only awarded to enlisted personnel and never to a commissioned officer. If, however, an enlisted person had earned a Good Conduct Medal then became an officer, he could still wear the award. This was the case with Griffin, and he wore the decoration proudly. What it signaled was that he had come up the hard way and made it. What it indicated to some misguided prima-donna types and Griffin could already detect that this light colonel of Marines was one of them was that an officer wearing an enlisted award was somehow tainted; that he hadn't been quite good enough to start out as an officer, but had somehow managed to finally get there.

As the colonel continued fixating on Griffin's ribbons, Griffin smiled and said, simply, "Thirty years of undetected crime." It was meant to be a joke, but was totally lost on this supercilious jerk. It was then that Griffin looked at the Colonel's decorations. Two rows of three. Six awards in all. The highest award, and not an insignificant one, was the Navy Commendation Medal, usually given for "superior staff work." The two men were of equal rank, though Griffin was clearly fifteen or more years the colonel's senior. And, apparently, the colonel had never been outside the confines of the CONUS-the Continental United States. He wore no ribbons for any overseas service or foreign campaigns. In short, he was, in slanderous military parlance, a "REMF" which stood for "Rear Echelon Mother Fucker." The colonel also wore a triple twist of gold braided on has right shoulder that indicated he was a senior aide to admiral somebody or other. Yep. This was instant dislike. But Griffin had been here before.

ID checked, metal (none) detected and palm print scanned, Griffin was finally allowed into the inner sanctum of the Pentagon's E-Ring. The Colonel led Griffin wordlessly, down and around a maze of corridors and checkpoints. Griffin knew he could never find his way out if he had to go back to square one alone.

They finally reached a secure area with a quadruple tumbler door marked "JTECHOPS 05-3-7." His experience led him to believe the letters stood for "Joint Technical Operations," but he had no idea what the numbers signified. The colonel punched in the proper code. The door clicked open. Griffin and the colonel locked eyes for a moment.

"The general is waiting inside. I'll come retrieve you when you're done."

"Retrieve, Colonel? Do I look like something you'd ask your dog to fetch?" Griffin whispered coolly.

The Colonel's face flushed. Griffin knew he had him. "No Commander. It's…it's just an expression we use around here sometimes. Sorry. My apologies."

"Accepted. Until later then." Griffin stepped through the door and closed it firmly. He had always had problems with officers like this no-name prick. He had to admit he enjoyed putting them in their place.

30.

The Lion's Den

The room was very dark. People moved from desk to desk, shuttling reports back and forth. Three giant consoles dominated the far wall. The left was a vid-map [video map] of Afghanistan, the right console was a vid-map of Iraq and the center console seemed to show status of forces throughout the Mediterranean and the Middle East. The cool air sang with electrostatic vibrancy. This was clearly a place where something important was happening, but Griffin couldn't tell as yet what that might be.

Then, over his left shoulder, he could feel Chalabi's presence. "Good Morning, Commander Griffin. Glad you could join us."

The oily accent of the man he loved to hate crawled down Griffin's spine like nails on a chalkboard. Griffin turned.

Chalabi stood there in Army greens, one shiny new star on each shoulder, both hands clasped behind his back sporting a shit-eating Mona Lisa smile. At first, Griffin said nothing. Then slowly, purposefully, Chalabi thrust his right hand forward to shake Griffin's. Perfunctorily, Griffin returned the gesture.

"Well, Colon…I mean General, I could say I'm glad to see you, but that would be a lie."

"I know." Chalabi released his grip. "So let's get down to business, shall we? Please step this way." Chalabi led Griffin across the room to a private office. As soon as the doors closed behind them, the ambient light rose automatically to normal levels, causing both men to squint in adjustment. The office was both plush and sparse. It was devoid of any decoration, but the chairs were leather and the desk mahogany, befitting Chalabi's new status as a general officer. He motioned Griffin to a seat on the visitor side of his desk. Griffin sat. Chalabi continued to pace behind the desk.

"What you may see or hear behind these walls stays here, Griffin."

"General, I'm an intelligence officer, remember? We burn everything before reading it." The joke fell flat. He was 0-for-2 on the day.

"Just want to be sure we're clear."

"We're clear. Now, what's all the urgency, what does it have to do with my current caseload and when the hell can I go back to New York? And by the way, the orders you threatened me with? They weren't ready for me as I got on your flight. The crew knew nothing about any paperwork for me."

Chalabi looked at Griffin intently for a moment, crossed his arms over his chest and cracked what served, for Chalabi, as a faint smile. "Then why did you get on the plane? Absent any official orders, you didn't have to take another step."

Chalabi had him, and he knew it. Why had he gotten on the jet? It had crossed his mind at the time when the crew chief had told him he had no paperwork to give the commander. And yet he'd mounted those stairs to the plane anyway. Was it a sense of duty? Maybe. Was it thirty years of experience telling him the military frequently fucked up the paperwork and using that as an excuse wouldn't cut it? Perhaps. Was it fear of Chalabi, the unknown? Unlikely. Was it that he simply couldn't resist finding out what the hell was going on? Was it his innate sense of curiosity and the rush he knew he'd feel if there was any mystery or danger involved? Absolutely.

Griffin relaxed, folded his hands on his lap and replied, "I just couldn't resist finding out what the hell you were up to. Sir."

Chalabi grunted in satisfaction. "I knew it." He moved back to his desk, pulled open the top middle drawer and took out a thin manila envelope. He handed it to Griffin. "Your orders."

Griffin took the packet and stuffed it down beside his right leg. "Thanks, I guess..."

"Aren't you going to check them out?"

"I'll read them later. I'm sure, knowing you, that they're perfectly in order and as bullet proof as possible, General."

"And signed by Sec Def himself," Chalabi retorted smugly.

"Well, that's interesting. But all it really tells me is that I'm probably going to be up to my ass in alligators and you'll want me to drain the swamp."

"Maybe. But I really don't know," Chalabi responded somewhat pensively. He finally stopped pacing and took his seat behind the desk.

"So, General, how about at least telling me what you know?"

"I'll tell you what I can. But it's not a complete picture."

"What a shock." Griffin smirked.

"I don't know as much as I'd like to."

"Fair enough."

Chalabi took a deep breath before proceeding. "Ten days ago, the night Petty Officer Carmody was murdered, an NSA satellite picked up a call between two Arab-speaking males. Not terribly alarming. This particular satellite intercepts dozens of Arabic calls a day and all of them are translated and transcribed. For once, some duty officer with a brain recognized that it was a call for help, not routine jibber jabber. So, it was interesting. Not startling, but interesting. Then the same bright lad happened to notice that the GPS location for the call was from a spot where we had never picked up any cell phone traffic in Arabic before. In fact, look at this." Chalabi pointed to the large center screen on the wall outside his bullet-proof office window and punched a key on his desktop PC. Griffin turned in his chair in time to see the large vid display change from the Middle East to a full scale overlay of the eastern United States. There were red dots, some isolated, many in clusters. The largest groupings were in and around the major urban areas like Atlanta, Tallahassee, Charleston, Philadelphia, Boston, Newark. The scale then changed to focus on New York City, the southern coast of Connecticut and Long Island. The City was a mass of red dots, smaller clusters of red dots showed in places like Greenwich, New London, Queens, Nassau County, then fewer and fewer in Suffolk and eastern Long Island until, way out at the end of the display, a lone red dot glowed in Montauk.

Chalabi continued, "Each red dot represents a verified telephonic intercept of interest to us. You'd expect places like Manhattan and the surrounding Boroughs to be awash in dots and, as you can see, they are. But way out there in Montauk, at a place called Camp Hero? What's that all about?"

"But one phone call…" Griffin shrugged.

"Yes," Chalabi continued. "Just one call, but it was a call for help, a call from what used to be a top secret military communications site."

"But that was thirty years ago," Griffin reminded him.

"True, but our whiz kid duty officer, in what can only be called a stroke of pure luck, maybe genius, also noticed in that night's message traffic that there had been a report of a murder involving a recently returned Iraq veteran that very night in almost the same location. He added it all up, and one and one and one can sometimes be four or five if you screw up the coordinates, but this kid didn't. He came up with three."

"Good guessing," Griffin had to admit.

"There's more."

"Go on, sir."

"You do remember Lt. Overton?"

Griffin's antenna went to full alert. "Yes, I do. He appeared out of nowhere that night. I had a conversation with him.

He was supposed to get back to me. He said he was going to report soon, become your deputy in Iraq."

"He did. Two days later he was in Tikrit. I believe you remember the spot."

"Unfortunately, I do, sir." Griffin frowned. "But I never understood why he didn't contact me as we had agreed."

"Perhaps he would have if he hadn't been murdered," Chalabi spat out.

"What!" Griffin came up out of his chair. "He's dead?"

"Shot in the back of the head, execution-style, two days after he arrived in Iraq."

"Sir, I'm sorry…I actually liked the kid. Do you have any idea…?"

"Some. And it's got something to do with your case and something Overton found out while he was in Southampton. But whatever it was, he didn't tell me, and he should have. Probably wouldn't have kept him from being shot, but at least I'd have more to go on. I think he picked something up he knew he could run to ground in Iraq, yet he kept it to himself. I think he wanted to impress me. It cost him."

"What do you think it was?" Griffin solicited. "What makes you think it has anything to do with my cases?"

"Believe it or not, when we found him, in his quarters in Tikrit, bullet to the back of the head, he was still breathing, so his killer or killers had just been there. An MP heard the shot. He didn't live another five minutes, because if wound like that, doesn't kill you instantly, you're dead in minutes, so the MPs just missed whoever it was that killed Overton. If the assassins had been able to stick around and search his quarters--or more importantly, his pockets--they would have found what I found. Which was this." Chalabi pulled a carefully folded packet from the same desk drawer that had held Griffins orders. He pushed it across the smooth surface of the mahogany until it lay in front of Griffin.

Griffin picked it up and unfolded it gingerly. It was a hiking guide to New York's newest State Park: Camp Hero in Montauk. One of the old coastal gun emplacement bunkers below the main radar communications tower was clearly marked with a red "X" and written below the "X" were the words, "tracked him to here." That was it. Nothing more.

"I had it analyzed," Chalabi said reading Griffins mind. "It's Overton's handwriting."

"But what does it mean?" Griffin was incredulous. "Who is the 'him' Overton refers to? And where did he track 'him' from?"

"I'd love to know. Any ideas? Any clues from your conversation with Overton at the Publick House?"

Griffin was stumped. "No, nothing. Sorry. But I'd sure like to know how a New York State Park hiking map ends up on the body of a dead Navy lieutenant in Iraq."

"It is curious. But Overton was ambitious and he wanted to run with this himself for a while, most likely. My guess is he kept the map with him to use to confront someone he was going to track down when he got to Tikrit. But who and where and for what reasons we may never know. In the meantime, we've had that bunker at Camp Hero under twenty-four hour surveillance by a team from Delta Force. Lt. Overton, despite his fate, certainly provided us with a piece of critical intelligence."

"How so?"

"We've watched ten-maybe a dozen- distinct and separate Arabic individuals come and go from that bunker, always after dark, and always on foot. They leave from parking lots at the perimeter of the park, which are sometimes a mile or more away, and go up and down the hiking trails to and from this bunker. We've only ID'ed three of these individuals so far. Unfortunately, we can't see into the bunker. All of our sophisticated technology –infrared, ground penetration, e-lint, microwave, whatever--can't get through the ten feet of concrete, dirt and ten inches of steel plate. Not without revealing our presence anyway. They really built those old gun emplacements well. They were meant to sustain direct hits from eighteen-inch shells. And there are always at least two guards on site, in the bunker, so we can't sneak and peek without tipping our hand."

"Well they're obviously up to no good, sir, why not just go in and clean them out? Take them alive. I've seen some of your interrogation techniques," Griffin said narrowly. "I'm sure you can get them to tell you what they're up to."

Chalabi sloughed off the criticism. "Maybe. I'm sure we could get some stories out of them, but I want to catch them in the act of almost doing whatever it is they're up to. I've profiled the three individuals we have identified. They're Al Qaeda and they're pros. They would die a thousand deaths before giving up much. They'll all have disinformation to throw at us if they're caught. No. I need to see where they're going and what the real goal is before we shut them down."

"That's a dangerous game, sir." Griffin scowled. "And I don't like that it's going down, so it would seem, in my jurisdiction."

"Another reason you're here," Chalabi countered. "And by the way, I should tell you that your second dead body, the one tied to the tree in Cedar Point Park, was probably one of these characters."

Griffin's blood ran a little colder. "These guys killed one of their own? Why?"

"Oh, he fucked up big time. He was probably the one who made the cell phone call for help the night Carmody was murdered."

"How do you know that?"

"Don't for sure, but he referred in his brief call to 'being hurt' and your dead guy had a busted ankle that occurred a day or two before he was found. My guess is he injured himself hiking into the bunker from somewhere, made a stupid mistake calling for help and suffered the penalty of getting snuffed. Probably served as a good example to the others, too."

"But this is all gross speculation…."

"Maybe. But there's more. One of the individuals we did ID, coming and going from the bunker, is a real bad-ass character by the name of Ottmar Germella, otherwise known as 'The Turk.' He was a high-up deputy to the late-great Al-Zarkawi. When the Air Force blew Al-Zarkawi all to hell last June, Germella went down a rabbit hole somewhere and we lost him. Until he turns up in, of all places, East Hampton, New York."

"East Hampton?" Griffin was stunned.

"Yep. Ottmar and his buddies go back and forth to this abandoned bunker at regular intervals. When they leave the bunker they only go to three other places. One is a trendy new restaurant in East Hampton where they wash dishes and bus tables. The second is a local synagogue where they pick weeds and mow the grass. The third is a private day school in Bridgehampton where they sweep the floors and clear the classrooms after each school day. Now, I'm sure they don't work at the restaurant for the tips or clean the school to get educated, and they damn sure don't pull weeds at the synagogue to partake in quiet worship. So what's the connection?"

"I haven't a clue, sir."

"Well, Commander, I do, and here's a bulletin for you: the trendy eatery is owned by the same man who co-chairs the board of the private school and sits on the board of directors for the synagogue. Much to my own shame and mortification he is a Jew and his name is Rubino. Ring any bells now?"

"Holy shit…" was all Griffin could manage.

"I believe you've met with Mr. Rubino recently."

"Yes, I have. And it wasn't pleasant."

"Tell me."

Griffin related the essentials of his unpleasant altercation with Milos Rubino from the previous afternoon. Chalabi sat quietly for a few moments, lost in his thoughts. Now it was Griffin's turn to do a little interrogating.

"Since you know about my meeting with Rubino I suppose you're having me tailed?"

"Watched is more like it. If I had the assets, I'd have you tailed. As it is, my team is stretched pretty thin up there and I'm having difficulties getting more people on task. That's another reason you're here. I need your help. Mostly, I need some of your assets. Feet on the street."

"Oh, really." Griffin paused. "You need me. That's rich. If this were such a high priority operation, if the SecDef was truly involved, you'd have all the assets you could stand. You're running a real black bag op aren't you, General?"

Chalabi had forgotten for a second just how smart his former deputy was. "Well, yes, and no. This op is way, way under the radar, that's true. But the SecDef is involved and the President has been briefed. But we can't afford to have any more exposure on this right now, either in this building or out there on the street. I believe we're on to something that could really blow the cover off of a major terrorist group, possibly seal off a major source of Al Qaeda funding and break the back of terrorist training in Iraq. That's why I'm back here and not sweating my butt off in that stinking hell hole in Tikrit. But here's the problem, as you will undoubtedly perceive in a moment if you haven't already. It doesn't look good to have the military operating under cover snooping and poking around in domestic issues. It makes the civilians nervous--police state overtones and all that. We have Homeland Security, the FBI, DEA, Secret Service and so on to track down all these domestic threats."

"But that's what you're doing anyway, running a military operation CONUS, against all the regs."

"Yes."

"You don't trust the Fibbies or any of the rest of the alphabet soup groups. You're afraid they'll fuck up your operation and you want to keep it under tight control: for the greater glory of General Achmed Chalabi," Griffin accused not too politely.

"I knew you'd figure it out. But you're wrong about one thing, Griffin."

"What's that?"

"Despite what you think of me personally, this is not about me. Yes, I'm interested in power and promotions, but only insofar as it helps me get what I want. And what I want is to avenge my family's honor, kill all the bastards who murdered my parents and raped my native country and, believe it or not, defend the country that welcomed me, adopted me and provided me with the means to meet my ends." Chalabi was breathing heavily and his temples were pounding. Griffin could see that and could also see that he was telling as much of the truth as he was capable of telling.

"I'm sorry, General. I am. But I still have to ask, what's in it for me?"

"More than you could possibly imagine."

"C'mon, General, I'm too old for the melodramatics."

Chalabi exploded. "Melodrama! Melodrama?! You think this is some sort of fucking game, Commander?" Chalabi came out from behind his desk, walked up to Griffin and got directly in his face. The two men were of equal height and could truly see eye to eye. Griffin got up and stood his ground. He didn't move an inch or respond verbally. He knew Chalabi was probably trying to bait him or maybe even use some of his very expert interrogation psychology.

"Griffin, you pulled my ass out of the fire in Iraq when you backed me up with our boss. You even saved my life that day when you spied that IED that nearly bought both of us the farm. I don't forget those things and that's why you got your Silver Star-from me. That's also why, next month, a Navy Captain Selection Board is going to pick your sorry old ass for promotion one more time before they kick you out to pasture. You will be able to retire with four fat stripes on your sleeve instead of these three. And as far as I am concerned, we are now even but in a few minutes I will be ahead and you will owe me more than you can probably ever repay, so I would appreciate it if you would sit yourself down, shut the fuck up and stop questioning my tactics, motives and methods."

After thirty years of taking orders, good and bad, Griffin was forced him to respond simply, "Yessir," and take his seat once more.

"I can't force you to cooperate, but if you do I'll see to it your department gets all the credit. The civilians and the press will never know we were involved. That'll be good for you, good for me and good for those who get a little too twitchy about the Constitution."

"I'm not in it for the credit either, Gen..."

"I said shut up."

"Yes, sir."

"You help me out, I'll get you the two choppers you've been wanting, Army surplus, of course. You'll get the $5 million mobile command center you've been bitching about not having, a hundred more recruits next year and a 15% budget increase."

Griffin sat silently.

"You may respond to that," Chalabi dictated.

"That's very generous, sir, but I have to ask again, what does 'help me out' really mean?"

"I will act through you. You will give all the orders. We will both agree on ops before proceeding but you will put your department and all its resources at my disposal for the next two weeks. Then we'll see where we are."

"General, surely you know you're asking me for the impossible. I just can't do that. The County Executive, my boss, would have my head and my badge. The Governor would go ape shit. The press would have a field day with this and you'd probably end up losing your job, too, if not your career."

"You don't need to worry about me. I've calculated all the permutations and combinations and the possible effects on my career. Bottom line, this is the most important op of my career and I'm willing to take the risk.

"You don't need to worry about your boss. He's in the Governor's pocket, and the Governor is retiring next year. Your boss wants his endorsement to succeed him and will do whatever the Governor says.

"You don't need to worry about the Governor. As you also know, he's a close personal friend of the President. And I have been assured by Sec Def that the President will call the Governor if necessary.

"And you don't need to worry about the press. We're already exercising some press control. But we're getting ahead of ourselves. None of this will be necessary if we keep this under wraps, as I believe we can. There's just one major problem."

"Only one? That's hard to believe."

"Well, it's the only one we know about, although we're working on some other possible challenges."

"Great."

"It's your deputy, Bethany Cantwell."

"Beth? What's her ...why is she a problem?"

"Rubino got to her."

Griffin was shocked. "What? What do you mean?"

"It certainly can't be any secret to you that she wants your job."

"No...but I'm not quite sure she's ready. I've been working with her and maybe in a year or two..."

"Oh, she's ready. Trust me, she's ready. There's no doubt in her mind she's ready and quite frankly, she's tired of waiting around for you make up your mind to die or retire, so she's taking matters into her own hands."

"What the hell...Is she planning on knocking me off or something?"

"Indeed she is, and in the worst possible way."

"C'mon, General, you've got to be kidding."

"I'm not. But she's hasn't scheduled you for a hit. Something worse."

"Couldn't be too much worse than a bullet between the eyes."

"For old farts like you there could be. She's after your pride and reputation."

"Oh, really. How so?"

"She's talked to Burke Edwards."

"Edwards? That shyster? What for?" Griffin's mind wrapped around the image of one of New York's nastiest, slickest, junk yard dog attorneys. His specialty was sexual harassment claims. He'd won many multi-million dollar judgments and some said that more than a few of his claims on behalf of his clients were false from the get go. Bling! Suddenly the light went on. Griffin sat bolt upright on his chair.

"No!" he exhaled. "You can't be serious."

"I am. The papers have been drafted and filed. Fortunately for you, the judge is in our pocket, too. He owes the AG a favor. But he can't hold what amounts to a routine filing for long. Another week at most."

"What is she alleging, for Chrissakes?"

"That you have made many inappropriate sexual advances

toward her over the last year or so, all of which she spurned, and that once you learned she was a lesbian, you turned her rejections of your advances into a personal campaign of verbal abuse and harassment based on her sexual orientation."

"That's bullshit!"

"Of course it is, and you'll probably be able to prove that in court eventually, but that'll take a year or two and in the meantime, the damage will have been done. As soon as the suit is filed--and the judge will pretty much have to let that happen--the County Exec will put you on administrative leave pending a full investigation. Beth, the feminist heroine, will be installed in your place, temporarily at first, but probably permanently."

"She'll never get away with it!"

"Sure she will. Rubino's paying her attorney's fees and he's a money pit. Edwards will bury you in paper, depositions and court dates. The press will have a field day. You'll find out who your friends are and you'll spend every nickel you have defending yourself because the county won't pay a dime. Eventually you'll run out of money and friends, you'll get tired of fighting a never ending battle and then you'll cave. That's what they're counting on. And by the way, Cantwell's new offshore Bahamian bank account has a balance, as of three days ago, of one million dollars. Courtesy of Milos Rubino."

"Shit, shit, shit. How do I fix this?" Griffin nearly roared.

"My advice? Do nothing. At least not now. I'm working on it. We've got a week, at least. I'll come up with something. But in the meantime, keep her close. Watch her every minute and always, always make sure that when the two of you are in the same physical space there is a third person with you, someone you trust."

"General, don't get me wrong, I'm grateful for the heads-up. But when you say you're working on something it can sometimes mean that something nasty could happen to someone. Beth may be warped more than I thought, and she's certainly crossed the line, but I'm not sure that physical harm--"

"Such a boy scout you are, Griffin. This woman is ready to cut off your balls and you'd sharpen the knife for her if she asked you. Jesus, get a grip, and let me handle this. I'm not going to whack anybody over this, at least not just yet"

Griffin stared at the floor. His mind fired in all directions. "General, you said something about 'press control.' The press in my part of the world is pretty wired in. How are we going to keep a lid on this?"

"Your biggest press threat is Miss Walden."

"Walden? Jenna Walden? How does she figure into this?"

"Just wait'll I tell you this one." And Chalabi did. Right through the scheduled evening news exposé that had been planned but sidetracked, and the crash that had killed Walden's cameraman and rendered Walden unconscious.

"…so, it was too bad about Walden's cameraman. We honestly didn't intend to kill him, but who knew he was such a shitty driver? We also didn't intend to injure Walden. My guys were just going to intercept her and scare the shit out of her. You definitely did not need to be on yesterday's six o'clock news, especially with the story she was going to run. She was injured, but not seriously—mild concussion and a few scrapes, I'm told. She'll recover fully but the accident played into our hands, thank goodness.

"I'm afraid to ask how," Griffin sighed.

"Look, whatever's going to happen out there is going to happen soon. My guess is within days--not weeks, but days. I'm just keeping Walden on ice until after all this breaks."

"I hope you don't mean that literally." Griffin had visions of Chalabi encasing Walden cryogenically until he was done with her, then thawing her out and trying to revive her.

"Partially."

Griffin swallowed hard, expecting the worst.

"We had her air lifted to Stony Brook Hospital. She's resting comfortably and she'll be there at least another week. Unconscious."

"My God, General!"

"It was easy. The senior neurosurgeon there is an Army Reserve colonel. I convinced him that Walden's condition and 'temporary incapacitation' was a matter of national security, so he's keeping her in a drug-induced coma until I tell him to wake her up. As far as her family is concerned, the coma is real and she's fighting for her life. In reality, she'll be none the worse for the experience but she'll have a helluva headache."

"Sonofabitch..."

"So, Commander, here's what I need you to do. First and foremost don't take a crap without consulting me. Second, reallocate your department's tactical personnel and SWAT assets, and all your spare hardware and extra vehicles to me and be ready to move at a moment's notice. Third, back off Rubino, as he demanded. Somehow he's the key to all this and I need him to think he's been able to push his weight around, so to speak. But watch him like a hawk. Put a couple of your best people on him but don't let him catch them. My team will continue to monitor Camp Hero and the suspected terrorists. You and I will be in constant contact. Last but not least don't say 'shit' to anyone, even though you've got a mouthful. A lot could depend on this, Griffin. Now get your ass out of here and back to work unless, of course, you have any lingering questions."

"Just one, General."

"And what's that?"

"How do you sleep at night?"

"I don't. And you better hope the other side never catches me napping either."

31.

Junk

"I wonder what all this means?" the junk shop owner pondered as he paged distractedly through screen after screen of what, to him, was mostly gibberish. He could speak pretty good English but his writing and reading skills were rudimentary. He was much more interested in what this heavy-duty laptop would fetch on the black market. He guessed maybe as much as a thousand in hard American currency. And he wanted only US dollars, no more of the increasingly worthless Iraqi paper. He had bought the computer from an Iraqi policeman yesterday for $25, U.S. The Iraqi worked as a guard at the American compound on the other side of Tikrit. Only Allah knew where the policeman had gotten it from, and the junkman didn't want to know the true origin, that was certain. His Iranian contact was the right one to approach with this prime piece of American hardware. The Iranian would pay top dollar.

The junkman knew how to turn the machine on, but not much more. He was somewhat surprised that he was able to access anything at all. He knew enough to know that getting beyond the machine's password should have been a problem, but somehow it wasn't. The computer had booted right to the files the previous owner had been working on before the machine was stolen. "Strange," he mused. "Maybe the machine is damaged…"

There was, to be sure, a rather obvious dent in one corner of the hardened case. "Maybe that was it…" But otherwise the laptop seemed to work perfectly and the screen and memory were intact. "Yes, it will fetch a fair price." The junkman knew the Iranian would probably turn it right around for twice what he paid, and that it would end up in the hands of one of the terrorist groups in the area that was desperate for such technology, but what concern of his was that? This war had created many opportunities, Allah be praised, and he needed to feed his family, too.

The LCD screen was flashing photos of what looked like routine shots of American hardware: Humvees, light tanks, jeeps, and smiling American soldiers in desert camouflage uniforms. Most of them were gripping rifles and otherwise mugging for the camera. Then some writings flashed by.

Maybe they were letters or correspondence of some sort. Or perhaps they were official documents. That would make the computer even more valuable, but he couldn't really tell. Then the machine stopped on one page in particular. The junkman's eyes saw two words larger than the rest of the text typed at the top of the page. They read: "TOP SECRET." These were English words he *did* know and suddenly he thought he would ask for $2,000 U.S. for the laptop. He only caught a few other words on the screen. Had he been able to parse all the text he would have read the following:

TOP SECRET

--Eyes Only—

FM: LT. Scott Overton, Deputy O-in-C

TO: COL. A. Chalabi, O-in-C

SUBJ: Report on Tracking Activities, Suspected Terrorist Camp, Montauk

VIA: E-mail

Immediately after reporting to Tikrit I was able to make contact, per your orders, with our inside source in the Al Qaeda training camp nearby. He did confirm that one Ottmar Germella, the man I followed from East Hampton to Camp Hero in Montauk last week, was actively recruiting from this camp for a "major terrorist event" to occur in New York. The contact was unsure of the exact target or the exact date, but he felt it was going to be late December. He also confirmed that six men have been transferred from this camp to the US, most likely smuggled into the country via commercial shipping passing into New York Harbor. All six operatives have been trained as suicide bombers. I am to meet my contact again later today, here in my quarters, and he is bringing me more information. I have the copy of a map to give him, the one of Camp Hero that he requested. I will update this message with the results of the meeting and e-mail it to you via secure internet immediately following.

V/R

Scott Overton

LT USN

Just then the junkman heard a noise in the front of his shop. Marines! It was a surprise patrol. In his fear and haste to hide his illicit treasure, he hit the "delete" key as he closed the laptop's lid. LT Overton's draft e-mail was scattered into an oblivion of bits and bytes, lost forever.

Or was it?

32.

Sweet Dreams

The stench inside the frigid bunker was becoming unbearable. Mansour was almost glad that today would be his last full day on earth. Paradise should be much pleasanter than this, and certainly much more fragrant. Seven weeks of close proximity to his fellow soldiers, their stale tobacco, body odor and fetid breathing was more than enough to make one want to blow oneself up—never mind the glorious cause. On top of this, the small chemical toilet they had managed to hump over the wooded trails had long since stopped absorbing waste effectively. These old bunkers had never been designed for habitation, only periodic guard duty; therefore, they were poorly ventilated, had no running water and, of course, no functioning electricity. A small generator provided minimal light for reading and at least some heat, but the cold still numbed. Mansour would take it over the heat of summer, though. Only Allah, bless Him, could know what this miserable place would have smelled like in the middle of August instead of now, in late December. This spot had certainly not been chosen for its comforts. But it was remote, absolutely out of the way, safe and quiet. No-one would ever know they were there. The secluded bunker was deep inside the boundaries of the park and the park's many trails and pathways had provided excellent opportunities to learn land navigation and stealth tactics in their new, non-desert surroundings.

They had all practiced many times finding their way about the park and its environs, mostly in the dark and always without lights. It was practice that would be made use of tomorrow on their final and ultimate mission. Only that stupid dung eater Ibrahim had failed the land navigation phase of their training. Mansour still shuddered remembering what Ottmar had done to Ibrahim, in front of all of them.

Mansour had been trained in one of the Al Qaeda camps in Tikrit. When they had asked for volunteers for a special mission in America he had eagerly stepped forward. He was taken through Syria to Jordan. At Aquaba he had been smuggled aboard a tanker ship headed to New York. He had no papers but would need none. The captain had been well paid.

Mansour was only nineteen. Before the war in Iraq he had

been training to be a butcher's assistant. The Americans wiped out his entire family one day with a misplaced 500-pound bomb, hurled from the skies. He had been having tea with some of his friends on his day off. He'd been at the Plaza down the street from where his family lived, just three blocks away, when the world around him exploded. Now, he smiled coldly to himself, he would become a butcher of a different sort.

He looked forward to seeing his parents and his little sister again, tomorrow, in Paradise. The seventy virgins would, of course, be nice to meet, too. He had yet to have a woman and starting tomorrow there would be dozens, just to serve him! His penis began to stiffen just thinking about it. Or was it that cute girl he had flirted with the other day at Rubino's restaurant? Maybe thoughts of her were making him hard. Since his English was the weakest among those in the group, Mansour had been given the fewest opportunities to journey away from the cursed bunker. He had been on semi-permanent guard duty, which made him hate the place even more. On the few days he was allowed out he had mostly cleaned rooms at that school. It was always at night and there was never anyone around so Ottmar had felt it was the safest place for him to be. But the other day had had finally gotten a rare treat—a chance to work at the restaurant, busing tables. It was to be one of his only exposures to recreational life in America and what he had seen had stunned him.

He could not believe the excess and the waste. There was food everywhere. More food than he had ever seen in one place in his life. And the people who ordered and paid for this food hardly consumed any of it. He watched in horror and fascination as huge plates of half-eaten dinners were bussed back to the kitchen and tossed in the garbage. What he saw thrown away during that one shift at the restaurant would have fed his whole family for a month. No wonder Allah hated these people so much and wanted them destroyed.

But he was sure this girl had flirted with him. At least it had seemed so. She was eating dinner with a couple he presumed were her parents. At least she called the woman "mother," but for some strange reason she called the older man, her father, "Steve." That seemed very disrespectful but since she was wearing a very open-necked shirt that revealed everything down to the tops of her little brown nipples, he was willing to forgive her disrespect. Mansour could not begin to comprehend what kind of parents would allow their female child to appear in public dressed in such a vulgar fashion, but he had to admit he enjoyed the show. And her hair! It was the color of light straw and fell over her shoulders. She looked to be about his own age, maybe a little younger. She also looked quite bored.

Her mother was dressed like a whore, and slathered in makeup, and she drank alcohol like water. Her "father" spent almost the entire dinner on his cell phone. They were seated in the area assigned to Mansour to clear and when the tables next to the girl turned over he took a little more time to bus them. Once—just once—he made eye contact with the girl. He smiled at her. She smiled back and then lifted her right hand toward Mansour's face with her middle finger extended upward. He did not know what this gesture meant but he was sure it was some sort of flirtatious greeting. He told himself he would ask Ottmar to explain this custom to him at the earliest possible moment, but so far he had been too embarrassed to ask.

She was not, of course, the kind of girl anyone could ever marry. Oh, no! She was far too tawdry and cheap, but she was certainly the kind of girl he would like to fuck and he had dreamed of her again and again for the next few nights. In those delicious dreams he had ravaged her over and over in every position imaginable: tied to a bed, from behind over a barrel, spread-eagled naked on the ground, hands and feet tied to stakes, and more. In his dreams he never stopped raping her until she begged Allah for mercy and his hard dick was red with her blood. Ah, those were sweet dreams, indeed.

33.

Drawing A Bead

Outside the bunker Navy Chief Warrant Officer-4 C.J. "Red" Connigliaro's Starlite sniper scope was carefully centered on the back of the head of the man who was hiking up the snow-covered trail toward the cave. He would dearly love to squeeze off just one round and send this sand nigger straight to Paradise. The double-jacketed 30-08 round would cause this asshole's head to exploded like a rotten pumpkin. There might be a few teeth left to send home to mother but that would be just about it. Because he was so sorely tempted he made sure his finger was nowhere near the trigger. No. It wasn't time yet. Their job, his job as Team Leader of Delta-Six, was just to monitor these fuckers. For now. Make sure they didn't fart without somebody on his team smelling it. But he'd damn sure like to get some different orders. Orders that would allow his team of four to hop and pop and clean out this nest of desert rats. *What the fuck were they doing here anyway?* Connigliaro swore silently. *God damn them, and on my own home turf!*

"Red" Connigliaro was twenty-six years a Navy man. Twenty-four of those years he'd been a Navy SEAL, eighteen enlisted, six now as an officer. He was a W-4, or Warrant Officer Four, the highest rank that could be achieved without actually being commissioned. He couldn't go any higher without getting a commission and that was something for which he had no ambition whatsoever. He figured that in four more years he'd retire at thirty. He'd only be forty-eight, and with his pension he could go back to the rough and tumble streets of South Boston where he'd grown up and finally get that auto body shop he'd always wanted. Yep. He'd tinker on his own cars and those of the customers he wanted to serve—no-one else. There'd be plenty of pasta, pizza, beer and Red Sox baseball. Life would be good! But in the meantime, he had this job to do and no one was better at it than "Red" Connigliaro. (Incidentally, his hair was not red. It was jet black Italian with a little grey at the temples. His nickname came from one of his many famous sayings he used in the training sessions he conducted for SEAL recruits and members of his own Team: "If you draw a knife on a mission, don't come back without some red on it—and be sure it's not your own."

This was a strange assignment, he had to admit. His Team had been pulled out of Iraq to come back stateside and sit on these suspected terrorists. Delta-5, the other Team with which they were alternating had been called up from Little Creek, Virginia. "Five" was headed by MSGT Tommy "Guns" Stankowski, US Army Rangers. Good guy. Solid. Dependable. Both of them had an immediate boss and he was Major Jack Evans, USAF Special Operations, one of the best officers in the whole Delta Force. Evans was Air Force Academy, a helo pilot by training, and a damn good fighter. He had pulled every kind of shit assignment from Somalia to Afghanistan and several places in between. Today, he was in a cheap room at the Memory Motel in Montauk with a pot full of commo gear and connected to every kind of listening device he could beg, borrow or steal. His room was an "HQ" of sorts for both Teams, who were now billeted in four huge RVs parked between the dunes at Hither Hills State Park. Major Evans reported directly to General Chalabi. "Now, there's one seriously deranged mother fucker!" Connigliaro mused. He had seen some of Chalabi's "work" in Iraq. "But I'm glad he's on our side."

They had been secretly monitoring the comings and goings of these twelve ragheads for a week now. Bone-chilling, shitty duty, four on, eight off, round the clock, hugging the frozen turf or sitting absolutely immobile behind carefully constructed blinds near the bunker and out over the trails. When any of these A-rabs showed, there was a bead on them from the time they left their cars to the time they entered the bunker and back again. Connigliaro would dearly love to take a peek inside that concrete cavern but they had not yet had the chance. Someone was in there 24/7.

His earpiece came to life. "Chief!" It was Major Evans.

"Here, sir,' Connigliaro whispered back.

"Somethin's shakin'. I have priority traffic here. Get your ass back to the motel ASAP."

"Roger, that, sir."

OK, Mr. A-rab. You live to fight another day, Connigliaro said to himself as he pulled the rifle up and off the back of the skull of the man he was tracking. With barely a sound and no more movement than a shadow flitting in the moonlight, Connigliaro was up, off, and down the trail headed to his carefully concealed rental car at the edge of the woods. He wondered what was so important that the major would pull him off his duty shift.

34.

Honeyed Dates

Germella couldn't shake the feeling. He could see the dim outline of the bunker ahead as he reached the end of the trail. For the last quarter mile he had felt as if a fly or some annoying gnat was buzzing around the back of his head. But that was ridiculous. There wouldn't be any such bugs this time of year. Yet he couldn't help it. His instincts told him there was something "bugging" the back of his head. Was he losing his mind? Was the pressure finally closing in on him? And then, in an instant, it was gone—as if someone had shut off a switch. He shook his head to clear the cobwebs. He reached for the cold steel handle of the bunker door and twisted it open.

Light from the inside could no longer escape. He had installed the scrim after the night that fool Ibrahim had almost gotten them all discovered. A large black curtain hung from the ceiling to the floor. He closed the heavy door as silently as he could then stepped through the curtain. In a glance he could see everyone was there, just as he had commanded. With all of them there the space was crowded, but it wouldn't be for long. As the men inside recognized Germella's face, each lowered his weapon and came to full attention.

Germella waved his arms in greeting. "Relax, my friends! Please be seated. Make yourselves as comfortable as possible. Let's have tea. And I have brought us a sweet treat." With that, Germella produced a large box of honeyed dates which the men eagerly passed from one to the other. Tea was passed. When all were seated, some on the cold floor on prayer rugs, some on supply bins, a few on ammunition boxes, Germella smiled at them.

"Tomorrow night, my friends, we will all sleep in Paradise."

A few nodded in agreement, several murmured "Praise be to Allah!" some sat in stony silence.

"Our glorious day of retribution and eternal martyrdom dawns tomorrow. You have all done well. Allah smiles on each of you, blessed be His name, and He will personally greet you with open arms after sundown tomorrow, when our work here will be done.

"I know that every one of you is ready. I know that each of you is eager to follow in the footsteps of our fellow heroes like Mohammed Atta, blessed be his name, who courageously and gloriously lead the strikes on the World Trade Center and the Pentagon. You have seen with your own eyes and heard with your own ears how honored and blessed he and his fellow martyrs have become in our homelands. When the sun rises again in two days time your names will be on the lips of millions of Arabs around the world. Our Muslim brothers and sisters will fill your ears in Paradise with praises to your names. Your names will be emblazoned on the rolls of the heroes to our cause and the world will speak of you in the same hushed tones they reserve for Atta and his heroic band.

"It is time, my friends, to leave this place. We must be ready in fifteen minutes. We will leave in pairs. Mansour and I will be the last to go. Take everything you will need for tomorrow, but nothing more."

The men started stirring, checking equipment.

"But there's one more thing." At this Germella beamed at them. "One small reward for your sacrifice in advance of attaining Paradise. Our generous patron wants all of us to be his guests tonight. We will be staying at his home. He has prepared a wonderful banquet for you and you will have warm beds and clean sheets to sleep on this night, before your labors begin. He has even promised companionship—male or female as you desire—to ease your way into tomorrow."

A chorus of cheers arose, with more praise for Allah.

"So, my brothers, let us be quick—and quiet. Now memorize these directions. You will need them to find Rubino's home…"

35.

Cave-In

Having quickly changed in his car from his camouflage gear to civvies, Connigliaro arrived at Room 6 of the Memory Motel about a microsecond before his counterpart from Team Five, Master Sergeant Stankowski. They nodded to one another in silent greeting and Stankowski knocked on the door.

"Enter!" they heard Major Evans acknowledge from the other side. The two men quickly stepped into the room to be greeted by their boss—and, in a real shocker, Brigadier General Chalabi. Both team leaders came to instant attention.

"At ease, men," the general offered.

Both leaders relaxed—a little, still wondering why HE was there.

"Let's not waste any time, gentlemen," the general went on. "I'm here because we've had a serious breach of security and I'm very concerned that we're going to have to move on this op, ready or not."

Evans and each of his team leaders glanced nervously at one another.

"The leak isn't on this end," the general explained. "Earlier today, Iraq daily fucking standard time, a routine US Marine patrol on the outskirts of Tikrit recovered LT Overton's laptop. Some dirt-bag black market operator says he picked it up from one of the Iraqi guards that are supposed to be securing my fucking compound! Jesus, I can't believe Overton was so fucking stupid as to put such sensitive shit on his laptop." Chalabi started pacing the room agitatedly. "Nonetheless, he apparently did. The laptop was not in his quarters when we found his body. We assumed he had hid it somewhere. But I guess he didn't. If I had known he'd do something this dumb I'd have shot the bastard myself."

All three men had no doubt whatsoever that Chalabi was capable of doing just that.

"Anyway, NSA is trying to unscramble the mess on his hard drive, but they say it'll take a couple of days. We don't have that kind of time. I don't know where that fucking laptop has been, who's had access to it, and what they may or may not know, but I'm concerned. Overton, as you can guess, had knowledge of our entire op here. Suggestions?" Chalabi stopped pacing and stared hard at the three of them.

Evans, as ranking officer, responded first. "Let's take what we can get. All these fuckers are right where we can bag 'em. Nobody's been hurt or killed yet. We may never find out what they were up to but we can be for sure certain it was no fuckin' good. If we take them now we can probably prevent something really bad from happening, sir." Both team leaders nodded in agreement.

Chalabi thought about it for a moment. "OK. Do it."

At that very moment, a radio sitting on the coffee table crackled to life. "Red! Red! It's Harrison. You out there?" a voice whispered from the speaker.

Evans looked at Connigliaro. "Answer him." Connigliaro strode quickly to the radio and grabbed the handset mike.

"Who's Harrison?" Chalabi demanded.

"Petty Officer Second Dan Harrison. He's on Red's team and he's on site outside the bunker right now," Evans responded.

"Go!" Red growled into the handheld.

Harrison came back instantly.

"Red! They're leaving—in pairs. The whole lot of them, I think. Eight so far. Looks like they're cleaning out the nest. What do we do?"

Connigliaro looked at Evans. He was their immediate commander.

Evans calmly ordered, "Have Harrison and his guys snag however many they can. Those they can't nab, take them out. Don't let any of them get out of the park."

Connigliaro keyed the mike to relay the orders to Harrison but before he could speak, at lightning speed, Chalabi slapped the handheld out of Connigliaro's hand. It clattered to the floor. The three Delta men froze in shock.

"Wait!" Chalabi ordered with upheld hands, palms out, "Just wait! That's an order!"

The other three stood there in stunned silence. Evans leapt to retrieve the handheld, and he scooped it up like a starved rat after cheese. He shouted, "But sir! They'll get away! We only have three guys out there right now. They can't secure twelve hostiles if we don't turn them loose now!"

Chalabi glared at Evans. "No, Major. I said wait!"

The room coiled with tension. Evans, Stankowski and Connigliaro knew they had no chance of getting close to twelve enemy if something didn't happen in the next few seconds.

Harrison's voice came back again, more alarmed. "Red! You there? What do we do, man? Come back! They're getting away from us!"

Chalabi held out his right hand toward Evans. He wanted control of the radio. "Give it to me, Major. Now!"

"But, sir!" Evans protested a little too strongly.

"Now! That's another order!"

Evans reluctantly complied.

Chalabi held the mike to his lips and pressed the transmit key. "Harrison. This is General Chalabi. Let them go."

Harrison hissed back, "Who the fuck is this? Where's Red? Major Evans?"

Chalabi handed the transceiver to Connigliaro. "Tell him to let them go, Mr. Connigliaro."

Connigliaro reluctantly took the handheld. He glanced at Major Evans, whose face was a stone mask. Connigliaro pressed transmit, "You know my voice, Harrison. You heard the General. Let them go, over."

There were five uncomfortable seconds of silence. "Harrison? You copy?" Connigliaro snarled.

"Yeah, I copy," Harrison came back. "We're letting the bunnies run off into the bushes. Now what, over?"

Chalabi addressed the small group in Room 6 calmly, 'Don't you see, gentlemen? They've fled the coop. We can finally get in that bunker! We can tear it apart and find out what their game plan is! And we know pretty much where they go. We can pick up their trails again. They can't get very far away. Now go get me some fresh intel!"

Evans took the handset from Connigliaro. "Harrison!"

"Yes, Major, can you tell me what the fuck is going--"

"Shut up, Harrison. Just get your team together and get in that bunker and do it NOW! Understood?"

"Yessir."

"The rest of us are coming to you. Be careful no-one doubles back. Leave a guard out. But get your asses in that bunker."

"Yessir. Harrison out."

"Get out there, Major, and get back to me ASAP. I'll wait here. I have some calls to make. I'm pulling in some local help on this," the general announced.

"General!" Evans nearly exploded. "Are you outta your...? Local help? Who? What? Since when do we need--"

"I'll brief you when you get back. Now get out there and tear that place apart."

"Yessir." The three Delta leaders left the room. Outside, once they were all in Major Evan's SUV, Stankowski and Connigliaro practically came unglued.

"What the hell was that about?" Stankowski pleaded incredulously.

"Ours is not to reason why, ours is but to do or die," Evans deadpanned.

"Yeah, but how many are gonna die because of what we're doing? We just sent a dozen armed terrorists out into the community. I don't think eastern Long Island is going to be happy about that."

Evans said nothing. He just threw the big SUV into gear and peeled out of the parking lot.

36.

The Only Way...

"It's the only way this could have been done, Centpied."

"But...but...It's so brutal, so disgusting!" Centpied moaned as he looked over the hideous display Rubino had dragged him out to witness. He knew he was going to be sick, and sure enough, he was. He ran to some bushes a few feet away, barely making it before tossing a very expensive veal dinner and half a bottle of $200 pinot noir in the brush. Shaking, his stomach still quivering, he wiped his mouth on the sleeve of his Burberry coat. He would take it to the cleaners tomorrow.

Rubino actually chuckled at the pathetic display being put on by this queer little man. *God, I do loathe him so*, Rubino told himself, *But he has his uses*. Rubino shook his head slowly from side to side, in mocking disdain. "C'mon. Let's get back. Quickly now."

Centpied trudged heavily back to the fat man's side, like a loyal little lap dog, which, indeed, he was. "Why?" he nearly cried. "Why did you want me to see this?" he begged.

Rubino shrugged. "Because you need to understand the gravity of the situation, my friend. We are too close to the end of our little game to have obstacles like this in our way. Besides, it'll distract our foes, like Mr. Griffin, and it will take the focus off of us just long enough for us to complete our tasks. After that, pah! Small potatoes like this won't matter much. The authorities will have much bigger problems on their hands. And you, dear Ivan, if you want to play in the big leagues, like me, these are the kinds of things that must be done. You need to see and understand this."

What went unsaid, of course, was the subtle message to Centpied: "Don't cross me, little man, or you could end up just like this."

Rubino's henchmen, the two who had created this macabre tableau, were finishing the rest of the cleanup. It would not do to have Rubino's large and expensive boot prints anywhere nearby, so all four men carefully walked back on the impressions they had made coming in. The thin crust of ice and snow would not give up any clues when it was examined later, as surely it would be. They slogged back to the

Bentley parked at the edge of the deserted field. As an additional precaution, the guards swept the snow away behind them with tree branches. Once Rubino and Centpied were seated in the back, one guard slid into the driver's seat and slowly backed the car all the way out to the asphalt surface that ran along the perimeter of the soccer field. The other guard carefully brushed the ground behind both himself and the car, all the way to the tarmac. The other car would be left at the scene. When the second guard reached the passenger side door he pulled himself in, branches and all. No use leaving any evidence that they didn't want to have discovered.

The wind had started to pick up again so it was entirely likely that Mother Nature would cover their tracks anyway, but the two hired killers fancied themselves as pros at this sort of thing, so they would take no chances.

With all four men back in the car, the driver pulled smoothly away. A light snow was predicted for later that night, but only an inch or two. Someone would surely spot the car left behind tomorrow. There could be little doubt about that. It was parked in a spot where no-one normally stopped. It would draw attention at first light and Rubino was counting on that.

In the warmth of the heated leather seats Centpied began to come around some. He stared out the window into the darkness and without turning said, "You're sure that was necessary?"

"Absolutely. Otherwise one of them could—and probably would—have betrayed us. It will also take suspicion away from Victoria and Vincenzo. By the way, they called. About an hour ago. They are safely on the ground in Geneva—out of harm's way and out of the grasp of Griffin and his cohorts. I'm having the jet fly back tonight. We'll be needing it tomorrow, no doubt." Rubino stopped talking for a moment and became just the slightest bit wistful. "This also solves my biggest money problem, too. But I will miss him dearly, that sadistic little spendthrift! Oh well, time to move on, I guess."

And move on they did, right down Butter Lane to Montauk Highway. Rubino knew he had a houseful of interesting guests to wine and dine and—who knows?—maybe one of them could be turned into a bedtime companion before the night was over.

37.

Rocky Raccoon

The abandoned car was spotted right after daybreak the next morning. The school's private security patrol noticed it immediately. It was not the norm by any means to park a car on the far side of the soccer field near the woods. The security guard carefully picked his way across the frozen field in his corporate jeep crunching over the tracks that had been there the night before.

The guard pulled up alongside the big blue Mercedes. An inch, maybe a little more, of new snow covered the sedan. If anyone was inside, they had been there all night because none of the snow had been disturbed. The guard began to get a little apprehensive. If someone was still inside, it could not be good.

He carefully opened the door to his patrol vehicle. He was not armed. His security company did not equip their people with firearms. Besides, as a convicted felon he wouldn't have qualified for the permit anyway. He walked around to the driver's side door. Carefully, gingerly, he wiped the snow off the driver's window with a gloved hand. He peered inside. Much to his relief, the car was empty.

Probably just some fuckin' drunk who lost his way home last night, he cursed to himself. He'd call it in, get a tow truck out here, and be on his way.

Just then a low, guttural snarl emanated from the snow covered brush ahead. He jumped at the noise. "What the fuck!"

Two large raccoons broke from the bushes, waddled into the snow and headed across the soccer field as fast as their short little legs would allow. They looked back over their haunches as they trundled away, seeming quite perturbed that they had been disturbed. It was almost laughable. Then the guard noticed something odd about the squabbling pair. What was that red stain on their snouts? A few red droplets fell away into the snow.

"Must have interrupted their breakfast," the guard murmured on frosty breath.

He was curious. *What the hell were those two varmints feasting on? One of the local chickens? A stray dog that had gotten in their way?* Raccoons were usually buried deep in their burrows this time of year. Still, if they had been disturbed, or were particularly hungry, they could be tempted.

The guard stepped through the brush where the raccoons had broken free. He found himself in a small clearing. His screams could be heard over a mile away.

38.

A Third Party...

It took Tartaglia and his crew most of the morning to sort everything out. Griffin, back from a mysterious day out of town, paced a new pathway in the snow, back and forth from the clearing to his car. Between growls at the forensics team and taking and making numerous calls on his cell phone, he looked as mean as an old grizzly.

"What's eating him?" Tartaglia's assistant grumbled.

"Who? Superintendent Griffin?" Tartaglia answered distractedly as he forcepted another long strip of stringy meat into an evidence bag. "Don't mind him. He's under a lot of stress—only to increase after word of this massacre gets out. What did that security jerk say? Raccoons? Was he sure about that?"

"Yeah. Says he likes to pop a few with his .22 now and again, over on his property. Says he knows a raccoon when he sees one."

"Hmm," Tartaglia mused. "Must be rabid. I've never seen them eat human flesh before."

"Sure made a mess of this poor bastard's innards, didn't they?" The assistant eyed the corpse at their feet with obvious revulsion.

"Probably more interested in what was already in this guy's stomach than the stomach itself. Looks like maybe steak and lobster, but I won't know for sure until we get this mess back to the lab. Does this guy look Japanese to you?"

"Nope. Looks like a middle-aged white guy. Why?"

"So, why does a middle-aged white guy kill himself by slicing open his abdomen like he's committing—what do they call it?"

"I think it's called 'seppuku.' Japanese ritualistic suicide."

"Yeah, right. Whatever you said. And what did the suicide note say again?"

"I don't remember exactly. Chief Griffin has it. Something about 'I'm sorry for all the pain I've caused. I can't take it any more.' The usual shit."

"Well, that's all we can do here. You can go ahead and bag and tag him. Funny though."

"What's funny?"

"Look at his eyes."

"Yeah, what about them?" Both men looked down at the cold dead face of Israel Sokolin staring straight up into the clouds, seeing nothing.

"He looks surprised."

"Huh? Surprised?"

"Yup. Surprised, like 'I didn't know it would be like this,' surprised. Why would he be surprised?"

"I dunno. Maybe it hurt more than he thought?"

"Nah. Despite the Jet Li movies, a large slicing stroke across the belly like this wouldn't hurt much. Not as much nerve area here as in other parts of the body. Besides, as you can see, blood and guts spill out pretty quickly. He lost so much blood so fast that he was in deep shock. He got beyond pain pretty fast."

Both men looked down again at the bloody mess that had once been the entrails and internal organs inside Sokolin's midsection. Sokolin was laying on his back, a razor sharp 12-inch fish gutting knife in his right hand. Bits of flesh, long stringy pieces of intestine, and parts of the stomach lining lay scattered around the body. The snow was also pockmarked by a hundred tiny little footprints, many of them bloody.

Tartaglia cocked his head from one side to the other. 'Anyway, he just looks surprised. As if someone did this to him rather than him doing this to himself. Just a hunch. And then, of course, there's the knife."

"What about the knife, boss?"

"It's wrong."

"Whaddya mean, 'wrong?' It's in his right hand...Oh! I know! He was left-handed!" the assistant yelped as if he had just solved a murder mystery parlor game.

"No...well, maybe, but I don't know yet if he was right or left-handed. "

"Then what about the knife?" the assistant inquired, somewhat defeated.

"If you're on your knees, as this guy apparently was when he was opened up, you'd want to be holding the knife backwards, against the belly, so you could stab inward, and pull the knife quickly across the abdomen. Look. He's holding the knife with the blade pointed away from him. It would be damn near impossible to stab yourself that way and get this kind of smooth, one-slice cut. I'll bet my next paycheck we have yet another murder on our hands."

"So, then, if that's true, what about the other guy?"

Both men looked up at the second body, tied to a large scrub oak tree a few yards away. The naked, bearded man, white, early forties, was just as dead as Sokolin. And he appeared to be the third victim of the mysterious homosexual rapist. Was Sokolin the murderer, as his remorseful "suicide" note, found under his body, would seem to indicate? Tartaglia was skeptical, very skeptical.

Griffin stepped back into the crime scene. He looked even more agitated than before, if that were even possible. He strode to Tartaglia. "So, I have a tentative ID on the guy tied to the tree," Griffin puffed, irritated.

"Who is he? The Head of the school? He was able to identify him?" Tartaglia asked.

"Yeah. Maloney's his name. Richie Maloney. Kids call him 'Phony Baloney Maloney' behind his back. Big glad hander and fund raiser. Anyway, says our dead guy tied to the tree is the PE teacher, 'Barry Logamin.' I'll have Garwood and Wysocki get the lowdown on him. So, whaddya think, Richie? What have we got in all this bloody mess?"

"I'm bettin' two murders, Chief. This bag of guts here on the ground is no suicide. The other guy, well, you know he was murdered, and probably made to look like the other two tree stiffs."

"Jesus, Richie..." Griffin frowned, pinching his eyes together with a gloved hand, signaling to all his intense fatigue.

"Hey, Chief! Mr. Tartaglia! Over here!" It was one of the local uniformed cops that had been poking around in the brush for any additional clues or evidence.

Tartaglia's assistant and an EMT began scooping Sokolin into a body bag. Griffin and Tartaglia walked the few yards to the brush where the sharp-eyed policeman had apparently found something of interest.

"OK..." Griffin glanced at the nametag on the Southampton cop's jacket, "Officer Platt. What have you got?"

"Well, sir," Platt responded, "I was just poking around in this brush with this stick when I stirred up this mess." Officer Platt directed the attention of both men to the point of his broken tree branch. The tip of the stick was turning over a half-frozen stew of regurgitated chunks of food.

"Well, well!" Tartaglia smiled as he bent down in the snow to have a closer look. "Seems like we have a third party at this crime scene. This will bag up nicely and I'll have DNA by noon, Chief."

"Harrumph," Griffin grunted. "You know it's going to be a shitty day when you're best evidence is a pile of puke."

39.

Love Letters

Griffin left his latest messy crime scene in Bridgehampton and sped off to Montauk. It seemed his worst fears were being realized. He had two more murders on his plate, General Chalabi was in his backyard, and a gang of terrorists wandered somewhere around the Hamptons. On top of this, a Delta Force contingent armed to the teeth was in town spoiling for a fight, his trusted deputy was in league with the enemy and Gracie wasn't returning his calls. Where the hell was she? Was she still pissed at him for the other night? Was she at their place in the City? He didn't know and he was starting to worry.

He decided to try one more time. He dialed Gracie's cell and after two rings got the automated answering service. Unfortunately, this told him Gracie had still not retrieved any of his messages. If she had gotten his increasingly frantic calls, even if she hadn't returned them, the answering system would have re-set itself and given her six—not two—rings in which to answer the call. Griffin ended the call and hit another speed dial button.

"Superintendent Griffin's office, may I help you?" Tilly's gruff but familiar voice answered.

"Hey, it's me."

"Chief Griffin, where are you? I've been getting calls. The County Exec is looking for you—"

"Later, Tilly. I'll get back to him. Right now I need you to do me a favor and to keep it quiet, OK?"

"Well, sure, OK, what's up?"

"I need you to call Dick Fagan and NYPD. Please have him send someone over to Gracie's, you know, just to check."

"Ohmigod! Is something wrong? Has Gracie—"

"No, I don't know. She's just not answering her phone and I'm getting a little worried."

"I'll call Chief Fagan right away. Shall I send someone out to your house, too?"

"Might be a good idea, Tilly, thanks."

"I'm on it. As soon as I get something—anything—I'll call you back."

"Great, thanks." They both signed off.

He pulled into the main entrance of Hither Hills State Park. This time of year the campgrounds were closed and there was no Ranger to collect the usual entrance fee, but the gates were open. Turning left he went down the old access road, behind the dunes, all the way to the end where four large RVs were lined up, side by side. Stopping by the first one, he switched off the ignition. A forest of antennas bristled from the top of this RV so he assumed that this is where he'd find the general. In their brief phone exchange the general had told him they were switching HQ from the Memory Motel to the park. All the comings and goings of these large, secretive men in and around the normally deserted Motel had caused too many tongues to wag.

As soon as he mounted the first metallic stair, the door popped open and he was motioned inside by a fierce looking, dark-haired warrior type in winter cammies. Chalabi and another man, also dressed in camouflage gear, were bent over a table in the center of the RV, pouring over a pile of documents. The general glanced at Griffin and motioned him to join the conference.

"Superintendent Griffin, this is Major Jack Evans, Special Ops, Delta Force," Chalabi indicated of the man standing next to him. The major was short, powerfully built with close-cropped sandy hair and vivid blue eyes. Griffin thought for a second that he had finally met the real "G.I. Joe" action figure come to life.

"The gentleman behind you is Chief Warrant Officer Connigliaro." Griffin shook hands with Evans and then turned to repeat the gesture with Connigliaro. "Mr. Connigliaro is a Delta Team Leader. Major Evans is on scene Delta Force commander and our other Team Leader, Master Sergeant Stankowski, is presently occupied on an errand, but he should be back shortly. I have briefed all three of these men on you. All you need to know about them is that they work for me, they are here under my orders, and they are thoroughly trained professionals. As for the other niceties, we can catch up on those later, as time permits. Now, Griffin, have you managed to arrange for the assets I requested?"

Griffin frowned but replied, "Yes, General, I have. The choppers are fueled and on station. One is at East Hampton Airport and the other is at the Montauk civilian airfield. Two full SWAT Teams are standing by, one in Southampton and the other in East Hampton. I have twenty extra detectives scattered around the East End and, unfortunately, I have a full forensics team already on site and at work in Bridgehampton."

"What about your deputy? Where is she?" Chalabi demanded.

Griffin blushed slightly. How much did these other men know about the plight within his own organization? Their impassive faces betrayed no knowledge one way or the other. "She's at the temporary command center we've set up at East Hampton PD."

"Good. Keep her there. I want her like a mushroom. Pile shit on her and keep her in the dark."

"But, General, shouldn't we get her out of the picture?"

"No. That could cause Rubino to have suspicions."

"But General…"

"Just do it, OK, Commander?" Chalabi reverted to Griffin's military title to emphasize his current hold over his ass.

"Yessir," Griffin replied, seething.

More feet were heard on the metal steps outside the RV's entrance. All four men froze. Evans and Connigliaro's hands instinctively went for their side arms.

"Stankowski!" a voice boomed from outside. Connigliaro checked the peephole and nodded in assent.

"Enter!" Evans commanded.

MSGT Stankowski came through the door carrying a large, open-topped cardboard box. He was followed by two more troopers, each of them carrying similar cartons. Introductions were hastily made. The other two with Stankowski were from his team, PO2 Danny Harrison and SSGT Patty Davis, USMC.

Whoa! Griffin said quietly to himself, *Did he say 'Patty' Davis?* Griffin looked hard at Harrison, then Davis. SSGT Davis had short, close cut brown hair and deep purple eyes but sure enough, beneath the camouflage gear one could definitely see the suggestive bulge of two well-shaped breasts. Davis stared straight back into Griffin's eyes, hard, and shot him a tight smile.

"Welcome to the 21st century fighting force, Commander Griffin." Chalabi smirked. "Now that Congress has authorized the full integration of female soldiers into combat operations we are able to take advantage of the considerable skills of superbly trained people such as Sergeant Davis. And I assure you, her skills are, indeed, considerable."

"Besides, now we can sneak a peek inside ladies' restrooms and not get into trouble with the Equal Opportunity Harassment weenies!" Master Sergeant Stankowski said with a laugh.

"Fuck you, Master Sergeant!" came Davis' quick reply.

Chalabi brought everyone back to focusing on the business at hand with a terse and no-nonsense, "What's in the boxes?"

MSGT Stankowski gave them all a quick rundown. "Well, sir, this is just some of the preliminary shit we picked up in the bunker. Sergeant Gutierrez is still on scene poking through more of their crap but we thought you'd better see some of this stuff right away."

"Go on," the general urged.

"Most of it is pretty ordinary shit, soldier stuff. No high value intel that I could see, at least not yet. Got this nice tin box…" Stankowski pulled a metal container about the size of a loaf of bread out of the cardboard container. It was labeled "Sweetest Honeyed Dates," from Sunkist.

"Should be a bunch of nice fingerprints on this baby, sir," Stankowski continued. He pawed through the contents of all three boxes, pulling out dog-eared copies of the Quran, a couple of small flashlights, a half-dozen old paperback books, all in Arabic and all decidedly anti-American. There was also a small solar calculator and a box of condoms. "Guess somebody thought they might get lucky." Stankowski grinned. "Or get very friendly with his cave pals." Sergeant Davis shifted uncomfortably.

"Ah! Here they are!" Stankowski announced triumphantly. He pulled a thick stack of small envelopes, held together with a rubber band, from box number three. "Looks like letters, General," Stankowski offered, trying to be helpful, "but none of us can read this rag head shit." Stankowski suddenly remembered he was staring into the face of a native-born Arabic speaking superior who could. "No offense sir."

"None taken, Master Sergeant," Chalabi replied without expression. "Let me see those."

Stankowski handed the packet to Chalabi. The general slipped off the rubber band and quickly tore into one envelope after another. He scanned the contents of several letters and as he did so, his olive-toned skin seemed to pale just a little.

"Shit!" was all he could muster.

"Sir?" Evans inquired.

"We were meant to find these letters, Major."

"What's that, sir?" Evans asked a little nervously.

"These are suicide notes. Each one is written by one of the men who were in that cave. They are meant for wives, family members, loved ones. Probably made some of them feel better knowing that their families might hear from them again. Fuck them!" Chalabi fumed. "And it means we've got one big, fucking problem. We've got a dozen terrorists on the loose somewhere nearby who are going to Paradise soon and try and take a lot of other people with them."

"Shit! General! I knew it!" Evans blurted out without thinking. "You shoulda let me take them out when we had the chance! Shit! Shit! Shit!"

"You may be right, Major," Chalabi said in a rare occurrence of self-questioning. "And you can write me up later if you want to, but right now we have to find these men again and do it pretty damn quick. I'll take any suggestions, people."

"Maybe this'll help." Stankowski rummaged again, this time back to box number one. He pulled a balled-up piece of paper out of the carton and carefully tried to smooth it out. "I found this scrunched up and tossed in a corner. Looks like a hand-drawn map." Stankowski laid it on the table and everyone present leaned in to look at the diagram. What few words were evident were in Arabic, except for one. There wasn't an Arabic word directly equivalent to "synagogue," for obvious reasons, so there it was, the word "synagogue" in plain English, with an "x-marks-the-spot" notation of some sort circled around it.

"Anyone recognize what this is?" the general asked in desperation.

"I think I do," Griffin replied solemnly. With his right index finger he silently traced the web of hand-drawn streets and road markings as they lead from what looked like a representation of the main gate of Camp Hero and Montauk Highway all the way back through the village of Montauk, straight down the Napeague stretch, right to Main Street in and through East Hampton. Another "x" appeared on an address that seemed to be somewhere along Newtown Lane, but it was not otherwise marked. The line drawing continued along Main Street to Town Pond, where the highway made a sharp jog to the right at a stoplight. Just after the light, on the right hand side of the road, was the "x" under the "synagogue."

Mechanically, Griffin said, "They're going for the East Hampton synagogue."

"And the other 'X'?" Chalabi demanded. Griffin and Chalabi locked eyes.

"I don't know, General, but if I had to bet, I'd say it was Rubino's restaurant on Newtown Lane."

"You're probably right, Commander...Oh, fuck!" Chalabi suddenly dropped into a folding chair and looked even more ill.

"What's wrong, General?" Evans quizzed.

"It's today! I just remembered what today is. How could I be so stupid?" Chalabi jumped up and started pacing.

"What, sir? What about today?" Evans inquired.

"It's the first day of Chanukah. The Festival of Lights begins at sundown today. That synagogue will be packed with families."

"Damn! It's worse than that, General," Griffin added, suddenly remembering what he had heard about a special meeting at the synagogue. His office had received a routine Homeland Security alert the other day—something about a gathering of prominent Jewish business and industry leaders, and movie moguls, to coincide with the Holiday. Homeland Security was nervous. They always got nervous when half the corporate leaders in America got together in one spot at the same time with half of Hollywood's elite.

"Worse? Why is it worse?" Chalabi stammered.

"Never mind, sir. I'll explain on the way. Sundown's in three hours. We've got to get a move on."

40.

Insurance Payments

The frightened boy had been easy. The middle-aged woman had proven to be a little tougher. She had fought, kicked, and tried to scream until a well-placed blow to the back of her neck finally rendered her unconscious.

Germella had simply trailed the bright yellow school bus at a respectful distance until it reached the boy's stop at the end of a private lane in East Quogue. The eight-year-old lad hopped off the bus, obviously glad to be free of the day's drudgeries. Now he could look forward to the Holiday, helping his mom light the menorah tonight and, of course, the gifts. Home was about one hundred yards down a dead-end lane, and hidden behind ten-foot high privet hedges. It was as safe a place as a boy and his single mother could want. So safe, in fact, that the boy's mother didn't even bother to walk the short distance to meet the bus. In a routine unbroken since kindergarten, the now second grader would have a few peaceful moments in the quiet lane, then greet his mother as he breezed through the door. She would play her part by instantly demanding a full recitation of the day's activities followed by increasing reminders to start and complete his homework. Except for today—today would be painfully different. Instead of stomping his snowy boots on the mud room floor, he would simply disappear.

Once the boy was bound, gagged and stowed in the trunk, Germella drove directly to the woman's house in Southampton. He parked in the gravel drive and withdrew a large vase containing a plastic-wrapped bouquet of roses. The red of the roses against the bleak backdrop of winter and the floral deliveryman's engaging smile allowed the woman to let down her guard just enough to open the door. Once the door was cracked, Germella dropped the pretense. He bulled through the door and tackled the woman before she could reach the panic button her partner had so considerately installed on the wall near the phone. The vase went clattering to the floor, scattering red petals, water and shards of glass everywhere. Sheer weight and brute strength made it a mismatch and within two minutes the woman, too, was bound and gagged. She was thrown roughly to the floor of the rear section of the car. Had she been conscious, she would have heard the soft sobs of a young boy she knew well coming from the trunk, two feet behind her head.

Half an hour later the boy was hidden in a vestibule far behind the main rostrum of the synagogue and the woman was on her way into a locked cooler at the back of a restaurant down the road.

41.

Facades

"Susan! You damn well better be ready!" Steve Kaye shouted to the top landing. His step-daughter, a disrespectful and sassy little bitch even on a good day, was making him crazy—again.

Kaye glanced at his watch, an oversized and gaudy Breitling. It was nearly five and the holiday services were scheduled to start in half an hour. He needed to be seen there and he needed to be on time. Then there was the all-important Board meeting right after services. He didn't give a damn about the outcome of the meeting itself. *Who cared who took over the running of the synagogue's Board? If it meant so much to Rubino to have control, let him have it.* Kaye thought to himself.

He needed to speak to Rubino about something else entirely. He especially needed to corner Rubino at the Board meeting before Rubino took off for the real estate reception at the big man's fancy new restaurant. It was vital that Kaye get to Rubino before his real estate competitors had a shot at him. The rumor was that Rubino was going to put the land underneath the Irving Center School on the market and that was prime property indeed. Kaye desperately needed that listing. He hadn't had a sale in over a year. Kaye also knew that he had a real buyer for the entire piece, a Chinese toy manufacturing baron who wanted a piece of the Hamptons pie. He was willing to pay top dollar and Kaye was convinced he could squeeze twenty-five million, a million an acre, out of his buyer. That was probably five million more than the property was worth.

What the fuck? Kaye reasoned, *the chink had no idea what things were worth out here and he had more money than sense anyway.* The commission on twenty five million would be a million and half. His cut of that would be six-hundred thousand, just enough to clear the back taxes, his delinquent mortgage on his over-leveraged house in Water Mill, his hundred-thousand dollar American Express bill, his gambling debts and a retainer on the divorce lawyer he was going to get as soon as the deal closed. He couldn't stand being married to a drunk any more and playing "daddy" to the spoiled little rich-bitch daughter, progeny of his present wife and her third husband, two husbands removed, including himself.

Goddamn it! He cursed to himself, *where are these women?*

A clink of ice into glass could be heard. He nearly ran down the hallway to the den with its expansive wet bar. His wife was pouring three fingers of straight Jack into an eight-ounce tumbler.

"Jesus!" He bellowed. "Can't you at least wait until dinner? What the fuck's wrong with you?"

Her eyes narrowed and as she raised the Baccarat glass to her lips. In one quick blink she tossed the entire contents back and swallowed with sadistic satisfaction.

"OK. Now I'm ready."

"Just bring your breath mints," Kaye sighed as he turned back down the hall.

"Susan! Now!" He roared again. "Get your ass down here *now*!"

"Fuck you, Steve," came the defiant reply from the top of the stairs.

Susan was taking one step down at a time, moving as slowly as she could. She didn't want to go at all, and was only going to prevent her mother from getting another beating at the hands of the man she refused to call "Dad." Susan hated Steve and all the hype, lies, cheating and money-grubbing he and his Hamptons real estate pals represented. All she wanted was to go back to North Carolina, live with her real dad and get laid and drunk as often as possible.

"For Chrissakes, Susan, you're going to synagogue dressed like that?" Steve was shaking he was so angry.

Susan had a mini-skirt on that barely covered her shaved snatch and she wasn't wearing any underwear. She was sporting a tube top that was one size too small and showed every outline of her braless chest.

"What do you care, asshole? You like to look up my skirt anyway. Besides, you're not even Jewish—you just pretend to be so you can get in with the crowd that has the money."

"Susan, I swear..."

"Swear all you like. I'm only going so you'll keep your grimy mitts off my mother."

The two of them stared at each other for a long minute. Susan's mother walked unsteadily into the foyer where her daughter and husband were glaring at each other.

Steve Kaye turned on his heel and said, "OK, let's go." One moment later he was out the front door headed to the driver's side of the Maybach that was scheduled to be repossessed next week.

Susan walked over to her mother and put her arm around the sad woman's shoulder.

"C'mon, Mom, let's get this over with. Just remember we've got that appointment with your lawyer tomorrow morning. We'll get this bastard. Trust me."

"Yes, honey, fine, I'm…I'm OK, let's go."

"Besides, maybe dickhead's deal will just blow up on him tonight. Wouldn't that be delicious?"

42.

Three Strikes

Griffin's cell phone handled three quick calls in succession—calls that would change his life forever. He was hurtling down the Napeague Stretch in one of Chalabi's SUVs, riding shotgun, Evans at the wheel. Three more SUVs loaded with fully armed members of the Delta Force convoyed right behind them. There were no sirens, but there were lots of flashing lights. All the vans were headed for the temporary command post at East Hampton PD. The balance of the Delta Force Team, as well as Griffin's SWAT Teams, assorted detectives and all the uniformed cops that could be spared were being summoned.

The first cell phone call went outbound, to his Deputy, Beth Cantwell. He tersely ordered her to meet him outside the back of the PD's rear entrance, to be standing at the curb when he arrived, and to be there alone. She seemed wary, but he told her he needed to give her some information he wanted no-one else to hear. "Wasn't that the truth," he grumbled to himself.

As soon as he snapped the flip shut, his phone rang. He glanced at the display. "Shit! Fuck! Piss!" he growled. "Don't I have enough trouble today already?" Evans shot him a sideways glance. The caller ID told Griffin it was his ex calling. They talked nearly every day, if you could call it talking. It was mostly a one-way series of directives emanating from the other end of a telephonic shotgun. But she was Kyle's mother and Kyle was the joy of his life, along with Gracie, and she could not, therefore, be ignored. If it wasn't for Kyle he was absolutely certain he'd never talk to or see this witch of a woman again—ever. He wouldn't have to and that would be just fine. He halfway thought about letting the call go straight to voicemail, but that seldom worked with her. She'd keep on calling until he answered the phone or his battery went dead, whichever occurred first. But he could—as he often had—blow her off with a "can't-talk-now-on-police-emergency-business' response. That usually worked, and that's what he decided he needed to do.

He opened the flip. All he heard was her screaming, "Kyle's missing! Our son is missing! James, do something!" His blood froze and he went numb all over.

"Calm down, Myrna, calm down!" he shouted back, "What do you mean Kyle's 'missing'?"

Between frantic sobs and irrational yelling he managed to understand that Kyle had gotten on the school bus to go home and the driver clearly remembered letting Kyle off at the end of her street, but then Kyle never made it to the house. A parent's worst nightmare now confronted him. He had no doubt Kyle had been taken and he was sure he knew who had done it. He told his ex-wife he'd put everyone he had on it instantly, as soon as he got off the phone, and he'd keep her posted. He pressed the "end" button, sweating profusely.

Rubino. It's fucking Rubino. God help him if he hurts my son. I'll kill him myself!" Griffin swore an oath to himself.

Jesus! He wiped his brow with a gloved hand. He was starting to feel nauseous. *I need help. Where the hell is Gracie?* His fevered mind raged. He went to hit the speed dial for Gracie's cell phone number, as he had done to no avail over the past few hours. But before he could hit the button his phone chirped again. It was Gracie calling him! *Thank God great minds think alike,* he managed to breathe. He flipped the phone open again.

"God am I glad to hear from you!" he shouted. But a man's voice laughed in his ear in response. It was a voice he recognized and it made him sicker still.

"I doubt that," Rubino said sarcastically into Gracie's cell phone.

Griffin came off the seat of the van. His brain was now on fire. "You fat fucker! I am going to kill you, you bastard!"

"You will never get the chance, Griffin, but I can kill your girlfriend who is tied up, shall we say, just a few feet away from me. I can also kill your precious little boy with just one more call. I have him, too, so just shut up and listen to me."

Griffin was wild-eyed and breathing hard. Evans was becoming very concerned that Griffin was going to have a stroke or a heart attack. "You all right there, Commander?" Evans stared hard as he dodged in and out of the slower, meandering traffic ahead.

Griffin briefly had the presence of mind to glance at the Major. Evans could see that Griffin was covered in sweat and not in good shape mentally. Griffin held a finger to his lips and silently mouthed "Shhh!"

"Rubino, you fucking Jew pervert, if you harm either Gracie or Kyle in any way I will track you down, wherever you are, and I will personally rip your heart out of your obese chest and feed it to the pigs!"

"I always knew you were a Jew-hating homophobe, Griffin, but I'm the one holding the cards now and if you want to see these two again on this side of hell you are going to do exactly as I say and you will do it NOW!"

Chalabi, who was sitting directly behind Griffin in the hurtling SUV, had heard the name "Rubino" and seen Griffin's gesture to Evans. He came to full attention upon hearing Griffin shouting at Rubino. It didn't take much to figure out what was happening. Chalabi pulled out his own cell phone and began a whispered conversation.

Griffin tried to take in a deep breath and clear his mind. He was so full of rage and fear that he knew he wasn't thinking clearly. He finally managed to choke out, 'What do you want, Rubino?"

"I'm in touch with your Deputy. She tells me you're on your way to meet her in East Hampton."

Griffin's mind spun again. He felt faint. He could barely absorb the waves of treachery, violence and panic that were crashing over him all at once.

Rubino continued dictating. "As soon as you hook up with Cantwell you will tell your companions that you are too ill to go on, which, about now is probably pretty close to the truth anyway, I would imagine. You will give Cantwell a complete briefing on whatever resources you are deploying including the identities of your traveling companions. You will tell her what your intentions are then you will turn over command of your complete operation to Cantwell. You will then go home and await my call. If you're a good little Gentile and do exactly as I say I will have your whore and your whelp delivered to your doorstep alive say, oh, by seven-thirty. If you don't do exactly what I say they will both be dead by six and you, too, soon thereafter. Your choice. Am I clear? Crystal clear?"

Griffin felt a light tap on his left shoulder. He turned in his seat slightly. Chalabi was holding his own phone to his ear with a shoulder while frantically writing something on a notepad.

"Griffin?" Rubino snapped impatiently.

"I'm thinking!" Griffin shot back. He was starting to regain a little control over his mis-firing neurons.

"There's nothing for you to think about!" Rubino bellowed.

Another frantic tap on the shoulder. Chalabi held up the notepad. It read: "SAY YES THEN HANG UP!"

What the fuck… Griffin's mind reeled again. Chalabi was somehow listening to his phone conversation with Rubino! How was that possible? Then he remembered that Chalabi had access to all kinds of satellites and gadgetry that could do just about anything with phone calls. He must have called Langley or NSA or somebody who had access to the very satellite that was handling this call. *Amazing…* was all Griffin could say to himself.

Evans, meanwhile, was telling Chalabi that they'd be on scene in about a minute. Chalabi slapped the pad on the back of Griffin's head and shoved it in his face again. Chalabi's wide eyes and stern expression told Griffin that he was being given a silent order—one that he didn't want to obey at all. This was an empirical, vital moment of truth. Trust your anger, trust your instincts or trust the man you love to hate. Which would it be?

Griffin spoke slowly and clearly into his cell phone, "I'll do what you want." Then he snapped the phone shut abruptly, severing the connection. He wanted to reach behind his seat and strangle the man sitting in back of him, but somehow he knew that Chalabi was thinking more clearly than he was at that moment. But even he could be wrong—dead wrong.

"General, I'm placing more than my life in your hands. You damn well better be right about this—this whatever it is!" Griffin almost pleaded.

Chalabi said nothing. They were pulling into the driveway in front of the East Hampton PD. Evans headed toward the back of the building. As they drew close to the back entrance Griffin could see Beth Cantwell alone, pacing impatiently.

"Pull up directly in front of her, Evans," Chalabi directed. At the same time he phoned the driver of the SUV behind them and told them to take the rest of the caravan back around to the front and park there. The three other cars pulled around the lead SUV obediently and went back to the front of the facility. Evans came to a slow stop in front of Cantwell.

"Ready, Major?" Chalabi nodded to Evans.

"Yessir," Evans responded crisply as he climbed from the SUV, leaving it idling, and went to open the passenger doors for Griffin and Chalabi. Both men stepped from the vehicle. Chalabi pulled Griffin by the elbow and moved him off to the side.

Beth Cantwell crossed her arms over her chest and gave Griffin a little "fuck you" smile.

"Well, hi, there, Chief." She smirked disdainfully, "You ready to--"

A bee suddenly whizzed by Griffin's head and twanged into the doorframe of the SUV. A quizzical little look seemed to flash across Beth Cantwell's face. Her right hand fluttered upward as if to reach for something, then her eyes went blank. It was then that Griffin noticed the small round hole in the middle of her forehead that seemed to grow larger in slow motion. The hole suddenly disgorged a torrent of bright red blood and small gray pieces of brain tissue. Cantwell's body began to pitch forward. Chalabi caught her from the front as Evans grabbed her from behind while simultaneously holstering his silenced .22. Beth Cantwell was dead in less than three seconds. The two men shoved her, face down, into the back of the SUV. It had all happened in the space of a truncated sentence. Griffin was stunned.

"Dump her in the bunker, Evans. Our story is that the terrorists got her and executed her."

"Will do, sir," Evans responded mechanically.

"General…" Griffin raised his palms upward in a gesture of perplexion.

"Had to be done, Commander," That was all the reply he would get.

"But…" Griffin tried to add.

"Commander, you always underestimate me. You should stop doing that."

"You just murdered--"

"Murdered? Murdered!" Chalabi was becoming excited.

Griffin backed up a foot. He had seen this look before. In Iraq.

"Neither Major Evans nor I murdered anyone. We executed a traitor! Plain and simple. And in case you're going to get all squeamish on me, let me remind you that the bitch had your balls in her hands until thirty seconds ago—and—

AND!—she was in cahoots with Rubino who has apparently kidnapped and is now threatening to kill the two people you hold most dear in this world. And in case you're going to get all legalistic on me, I should remind you that OPSEC 50-11-9, signed consecutively by each and every President since Harry Truman, a Presidential Directive of which I know you are at least conversant, allows the designation of one dozen, maximum at one time, legal, United States government, no-questions-asked assassins who have the right to shoot or otherwise dispose of anyone they see fit to kill as long as it is done in the line of duty and under strict and direct authority. I have that authority and Major Evans is one of our government's designated 'Dirty Dozen.'"

In his line of Navy work Griffin had, indeed, known of this top secret directive, but had always given it an "urban legend" sort of respect and had never believed he would ever see it put to use—until now, that is.

"General," Griffin continued to plead, "Even if I were to agree with your assessment, you've just cut our contact with Rubino, which is my only contact now with Gracie and Kyle. You can't--"

The back of the SUV opened. Out stepped a living Beth Cantwell. For the second time in the same day, Griffin nearly fainted. Was he seeing a ghost? Griffin glanced back into the SUV's rear seat where Beth Cantwell's body had been placed.

It was still there, but now minus the overcoat and red dress. Griffin stared more closely at the "Beth Cantwell" that was still breathing. The resemblance was close. Very close. The make-up and prostheses were superb. Unless nose-to-nose, anyone would believe that this was Beth Cantwell.

"Well, hi there, Chief!" The voice was a near perfect imitation of Beth Cantwell's Southern drawl.

"How?" Griffin's mouth was still agape.

Chalabi said triumphantly, "I believe you've already met Sergeant Davis?"

"It's…it's unbelievable!" Griffin stammered.

"I told you her skills were considerable, didn't I? And I also told you not to underestimate me. Now, let's get this party rolling, shall we?"

43.

The Hunt Begins

Griffin, Chalabi, Evans and 'Cantwell' walked into the East Hampton PD Operations Center and were immediately besieged by the Chief of Police, the Town Supervisor, and the Director of Emergency Services. Everyone clamored to find out what was going on and why all the County police and military were roaming around. It was chaos.

Chalabi shouted to get their attention. Every eye was on the General, who passed the buck neatly. "Major, please take these folks and give them a briefing, exactly as we discussed."

"Yessir." The Major saluted. "I am Major Jack Evans, United States Air Force, and I'm prepared to give you all a complete rundown on our current situation. Is there a place we can talk?"

"Our conference room is right down the hall to your left, major," the Chief of Police offered.

"Thank you, sir. Shall we?" Evans parted the group in the room like Moses at the Red Sea and headed for the conference room. The crowd turned to follow.

"Chief, a moment, please," General Chalabi called after Peter Duryea, the head of East Hampton's police. Duryea turned back toward the General. "Could you please join us? And maybe find us a quiet spot to talk?"

Duryea was conflicted. He ran a very tight and efficient operation. He was clearly uncomfortable with all this high level activity and its accompanying uncertainties. Duryea hesitated for a moment then said, "Sure. Let's use my office. It's over here—and secure." The smaller group peeled off to the right and headed to Duryea's private spaces.

Once the general's retinue and the Chief were behind Duryea's doors and comfortably seated, Duryea turned to Griffin, whom he knew quite well and demanded, "Superintendent, you want to tell me what the hell's going on here? And why you have the entire East End in an uproar?"

Griffin started to reply, then realized he didn't know where to begin or how much to say. Chalabi stepped into the breach. "I'll handle this, Griffin." Chalabi gave Duryea the *Reader's Digest* version, which still lasted a good five minutes. It was clear, concise and complete. Duryea was dumbfounded.

"We can't…I don't have… How are we?" was all a pale and shaken Duryea could manage.

"Yes, Chief, it's a mess, but we have assets standing by, both military and civilian. I will admit, though, that I'm not sure what our next steps should be yet," Chalabi said with genuine candor.

Griffin suggested, "Why don't we start by arresting Rubino?"

Chalabi shook his head. "No. Can't do that. We don't know what his next moves are either, but I'm sure he's been smart enough to give instructions to proceed if he's picked up. Besides, he doesn't know what he's up against. You heard him say that he wants Cantwell to find out who 'your companions' are. He has no idea that there's a significant military presence on scene. With all due respect he thinks he's dealing with a bunch of local cops and some county Mounties, not the Delta Force. He thinks he's got the pros on his side."

Duryea bristled. "Now just a minute, my men and women…"

"Chief, I know, I know. I'm sure your people are all very good at what they do." Chalabi waved him off. "But they don't have to handle these types of situations all the time, thank God, and my people do. I'm just trying to get into Rubino's head, that's all." Chalabi started to walk the office, side to side, planning out loud. "We also know that Rubino has the Commander's son and girlfriend. He's trying to take Griffin out of the picture. Let's let him think you're caving, Commander, so we don't force him into too small a corner. Don't you agree?"

"Yes, yes, I do, but shouldn't we throw a protective screen around the synagogue?" Griffin added.

"I don't think we can do that either." Chalabi continued to pace, forcing himself to think the problem through. "We can't tip our hand too much until we know more about his plan. But there's a way, I think, to get some of the information." Chalabi stopped pacing for a moment and looked directly at SGT Davis/Beth Cantwell.

"I'm ready, sir," Sergeant Davis responded calmly.

"Good. I'm sure Rubino will be contacting you shortly."

"What about Rubino's restaurant?" Griffin pressed. "Couldn't we at least station some of our people there—maybe sit a couple of guys at the bar? Have a couple seated at a table for late lunch or early dinner?"

"Can't," Chief Duryea interrupted, "Place is closed today. Private party. Starts in about an hour. I was invited. Guess I won't be going."

"Party?" Chalabi demanded clearly interested, "What type of party?"

"Big holiday party. Hosted by Rubino and his partner, Sokolin."

"I can pretty much guarantee Sokolin won't be there," Griffin deadpanned.

"All the local politicos will be there, and most of our local real estate moguls, too," Duryea added. "Rubino has promised a major announcement, something about a huge real estate development deal. The land sharks are circling what they think is another deep commission pool. Anyone who's anyone around here is curious about what Rubino is up to—and they want to eat and drink at his expense, too."

Griffin began adding things up in his head. "What times does that big board meeting at the synagogue start?"

"Same time as the restaurant party. In an hour. We were asked to provide some security and parking control. I have six officers headed that way in about five minutes."

"Stop them!" Chalabi ordered.

"Why?" Duryea wanted to know.

"Chief, again, don't take this wrong, but I want six of my Delta Force people to go instead. Can you get them some of your uniforms?"

Duryea did feel slighted for a second but then quickly realized where Chalabi was going and that the General's people were much better trained for this than his people were. "OK, let me get on that."

"Thanks, Chief. I appreciate it." Chalabi was, indeed, grateful. Duryea left the office to make the appropriate arrangements. As Duryea left, Evans returned.

"How'd it go, Major?" Chalabi asked.

"About as well as could be expected. I told them we had received a credible report of a possible terrorist plot involving stealing a couple of private planes from East Hampton Airport then trying to fly them into the germ warfare lab at Plum Island. I think they bought it. At least enough of it to give us a little breathing room. And they're more than happy that we're handling it. They admitted they're not prepared for something like that and they really don't want any part of it."

"Good, good." Chalabi smiled. "Well, I guess we know why there was a second X on that map we found, don't we?"

"You're thinking he's going to blow up his own restaurant?" Griffin asked with some incredulity.

"What better way to throw suspicion off yourself? But I don't get the real estate angle. Not yet anyway. Why does he want to wipe out the local real estate hot shots?"

"And I don't get how he's going to be two places at the same time," Griffin added. "Isn't he deeply involved in the synagogue crisis? Doesn't he have to be there? How's he going to pull that off while hosting the party at his restaurant?"

"I can promise you he's not going to be in either place," Chalabi replied. "Whatever is going to happen at those spots is going to happen without him. Later, after it's all over, it'll be easy to explain why he wasn't in attendance at one or both events."

A cell phone rang. It took a few seconds for all of them to realize the phone was in the coat pocket formerly worn by recently deceased Beth Cantwell.

"You're on, Sergeant." Chalabi nodded to Patty Davis. Simultaneously he pressed the speaker button on his own SAT phone. "Answer it. We'll all be able to hear the call."

Sergeant Davis reached into the coat pocket, retrieved the phone and answered, "Cantwell."

"Has Griffin turned over command to you yet?" Rubino's voice came through Chalabi's speaker phone clearly. Rubino would not be able to tell that he wasn't on a totally private call. All he would hear was Davis acting as Cantwell.

"Yes."

"Good. Has he left?"

"Yes."

"Excellent. Now here's what I want you to do. Don't respond, just listen or say 'yes' or 'no.' I know you're probably surrounded by people and can't respond to questions. You won't have to. Then when we're done, just say 'goodbye' and hang up. Got it?"

"Yes."

"Are those people who were with Griffin military? Maybe some of his Navy buddies? Seals?"

"No," Davis lied.

"Good. Just local yokels?"

"Yes."

"Even better. Are they on to us in any way?"

"No. Not really."

"Just 'yes' or 'no' dammit!" Rubino boomed.

"Yes," Davis winced.

"You mean 'yes' they're on to us or 'no' they aren't?" Rubino shouted.

"Look," Davis dared to reply using a near perfect copy of Cantwell's voice, including the Texas accent, "cut the crap,

OK? I'm not some stupid airhead and I happen to be in the ladies room, all by myself. I meant what I said, which was 'No, not really.' They certainly know something's up but they are clueless as to what and I'm doing my damndest to send them in the wrong direction. Now, I've got a lot going on here and I'm trying to help you out, so let's move on, shall we? What's the plan?"

Chalabi smiled at Davis' bravado and acting skill. He flashed her a big 'thumbs up' from across the room.

"Very well, Miss Cantwell." Rubino chuckled. "You've got more balls than I gave you credit for, certainly more than that soon-to-be ex-boss of yours."

Griffin seethed in silence.

"Let's review what I want you to do. Nothing has changed. It'll be just like we discussed," Rubino resumed. "I want you to tell our friends that you've just received a tip that a group of Arabs have taken some children and teachers hostage at the Irving Center School in Bridgehampton. This is, in fact, now true. Several of my operatives are holding the Head of School, some of his staff, a couple of teachers and some students. One group is in the school gym, another in the admin building. Take all your available forces and surround the place. Negotiate, talk, beat each other off, whatever, I don't care, but make it look like you're trying to resolve this crisis, but don't do it too quickly. I need you to keep as many cops as you can away from the East End Synagogue and my restaurant in East Hampton for at least the next hour. Are we on the same page so far?"

"Yes."

"At precisely six p.m. my people at the school will come out shooting. They will try and kill as many of you as they can. I suggest that you, Miss Cantwell, stay out of the way and keep your head down--if you want to enjoy my money, that is. As for your people, have them kill mine. They are prepared to die and they know you will kill them. They expect it. They are a diversion, a very important one, and they know this, too. When it's all over, you'll look like a hero. Any questions?"

"No."

"No questions at all?"

"No. You bought yourself the right girl."

"Excellent. Now, you're sure Griffin went straight home?"

"Yes. One of my people is dropping him off there now."

"Perfect. One of my men is waiting there to kill him."

"Good riddance." Davis winked at a horrified Griffin. "Oh, I do have one question. Where are you if I need you?"

"Don't worry about where I am. You just hold up your end of the bargain. Now move, Cantwell. I'll call you again at five-thirty to see how it's going." The line went dead.

Duryea's office was silent. Chalabi glanced at his watch. It was five after five. "Ok…Ok…Ok…" Chalabi was pacing again, his mind racing against the clock.

Chief Duryea re-entered his office. "I've got six of your men decked out in our uniforms and on their way to the synagogue," he announced proudly.

"Good. Now, what to do about the restaurant?" Chalabi asked to no-one in particular.

"How many invites do you have to that party, Peter?" Griffin asked Duryea.

"Four. Me, my deputy chief and two senior lieutenants. Why?"

"Well, I suggest we show up," Griffin offered.

"Where are you going with this, Commander?" Chalabi wanted to know.

"If Peter and I and two of your shooters show up at the party dressed as East Hampton cops you'll have four people on the inside of a bad situation. You game, Peter?"

Duryea smiled broadly. "I've handed out enough parking tickets, James. Let's do some real police work."

"I like your plan, Commander, but you're forgetting one thing. You're supposed to be going home," Chalabi challenged.

"To stop a bullet? No, thanks."

"But if you don't show up, Rubino will get suspicious. His guy will call and tell him you didn't arrive."

"Then, General, I'd get that expert in makeup and disguises busy again," Griffin suggested. "Make up one of your shooters to look like me. Close enough will do. It's not likely Rubino's man will know me well enough to recognize a possible fake until he's close, and close is all you'll need, right? Here, let's get started." Griffin began stripping off his suit jacket, tie, shirt and pants until he stood there in his skivvies. Griffin picked up the clothes and tossed them to Evans. "Peter, get me a lieutenant's uniform, please," Griffin ordered.

"Roger that!" Duryea responded and left the room.

Chalabi nodded to Evans. "Get Harrison. He's about the same size and build as the commander."

Evans exited the room with Griffin's clothes.

"Our makeup expert is in the second SUV," Chalabi admitted. "But you're taking a risk being recognized at that restaurant."

"General, by your own analysis, Rubino won't be there and

for once, I agree with you. As far as being recognized by others? I doubt it. I don't hang out with this crowd—not with what the County pays me—and these people won't pay much attention to a lowly police lieutenant."

"OK, I'll go with it. It's your neck. We're running out of time and options anyway. Now, what do we do about the school?"

"Give me the rest of your shooters, General," said SGT. Davis. "Rubino's expecting 'me' there anyway, with a whole lot of assets. I'll take all that you can spare, and make it look good. That should keep him happy."

"OK, and I'll send Master Sergeant Stankowski with you…"

"Sir," Davis stopped the general.

"Yes, yes. You're right. You've earned it. You lead the team at the school. I can use Stankowski better anyway at the restaurant. Connigliaro's leading the team at the synagogue, so that leaves you, Staff Sergeant. Do me proud, OK?"

"Yessir!" Davis responded with pride.

"And for God's sake, get those civilians and those kids out of there if you can."

"I'll do my best, sir," Davis said, coming to attention stiffly.

Evans came back into the room to report that Harrison was

on his way to Griffin's home, and Duryea returned with an appropriate uniform for Griffin.

"Major Evans, you're with me," Chalabi ordered. "We'll take SUV Two. Davis, you take Three, Griffin Four. We'll leave SUV One where it is for the moment since it has…ah…a dead body in it. I'll worry about that later. Let's stay in touch and keep all channels open. Let's move."

"General!" Griffin called after Chalabi, "Where are you going to be?"

"I'm retaining tactical control and I'll be on the radios with all of you, but the Major and I are going hunting. Thanks to satellite triangulation, I know where Rubino is. We're going to bag us one big, bad asshole."

44.

Very, Very...

The very solemn man sat quietly on the large blue couch lovingly caressing his worn copy of the Q'uran. Inside its front cover was a photo of the man he was to kill. Positioned across his knees was the big Sig Sauer P220 pistol he would use. Silencer attached, of course. He was going to be very careful to allow the man to enter by the front door. As soon as he was fully inside the room he would fire. Once he confirmed the man was dead he was to return as quickly as possible to the school in Bridgehampton. He wanted to be there to help his comrades in their glorious fight. If his target got here in the next few minutes, there would still be plenty of time. He'd race to his car, which was parked in the empty lot down the street, and speed off to the fight.

A clock ticked somewhere in the background. This very religious man absently wondered why there was so much broken glass on the floor. Someone had dropped a large vase of red roses and had not cleaned it up.

A car door slammed. This very pious man came to full alert. Shoes crunched on the gravel in the driveway. The blue couch had a full picture window view of the steps leading up to the house. Through the slightly frosted panes he mentally compared the dark haired figure of the man approaching the front door with the photo inside his Q'uran. Yes. It was him. This very faithful man picked up the pistol from his lap and noiselessly slipped off the safety. A key turned in the lock. The door knob spun counter clockwise. The front door opened an inch. He aimed the pistol at about where he thought his target's heart would be.

A small glint, a tiny sliver of light from the kitchen window to his left was all this very God-fearing man noticed before he felt a pounding thud in his chest. Then another. And another. Glass shattered somewhere. He looked down to see a pool of blood spread across his shirt and then his eyes exploded as the fourth bullet smashed into the bridge of his expansive Arabic nose. The very solemn, religious, pious, God fearing man was now only a very dead man.

The front door opened fully and Danny Harrison peeked through the opening, dressed in James Griffin's suit.

"Nice shooting, Gutierrez. He's down. Let's go."

Harrison closed the front door and walked back down the driveway. Gutierrez walked out from behind the back of the house to join him. They got into Griffin's Mercedes and sped away.

45.

Pillar of Fire

Rubino sat in the back of his Learjet in expansive leather comfort. He glanced at his watch. Five fifteen. The aircraft was idling quietly just outside Rubino's hangar along Industrial Road on the apron to East Hampton Airport. Both pilots were in the cockpit, ready to fly at a moment's notice. He planned to be airborne and above suspicion as the bombs went off. He wanted to see the explosions from the air, but mostly he wanted to be beyond reach and headed for Brazil if there was trouble.

Rubino dialed a number. The phone was answered, but silently. "Proceed," Rubino said, then he hung up.

In the carefully planted and thickly wooded lot bordering the synagogue's north side Ottmar Germella knelt in the thin layer of snow. He closed the cover of his phone and stuffed it in his coat pocket. Behind him, also crouched and at the ready, were four suicide bombers, each wearing thickly padded vests with twenty pounds each of C-4 plastic explosive. Any single vest would be more than enough to blast the synagogue to oblivion. Four such vests would be overkill, but that was exactly the point. Germella was also wearing a vest but in his case the padded pockets were filled with harmless plasticene. His men believed that he, too, would soon be blowing himself to Paradise but Germella had other plans. He would not be a stupid ox to such mindless sacrifice. As soon as the others had atomized themselves he planned to be on his way to somewhere warm and inviting. Maybe St. Barth's. He had heard that this paradise was the place to be this time of year. Germella was packing some lethality, however. The bombers beside him could clearly see the big pistol he held in his hand--insurance, they knew, against any one of them having last second thoughts of survival. Truth be known, only Mansour, among the four of them, was quivering from within. He'd had his first taste of carnal pleasure last night at Rubino's home, courtesy of a big-breasted whore. He had liked it. A lot. And now he was not certain that he wanted to go straight to Paradise without sampling more of what this earth had to offer. He crouched there, sweating, panicked, waiting for an opportunity to bolt and run.

Multiple streams of headlights could now be seen pulling into the parking spaces near the synagogue. The faithful were gathering. Germella motioned for each man to move toward his position. The plan was for each bomber to enter the building from four different doorways. Providently, in addition to the main entrance, there were doors to the sanctuary from either side and one conveniently placed in back. As soon as a large crowd was inside, the bombers would race into the meeting, each from a different direction, yell "Allah is great! Allah is Merciful!" then pull their respective cords. A slaughter would ensue.

The sanctuary began to fill up. The fading daylight turned to full night. A couple of local cops directed traffic and two more stood near the main entrance. *They will be no problem,* Germella mused.

"You see anything suspicious yet?" Chalabi breathed into Connigliaro's earpiece.

"No, sir. Just a lot of people arriving. Tower and Sipalla are on the street directing traffic. I'm at the front door with Oates. Santos and Shockley are in the bushes with night vision on. These people sure drive some expensive tin, sir. More Jags, Rolls and Bentleys than I've ever seen in one place at one time."

"Just be alert. We've got less than 30 minutes."

"Red." It was Shockley.

"Go."

"I've got two bad guys. One's crouching to your left, right side entrance. Other guy looks like he's headed to the back."

"I've got two more," Santos whispered into his mike, "one on your right, one moving toward the street. Jesus, one more! He seems to be sitting tight. Way off to your right, behind the trees over your right shoulder."

"You copy, General?"

"Roger, take them out."

"Yes sir."

"Tower, Sipalla. Block the traffic. Take the two on the left. Santos. Shockley. You've got the two on the right. Oates. You're backup. I'll take the guy in back. He's probably their leader. Head shots only, gentlemen. Don't want any rounds hitting explosives."

"Everybody ready?" Connigliaro got five "Rogers."

"Execute."

Oates took position covering the front of the synagogue ready to jump in whatever direction he might be needed. Tower, Sipalla, Shockley and Santos all had night goggles on, and had their targets in sight. Connigliaro calmly turned and walked to where he thought his target might be. Red had decided not wear his night vision goggles. If his target was indeed the group's mastermind, he was watching carefully--and seeing special equipment in play would alert him in an instant that they had been compromised.

Germella observed the two cops who had been directing traffic move away from the front and off to one side. *Must be headed into the cursed Jew-hut*, he theorized. He also noticed one more cop move out and to his right. *Where is he going*? he wondered. The big cop, he must be their leader, the one who was standing at the front had turned and was now walking slowly in his direction. Something was beginning to feel wrong but he couldn't wrap his brain around it. Not yet. *Where was that other cop?* Germella could no longer see him. The hairs on the back of his neck began to stand.

PO3 Miguel Santos and LCPL Steven Shockley were both expert marksmen. They knelt quietly, nodded to one another to confirm that each had a target, simultaneously lifted their long-barreled and silenced Smith & Wesson police specials to eye level and squeezed off two shots each. Both targets took two fatal taps to the head and crumpled to the ground.

"Two bad guys down," Shockley breathed softly into his lip mike. He and Santos raced quietly to their targets to disarm the explosives.

Sgt. Tony Sipalla dropped one more nearing the left side entrance. CPL Jerry Tower's shot was slightly off. It grazed the back of Mansour's neck, leaving a hot, burning and bloody trough that made him yelp and leap toward the synagogue's back door.

Germella saw Ali-Phar drop to the ground.

Stupid fool! Germella cursed to himself. *Get up you son of a whore!* But Ali-Phar did not move. He then heard someone cry out in pain and he saw Mansour fall into the synagogue's back doorway. Now he knew something was wrong. Suddenly the big man he had been watching broke into a run and headed straight for Germella. Instinctively, Germella flattened himself on the ground, and just in time. Three bullets smashed into the branches just above him. His head had been there one split second before. Bark, needles and splinters of wood flew all around him. In a flash he had his pistol out and fired back, wildly, in the direction of the big cop who was charging toward him. He got off four shots. The cop went down hard, on his back. Germella knew there would be others on him in seconds. He had to get out. Now. He came to his knees and looked around carefully. The cop on the ground wasn't moving but he could see shadows coming from the front of the synagogue. Germella began a crouching jog, back toward the utility shed twenty yards away. He'd pick up his insurance policy and then be gone. Abstractedly he wondered why none of the bombs were going off. He knew Mansour, at least, was still alive. And all they needed was one. He also began to wonder why the police were trying to stop this. Rubino had assured him that the cops were in his pocket. Something had gone very wrong, this he knew, but it wasn't the first time, and it wouldn't be the last. His goal now was to escape from here and live to fight another day. He'd figure it out later.

"Red! Red! Come back, Red!" It was Sipalla that he heard, seemingly a thousand miles away, rattling in his headset. Connigliaro was on his back starting up at a starry, moonless night sky. All he could think of was, "Thank God for Kevlar." He knew that his target had gotten off three or four rounds in his direction. He'd heard at least two go whizzing by his left ear, uncomfortably close. In fact, as he now felt a warm trickle of something pooling in his shirt collar he realized that one of those shots hadn't missed completely. He reached for the left side of his head with a weak but working left hand. *Shit*, he said to himself, *I've got to retire. My luck is damn near out.* His left ear was a mess, and hung down to his collar by a thin strip of flesh. Either the third or fourth bullet –he wasn't sure which – had caught him square in the chest, just above the diaphragm. Thanks to his bullet proof vest he'd only have a bad bruise and not an air-sucking hole clear through his right lung. The bullet had stopped him cold, though, like someone had swung full force at his chest with a metal baseball bat. *Damn, it hurt!* he told himself as he struggled to raise himself up on one elbow. But worst of all, he was sure his target had gotten away, and that couldn't be good. There was that insistent little voice yelling at him again.

"Red! Red! You with us, man? Where are you? Whadda we do now?"

Fortunately his earpiece and lip mike were anchored in his right ear, and not the left. Otherwise they would now be plastic splinters and utterly useless. He coughed into the mike, "I'm down, hit. But I'll be okay. Shot to the vest. My bad guy's still loose. Have no idea where. I'm towards the back. Left side."

"OK, I'm on the way," Sipalla responded.

"No!" Connigliaro shouted as best he could. "Make sure we have them all. There were five, weren't there?"

"Confirm three KIA," Sipalla shot back. "Plus Tower thinks he at least wounded a fourth. Santos says he saw your guy drop his vest and beat feet to the boonies out back."

"Well, shit, guys, the party's not over. Find that fifth guy, now—he's still hot and probably mad as a hornet. He'll blow for sure! Get him! Get him now!" Connigliaro groaned into his mike trying to get his legs working again. "And Oakes!"

"Yeah, boss."

"Get those people out of that fucking building!"

"You got it."

"Sipalla!"

"Yeah, Red?"

"Take over will you? Until I can at least stand the fuck up."

"No prob."

Mansour was not mad. Just scared and in a lot of pain. Something--a bullet, probably--had raked across the back of his neck. It burned beyond belief and he could still feel hot, sticky blood leaking into the back of his shirt. *But who shot me?* Mansour wildly grappled with his own thoughts. *And where were the others? What was going on?* He peeked out from his hiding place. He was completely inside a wide double-door frame of steel and glass. He could hear shouts now, a few panicky female screams. People who had been streaming into the synagogue a few minutes ago were now fleeing outward, toward the street and the parking lot. They were desperately trying to get to their cars and get the hell away. The first few who had managed to make it to their vehicles drove away madly. Fancy cars slammed and crunched into one another as the urge to flee grew in intensity. Cars smashed through hedges, running wildly through carefully landscaped beds, spinning across wide expanses of snow-slick lawn. Mansour even heard a sickening thud and another agonizing scream as somewhere out there hurtling metal came into contact with vulnerable flesh. *Good,* Mansour thought to himself. *This confusion will aid my escape.*

Mansour was panicked, scared and hurting but clear-headed enough to know one thing with crystal clarity. This was madness and he no longer wanted any part of it. He bolted from the door frame and headed toward the largest mob of fleeing people he could see, unbuttoning the cursed vest he was wearing as he ran.

"Sarge! I got him! One bad guy just ran out from behind the building. He's headed toward the parking lot." It was Jerry Tower. "This is the guy I nicked. I'm sure of it. Let me take him out." Corporal Tower wanted redemption for his previous errant shot.

Sergeant Sipalla, with Connigliaro down, was now in command of the team. "OK…OK. You just be damn sure you don't miss this time."

"No need to worry, Sarge. The bad guy just peeled off his vest and flung it into the bushes. Looks like he thinks it's not a good day to die, but he'll be dead in another sec--"

"Hold it! Hold it!" It was Chalabi, who had been listening to everything as it unfolded. "This is the General. Tower?"

"Yes, sir?"

"Did you say he's dropped the vest?"

"Yes sir, but he's running--"

"Then shoot him, but try not to kill him. Do you read me? I want one of them alive."

"Yes, sir." Tower squeezed off two shots, this time perfectly aimed, and the bad guy fell screaming, one bullet in or at least near each kneecap.

Tower was disgusted. He wanted to kill the bastard. *Isn't it fuckin' typical?* he grumbled to himself, *the pencil pusher who's not out here on the front line gets to call the shots, so to speak. Another fuckin' instance of leadership from the rear.* Tower spat into the snow as he headed to where his target writhed in pain. Tower was angry he couldn't notch a kill, but the consequences of Chalabi's decision were about to have much more tragic outcomes.

One second Mansour had been running toward the crowd and safety, the next second he was slammed to the ground. He could not figure out why his legs would not obey him. Why had they stopped running? His brain was still sending them "run!" signals. Then his brain began to send him different signals, ones Mansour could not control. And they were painful—mind-tearing, excruciatingly painful. Mansour looked down. Even in the dark he could see large, bloody tears in the fabric covering his knees. And every attempt to move only brought more pain. He screamed again and again in agony. He would be a man without legs! He would be crippled for life! *What kind of woman would fuck a man like that?* he thought to himself. *Only a toothless old whore who has diseases!* his brain told him, between waves of pain.

People were still rushing by, remnants of the desperate crowd stampeding from the synagogue. Suddenly, Mansour was aware that some people had stopped to stare down at him as he writhed and screamed in pain. He forced himself to look at them. They simply stared back at him.

"Please! Help me…" he managed to croak in broken English.

A young girl stepped forward and glared down at him, eyes wide in anger as well as terror. "No!" Mansour gasped. "You! It is you, the blonde girl from the restaurant! Allah has sent you to help me! Allah is merciful! Allah is great!" he shouted.

"No!" She shouted down at him. "Allah sucks you fucking, stupid raghead!" And with that she kicked him, hard in one of his shattered knees. Mansour felt that greatest wave of pain yet wash over him. He nearly passed out and probably would have if his anger had not also begun to return to him. Anger had always brought him clarity.

She cursed the name of Allah! his brain reeled.

"Susan! That's enough! Let's get out of here!" Then Mansour recognized the man grabbing the girl by the shoulder and tugging her away. It was the father she called "Steve." And the mother was there, too, still looking drunk, eyes puffy and mascara running down her cheeks. She was sobbing.

Steve kept tugging. The girl kept shouting. "Fuck you! Fuck you! Fuck you! Die, asshole! Die!" She shoved her hand in Mansour's face, middle finger extended upward, "Fuck you!" Steve finally managed to pull the girl away and they started to disappear into the night.

Mansour rolled over on his back and stared up at the heavens. *So,* he told himself quietly, *that's what that gesture means.* He was beyond pain now and going into shock. A grim little smile crossed his face. *We'll see who's fucking who, you little whore!* Mansour giggled in his delirium.

Corporal Tower leaned over Mansour, pointing the barrel of a long-nosed pistol in his face.

"Well hi, there, Mr. Asshole. How's you're night working out so far?" Tower needled sarcastically. Tower noted that Mansour's right hand was in his right pants pocket. Tower suddenly jammed the barrel of the pistol in Mansour's cheek. "Hold it right there, asshole," Tower growled. "Bring your hands up slow and empty."

Mansour smiled brightly at the Marine and raised his left hand slowly until it was a fist in Tower's face. He then uncurled the middle finger of his left hand so it pointed straight up and with a laugh said, "Fuck you!"

Simultaneously with the right hand still in his pocket, he pressed the remote detonator for the vest full of explosives.

The night was ripped apart by a horrifyingly loud and vivid explosion.

46.

"When Pigs Fly..."

A mile away, still sitting in comfort aboard his aircraft, Milos Rubino saw a bright ball of light flash through the trees. Three seconds later, the sound wave struck like a violent clap of thunder. The jet shimmied and shook. Rubino glanced at his watch. Five minutes to six. Damn, a little early, but, OK, it's done. He pressed the intercom button for the cockpit.

"Let's go," he commanded.

The plane had been idling for nearly an hour so it only took seconds to begin the taxi procedure. The pilot in command called East Hampton tower for clearance, based on their previously filed flight plan for Miami. But the controllers were a little hesitant. They, too, had seen the bright light and felt the shock wave.

"Lear 708, East Hampton Tower, maybe you should shut down until we can figure out what's going on. Did you see that light? Feel the--blast?"

"Tower, 708. Yeah, we caught it. And we have a nervous owner in the back. He wants to get the heck out of here, copy?"

"708, Tower. Well, OK...if you're ready we'll clear you."

"Roger. Thanks. We're rolling."

With that the Lear took the active runway. The pilots spooled up the engines and started the take off roll. Eight seconds later they were airborne. As previously instructed by Rubino, the pilots banked right, not the usual left as the plane got airborne.

"708, Tower. Sir, you're heading...it's wrong.."

"Tower, 708, yeah, OK. We know. We're heading back the other way. Sorry."

But the jet took the long way around to get out over the Atlantic, just as Rubino had instructed. It would take the plane right over where the synagogue used to be.

Rubino stared intently out his porthole. He could see a giant, dancing fire just ahead. The plane rolled level for just a moment. Rubino could see that there had, indeed, been some sort of explosion but the light from the fire also clearly showed that it was not in but near the synagogue. Rubino had one moment to panic. "Jesus! The building's still stand--" before he was blinded by another flash of light. The sounds of metal ripping apart were all about him. Hot slivers of aluminum began to tear huge chunks of his flesh away. He felt himself tumbling...and then ...nothing.

In one of the grand ironies of this whole besotted game what was left of Milos Rubino's Learjet, and Rubino himself, fell flaming from the sky right on top of the empty synagogue. Aircraft and building imploded in one more horrific blast.

Back at East Hampton Airport Major Evans hurriedly stowed the Stinger missile launcher he had used to shoot Rubino out of the sky. He shoved the extra rocket and launcher into the rear of SUV Two, which he had parked in the woods at the far end of the main runway. Chalabi's trace on Rubino's encoded cell had proven to be dead on. *Dead on! That's rich!* Evans chortled to himself. Thanks to NSA and FAA Chalabi also knew that Rubino's pilots had filed a flight plan for Miami and then on to Brazil. Chalabi put Major Evans on Rubino's tail with orders to shoot him down if it appeared he was trying to escape. As soon as the first explosion had occurred at the synagogue, Chalabi had confirmed his order to Evans. The rest was easy. It was a clear shot on a slow target. Evans couldn't miss. He was a little concerned the plane had banked right instead of left. Evans knew there were some houses out that way. He could only hope the plane had fallen in the woods and not on any of the homes below. He would feel bad about that. "Oh, well," Evans sighed. "Collateral damage."

He also knew that the NTSB, which would have the inevitable task of investigating the crash, was already "wired" to determine the cause as "catastrophic engine failure at take off." There would be no mention of "missiles" or "explosive residue." The NTSB and CIA had learned enough from the TWA Flight 800 debacle ten years back. A trickle of missile damage evidence had somehow escaped back then and it was mostly because the investigation took too damn long to wrap up. If you let people poke around long enough, they're bound to find something. The Flight 800 "Conspiracy Theorists" were still looking, for heaven's sake. And they were right! A new type of heat-seeking missile from a highly secretive USAF stealth fighter had somehow cooked off on a low-level open water test run over Long Island Sound on that fateful summer night in 1996. The errant super-secret bullet had no warhead, but that didn't prevent it from auguring into

the big, lumbering 747 and then blasting itself cleanly through the jumbo jet, just aft of the cockpit. No, this time the NTSB would be in and out of East Hampton in 48 hours, case closed, no leaks.

Ottmar Germella was just getting into his car when he was knocked off his feet by the explosion. "Praise be to Allah!" he shouted, as he picked himself of the ground. "At least one of those worthless fools had managed to kiss his dick goodbye!" By the time it happened, he was a quarter-mile away, where he had parked his car. The blast radius and fallout would not reach that far with the exception of some dirt, small stones, broken sticks and other assorted debris that now began to rain from the sky. So the deed was finally done. Rubino would be calling him any second. There would be much to do. Germella stuck the key in the ignition. He heard a loud whooshing sound, like jet engines. *That would be Rubino circling above his kill, the sick Jewish pig!* he said to himself. But something was wrong. *The engines don't sound right*, he thought.

What seemed like a flaming meteor roared overhead and came whining and crashing from the sky. It landed behind him, from where he had just come. There was another explosion. This time large chunks of metal, wire, rubber and plastic began to fall from the sky. Then a large piece of what looked like charred meat slammed into the hood of Germella's car. The impact even cracked the windshield. Clinically, Germella examined it with his pocket flashlight. It was a human leg, from knee to foot, including a shoe. It was very large. Germella knew there wouldn't been too many human calves that large flying around the Hamptons that night. He also thought he recognized the brand of shoe—one that Rubino favored, hand-stitched in Venice.

Germella got out of the car and pushed the smoking flesh off the hood. It plopped sickenly on the pavement. He was now even more thankful he had taken out this insurance. He leaned over the back seat to make sure it was still there. It was—and it was awake. The boy was bound and gagged, and looked terrified. He was only eight, far too young to be a pawn in such a grownup game.

47.

Flights of Fancy

Medical experts have somehow concluded that the human brain can continue to function for anywhere from seven to fifteen seconds after someone's head is physically separated from their body. Sight is definitely possible for most of that time. Hearing can last a little longer. Thus it was that Mansour, in the last ten seconds of his life, understood fully that the explosion had torn his body apart. He sensed his head rocketing skyward. Toward Paradise, perhaps? But he also saw, with the light fading from his very own eyes that the girl called Susan was also ripped to pieces, her various body parts flying outward toward the perimeter of the corona of the blast. Others, too, were swept away in this maelstrom, including the cop who had shot him, cars, trees, paving stones, dirt, gravel and, he noted with calm precision, at least one stray cat. His very last thoughts were of great satisfaction for what he had done, pride in his own bravery and a deep, fervent wish that Allah would somehow be able to reassemble all of Susan's body parts in Paradise so he could consummate his passion for her. He would trade her for the seventy virgins. With that last echoing memory Mansour's life faded to black.

Connigliaro had been shielded from the worst of the explosion simply because he was on the far side of the building. Still, the concussion had been enormous. He reasoned, with an expert's knowledge, that one of the suicide bombers had somehow managed to detonate his vest and that the sound and fury of the subsequent blast must have equaled or exceeded fifteen to twenty pounds of C-4. Dirt and dust settled everywhere. Sirens were heard in the distance. People screamed and shouted. Where was his Team?

"Sipalla!" he shouted into his lip mike. Static.

"Tower!" Static.

"Santos!" Static.

"Shockley!" Static.

"Boss..."

"Oakes! That you? Where the hell are you?" Red staggered to his feet.

"I'm in the synagogue. With Shockley. The blast blew him back into the building, Red. It's not good. He's…he's…missing his legs."

"Shit!" Red choked on his mike. "The others? You?"

"I'm…I'm OK. Just a few cuts. I don't know about the others. Tower was with the fucker who fled, so I'm pretty sure he's gone. I haven't seen Sipalla…or Santos."

"OK, I'm coming. Hold on."

"Hey, boss, you hear that?"

Connigliaro was suddenly aware of a loud ripping sound over his head, like bed sheets being torn apart. Then he heard airplane engines cycling up and down in a sickly whine. He looked up in time to see what was left of a small jet, one wing, half the fuselage, the cockpit arcing downward, trailing a stream of flame. He though he saw a body tumble out of the falling wreckage—a big body, all on fire, frantically flapping its enormous arms. It was like a sick cartoon. All Red had time to scream was, "Oakes! Incoming!"

The mass of fiery aluminum and jet fuel landed squarely on top of the synagogue. The entire roof of the structure, with what was left of the aircraft, crumpled inward and for a second, just a second, the entire mass sat there quietly. Then the remainder of the jet fuel exploded all at once. In the following seconds Connigliaro realized he would never be tossing back brewskis in his South Boston body shop. He knew he was dead. And sure enough, the walls of the synagogue began to expand outward like a hideously inflated balloon. As the flaming shock wave swept him off his feet, tossing him like a rag doll into the night sky, he could feel his clothes being burned off his body as he flew through the air. Then, strangely, there was nothing but a peaceful drifting…

48.

Chaos

The crowd at Rubino's on Newtown Lane was in a very festive mood, aided considerably by liberal quantities of free alcohol. It was five thirty-five and Chief Duryea with his "police escort" had just arrived. Posing as Duryea's deputy was PO1 Gino Pirelli, and acting as Duryea's two Lieutenants were GYSGT Mack McConnell and James Griffin. A few of the partygoers were offended by cops carrying firearms attending "their" soiree, but most didn't notice or care. The four men were not there for fun and being ignored was just perfect. They sported ear buds and lip mikes, but not even that caused any extra notice since anyone who did care would probably think the devices were for security at such an important event.

The area's only Congressman, a local boy, was in attendance, along with just about all the town and village mayors, supervisors, state legislators, and politicos of all stripes from both sides of the aisle. The star attraction from the legislative world was one of New York's two famous senators. Mrs. Clinton had declined due to a previous commitment but her senatorial sidekick was there, persuaded to attend when told that the party was going to have massive media coverage. It was said that this senator could hear a camera shutter click a mile away and the local joke was that he'd attend the opening of an envelope if it happened on the six o'clock news. The media was, indeed, there. Half a dozen vans, relay antennas extended, were parked on Newtown Lane or in the town parking lot behind the restaurant. Several well-known local reporters circulated through the jovial crowd, jamming microphones in important faces. The press, like the rest of the guests, was drawn as moths to flame by the presence of so many glitterati at a Hamptons holiday party and the promise of some fabulously newsworthy announcement from their host. Griffin estimated the crowd at somewhere near three hundred. Private security was in evidence everywhere, struggling to control the flow of invited guests and the curious holiday shoppers strolling by. Griffin wanted desperately to clear the place and get everyone to safety but he knew he couldn't without tipping his hand, which was likely to cause an instant and fatal response. No, they would have to figure this out themselves, and pretty damn quick besides. Not content to rely solely on Chalabi's forces, Griffin had quietly summoned Tim Garwood and Gerry Wysocki to the scene. He had quickly briefed his trusted detectives and now they, too, worked the crowd. Griffin glanced at his watch: five forty-five.

Gerry Wysocki sat at the crowded bar sipping a club soda and lime. He eyed the throng intently. Tim Garwood had stripped off his coat and tie and had donned a serving apron. The apron neatly hid his .38 which was now stuffed in his waistband. He shuttled trays of hors d'oeuvres from kitchen to main dining room with ease. He had paid his way through college waiting tables at the old Chart Inn, so the ruse came easily to him. And it was Tim who first noticed them.

Among the crowd of servers was a small coterie of four dark-skinned men who looked Arabic to Tim, but who could also have been Hispanics or Brazilians given his limited ethnic experience. They seemed a bit edgy, though, and he noticed as he plodded back and forth that the four men never spoke to any of the other staff, only to each other, and two minutes ago, they had huddled to one side of the room and spoke together. Garwood went to find Wysocki and compare notes on his observations.

Machmoud Al Tafari was nervous, but not for himself, only for his mission. The Turk had left him in charge of this part of the operation and there was no doubt that this extremely religious and utterly devoted man would carry out his assignment. No, that wasn't an issue. It was the crowd. It was bigger than they had anticipated. It was going to be difficult to push, shove and maneuver through this many people and properly coordinate the activities of his three other partners.

The plan itself was relatively simple. Since the Turk was in close partnership with the restaurant's owner and had been able to come and go as he pleased for weeks, it had been easy to hide the necessary explosives and stash the weapons. Four fully loaded AK-47 assault rifles were tucked away carefully out of sight but within easy reach: one under the bar, one in the coat room off the foyer, one taped to the underside of the server's counter connecting to the kitchen, and one behind the banquette in the back. Fifty pounds of C-4 in five-pound chunks, all equipped with remote blasting caps, were hidden in the hollowed out undersides of ten separate tables evenly spaced throughout the facility. At exactly the right moment, Machmoud would give the signal and each of the four terrorists would secure their weapons, fire one burst into the air and get the attention of the crowd. Before panic set in, Machmoud would jump up on the bar, give a short prepared speech on the evils of America, Israel and Jews in particular, which would certainly be captured by all the media present, and start firing with his partners into the crowd. Neither Machmoud nor any of his brothers in arms would have extra magazines or other weapons.

When all their bullets were expended, Machmoud would press the remote detonator in his shirt pocket. The restaurant and any survivors within 100 yards would be vaporized or torn apart. Machmoud looked out at the crowd. He put down the last serving tray he would ever carry, and walked toward the bar.

Wysocki and Garwood shared their observations with the rest of the team. Pirelli and McConnell each took one of the four suspects under positive watch. Wysocki and Griffin took the other two. Garwood was dispatched to the back of the restaurant to see if anything else was brewing. Glad-handing was left to Chief Duryea, who knew most of the people there. He would act as backup. Griffin tried to raise Chalabi but got no response—at least nothing he could hear amidst the roar of the crowd. Griffin decided to proceed as if they were on their own, which actually gave him some comfort, as if he were at least semi-in charge of something.

Strange, the sous chef wondered to himself as he tried to open the cooler door. *Why is this thing locked? It's never locked!* He looked around for a key even though he had no idea where to find one. *Where's the damn key? What am I supposed to do for heavy cream? Shit! I'll have to run next door to Waldbaum's.*

Inside the walk-in, which was set at a numbing thirty-eight degrees, Gracie was desperately trying to keep warm. She was bound by the ankles, gagged and her hands were tied behind her back. She'd managed to roll away from the blower, to the other side of the freezing space, and wedged herself between two large stacks of cardboard cartons. She was somewhat shielded but could feel her core temperature dropping. She'd been in the box for most of the afternoon, and knew she couldn't last much longer.

Griffin almost had to shout into his lip mike to be heard. He gave final instructions to the team, "Do not fuck around with these people, gentlemen. If anyone, I mean anyone, makes a strange move, shoot first. I'll clean up the mess and take the questions later. Am I clear?"

Everyone rogered, "Clear."

He went on: "I haven't seen anything that looks like a suicide bomber vest yet, so I don't know what they're planning, but don't count it out. If any Ayatollah jumps up with a vest on, shots to the head only."

Five "Rogers."

"It's almost show time, boys, its five to six--" At that second, Newtown Lane was bathed in a flash of light that lasted three seconds, and then the entire building rumbled, as if a small earthquake had passed beneath their feet. The crowd went eerily silent in the space of two heartbeats.

Machmoud was now behind the bar. He shoved the bartender aside and bent down, underneath the highly polished walnut top. Coming up cradling an assault rifle, trigger finger at the ready, he opened his mouth to shout "Allah is great!" Unfortunately for Machmoud, he had stood up behind the bar directly across from where Gerry Wysocki sat. Before Machmoud could utter a word, Wysocki stuck the barrel of his .38 in Machmoud's mouth and pulled the trigger. A large chunk of the back of Machmoud's skull cracked the highly polished mirror behind the bar. The piece of skull was followed by most of Machmoud's brain and a fair amount of blood. Machmoud's lifeless corpse stood rigid for three seconds before collapsing to the floor.

The reverberations from Wysocki's shot had just stopped echoing when panic finally erupted. People started diving under tables and seeking any available cover. A huge section of the crowd surged for the front door, which was only wide enough to allow three or four people to pass at one time.

Another terrorist became trapped between the front entrance and the large picture windows fronting Newtown Lane. He was desperately trying to wade through the onrushing crowd. He had to reach his weapon! A small table flew by his head and shattered the window behind him. Then two chairs flew by and another window exploded outward. The panicked crowd surged over him. He was no match for the hundred or more desperate people clawing and clamoring to get by. Slipping on some broken glass he fell directly backward. His back struck the sharp aluminum frame that had, until seconds ago, held a large expanse of glass. Something cracked and then he felt a stabbing pain. He looked down to see a six-inch dagger of broken glass protruding form his sternum. And on they came, hordes of hands and feet, bodies large and small, all washing over him, crushing the life out of him in their desperation to flee the scene and save themselves.

In the ensuing panic the last two terrorists could not get to their weapons either—but they knew where Rubino kept his pistol, so they slipped down the darkened hallway to Rubino's office.

Griffin stood in a perfect tsunami of bodies trying to rush past him, or knock him down. He screamed into his mike. "What happened? What the fuck happened?"

"I shot one, boss." Wysocki could barely be heard in Griffin's earpiece "He's down. Behind the bar."

"Others?" Griffin demanded.

"My guy got pushed to the front," Pirelli shouted back. "I'm moving toward him. I saw him fall."

"Lost my guy," McConnell muttered, "Shit!"

"Don't feel bad. So did I," Griffin confessed.

"Peter!"

"Yes, James?"

"You OK?"

"Trying to be. I think my arm's broken. Fucking sheep! Bowled right over me!"

"Can you get your guys in here now? Crowd control?"

"Yeah, think so. I'm on it."

"Garwood! Where the hell are you?"

"I'm on two bad guys. They ran down the back hallway into some office."

"Stay there! Don't move! We're on the way. Don't engage until we get there!"

"Too late. They're coming back out. Looks like, oh, shit!"

Griffin heard two shots echo in his headset. "Garwood! Garwood! Tim! You read me?" Silence. "Pirelli! Stay on your guy. McConnell, Wysocki, Move! Down the hallway!" Griffin commanded.

Griffin hit the end of the hallway first, just in time to see two shadows dart to his left, and hear a bullet smack into the wall six inches from his head. Wysocki and McConnell materialized behind him. Light was nearly non-existent. Cautiously, they inched down the darkened corridor. Griffin's shoe struck something soft and he heard a whimper. "Please! Don't shoot!" It was the voice of a very frightened girl. Griffin reached down with his left hand and hauled the girl to her feet. She was dressed in a waitress uniform and very scared. "Miss, you ok?"

"Please don't hurt me," she sobbed.

"Don't worry. We're the good guys. Where does the end of this hallway go?"

"To the kitchen," she could barely choke out.

"Is there an exit from the kitchen?"

"No. You have to cross the back through the hallway, to the loading dock."

"OK, now quietly as you can, get behind us, then get the hell out of here."

The girl didn't have to be told twice. Like a frightened rabbit, she broke and ran.

"OK, guys, they haven't come back out yet, so they're trapped in the kitchen. Let's go but let's be careful."

With Griffin on point they crept slowly down the hall,

Wysocki behind Griffin, McConnell flattened against the wall on the opposite side. Griffin's shoe stumbled on something soft again.

"Shit! Another…?" But the form lying at his feet did not move or utter a word. Griffin knelt to take a closer look. The light was dim but sufficient for him to recognize Tim Garwood. Then he caught it, the soft, gurgling sound. He leaned closer. There were two neat bullet holes in Tim's chest, one just above his heart and one under his right nipple. The lung shot was foaming and blood pumped out in small slugs of dark crimson. He felt for a pulse. It was light and thready, but at least he had one. "Wysocki, drag him out of here. McConnell, stay with me."

"But--" Wysocki began to protest.

"He's your partner, Gerry, and he'll be dead in five minutes unless you get him some help. Now do it. We'll handle this."

"Yes, Boss." Wysocki put his hands, under Garwood's armpits and began dragging him back down the hall. McConnell and Griffin continued toward the kitchen.

The double doors to the kitchen were open. The room was quiet but still well-lit. Pots of bubbled on a stove. Water streamed from a faucet that had not been shut off in the haste to evacuate the kitchen.

Griffin and McConnell looked at each other, weapons at the

ready. Griffin pointed "right." McConnell nodded and pointed "left." Griffin shouted "Go!" It was an old but effective tactic to distract a target ready to experience one thing, but then see another. It buys a fraction of a second and often that's all that's needed. The man on "right" comes in from the left hand side of the entrance, dives, rolls to the right, and comes up firing from the crouched position. The man on left does just the opposite.

Griffin dove through the doorway from the left and rolled to the right just as he heard the first shot. He came up to a crouch, finger on the trigger, and froze.

McConnell dove through the doorway from the right, rolled left, heard a second shot, and came to his knees, pistol leveled at a man lunging toward him with a meat cleaver. McConnell's first shot smashed the man's right elbow and the cleaver went pin-wheeling into the wall behind McConnell's head. McConnell's second shot hit the man square in the throat, shattering his Adam's apple, clipping his right carotid artery and exiting his neck. The wound sent a shower of blood everywhere.

The other terrorist, the one with the gun, took careful aim at the head of a distracted McConnell. The man would have already been dead if Griffin hadn't frozen, but Griffin had chilled for a very specific reason. The terrorist with the gun was using Gracie, his dearly beloved, soul-connected, beautiful Gracie as a human shield. He simply couldn't shoot. Instead, he pointed his pistol at the ceiling and fired. It was enough. The terrorist jumped and shoved Gracie and his weapon to the left, at Griffin, and away from McConnell. He fired once. The bullet kissed Griffin's left cheek but Griffin didn't feel it. He concentrated only on Gracie's face.

Gracie, for her part, was rightly terrified, but to her great credit she neither screamed nor struggled. She was still partly immobile from her chilling experience, but she instinctively knew events were out of control and there was damn little she could do.

The terrorist ducked back behind Gracie's left shoulder. His left arm firmly encircled her waist; his right hand brandished the gun which he had thrust between her bound right arm and torso. Griffin had distracted the shooter but only for a microsecond. With Gracie as a hostage and an effective shield, both he and McConnell were perfect targets. The pistol moved again, another fraction toward Griffin, and the terrorist, peeking out from behind Gracie's left shoulder, took careful aim.

Griffin made one of those split-second decisions you can't stop to analyze. Silently, he begged, *Forgive me, Gracie, my darling, forgive me*, and squeezed off what he hoped was the most carefully aimed shot he had ever fired. His pistol, he knew, held penetrating rounds, not hollow point. Penetrating rounds went through things. They were neater and cleaner than hollow points, which were meant to smash, mash, tumble and maim.

Griffin's round passed cleanly through the fleshy part of Gracie's left shoulder, just below the clavicle, exactly where he wanted it to go. Without destroying muscle or touching bone, it exited cleanly out her back. The bullet continued, at a speed little reduced by contact with Gracie, squarely into the right temple of the terrorist, where it finally ground to a stop somewhere in the middle of his brain. The terrorist slumped to the floor, still clutching a wounded and now screaming Gracie.

The first shrieks from the media were just then reaching control booths at all the networks. It seemed that the Hamptons were being bombed, victimized by falling airplanes, experiencing meteor showers or maybe earthquakes all at once. No-one knew what was really happening and it was total, utter chaos.

49.

The Quick Change Artist

What had been intended as a sideshow was about to become the main attraction. Totally oblivious to what was happening at the synagogue or Rubino's restaurant, the four terrorists assigned to the diversion at the Irving Center School continued carrying out their orders. They understood that they were necessary but expendable, meant to pull resources away from other actions where far more important people would be killed. That was OK with them. Along with all of their brothers in arms they would ascend to Paradise this day and Allah would write all of their names on the scrolls of the holy martyrs. It was 5:33 p.m. and everything was in readiness.

Abou Said and Medulla had quickly and quietly rounded up the Head of School and the staff that remained in the administration building. In addition to Dr. Maloney the hostages included the head bookkeeper, the director of instruction, and Morton Rivkin. These four thoroughly frightened individuals were now bound and gagged in Dr. Maloney's office. Maloney was so terrified he had already wet himself.

Rafsanjani and Ibrahim the Elder had taken three teachers and six middle school students hostage in the gym, and all the captives sat in a huddle in the center of the basketball court. Fully armed with AK-47 assault rifles and vests full of explosives, the terrorists quietly circled the frightened group like sharks swimming around a potential kill. On a practical basis, it allowed the two armed men to constantly watch all the doors to the large fieldhouse in case anyone tried to storm in. The duos were in touch via walkie-talkie. The Arabic flew back and forth constantly as the terrorists pumped each other up for their imminent martyrdom and exchanged notes on the opposing forces gathering outside.

Those outside forces were formidable indeed and gaining strength by the moment, just as the terrorists had hoped. The more cursed infidels there were, the more they could kill and send to whatever hell they may believe in. The more police they attracted, the less their brothers would have to contend with at the other target sites. It was happening exactly as the Turk said it would.

"Beth Cantwell"/Sgt. Patti Davis was outside standing next

to SUV Three, directing the situation as best she could. It was a difficult role. Not only did she have to pretend to have the persona of Deputy Director Cantwell, she had to shoulder the responsibilities of a much more seasoned cop who had been in these situations before. Sgt. Davis had not been under this type of strain or pressure ever and she was struggling to keep it all in perspective and under control. She was beginning to regret insisting she was ready to direct her own "op."

Davis knew there were two groups of hostages, and terrorists, and roughly where they were located. She didn't know for sure how many bad guys there were. She guessed at least four, maybe as many as eight. Two teachers and a librarian who had barely escaped the roundup were being questioned but they all clearly remembered seeing "rifles" or "big shotguns," all of the terrorists wearing "bulky black vests," and one vest had "visible wires."

On scene, Davis had one full SWAT team from Suffolk County, which consisted of eight highly trained and capable shooters; three of her Delta Force mates, five Suffolk County detectives and nine local cops. The gym and Administration Building were both virtually surrounded with at least one pair of eyes on each door. No demands had been made by the captors, and no face-to-face or voice communications were underway, which, to Davis, seemed odd. "What do these assholes want?" she wondered aloud.

"Nothing," a voice replied from behind her, giving her quite a start, "Except to die bravely." She turned to face a tall, bearded man dressed in a small black turban and flowing white caftan. He appeared to be a holy man, or Mullah of some type. Then Davis looked a little more closely, directly into the Imam's face, and his cold, hard eyes.

"General?" She gasped.

"Not so loud, Sergeant. A word please. Come with me behind the SUV."

"It is the general!" She breathed a sigh of relief, actually glad to see him. She quickly followed him, ducking around the far side of the large van. He was there, along with Major Evans.

"Sir, am I glad to..." she was motioned to stop by the general in disguise.

"Yes, yes, no time. I've looked over your dispositions, Sergeant, and the Major and I agree you've done an outstanding job."

The Sergeant was even more relieved. "Thank you, sir, but we've still got a stalemate."

"Not for long. I know what they're up to," the general stated confidently.

"But, how, sir?"

"Never mind that now. Have they communicated with you at all?"

"No, sir. Nothing. No demands, no talk, no requests. They seem to be waiting for something or someone."

"They are. They're just waiting until six p.m."

"Six o'clock? What happens then, sir?"

"Something we have to try and stop."

"I'm ready, sir. What are your orders?"

"Just keep your current positions intact, Sergeant. I'm going in."

"In?! In where?"

"Where are the students?"

"In the gym, we think. At least that's where any students might be this time of day. You're going in there?" Davis demanded again. "Why?"

"To pray. And maybe save some kids. Stay here with the Major and don't do anything until you hear from me. Understood?"

"Yes, sir."

With that, Chalabi spun on a heel and boldly walked out from behind the SUV and headed toward the gym's main entrance. Sgt. Davis's headset crackled to life and a dozen voices tried to get her attention.

"All units! All units! This is Director Cantwell. Stand Down. I say again, stand down!" she barked into her mike. "I'm sending in a negotiator. Everybody relax. Stay alert, but do nothing except on my orders." She could hear a dozen trigger fingers ease up, just a hair.

"Nicely done, Sergeant," Major Evans whispered.

"Thank you, sir. But what the hell is he doing?"

"I don't know exactly, but you can be sure he's not going to be negotiating anything."

From inside the gymnasium the two members of Al Qaeda heard the shrill call of someone outside summoning them to prayer. In truth, they had not prayed at sundown and they were way past due. But who was calling to them? Ibrahim carefully walked over to the main door and cautiously peeked through the partially frosted glass. "What's this?" he nearly cried. He saw an Imam walking toward the door, both arms raised skyward and calling to them to join him in prayer. The Imam approached slowly. He stopped two yards from the main door and called out, in Arabic, "My Brothers! The Turk has sent me to you! He has a final word for you and also bids me to pray with you one last time before your glorious sacrifice!" The Imam then stood there, silent, hands raised high.

Ibrahim, superstitious and ignorant as he had been all his life, reasoned in his limited mind that he could not disobey an Imam-or the Turk. He opened the door, bowed to the Imam, and bade him enter.

Rafsanjani shouted at Ibrahim from across the cavernous hall, "You fool! What are you doing?" He raised his rifle and pointed it directly at the cloaked and bearded man.

"It is OK, my brother!" Ibrahim shouted back. "This Imam brings news from the Turk! And he wishes to pray with us before our sacrifice!"

Rafsanjani was smarter than Ibrahim, but only just a little. He was not totally convinced, but even far across the hall he could feel the power behind the eyes of this imposing cleric. A thousand years of mindless conditioning took hold and Rafsanjani obediently lowered his weapon. The tall Imam beamed at him and held out his arms as if to embrace them. "Come, my brothers! I have glorious news. But first, we pray."

The minister glanced around. He saw what he needed. He walked over to one side of the gym, to a stack of floor mats. He picked one large enough for all three of them and rolled it out on the hardwood, facing east. He quickly knelt, motioning the other two men to join him. Ibrahim obediently put down his rifle and dropped to the mat, head bowed low and on the surface of the vinyl. Rafsanjani hesitated. He glanced back at the circle of hostages. They were all wide-eyed, terrified and securely bound. They weren't going anywhere and Rafsanjani reasoned it would be good to have one last comforting prayer, to cleanse his mind of impure thoughts, before meeting Allah in person. He, too, carefully laid his weapon on the floor and joined Ibrahim and the Imam on the mat.

One last prayer was all Rafsanjani got-Ibrahim as well. Neither had stopped to think about searching the robed teacher. The thought would never ever have occurred to them. Imams were holy men. Above suspicion. That's exactly what Chalabi had counted on.

As both terrorists prayed, foreheads to the mat, Chalabi quietly reached underneath the folds of his robe. He slowly removed a silenced Luger and when it was fully exposed yet still out of sight of both praying penitents, he quickly fired a single shot into the back of each man's skull. Ibrahim pitched forward, splayed across the floor. Rafsanjani froze in his prayerful position. A pool of dark red blood spread rapidly from his shattered all across the mat.

Chalabi stuck the pistol back in his holster, under the robe, and rose to his feet. "Greetings to Allah from me," he murmured to each dead man's back. Some of the hostages were able to see the executions directly and several scrambled and struggled to get to their feet and run. Chalabi held up his hands and shouted at them, "Stop! I am General Chalabi, United States Army! Stay where you are! You're safe now. Sit, please. I will get help."

They all obeyed-instantly.

Chalabi looked at his watch. Eight minutes until six.

Not enough time to get out of here and get across campus to the other building to run this drill again. Think, man! He chided himself.

He noticed the walkie-talkie lying beside Rafsanjani's body. A small red eye blinked on and off every few seconds, indicating it was on and "live." He picked it up and keyed the mike. In Arabic he whispered, "My Brothers! There's an Imam outside! Do you see him?" Chalabi had no idea, of course, if anyone would respond, and if anyone did, who it might be, but he counted on a whispered voice being indistinct. A few seconds later Abou-Said answered.

"Rafsanjani! Is that you? Why are you whispering? I see no Imam! What is happening?"

"Of course it's me, you idiot!" Chalabi boldly answered. "I'm whispering because I think the infidel police are behind the building now, ready to rush us. Wait, wait. The Imam is calling me. I'll call you back in a moment." Chalabi clicked off and calmly waited for sixty seconds to tick off his watch. He keyed the mike again. "My brothers! This is the Imam Achmed Ben Said." Chalabi transmitted, in his own voice. "I bring new instructions from the Turk, who has sent me to pray with you."

Abou-Said was skeptical: "What new instructions? How do I know you are not tricking us? Let me talk to Rafsanjani again!"

Chalabi had a moment of panic as he looked down at the two corpses at his feet. He keyed the mike again: "He cannot! Someone is trying to break in by the back door. He is going to stop them!"

"Then let me talk to Ibrahim," Abou-Said demanded.

So, Chalabi breathed to himself, *That's the other assholes name.* "Ibrahim is with Rafsanjani. He cannot talk. You must listen to me!"

"I don't need to do a cursed thing except carry out my instructions!" came the defiant reply.

"Very well, but Allah will not be pleased," Chalabi shot back, taking a huge gamble. A few seconds passed.

"How do I know you're not with the infidels?" Abou-Said demanded.

"You don't, but how would I know about the Turk if I were not one of you? I pretended to be a local Teacher and offered my services to the infidels, to try and negotiate with you. The fools were all too eager to try."

Abou-Said bought it. It made perfect sense to his limited brain. "There are six minutes left, Imam."

"Then listen. The infidels do not know your plan. They think you have some demands, something to negotiate, that you want something. They are sending someone to talk to you."

"So? Then he will be dead in five minutes, too."

"But that is precisely the point!"

"What do you mean?"

"You must be sure that the man they are sending to you dies. Rubino desires it. The Turk desires it. Allah desires it. These are the new instructions." Chalabi pressed all the man's possible buttons, hoping he was right.

"Who is this man?"

"His name is General Achmed Chalabi. He is a traitorous Arab in the military of the United States. He is here. They are sending him to talk with you. Allah wants him dead."

"As do I!" Abou-Said hissed back.

Chalabi, who was clearly stalling and making this up as his mind flew forward, was stopped cold. "You know the man?"

"Yes, Imam, I do. He tortured and killed my brother, a loyal Iraqi patriot."

Chalabi's heart skipped a beat. "What is your name, my son?"

"Abou-Said Tikriti. My brother was Machmoud."

Well, well, Chalabi's mind spun back. *It is indeed a small world,* he told himself as he recalled a dark afternoon in a small room in a hot tin shed in Tikrit.

"It is also why I got close to him, pretended to be a spy and betrayed Al Qaeda from the inside. I was ready to kill him, but then I was ordered here and he eluded me. I did manage to kill his deputy, though, a young Navy Lieutenant that was sent to help him. I shot him in the head, just like he shot my brother."

Another mystery solved, Chalabi told himself.

"And now you say he's here? Allah is truly great! He is letting me fulfill my mission and my dream of revenge! Where is this man?"

"He's on his way to your location at this moment. You will no doubt recognize him?"

"Oh, yes, Imam. I certainly will. And I will greet him with open arms, and when I have my arms wrapped tightly around him, pretending to be a comrade, I will press the detonator."

"Good, good. Then you must wait for him, even if it delays you a few moments past your time."

A light brightened the sky for a second and the ground beneath them trembled. East Hampton Synagogue was five miles away, as the crow flies, but the explosion was very powerful.

"Imam! Did you see! Did you feel? It is a sign from Allah!"

"Yes, my son, it is. Now wait for this man."

"Oh, yes, Imam, I will wait."

Chalabi tossed the walkie-talkie to the mat. He hurriedly stripped off the turban and caftan. He tore at the fake beard glued to his face. Once again looking like himself, and revealing his Army fatigues with General's insignia, he trotted from the gym and headed across campus to the main office where his former spy, a man he had known as Ben-Salim, awaited him. He placed the headset in his ear once more and keyed the mike.

"Davis."

"Yes, sir! Good to hear you. What's going on?"

"Get some people in that gym. It's secure. Take care of the hostages."

"Right away, sir."

"And listen very carefully. You've only got once chance to get this right."

Abu-Said Tikriti told Medulla to stay with the hostages.

"But, Abu-Said, where are you going?" a confused and edgy Medulla asked.

"I am going to greet a very special visitor," he grinned. "When you hear me shout, 'Allah is great' you pull your cord, like we planned. Nothing has changed except I want to include this man in our party. Do you understand?"

"Yes, Abou-Said. I will do as you say. Allah be with you."

"And also with you."

With that, Abou-Said laid down his weapon and walked

slowly out the Headmaster's office, down the hall, and to the front door.

Outside, under the single lamp used to illuminate the school's main entrance at night, stood General Chalabi, bathed in the light. As a target, he couldn't be missed.

In the next instant, on the second floor landing, at the top of the stairs, Abou-Said appeared. Abou-Said gazed out the picture window and down at the perfectly silhouetted form of the man he hated most. There was a sublime moment of instant recognition as each man's eyes met the other.

Abou-Said's view of General Chalabi suddenly blinked out in total darkness, as if someone had shut off all the lights. He thought, *What...?* It was his last thought.

Sgt. Patti Davis sniper rifle had coughed once. She was perfectly positioned outside Chalabi's circle of light behind a large spruce tree in front of the building. Aiming upward, the 30-06 hollow point shot blew through the plate glass window and slammed into Abou-Said's forehead on a slightly upward trajectory. The top of Abou-Said's skull came off followed by a shower of blood and brains. The impact sent Abou-Said's corpse upward off his feet an inch and tumbling backwards, hitting the carpet on the landing with a considerable thump.

Down the hall, Medulla heard a small tinkling of broken

glass followed by a muffled thud that he could feel as a slight quiver beneath his feet.

He poked his head out into the hallway. He could see, in the semi-dark, someone lying on the floor near the top of the stairs.

"Abou-Said?" he shouted, wondering what was going on.

Morton Rivkin had never, ever, done a brave thing in his life. He had let bullies beat up on his skinny-as-a-rail body in grade school. He had let the Goyim steal his lunch money in high school. He had avoided confrontation all his life and was particularly frightened of bees, wasps, and any and all stinging insects. That is why what he did next was so extraordinary, so atypical, so out of character. It would continue to shock him, and anyone else who knew him, until the end of his life.

Morton, his bookkeeper, the headmaster, and the school's director of instruction were seated in high backed chairs, with gags in their mouths and arms bound behind the backs of their chairs. They could not speak, but their feet were free. When Medulla cautiously peeked into the hallway, Rifkin lowered his head, pushed upward with his feet, and ran, bent over, barreling toward Medulla like a battering ram. *What the hell?* Rifkin later remembered thinking, *We're all dead anyway.*

The top of Rifkin's head hit Medulla in the middle of the spine. Rifkin's forward momentum carried him, his chair and Medulla into the hallway where Rifkin fell on top of Medulla in a heap. Medulla dropped his rifle as his head hit the floor savagely with an audible crack.

At the same moment, the back door at the top of the stairs blew inward, shattering the doorframe. A flash-bang grenade exploded in the hallway. Rifkin went deaf and blind in an instant, as did everyone else on the floor. Four large men in black suits flew into the room. They carried what seemed like a vast array of mobile weapons. One of the men kicked Rifkin, chair and all, halfway down the hall. Something broke. Rifkin thought it might be a rib. Two more men slammed one heavily booted foot on top of each of Medulla's splayed out hands, pinning them to the floor. The fourth man sat fully on Medulla's back, practically squeezing the life from his lungs. Carefully, hands searched Medulla for the remote detonator he could no longer reach.

On his back, still tied to the chair, his chest aching, his eyes unfocused and his ears ringing, Rifkin could still hear one of the men say, "We're secure! We're secure! And we've got a live one!"

50.

Neat Tricks

"You bastard!" Gracie groaned from her prone position on a gurney in the back of an ambulance, "You shot me! On purpose!"

"Sweet pea…" Griffin tried to soothe her wounded pride as he stroked her auburn hair. He sat next to her, on the floor, a butterfly bandage covering his burning cheek.

Peter Duryea stuck his head in the back door and handed Griffin a cell phone. "I don't know how she got through, but you'd better take this," he sighed.

Griffin grabbed the phone.

"You bastard!" Myrna, his ex, screamed into his ear.
"Where's my son!"

Griffin paled. Caught up in the moment, he had completely set aside his concern for the other most important person in his life. "Look, Myrna, it's a little crazy here right now…"

"I know! I have CNN on one TV and News 12 on the other! Where's our son?" she wailed.

"I have a pretty good idea, but I'm also convinced he's safe. [Griffin certainly didn't want to add, "as long as he's still useful as a bargaining chip."] Look, we're getting close to wrapping this up right now [another outright lie] so, let me call you back. If you want to be helpful, why don't you come out to the East Hampton Police Station. I'll meet you there as soon as I have Kyle with me." [Griffin knew, things being what they were right now, absolute chaos and confusion, that it would take hours for her to travel the fifteen miles, if she could get through at all, but at least it would give her something to do.] "I gotta go…" A string of obscenities flew through the air as he closed the flip.

"She'll just call back," Peter Duryea shrugged.

Griffin placed the cell phone on the steel deck of the ambulance and ground it under his left heel until he could hear plastic crack and glass crunch.

"I'll buy you a new one," Griffin told Duryea.

Duryea smiled. "Don't hurry. Hate the damned things anyway."

Static clicked in Griffin's right ear. He had forgotten he still had his headset on. Then a voice came through the static.

"You're a bastard, Griffin, but a clever one."

Jesus! Griffin muttered to himself. *I must be in the running for bastard of the year.*

"Who is this?" Griffin keyed back. He did not recognize the heavily accented voice.

"Never mind who I am. Pay attention to who this is!" The voice growled back. The headset crackled again.

"Dad!"

Griffin leapt to his feet nearly slamming his head on the roof of the ambulance interior. "Kyle! Is that you?" he shouted back.

"Dad! It's me! Help me, Dad!" a frightened little boy blurted into the mike.

"Are you OK? Kyle? Are you OK?" Griffin pleaded. Gracie raised herself up on one elbow, obviously concerned, and placed a hand on Griffin's arm.

The accented voice came back. "He'll live. For now, and maybe later, if you do exactly what I say."

"Who is this?" Griffin barked. "Where's my son? I want him back now! How'd you get on this frequency?" Thoughts came tumbling out, all disconnected.

"I took this headset off the dead body of one of your soldiers, Griffin, that's all you need to know, except that I have your boy, of course."

Griffin took a deep breath. "OK, what do you want?"

"I want off of this fucking island, Griffin. Safe passage. That's a fair exchange, I think."

"Don't do it, Griffin." It was Chalabi. He was obviously on the same frequency.

"General, let me handle this, OK?"

"Not if it means giving in to these bastards."

"General, we're talking about an eight-year-old boy, my boy. I'll do whatever--"

"No you won't, that's an order!"

The circuit went silent for a few seconds. Then Germella laughed.

"I see we are at odds. No matter. Do as I say or the boy dies. Simple."

Griffin tried reasoning again. "General, please, we've taken these guys down, their plans are in shambles, what difference--"

"Shut up, Griffin. We do not negotiate with terrorists. We kill them."

"No, General, you shut up, dammit! This is my son we're discussing--"

"Griffin you're insubordinate! I'll have you court-martialed."

"Fuck you, General. OK, whoever you are, what do you want?"

"A helicopter—and a pilot to fly me to a location of my choosing. Have it fully fueled and ready to meet me. Contact me when you have made the arrangements and I will tell you where to meet us."

"Tell me now," Griffin begged, "so I can tell the chopper to go direct."

"And send a squad of your men in advance to greet me? I don't think so."

"I'm telling you, Griffin, don't do this!" Chalabi shouted.

"General, I already have a bird standing by at Montauk Municipal. I can--"

"Traitor! You are giving in to terrorists! Have I not trained you better? Have I not taught you to keep a fish on the line until we can reel it in and take it as a trophy? We must keep this one on the line and capture him, and make him tell us what he knows, just like in Tikrit, do you remember?"

"What the hell are you talking--" Griffin started to say, and then it hit him. *Shit!* He wasn't thinking. The danger to Kyle, which was real enough, had clouded his judgment. The general was trying to tell him something. What was it? Fishing? Tikrit? Trophy? Yes! He finally had it. Chalabi was playing good cop/bad cop, with Griffin as the good cop, and all to keep this guy, whoever he was "on the line." Chalabi's using his electronic magic to triangulate the position of the headset. In order to do that he had to keep the connection open.

"General--"

"I have heard enough! You're a traitor!"

Good! Griffin said to himself. *He's heard enough. That means they have a fix.*

"OK, Mr. Raghead, I'll get your chopper ready. But if any harm comes to my boy, I promise you there will be no place on this planet where I can't hunt you down and rip your balls off before cutting out your heart."

"No need for insults, Griffin. Just do as you are told. By the way, I am not-as you say- a 'raghead'." I am Turkish, and proud to be so. I will call you back soon." The connection to Germella was lost.

Griffin's cell phone rang instantly. It was Chalabi. "Jesus, James, it took you long enough to pick up on the act!"

"Yes, sorry, but, my son is--"

"I know, I know. Now let's go get him back. I'll meet you in three minutes. I'm on the way."

"You know where this guy is?"

"Yes. GPS says somewhere very close to the Montauk Lighthouse. And I also know who he is, and he's a bastard."

"Guess that makes two of us," Griffin sighed heavily.

Minutes later, Griffin, Chalabi, Evans and Sgt. Davis were hurtled down the Napeague stretch in SUV Three at speeds approaching ninety. Fortunately, the road was dry and traffic was sparse. Evans was behind the wheel.

"Were you a NASCAR driver in another life, Major?" Griffin asked, hanging onto the passenger side grab bar for dear life.

Evans grunted in obvious enjoyment. Griffin's headset came to life once more.

"Is my helicopter ready yet?"

"It is. It's on its way now. You just need to tell us where to send it."

"There is a big parking lot in front of this Montauk Lighthouse. That is where I wish to be picked up. Tell him to be there in fifteen minutes. And just you, Griffin, and the pilot. No one else. If you play fair, I will exchange you for the boy and we'll be on our way. If not, I will kill the boy instantly. The same is true if I see flashing lights in the distance or if anyone else approaches. Do you copy?"

"I do, but exchange?"

"Yes. I will exchange you for the boy, then you and I and the pilot will take a little ride."

"Where to?"

"This is for me to know. All you need to concern yourself with is saving your boy. Fifteen minutes. Goodbye." Silence.

Griffin turned in his chair to look at Chalabi, who gazed out his window into the night.

"What do you make of that, General?"

Chalabi ignored Griffin for a moment and spoke directly to Evans. "Major, radio the helicopter. Tell the pilot to set down now, wherever he can. We'll meet him."

"Yes, sir."

"What's your plan, General?" Griffin asked a little nervously.

"We'll put you on that chopper, so you can make the exchange for your son, if that's what you really want."

"It's not what I want, but I'll do it for Kyle."

"Don't be so quick to say that. You know he's going to kill you, don't you? He may-I say 'may' exchange you for the boy, if he's in a charitable mood—which after today, I doubt. My guess is he'll have a gun, force you on the helo with your boy, then take you fifty miles out over the water, shoot you both, and dump you in the ocean. Maybe he won't even shoot you. More likely he'll throw your boy out the cabin door and you'll leap after him. Then he'll shoot the pilot."

"Why the hell would he do that? Who'll fly the thing?"

"He will. I've read his file. He's a qualified chopper pilot, courtesy of the Turkish Air Force."

"Fuckin' great. Just fuckin' great.""

The pilot of County -2 set the Bell Ranger down in the main parking lot of Hither Hills State Park. In a flash, he was replaced by Major Evans with Griffin in the co-pilot seat.

"Looks like you're the designated driver all around tonight, Major." Griffin glanced at Evans.

"Cut my teeth on these babies at the Academy, Commander. Ready?"

"Yup, let's go." They leapt into the sky.

Five minutes later they hovered over the main parking area

in front of the Montauk Lighthouse. Chalabi had quickly and efficiently closed down the entire highway, all the way back to the village itself. Any civilians in the zone were quietly being rounded up and pushed back toward Main Street.

Griffin heard the voice in his headset. "I will turn on a small flashlight now. Set the chopper down as close to it as you can."

"Over there!" Griffin pointed to a spot below and to the left. Evans had seen it at the same time. He flicked on the landing lights, crabbed the helo to his left and settled to the pavement. Instantly, Griffin was out of his seat and on the ground. He scanned the parking lot, trying to peer into the darkness. A form began to emerge.

A few yards away, Germella walked into the circle of light provided by the chopper. He held Kyle in front of him, a large pistol under his chin. He smiled with obvious malevolence.

"You have done well, Griffin. Now get in the back."

"I will, if you release my son first."

"You do not make the demands here, Griffin. Now get in the back!" Germella growled.

"Look. Your argument is with me, not a little boy. You are going to live to fight another day. Just let him go and you can have me. It's more than a fair exchange."

"Daddy!" Kyle whimpered. "Don't leave me."

"It's going to be OK, Kyle. Now just move away from that man and run to the lighthouse office. Stay there. Someone will come along soon to meet you. I promise."

Kyle tried to move. Germella's grip held tight.

"Allah, as I understand it, doesn't make war on children. Let him go," Griffin said evenly.

Germella shrugged and released his grip. He turned his weapon on Griffin.

"Run, Kyle!" Griffin barked.

In an instant Kyle was gone, out of the circle of light. Griffin could hear his sneakers continue to slap the asphalt for several seconds as he ran.

Germella's face returned to a stony mask.

"Now, get aboard, in the back."

Germella aimed his pistol squarely at Griffin's head until he was in the rear passenger seat and strapped in. Germella then opened the passenger side cockpit door and aimed the pistol at the pilot. Only there was no pilot. The seat was empty. Had Evans been there, Germella would have shot him dead. Instead, the bird sat humming quietly, waiting for someone to take the controls.

For a second, just a second, Germella was non-plussed. Then he laughed. "It seems your brave pilot has flown the coop! No matter." With that, he walked around to the pilot's side of the cockpit, opened the door and placed himself at the controls. He glanced back at Griffin, seated behind him and to the right. "Don't worry, Griffin. I'm not going to kill you. At least not yet. I actually need you. I'm banking on your friends not wanting to kill you by blowing me out of the sky, as they did our fat Jewish friend." Germella chuckled, and then fiddled with the stick and gauges. "There's a freighter 200 miles offshore with a helo platform. They are my friends. They are waiting for me to join them. Let's say hello, shall we?"

The Ranger lifted off smoothly, circled the lighthouse once, gaining altitude, then turned seaward. At three-hundred feet the seemingly impossible occurred. The helicopter rolled violently to its left until it rested on its side in mid-air. The pilot's door magically flew off its hinges with two little pop-pops and dropped away. The pilot's seat, with Germella strapped securely in it, also blew off its rails and tumbled through the opening. Ottmar Germella grabbed at handfuls of dark night air as he fell screaming onto the jagged rocks surrounding the lighthouse. Inside the protesting airframe Griffin was thrown violently against the left bulkhead.

Something cracked. He knew he was going to die. Then, with just as much violence as before, the chopper rolled right, leveling itself. It hovered in place. Griffin was truly frightened. One thing he had never learned was how to fly. He was now in a death trap without a pilot. He reached over the seat to try and at least grab something that looked like a control mechanism. A searing pain in his left elbow stopped him cold. Panic would soon set in. Then, as if by magic, he watched in morbid fascination as the controls seem to come to life on their own. The helicopter steadied, turned itself around, flew forward a quarter mile and gently descended to the point in the parking lot where it had taken off just moments ago. The engines started to wind down to a complete stop.

Griffin was stunned. Major Evans opened the door to the back compartment.

"You OK, Commander?"

"Yes…I think so…I think I broke…how did?"

Major Evans grinned broadly. "Here. Let me help you out." The Major unbuckled Griffin's seat belt and gently helped him out. "Where does it hurt?"

Griffin cradled his left elbow in his right hand. "I think I cracked it pretty good. But how did you…?"

"With this." Evans held up a small black box about the size

of a child's school lunch box. It had a few tabs and what looked like a joystick. "While you were jabbering with the asshole, I was booby trapping the bird. I placed pads of C-4, each about the size of a wad of gum, on the door hinges and the seat mounts. As soon as you were safely in the air, I took control of the chopper with this little toy. I flipped the bird on its side with this joystick, blew off the door, blew the seat off the rails and bye-bye Mr. Bad Guy. Neat, eh?"

"I'm glad you're on our side, Major, that's all I've got to say."

"C'mon Commander, let's get your son. He's safe. Right over there. He really wants to see you."

51.
Debrief

At three p.m. the next afternoon General Chalabi, Commander Griffin and Major Evans were all seated at a large leather-bound conference table in the Situation Room, the secure briefing center three levels underneath the White House. On Chalabi's right was the Army Chief of Staff. On Griffin's right sat the Chief of Naval Operations. On Evans right was the Chief of Staff of the Air Force. Across the table sat the Directors of the FBI, CIA, NSA and several of their principal aides. Griffin was in his Navy Blues but his left arm was pinioned by a shoulder sling encasing his shattered left elbow. He was itchy and uncomfortable. His cheek still stung and was broadly bandaged. H also suffered from a number of aches and bruises he didn't know he had incurred until all of the fast and furious action had subsided. In short, he was a mess and hurt like hell. All he wanted was a stiff drink and about ten aspirin. He also squirmed under the gazes of the others across the table eyeing him with such curiosity.

At one minute after three the double oaken doors at the end of the room opened widely and the President's National Security Advisor (NSA) breezed through with the Chairman of the Joint Chiefs and the SecDef in tow. Everyone stood to attention. Griffin found it extraordinarily difficult to get to his feet. The slow, crippling, unwinding of his frame caught the NSA's attention and he quickly motioned Griffin and the others to "Sit, ladies and gentlemen, please."

Although the SecDef was senior to the NSA, he deferred the running of this meeting to the NSA. The Sec Def and the Chairman of the Joint Chiefs took seats at the head of the table on either side of the Honorable Jeremiah T. Johnson.

Johnson was an ex-military man himself, having won a Navy Cross in Vietnam as commander of a company of Marines who had fought their way out of a nasty envelopment on the second day of the notorious 1969 Tet Offensive. Johnson had lost an eye and three fingers of his right hand in the battle which, of course, made him unfit for continuing a career as an officer of Marines. He went back to law school at Yale, landed on Wall Street, and made a fortune in mergers and acquisitions before he was 35. Returning to his native Texas he joined a powerful law firm in Houston that had big connections to Republican politics becoming legal counsel to a relatively unknown oil baron who had also attended Yale. The two men became fast friends and Johnson took a ride on his client's coattails all the way through the Texas Governor's Mansion to and through the White House.

Johnson's black eye patch, his penchant for Marine Corps red vests for his finely tailored suits, and his ruthlessly efficient approach to the law and government, had earned him the nickname of "The Crimson Pirate." He loved the sobriquet and his dashing reputation; plus, he also had the charm, good looks and brains to back it all up. Looking squarely at James Griffin, he began, "Commander Griffin, General Chalabi, Major Evans, it seems the nation owes you three and your people an enormous debt of gratitude for your actions over the past several days. The President wishes to have me convey his thanks to all of you. Appropriate notations will be made in each of your permanent records." Johnson's warm smile faded. "But that's not why we're here today. We want to know how the hell this happened, how we were blindsided yet again by these terrorist bastards and how we're going to explain this one to the American people. Comments? Ideas?" Johnson entwined the remaining two fingers on his right had with those on his left and placed his hands on the table in front of him, awaiting answers. His single grey green eye glowered like a smoky emerald, its gaze landing on Evans, Griffin and Chalabi, in turn. A long uncomfortable moment passed in silence.

Griffin and Chalabi had worked up some mental notes, with Evans providing additional tactical background. It was all they had, and it wasn't yet a complete picture, but they had all agreed they would lay it out, unvarnished, and let those way above their pay grades sort chicken shit from chicken salad. Chalabi cleared his throat and stood.

"Ladies and gentlemen, Commandeer Griffin, Major Evans and I have pulled together all that we do know and what we can reasonably surmise. I have no charts, PowerPoints, notes or briefing books to share with you. Most of that is because we didn't have time to prepare much of anything but some of it is also because, quite frankly, we didn't know how much you wanted us to put in hard copy. At least not yet."

Chalabi looked down for a second, took a deep breath, looked up and continued. Griffin had the distinct impression that Achmed Chalabi was going to relish this moment but Griffin knew, too, that Chalabi was also a prisoner of the moment and was being genuinely affected by it.

Chalabi shook his head slowly. "It's complicated. We have issues touching on international relations, religion, sexual orientation and; of course, terrorism."

Johnson interrupted, "Just spill it, General. The rest of us will figure out how to dress it up and take it to the dance."

Chalabi smiled weakly. "Yes, sir." Chalabi began to pace behind his side of the table once again incapable of deep thought or conducting briefings without some physical movement.

"The bottom line is this: we have--or I should say 'had'--a well-known Jewish gay man, Milos Rubino, whose resources were almost unlimited, waging war on the Hamptons. For reasons that are only now becoming clear he decided to use his money to finance a terrorist operation here in the United States, principally against prominent men and women of his own faith. He smuggled a dozen suicide bombers and their leader into this country and hid them in an old, abandoned military facility in Montauk. He saw to it that they were trained, equipped, entertained and supported but the terrorists themselves knew little, apparently, about Rubino's agenda. They themselves believed that they were on a true Jihad on behalf of Al Qaeda. Rubino's plan, it seems, was to use the terrorists to bomb a synagogue, blow up his own restaurant and attack a children's school in which he had a substantial interest. We suspect he wanted to wipe out a number of prominent Jewish business and community leaders by destroying the synagogue while many of these same people were attending a meeting that he, himself, had precipitated by generating a leadership crisis in the congregation via its rabbi. We also feel he intended to assassinate a number of non-Jewish local politicians and business people, real estate people in particular, by simultaneously blowing up his restaurant. We believe he wanted to attack the private school as a diversion, but also possibly because he wanted to get the land the school owned firmly in his control for future real estate development.

"The terrorists were to die, leaving no eyewitnesses to his perfidy. All of the actions would focus on properties or entities owned or controlled by Rubino. He would thus gain enormous notoriety and sympathetic support. All or most of his principal rivals would die. People would flee the Hamptons in droves. This formerly safe and secure garden of upper crust peace and financial tranquility would be in ruins. Real Estate prices would plummet. The local economy would be destroyed. All or most of the best real estate professionals in the area would be dead. He could buy up huge chunks of formerly stratospherically priced property for distress sale prices. He could then sell the pieces of property to his –ah--sexually oriented friends from around the world and make a killing in the process. We also know that he and his principal lieutenant were involved in a shady deal to bring a major casino to the Hamptons-something that could never happen unless the economy was so shattered by events that there would be very little chance to revive the local economy unless a casino or something like it were built. To make this happen he secured the backing and loyalty of the local indigenous Indian population, without whose endorsement a casino could not be built. And that's pretty much the bottom line, sir."

The room went deadly quiet. It was difficult to read the faces around the table but Griffin surmised correctly they were all saying to themselves that it sounded more like a bad Nelson DeMille novel than reality.

"General," NSA Johnson finally broke the silence. "This is a pretty bold plan, a diabolical plan. What on earth does a man like Rubino, with all his money, need with all this nonsense? What was he thinking?"

"Well, sir, that's really beyond my expertise. I can only give you an uneducated opinion, and then I'll have to defer to the psych profilers who will, I am sure, be studying this one for a long time. Actually, sir, I'd like to have Commander Griffin handle this part of the discussion. He had direct contact with Rubino, and has studied his background more than I have."

Goddamit! Griffin said to himself. *He didn't tell me he was going to throw that one at me!* Griffin squirmed in his seat. All the eyes in the room immediately shifted their gaze. Griffin pushed his chair back. His boss, a four star admiral no less, offered to help him stand. "It's OK, sir, thanks, I'm fine," he protested, although he wasn't.

Griffin began nervously. "Well, as the general said, I had occasion to meet with Rubino, and I did some background investigation on him and his family. I also checked with a couple of people from his social circle, shall I say, that know him or of him. We started looking into him, or rather his family, as part of a murder investigation."

"Murder?" NSA Johnson's single eyebrow arched high. "Rubino was also involved in a murder?"

"Yes, sir, well, actually, we think members of his family, his wife and son specifically, were involved in a murder, then one of his hired guns precipitated a copycat murder to get rid of one of the terrorists who apparently failed to live up to their exacting requirements. Then Rubino ordered a third and fourth killing to get rid of a loose cannon at his school and his own spendthrift lover, of whom he had grown tired, it seems."

"My God, this gets worse by the moment." Johnson shook his head.

"Yes, sir, it does. Anyway, yes this guy's got more money than God—hundreds of millions to play with, yet he's not happy, apparently, with his lot in life. You said, sir, I believe, his plan was 'bold' and 'diabolical'. Yes, it was all that, but it wasn't really clever. And that was his downfall. Rubino, after all, was not a very smart man. He inherited all his money. He never had to work a day in his life. Yet in a curious way that seemed to rankle him, too. He was thrown out of the family business for his personal peccadilloes and his basic lack of business skills. He was angry. He had something to prove. He tried to be a successful businessman but failed at everything he attempted. I'm certainly not qualified to render psychiatric opinions but I have run across this profile before in my years of police work and it seems to me he suffered from a type of "little big man's" complex. He could have anything money could buy, but what his money couldn't buy was talent and recognition. He apparently grew more unhappy—morose even—as he was continually reminded of his shortcomings. Somewhere along the way he apparently decided to take by force what he couldn't build and then, as an extra added measure of revenge against his family and anyone who was laughing at him behind his back, he decided to simply wipe away his competition. Bold, yes, but not smart. What made it work, in my opinion, and what let him get as far as he did get, was the money. He dangled tons, scads of money, in front of people to get them to do his bidding, no matter how outrageous the request, how far-fetched the idea. Frankly, I'm not surprised. He bought a school, he bought a restaurant, he bought a synagogue, he bought people, he bought politicians, and he bought property, all to try and legitimize his unhappy, unsuccessful life and to gain status and credibility among people like those who dominate in the Hamptons. But eventually he overextended and events began to move faster than his limited intelligence and even his money could manage. Ultimately, I think he was a sick man, mentally unbalanced by a life of excess, but that's certainly just a layman's observation. I guess we'll never know now but it's a shame he had to hurt so many people in the process. And, well, that's about it on this point, I think." Griffin was beginning to feel a little weak. He sat heavily.

"Thank you, Commander. That certainly helps paint the picture," Johnson said. "So, what is the butcher's bill on this General?"

"Major Evans will speak to that, sir."

"Major Evans?"

Evans leapt to his feet. He was the junior officer in a room full of stars, stripes and important "suits," and he knew it. "Twenty-three people were killed at the synagogue, sir, including all six members of my—er—our Delta Force contingent on scene, and may I say, sir, they were all brave and excellent men."

"Yes, you may say that, Major, and it is a sad loss, a regrettable loss, and the President has told me he will be contacting each of these brave men's families personally."

"Yes, sir, thank you sir. The assho…I mean, Rubino, sir, he died there, along with both of the pilots of his private jet. Four suicide bombers were killed; three shot by my men and a fourth managed to blow himself up. Ten civilians were killed, too, unfortunately, including the Rabbi. We also have forty-one wounded civilians--seven are critical and one or two of those will probably not make it. "Four terrorists were killed at Rubino's restaurant, thanks to Commander Griffin, two more of our Delta Force men and some excellent support by local law enforcement. Fourteen civilians were injured, mostly cuts and bruises, broken bones, except for one civilian who was-ah-shot incidentally, caught in the line of fire, so to speak."

Evans gave Griffin a wickedly playful glance. Griffin caught it and shrunk a little lower in his chair.

"Glad to say no friendly fatalities there," Evans went on. "Three terrorists were killed at the school site. There was a bit of a shootout there, sir, but we were fortunate to be able to rescue all the hostages, including the children, without any injuries, but we did lose one of our own, sir. Deputy Superintendent Cantwell, Suffolk County Police, Commandeer Griffin's right hand lady, was on scene commander, sir, and she acquitted herself bravely but in the process of trying to free the hostages she was gunned down by one of the cowardly bastards and she expired at the scene."

Griffin tried to look at his shoes. Chalabi said nothing and didn't move a muscle. Evans was incredibly poker-faced. No one questioned the account. Evans moved on.

"The good news from the school site, other than getting all the hostages out unharmed, was that we also managed to capture one of the terrorists alive. He's—ah—being questioned as we speak. Rubino's guy who was controlling the terrorist cell, a well-known Al Qaeda operative by the name of Ottmar Germella, was also killed. We tracked him down after the synagogue blast and found him trying to flee in a helicopter. He was successfully extracted from the chopper, but didn't survive the landing." Evans was again straight-faced. Griffin grimly thought that after Evan's military career of murder and mayhem he might have a future in stand up comedy. "Attila the Hun" plays the Improv. Evans sat down abruptly. He was done.

The Sec Def then spoke: "General, this terrorist you captured. Are you absolutely sure he belongs to Al Qaeda?"

"Yes, sir, no doubt about it. He admits it and some of my records from our base in Tikrit support it."

"And General," the SecDef went on, "Please don't take this the wrong way--this is not in any way, shape or form a criticism or accusation—but this man, this member of Al Qaeda is cooperating with us freely and without coercion?"

"Yes, sir. We are, of course, questioning him, but we are using only approved DOD interrogation guidelines. I have to say though, sir, this guy is only eighteen years old. He's a poor Arab kid, really, and not much of a dedicated freedom fighter. He's scared to death and all he wants is to see his family again."

"Good, good." The SecDef smiled. "This is excellent political capital we can use."

"Major," Johnson said, "how is it that Rubino's aircraft ended up crashing into the synagogue?"

Evans was on his feet again, nearly snapping to attention. "Well, sir, best we can guess at this point is that Germella shot him down with a shoulder fired missile. We found a used launcher in the rental car Germella used to drive out to Montauk to try and make his escape."

"Why would he want to kill his benefactor, Major?"

"Good question, sir. Unfortunately neither lived to tell the tale, but I'd speculate that; A, Germella was a known hater of Jews; B, by the time Rubino was flying overhead to inspect the hoped for bombing of the synagogue, Germella knew his plan had been shot to shit, and most of his pals were dead, so he probably expected treachery on Rubino's part so; C, Germella might have done it just to cover his tracks. Rubino was one of only a couple of people who knew Germella had been involved. Yesterday, the Coast Guard boarded a Syrian freighter off the coast of New Jersey that they had been tracking for several days. It was just steaming up and down the coast, going nowhere except toward Nantucket and back toward Barnegat Light. The freighter had a makeshift helo pad on the fantail and NSA had picked up two radio intercepts from Germella that were beamed in the direction of the freighter's track. Two and two is four to me, sir. Germella was definitely planning a getaway, wanted to live to fight another day and he may have decided Rubino had outlived his usefulness."

"I see..."Johnson rubbed his chin. Perhaps he did see but more likely he decided he had heard enough and wasn't going to pursue it further. "Now, General," he said staring back at Chalabi, "you seem to know, or perhaps you even knew then, a lot about Rubino's intended movements, maybe even some of his plans. How was that possible? And please don't tell me it was 'good luck' because, knowing you, I won't believe it."

"No, sir. I mean, yes, sir," Chalabi was temporarily flustered. "We had excellent electronic intelligence, sir. NSA's new selectable intercept equipment was invaluable, sir, especially the new CRAY computer and its associated satellite dedicated to cell phone traffic."

The Director of the NSA shifted in his chair a bit and smiled demurely. *Nobody on the Hill or in the White House would ever question that billion dollar program again,* he said to himself contentedly.

"But I do admit I had a little inside help." With that comment, Griffin's aches and pains suddenly disappeared as his foggy brain wrestled with that revelation. *Did he say 'inside help'? What the fuck?*

"And would you care to share that information with us, General?" Johnson queried.

Chalabi would definitely prefer not to share it. There were too many people in the room. Someone would undoubtedly get flannel-mouthed about it. But Chalabi also knew that Johnson's request was not casual. It was couched it in polite tones but it was an order. "Well, sir, I was able to turn one of Rubino's trusted insiders, at the last moment, and that source was very helpful." One glance at Johnson's stone cold stare told him that he wasn't going to be able to stop there. Johnson was silently demanding more—the whole truth.

"His name is Ivan Centpied, sir. He became Rubino's associate when Rubino first moved out to the Hamptons. Centpied is well connected to a certain segment of the Hamptons social strata and Rubino needed someone like that to introduce him around. Centpied comes from 'old money', although most of it is gone now. Centpied needed an 'angel' to reverse his sagging financial fortunes. The two were a good match, for a while."

"How did you turn him, General?"

"I'd like to tell you it was by my brilliance, sir, but in truth it was a stroke of luck."

Griffin thought, *My, isn't this refreshing.*

"Two days ago, just after noon, I got a call from Chief Griffin's head of forensics, Frank Tartaglia." At this, Chalabi glanced at Griffin, almost apologetically. "He was trying to reach the Superintendent to give him the results of some tests he had conducted on a sample of vomit recovered from the most recent crime scene in this case. The Chief wasn't answering his cell phone at that moment."

Well sonnofabitch, Griffin exhaled under his breath. *Where the hell was I?* He frantically began mentally retracing that time period of that fateful day. He reckoned he had been somewhere between witnessing Evans blow Cantwell's brains out and the meetings in Peter Duryea's office. Had Chalabi been there the whole time? He couldn't remember with any real clarity. He did remember doing one simple thing, though, as he always did, out of respect for other people's meetings. He had turned his cell phone off.

"....so Inspector Tartaglia asked me to relay the message to Chief Griffin. That message was that the DNA recovered from the sample of regurgitated food belonged to one Ivan Centpied. Centpied had been arrested three times for DWI, twice for domestic abuse and once for securities fraud. He plead all the cases out to fines or censures but his DNA was still on file. At that point, I knew he was involved, somehow, in the murders of Rubino's partner, Sokolin, and the day school's coach, both of which had occurred the day before. We also did a data dump of a cell phone we had picked up that we thought belonged to one of Rubino's co-conspirators."

Griffin's mind was raced. *What cell phone? Oh, shit! Beth Cantwell's!*

"Centpied's ID and cell number were in the phone's address book. I hit the number. After three rings, Centpied answered."

Like hell! Griffin snorted a little too loudly to himself. *The only reason he answered was because he thought a trusted ally—Beth Cantwell—was trying to call!*

"I identified myself, and Centpied immediately agreed to meet. He was very frightened and didn't know quite what to do."

Oh, Achmed, you're good! Griffin smiled. *Sure, you told him who you were, and you told him you had DNA placing him at a murder scene and you told him you were on the way to get him and if he didn't spill his guts voluntarily you'd simply rip them out for him.*

"As it turns out," Chalabi continued, "Mr. Centpied had, indeed, been privy to the murder scene and had gotten a pretty clear message from Rubino that if he didn't keep his mouth shut forever, he, too, would soon be naked, tied to a tree and whacked. While you were on your way to Rubino's restaurant, Commander, Mr. Centpied and I had a brief chat. That's why you were unable to reach me on my cell or my headset."

Brief chat, my ass! Griffin laughed internally. *I'm sure you showed him what life would be like inside one of your sweaty little rooms in a tin shack and that was enough to get that worm to turn.*

"In exchange for my protection, Mr. Centpied agreed to cooperate. As events were developing very rapidly, I doubt we could have reacted as well to each situation without Mr. Centpied's insight to Rubino's plans."

"And where is Mr. Centpied now, General?" the Director of the FBI spoke up. As a domestic terror matter, this case would normally be in the FBI's bailiwick.

"He's being questioned further, Director. My people should be done with him shortly and then he will be turned over to your people promptly. But I will say he's singing loudly and without hesitation."

"Thank you." The Director was temporarily satisfied.

Griffin was sure Centpied would not be turned over to the FBI without some 'incidental damage'. He envisioned a small pile of bloody fingernails collecting on a cement floor somewhere.

"Well, gentlemen, that's quite a tale." Johnson sighed. "We were lucky. We were staring another 9/11 in the face. The deaths and injuries are tragic and unfortunate, but I guess it could have been worse. OK, then, we'll take it from here. I will brief the President and the Cabinet and work up a response. How are things on the East End today? What are people believing or thinking?"

Chalabi and Evans looked at Griffin. He was the "local boy." This time Griffin did not try and struggle to his feet.

"Well, sir, people are scared. We have put a big, fat lid on the story. We're only releasing dribs and drabs, telling the media we're still investigating. We can't cover up the fact that there was some sort of terrorist attack. It was too extensive; there are too many civilians who have seen at least something, like dead bodies of Middle-Eastern- looking men. We have people who have been hostages. They will talk or sell their stories to the media. But I am pretty sure no one knows how extensive the plan was—the actual scope of the intended mayhem. There's no general panic, but people, as I say, are scared. They need information, sir, and they'll need it quick. They'll need some reassurance from their government, too, sir."

"Then we will give it to them," Johnson vowed. "Excellent work, gentlemen. Again, our thanks. I think we're done here." Chairs scraped the floor, people began to stand. Johnson turned toward the double doors, then quickly turned back. "Oh, gentlemen. One more thing. No notes, no reports, no e-mails, no secret memoirs, no discussion of any of this to anyone without our prior approval. Ever. Am I clear?"

All three officers answered in the affirmative despite knowing the directive was a practical impossibility.

52.

Epilog

Things in the Hamptons quickly settled back to a fairly normal routine. There were a few panicked sales of properties but by the following spring the rental market was once again brisk in anticipation of the coming summer season. The home buying market was a little slower to recover--prices didn't drop, but they did slow their unreasonable acceleration to idiotic levels.

A memorial was being constructed to those who had died in the tragic crash of Milos Rubino's plane into the East End Synagogue. His name would be placed at the top of the monument even though it was his unfortunate crash that had caused so much death and destruction. It wasn't his fault, after all, that terrorists had shot him down as he was hurrying to return to East Hampton to attend Chanukah services at the very same synagogue he would innocently destroy. He had been a very generous benefactor; in fact, several million dollars of the money he had donated were going to be used to rebuild the temple. Rubino's fiery death by immolation in the temple was actually seen by some as a sign from God that Rubino should be honored. The Temple had already had its first sacrifice, so to speak, and the ground upon which the temple would be re-built was stained with sacred blood.

Rabbi Feldman's name would also be inscribed on the new Temple's memorial, for although he may have strayed a little, he was still, overall, a good man, deserving of recognition for many good deeds, not the least of which was dying at his post.

The names of the six Delta force commandos who had quietly saved hundreds of lives before the Temple imploded would not be inscribed on the memorial because they had not been there as far as anyone connected with the rebuilding program knew. But they had certainly not been forgotten.

The bodies of all six men had been recovered, or at least most of their body parts. Each of the brave Delta warriors would have a marker erected at Arlington National Cemetery, listing name, rank, branch of service, date of birth, place and date of death, and any extraordinary military honors received. Place of death was simply listed as "Iraq." Included on the tombstones for CWO4 Connigliaro, LCPL Steven Shockley, PO3 Miguel Santos, and CPL Jerry Towers were the notation "NC" for "Navy Cross." On the headstones of Sgt. Anthony Sipalla and Sgt Kevin Oates were the initials "DSC," for "Distinguished Service Cross." All were, of course, awarded posthumously. Each grieving nearest relative received a letter from the President, a burial flag and the standard Serviceman's Group Life Insurance death benefit check for $25,000. Each family also received, mysteriously, six months later, additional cashier's checks for $166,666.67 exactly. There was no return address, no traceable bank number, just a cashier's check. Griffin had made sure that each man's family or closest relative had received one-sixth of Beth Cantwell's million-dollar Bahamian account. Beth Cantwell's female partner received nothing. Her partner was even forced to file for Beth's survivor pension, which had now been denied three times and was in the fourth appeal. As far as Chief Griffin was concerned the appeals would drag on until hell froze over.

Tim Garwood was in the hospital for over a month. He nearly died several times. He retired on disability, went back to school to get a Coast Guard Master's Certification and now skippers a fishing boat in The Keys.

Gerry Wysocki's still on the force. He's three years from thirty and will definitely retire. He's planning on opening a bar in Islip. He'll have a lot of stories to tell as he mixes the drinks.

Morton Rivkin moved back to Plainview. Appearance fees from several television interviews and stipends from a number of magazines concerning his experience as a hostage left him with more than enough for a fat down payment on a four-bedroom on a quiet cul-de-sac. He also put up two years advance rent on a nice new office for his private practice CPA firm. His daughter now attends public school, and eagerly looks forward to college and getting away from her nudge of a mother.

The Irving Center Day School quickly and quietly changed its name back to the East End Day School, but its notoriety under the Rubino regime and the rumors of "goings on" at the school while under Rubino's oversized thumb were enough to keep applicants away in droves. The Board of Trustees was forced to close the school for financial reasons and sell the land to a local developer to pay off the school's debts.

Rubino's restaurant sat vacant and some say, haunted for nearly a year. It was purchased for next to nothing, as far as East Hampton properties go, by an enterprising Italian family from Brooklyn who obviously didn't believe in "ghosts." They turned it into a thriving pork store and deli now known as the best of its kind on the East End.

Jenna Walden awakened miraculously from her coma. It was two days after "The Events," as that day came to be known in the Hamptons. She hurried back to work the next week but was promptly fired for "gross incompetence." She is now the "weather girl" at the NBC affiliate in Tucumcari, New Mexico. She seethes to get back in the game.

"The Cave" at Camp Hero became a hiker's and ogler's mecca. Park entrance fees increased so substantially that the state was able to complete its extended Master Plan for the park five years early.

Frank Tartaglia wrote a book on the Hamptons murders and became nearly as famous as Patricia Cornwell. He teaches forensic science at CUNY now, thanks to an endorsement from Gracie, and loves spending his money on fast cars and weekends at Foxwoods.

The FBI spotted Ottmar Germella's broken body, still strapped in the pilot's seat, wedged among some granite blocks at the foot of Montauk Lighthouse. They sent a recovery team to retrieve his bloody remains, but high tide beat them to it. Before the EMTs could get to the body a large swell popped it out of its crevice and washed it out beyond the rocks. Just as the body began to sink out of sight, two thresher sharks began to circle and rip at the bloodied flesh. Ottmar Germella's mortal remains were quickly turned to chum.

"Brawny" Harris still gets around, still slides his hands up women's skirts, and still likes Stoli Bloodies and too many cigarettes.

Sgt. Patti Davis is now 2nd Lt. Patti Davis, her application for OCS having been rapidly approved. When she finishes her degree and then her masters she figures she'll be ready for the President's secret service detail, and in all likelihood, with her record, she'll get it.

Kyle Griffin, after a little judicious psychological counseling, returned to being a rambunctious, active pre-teen with a healthy interest in tennis and pre-pubescent girls. He seems to bear no emotional scars from his ordeal and longs to spend as much time as possible with his dad.

MSGT Tommy Stankowski retired from the Army and moved back to his hometown of Fresno, CA. After a lifetime of guns and violence, he and his wife run a shelter for abused mothers and their children. They hate the need, but love the life.

Major Jack Evans is now Lieutenant Colonel Jack Evans. He instructs English and coaches the rifle team at the Air Force Academy. He doesn't discuss how he won the Air Force Cross he wears proudly above the other four rows of ribbons on his bright blue tunic. He can't. He likes what he does but longs to get back out into the field and get his "hunting license" reinstated. His superiors think he still needs to lay low for at least another year. He fumes and drinks too much beer.

Vicky and Vincenzo Rubino mysteriously disappeared from their villa in Geneva one night and somehow ended up on a train going over the Italian Alps. Italy and the US have an extradition treaty, and as soon as the overnight train pulled into Milan, Vicky and Vincenzo were awakened from what seemed like a drug-induced stupor and taken into custody by Federal Marshals and some very cooperative Italian police. They were on a plane to New York within the hour. Vincenzo is in a mental institution for criminal juveniles in upstate New York. His rehabilitation is certainly many years away –if it ever comes. Vicky somehow managed to get a substantial quantity of Quaaludes smuggled into her detention cell just hours before being arraigned on murder charges. She never made her court date and is now buried beside her "loving" husband, Milos, at Greenlawn Cemetery in Brooklyn.

The extent of Milos Rubino's nefarious plan went to his grave as a dreaded family secret. His parents and older brother were mortified beyond words when Achmed Chalabi favored them with a personal visit. Even the Israeli government got into the act. The Rubinos had been extremely generous givers to Jewish causes in Israel and to Jewish philanthropies around the world. The Israeli Ambassador to the United States, speaking for his premier, practically begged his good friend the American Secretary of State to use her influence with her boss, the President, to intervene. The Israeli Ambassador nearly cried in the Secretary's arms. He felt letting this story fully emerge--that the son of such a prominent Jewish family was supporting terrorists in plots against the United States on its own territory--would set US-Israeli relations back a thousand years and encourage terrorism around the globe. The Secretary and the President agreed--for a price.

The Secretary of State, the Prime Minister of Israel and the Director of the CIA paid a secret and surprise visit to the new President of the Palestinian State. He was confronted by proof positive that Al Qaeda was actively waging war against the United States and using secret training camps and staging areas in Palestine, Iraq and Syria. The Palestinian President was asked if he wished to wage war, outright, right now, with the full military forces of both Israel and the United States. He declined. The US and Israel backed down--for a price.

The price was immediately paid. The new government of Palestine officially denounced both Hamas and Al Qaeda as terror-based organizations and dismissed all members of both groups from any and all government positions their members occupied, right down to dog catcher. Before the terror groups could even stage an anti-government demonstration the Palestinian government passed a resolution recognizing Israel's right to exist, and opened active, meaningful peace talks to try and settle their 2000-year-old dispute. This was certainly something that would cause Milos Rubino to roll over in his grave, if it were wide enough for him to do so, which, due to space limitations at Greenlawn, it wasn't.

Henry Brother Fox had felt all along that a casino in the Hamptons was as likely as a ham sandwich at a Bar Mitzvah, but if any white man came along with enough scratch to try and make it happen, he'd ride the wave. It finally happened with Milos Rubino, a man with more money than sense. The Shinnecocks got $45 million free and clear after Henry's cut, plus the generous donation to the leaders of the Tribal Council. The tribe went on a wild spending spree, delirious in their good fortune. When the lawyers for Milos Rubino's estate came around, Henry was fearful they wanted ol' Milos's money back. Instead, astoundingly, they said the tribe could keep it as long as Henry and the Council signed papers agreeing to forswear, in perpetuity, the source of their new-found wealth. Henry extracted another half-million from them for his promise, which, to him, amounted to one more worthless piece of white man's paper. Henry went out and bought himself the biggest Harley ever made and got drunk. He promptly drove the Harley into the right hand abutment of the old steel Shinnecock Canal railroad bridge. He was doing something like 80 MPH. It took three days to scrub Henry off the columns. His share of the loot went right into the tribe's general operating fund but the bridge got a fancy new copper sign: "The Henry Brother Fox Memorial Bridge…Ride on, Brother!"

The BIA adjudicating officer responsible for Shinnecock tribal recognition fell off his sailboat and drowned in the Potomac River under mysterious circumstances just days before rendering his decision on tribal recognition. As a result, a new case officer had to be assigned and the process started all over again. It could take years, certainly long enough for $5 million of Milos Rubino's bribery money to cool and "get lost" in that Bahamian bank account. The new case officer figured ten years ought to do it. He considered he was now earning more than half a million a year-plus interest!

The summer people who flock to the Hamptons each season are generally clueless. The old-timers and year-round residents are generally not. The "locals" have a favorite bumper sticker: "Summer people--Summer not." Despite all the public paeans to Milos Rubino's generosity, despite the new synagogue and the monument with his name at the top, despite all his $5000-a-plate dinners for famous senators, the locals had always been suspicious of the "big man" who had not been afraid to throw around his money or his weight in an effort to gain acceptance. This is, after all, an area where you aren't a "native" until your family has been here for at least ten generations, no matter how much money you have.

There was always something about Milos Rubino that didn't smell quite right, and many locals now said, "I told you so." The Hamptons are a generally tolerant and avant garde group of communities. The tone is generally liberal and wide open. It is definitely a place where alternative lifestyles can be accommodated. But even in this crowd, Milos Rubino was too-too: too rich, too pushy, too gay, too Jewish, too anxious for acceptance, too eager to "be in control" and definitely too obnoxious when he couldn't get his way. Having cast his lot with Rubino, Ivan Centpied was now strapped with his legacy and for Ivan that turned out to be too bad. "You know, Ivan's the one who..." became a popular catch phrase at Hamptons cocktail parties and summer benefits. Without Rubino's financial support and now without the moral support of what Ivan used to call "my people," he had really fallen on hard times. He had been forced to sell the family retreat in Montego Bay. His prized collection of '50's Cadillacs was gone. The home in Bridgehampton was mortgaged to the max. His latest business venture, a scheme to deliver catered picnic baskets to beach goers too lazy to get up and go to the store, had failed miserably. His wife and kids elected to live with his mother-in-law most of the year. He could no longer afford their private schooling and Rubino had destroyed the school they had attended anyway. His boyfriend, who, unbeknownst to his wife was actually her brother, was in drug rehab. Ivan himself was drinking too much, out of work and an insomniac. If this wasn't bad enough, he also had Achmed Chalabi to contend with. It was only by Chalabi's forbearance that Ivan was not in jail or Guantanamo. Chalabi had not yet told him for what purpose he had been spared prosecution. He had pleaded for Chalabi's protection-and his life- and had secured both, but he now twisted slowly in the wind waiting to see what

Chalabi would do. On his part, Chalabi was in no hurry to summon Centpied for any purpose. Chalabi was simply enjoying watching Centpied's life fall apart. He knew that this was even worse punishment for Centpied than incarcerating him. And Chalabi knew one more thing that Centpied did not yet know. Centpied's male lover, after checking into rehab, had been given a blood test. He had tested positive for HIV. Chalabi was waiting for the right moment to drop that bomb on poor old Ivan.

Achmed Chalabi got a second star and a Distinguished Service Cross. Major General Chalabi is now Deputy NSA, which meant he had to give up his post as Director of the "Black Bag" tech force at the Pentagon, a job he loved. To be persuaded to take his current assignment he wrangled out of his new boss, Jeremiah Johnson, the right to name his successor at Tech Ops. The new director was a guy named Griffin, recently retired Chief of Detectives of the Suffolk County Police Department. The Navy Captain selection Board that had met this last time did not have James Griffin's name on their list of candidates, as Chalabi had promised. By special Presidential order, James Allen Griffin's name was placed instead on the selection list for Rear Admiral with a very strong recommendation that Commander Griffin be selected. Naturally, this "totally unbiased" Board found some way to reach way down deep and pull a lowly Commander all the way up to Flag Rank.

Admiral Griffin is a little grayer now, but fit and imposing with a rakish scar across his left cheek. He still suffers from the bad left elbow, though. His impressive array of fruit salad has a band of blue-white-blue at the top signifying an award of the Navy Cross. He and Gracie have a two-bedroom brick townhouse in Georgetown and love escaping to the Hamptons for long weekends and extended summer stays in Montauk.

Gracie, who recovered fully from her shoulder "insult" as she calls it, instructs part-time at George Washington University. She also has a fat six-figure consulting contract with Homeland Security and develops programs for teaching criminal justice basics to new hires.

Gracie has forgiven James, mostly, for shooting her. She's even contemplating his semi-serious marriage proposal. They are still very much in love and still sexually frisky. In fact, when they are feeling especially in the mood, Gracie will stroke the wicked scar on James's cheek. He'll fiddle and fondle with her clothes until he can gently push a fingertip a quarter inch into her shoulder scar. At that second of remembrance of the most terrifying and exciting day of their lives, Gracie will whisper, "Shoot me, you bastard!" and they'll be naked and screwing like teenagers in heat.

The End

ACKNOWLEDGEMENTS

I have come to the craft of writing for pleasure later in life than most. I hope that this will make me a better writer, for all my experiences, although it will definitely shorten the number of books that I can be expected to write. Patrick O'Brian, the wonderfully talented spinner of sea tales, notable the "Aubrey/Maturin" series that spanned over twenty books, was "in harness" when he died at 86 and he didn't really start to write the series until he was in his late 50's; so, you see, there's hope for me.

The one writer I wish to thank over all others, though, is my friend Nelson DeMille. He had the good sense to go after this business when he was a lot younger, he worked very hard at it and he got it right. His novels (which now number fourteen) have sold millions of copies all over the world and have entertained countless readers with vivid stories for several decades. After I settled in the Hamptons I went to a book signing Nelson did at a store in Water Mill, New York, for his book "Plum Island." I was writing, at the time, an annual tongue-in-cheek look at the Hamptons called 'The Hamptons Survival Guide." It was a success for ten straight years until it was bought out by an Internet publishing wannabe who promptly blew it up in the dot.com bubble of the late 90's. In any case, Nelson supported me generously in that enterprise via Warner Books and I have always been grateful for that support. I was delighted to be able help him with some background and research for his wonderful book "Night Fall." He, in turn, kept encouraging me to write. He knew, I think, that I had at least one good novel in me. So, here it is. I also say, without apology, that I have tried very hard to write in Nelson's style, which happens to be very comfortable to me. I have also presumed to create a character in James Griffin that I equate to Nelson's delightfully roguish Detective John Corey. So, on many levels for many things, thank you my friend, Nelson DeMille.

Laura Lyons, my partner in life, to whom this book is dedicated along with my incredibly wonderful son Pierce, was the true inspiration for getting his thing done. It was her knowledge of local lore that created the basic premise for the book. It was her that kept me going through some pretty dark moments when I felt like giving up and it was Laura who actually did the initial word processing because, even though I'm pretty computer literate, I can't use the keyboard to write—I still do it longhand on yellow lined tablets (another DeMille trait). She also did the initial edits and held my hand as rejection after rejection came back from agents and publishers alike. Thanks, My Love. I couldn't have done it without you.

I want to add a note of gratitude to Paula Godfrey who took on the job of handling the first "messy" edits. Paula made many invaluable suggestions on style and helped clean up the manuscript considerably.

Next, Tricia Rayburn took a crack at it. Tricia is a fantastic writer and has the Simon & Schuster book deals to prove it. She is also a professional editor and I am grateful she accepted my offer to review this book. When I received her initial edits I was floored that she had read the book four times and found many, many necessary corrections. She also made numerous suggestions on flow, timing and content. This is a better book for Tricia's input.

I also want to say a heart-felt "Thank you for your service" to all my fellow Veterans. My time in hell came during Vietnam and the impact of that war changed my life forever, in ways both good and bad. As this book goes to press America's best sons and daughters continue to struggle with the foe, this time in Iraq, Afghanistan and with terrorism everywhere. Just remember that even if you are not always honored as you should be, you are never forgotten.

ABOUT THE AUTHOR

Phil has a degree in History from Harvard and would have become a professional historian if the Navy hadn't called him to duty the day after graduation. Flight School, designation as a Naval Aviator and three tours in Vietnam followed in rapid succession. He left the Navy with the rank of Commander and embarked on a career in business. Phil worked in sales and marketing for three Fortune 500 companies. Since then he has been a Professor of Business, globe-trotting consultant, licensed Coast Guard Masters Mate, a CEO, CFO and COO and is currently chairman of the Town of Southampton Transportation Commission. As a writer, he authored the very successful "Hamptons Survival Guide," collaborated with good friend Nelson DeMille on the best-seller "Night Fall," and he has recently finished this, his own first novel, "Animus," a terrorist thriller that occurs in the Hamptons. A second novel, a text on professional selling and a revival of the "Survival Guide" series are also underway. Phil is also the history correspondent for VOX Magazine, a regular contributor to "Hamptons On-Line," and the Southampton Press; and, Adjunct Professor at RISD (the Rhode Island School of Design) and Roger Williams University. He lives full-time in Southampton, NY, with his partner Laura and son Pierce and part-time in Rhode Island.

Printed in the United States
206849BV00004B/1-51/P

9 781419 699627